THE
SILENT
CRY

Diamond Glenn Publishing

Diamond Glenn Publishing

ISBN: 978-0-578-18305-3

PRINTED IN THE UNITED STATES OF AMERICA

Special Dedications

First of all I will like to give thanks to God, for keeping me alive even thou I did not know it and for not letting the original manual stripe to this book burn. I can say, "God is good all the time," because He was in my life all the time, I just didn't know it.

I would like to give a public dedication to some very special people whom I feel is such a pleasure and an honored for me to have them in my life.

She and her husband were true friends and neighbors of mine. They were always there for my family and me anytime I needed them regardless of the situation, good and or bad. They went beyond the meaning of a real friend and not only open the warmth of their arms, their sincere hearts of gold and their unconditional love but the extra extension of their respectfully, loving and caring family. I look and received the genuine acts coming from them and accept them as part of my family. I thank God for allowing me to have met these two loving and caring individuals and I want the whole world to know how much I love you, Earl and Tracy. Thank you.

To my grand babies whom I love with all my heart you all have your own special place in my life that made and kept me together. I would like to say to Fatta, Momo and Nono, I know you could have found lots of things to do with your teenage life besides retyping Nana's book but it means so much to me that you girls took out your busy life to do this for me. I hope while typing and reading my words that maybe something was in the chapters that could and would help you in your decisions making in different situation in your life and remember to always keep God in your life. I love you so much. Thank you so very much.

What can I say? To my oldest daughter, I am overflowing with the utmost fulfillment that words that can't express. You are so dear to me that I am choked up as my heart cries with tears of joy and happiness. Out of the overload, the kids, school, work, your health and then all life other problems that it dumped in your lap. Where did you find the time? Always thinking of others before your self. That is Jesus, which is love. These words I wrote to, for, about and dedicated to my daughter. I never finished what I wanted to say. My daughter passed January 10, 2015. Tee, I know you are looking down on me from Heaven installing in me to put my book out there. None of this would had been possible without you. Walking in this awaken nightmare my heart will forever be heavy. I love and misses you so much My Baby, "R.I.H." Love your Mommie..

"The birth of a little girl"

MAY 30, 1959, is when it all began!

First, let me give you, my reader, a little information on my family's background. My parents had two boys already and wanted a little girl very much. They decided to bring one more child into this world, which was a girl and that was me. Both my parents were hard workers and were very well respected everywhere they lived. As far back as the first day of my life, we always had a very close knit type of family. Our family was full of love, happiness, and understanding as a unit; as a whole, a mother, a father, children, and a lovely and loving home.

My mother's role in life was that of a mother, a wife, a nurse, a friend; a shoulder to lean on, and a helping hand to anyone in need. My dad held two to three jobs at a time. One job held was a cab driver position. I can remember how we always worried about him when he drove the cab. Just knowing the type of parents I had through the lens of a toddler, my parents raised my two brothers well. They, that is my two brothers I've yet to meet, were very well taken care of and well mannered too!

On Memorial Day, 1959, my family was having they're usual holiday barbecue. On that day the grass was beautiful; green and full of life. The sun was bright and the park was thriving with the sounds of happiness in the air. The picnic and everything was going along just fine, until early evening. My soon to be father noticed my mom was not her normal happy self. She didn't want to spoil everyone's great time by announcing she was in labor. I was ready to see the world and could not wait. Therefore, they had to go to the hospital so I could be born.

After a long, hot labor my parents marveled at the birth of their 14-pound baby girl. I am told my older brother was overly happy! You see, my mom promised him, he could name her first girl. He held my mom to her word and reminded her of the promised she made to him. I remember how my mom said my brother was jumping around saying, "Her name is Lovely!" I want to name her Lovely!" Now that I have had kids of my own, I could understand the joy my family had experienced the day I was born.

The stay in the hospital was ok, I guess. My parents never told me we, my mom and I, had to stay in the hospital for any complications after my birth. However, the best part I felt as a newborn was being at home. My best thrill about being at home was the cuddles and love I received from each one. Everyone loved my parents' big, bald-headed baby girl. I was loved so much that a few families living in Chicago were competing with each other to see if they could convince my parents to let one of them adopt me.

My mom was proud of her big baby girl too, but I believe my dad was even more proud. He took me everywhere he went when he didn't have to work. Yes, with his busy workload, he still made time for his baby girl. Everyone loved me unconditionally, except for one person who loved and envy me very much! At the same time this person loved me, but he didn't really understand why. All he knew was the attention he once had suddenly was being took away from him. I guess in his little mind he was thinking of a way to get rid of me; revenge!

I didn't understand what was going on! I now know what they

call assault with a deadly weapon was part of abuse. I used to be afraid to go to sleep because I never knew when he was going to attack me. As long as my mom and dad had me I was happy. I never wanted to leave their arms or their sight! They played with me morning, noon, and night. I really enjoyed it a lot.

Little did they know I was willing to get up and dance for them if I could but unfortunately, I could only lie there and fight sleep as long as possible. I had to leave my only means of security, which was my parents and go into that room once I fell to sleep. My room was not your typical nursery. It had all those pretty little stuffed animals, carrousels on the crib, dolls, and other toys that turn into your baby's worse nightmares whenever the room was dark.

I could feel my heart beating faster and faster as I awaited my attacker to make his move. The moon was bright, still and cold looking. It also looked as if it had a face, which was smiling and laughing at me because it knew what was about to happen. Suddenly, I heard a bump, and became afraid. I begin wondering if my attacker was approaching me. Not able to talk or run away I lay there hoping he would think I was dead asleep and leave. A squeaky sound started coming out of the darkness. It came closer and closer! I said to myself, "Oh my God, where is my mommy or daddy? I need you. I'm so afraid! Somebody, anybody, help me, please come help me!" Maybe this time it will kill me"

Now the squeaking noise is so close it seems as if it's right by my crib. "Oh, my God," I replied to myself. The shadow was now over my head. It's moving to my side! I cried, "God, please don't let it hurt me." POW, POW! I screamed to the top of my lungs. I started to cry so hard that tears covered my face like a pool of water. I wonder to myself, "Why me? Why me? Why does it keep doing this to me? Why this shadow in the dark doesn't leave me alone!"

For 2 1/2 years I've gone through this horror everyday and night. It seemed like the louder I cried, the angrier my attacker became. I began to hold my tears in and just hurt on the inside. As I silently cried I prayed to myself asking God to end this horror. Needless to say, once he realized he wasn't hurting me, hearing my screams of fear, and seeing my tears of pain, he started slowly slacking up on his abusive attacks.

Yes, my reader, from that moment that's when I can say, "My Silent Cries" began.

Chapter One
"A voice that was not heard"

ONCE I BECAME old enough to talk...

As a child I was different; they said, my parents that is! When all the other kids were out playing, I wanted to help in the kitchen and cook; make cakes, bread, and pies. I would run around in the pantry gathering the different pots and pans my mom and/or grandmother needed to cook or mix something in. What I enjoyed the most about being in the kitchen was being nearby the ones I knew really loved me.

I was willing to do anything to keep from being with the other kids, and around other people. Considering, I did not trust anyone. I stayed to myself and played alone. I think deep inside I still relived the fear my mind held as a baby. So, I felt if I were alone, I wouldn't have to worry about anyone being next to me to do anything to me that would hurt me.

By this time my little sister was born. A few years went by and she could get around. I kept her with me at all times. I was kind of like the bodyguard she didn't know she had. I would watch her all day while she was awake and at night while she slept. My parents use to turn off the lights, after they would put my sister and me to bed! As soon as they'd go into their room and close the door, the squeaking and creeping noise would start. I'd jump up and run to turn on the lights while saying, "You're not going to get, hit, or hurt my little sister the way you did me!"

I would sit up watching and waiting for the shadow attacker of the darkness. You know what? I never saw him come into the light! He was afraid of the light! I kept the lights on in our bedroom. I can remember hearing my mom and dad saying, "I know I turned off the lights in the girls' room!"

Not being to sure, they would look into our bedroom and just say something like, "oh well, as long as they're sleep," and close the door. They just didn't know, I was so glad they left the lights on as I would lie in my bed with the covers over my head pretending I was asleep. I became good in pretending like I was sleep; my only concerned now was how good I really was at pretending I was sleep.

It was that time now, the first day of school. I was so afraid; I cried, fought, fell out, and begged my parents not to send me. I knew it would be a lot of strange people there, and I felt they were going to attack me. I guess the first few weeks were fine; but then it started. The fear of all fear! I had become the victim of another attacker, and he wasn't anything nice. As I think about it now, I believe he picked me out of the whole class because I was a loner.

Even at school I stayed to myself. My shy-shamefulness and quietness drew more bad than good my way. My teacher would ask me questions over and over again. I'd cry each time before I would answer her! That caused me to be put in the corner or sent to the coatroom until I was ready to answer her questions. That's where it all began!

I was crying, awaiting, not knowing what was about to take place. He would come into the coatroom as if he needed to get something out of his jacket pockets. All the time he was really checking me out, but I didn't know it at that time. Oh, but now I remember it well! He'd pull my hair until I cried. The teacher would ask me what's wrong with me, and he'd lie and answer for me. He would say,

"Nothing! Ain't that right!" I wouldn't say anything. I'd just shake my head up and down meaning "yes." Oh what did I do that for? I had to deal with his abuse for months, and as the months went by his vicious attacks got worse.

He started doing really mean things such as knocking me out of my chair, pulling my seat from under me, and then he had the nerve to try to help me up. The teacher thought he was such a good little boy for helping me when all the time he was the reason why I fell on the floor in the first place. I can still remember how my teacher used to yell at me. She would say, "Lovely, stop being so mean, all the boy is trying to do is help you!" Man, I use to think to myself how I wish I could kill her too because she made me cry all the time. When I cry she would call me a big crybaby in front of the whole class. I couldn't wait to leave school.

When it was time to go home, I always went to the end of the line so that I could run out a different door from the other kids. I started to believe I was a big crybaby, and I didn't want to be around anyone after school because I felt they were going to do was tease me. The overly evil coatroom attacker had me so afraid that I had to pay him to stop attacking me. He had me lying to my parents to get money so I could give it to him. Everyday I had a different fieldtrip to go on.

He could have bought school supplies for the whole school with all the money I had given him. His orders and needs became more and more costly each day. All I could think about was if my parents run out of money, then I was good as dead! The dude was good! I mean real good at what he did. One day after waiting for me after school, he realized that I was going home a different way. He would catch me going out the back door and beat me down into the mud. Once he did his damage, he'd take me home and lie to my parents. Of course, I was young and scare; therefore, I would shake my head agreeing with whatever he said. I felt so stupid as I cried inside with fear, while nodding my head, "yes" to his lies! Again, I asked God, "Why me?" as I stood with fear and terror in my eyes while looking at the ground.

Most of my life as a young girl was basically the same. I had all kinds of attackers. I can remember as far back as an infant laying in my crib the pain and torment my attackers inflicted upon me. It had gotten to the point that even the girls became abusive. Being born a "big baby" meant some disadvantages for me! I looked older than my age group both as a newborn and a child. Things just got worst for me. Being older looking, cause me to become a mature looking child. The girls picked at me and teased me about my chest, because I had breasts at an early age. The girls my age would say things like, "Lovely had a baby because my mom got those and she has two babies." Having breast at a young age was confusing to me. I didn't understand what was going on with my body.

I was so ashamed of my overly developed body. When it was time to take a shower after gym, I would wait until the last girl left the shower room before I would take off my clothes and shower. I'd go and sit on the toilet seat with both my feet up until there weren't any more voices to be heard. Then I knew the coast was clear and I'd come out. I would take me a quick "wash me up" shower. Because my body looked different from the other girls my age I felt I didn't belong.

All I knew I was different from the other girls! I used to be called a giraffe with breasts, a freak of nature, and any other names classifying me as abnormal or ugly. I used to wonder if there was truly a God who was so great, so good, so perfect, and truly love me because I didn't understand why he allowed these things to happen to me if he was all these wonderful things. I was a nice girl who did not give my parents any problems whatsoever! Why must I live such a sad, confusing, and painful life? I couldn't understand why anyone didn't like me.

Being young, every time I saw a person in Chicago bleeding, they usually died. At nine years old I thought I was dying. I can remember the moment I thought I was going to die as if it was yesterday. On the other hand, I can honestly relate to this movie I remember seeing. Especially, the part when she was in the shower. No matter how many times I see the movie, I still cry because I know how she feels. One day after gym I decided to run in and take a quick shower after everyone had left. The moment I thought I was about to experience death happened!

I was washing and my soapsuds were constantly turning a pinkish red color. I couldn't understand why? So, I rushed through my shower faster than usual. I started drying myself off and that's when it really scared me. I turned the water off, and reached for a dry towel. As I began to pat the water from my womanly-developed body, I started down my thighs, up my leg than I wiped my inner thigh. Man did I cry! I was so afraid of what I saw. Blood was all over the towel. I remember crying and saying to myself, "I didn't do anything to die! God, why me? Everyone picked at me and hurt me!" Not realizing I had over stayed my time in the shower; a few of the girls came back into the shower room.

I never knew why they came back; but that was one time I was glad to see them. I don't know if it was so they could see me dying. Therefore, they could tell everyone how and why I die. Regardless of the reason, I was glad they were there because I wanted them to see what they had done to me. I wanted guilt to eat them up so bad; however, having them there was somewhat sad to me. One of the girls, who use to call me crazy, ugly and other hurtful names were standing there too. I started to feel kind of sorry for her. I also start wondering maybe she wasn't evil after all and maybe she did have feelings because she was crying!

I really was surprised because they were really concerned and afraid for me. They ran out and brought the teacher back to help me. I was glad to see the teacher, but the anger I had in my heart against them wouldn't let my lips form the words to say thank you to them. I can remember that incident well! After waiting for me to get dressed, the teacher then took me home. Back in those days, if a teacher had to take you home it was an indication you must have done something real bad. You knew what was going to happen once the teacher left your house. I was so afraid even though the teacher kept telling me everything was going to be alright. I was hoping I would die before she'd get me home! I couldn't stop wondering what was going to happen to me when we got to my house.

Once we made it to my house I saw the expression on my mother's face as she look at the teacher who was bringing me home. The first thing I said was, "I didn't do nothing," as I cried big crocodile tears trying to convince her of my innocence. My mom didn't want to hear it. She sent me to my room while she and the gym teacher talked. I remained in my room, still bleeding alive. I was wondering to myself when I was going to die. I lay balled up in my bed crying until I fell asleep.

My mom finally came into my room and woke me up. I just sat there looking with my eyes frozen open and scared to blink; terrified of what was about to happen. As she walked closer my heart began to race very fast, but then I was really surprised at the same time. That day led to one of those mother-daughter serious talk moments. Since it was almost summer vacation time and so close to the ending of the semester, it was recommended I start my vacation early. As a result, I would return to school in the fall. A break from school during the summer meant time to go down south. Like the birds fly south every year for the winter we drove south every year for the summer. I used to love when school let out for the summer, but now I hated when that time of the year came! It's funny how a vacation that's supposed to be fun and full of enjoyment can become a trip of horror and the picture of hell for me.

It's funny how a vacation that's suppose to be fun and full of enjoyment can become a trip of horror and the torque of hell for me.

Chapter Two
"The vacation from Hell!"

FOR US, DRIVING south has always been a family reunion type of vacation; everyone came! I remember sometimes it would be three to four car loads leaving one state to meet up with a car or two in another state along the way. The ride was long and exhausting to me. Maybe because I was a child and there really wasn't anything to do during the ride. Sometimes younger ones had to sit on the lap of the older ones. Knowing what I know now, I realize how dirty some of those minds were that belong to some of those laps I sat on. Being a young girl, mentally I did not know what was going on when sometimes I felt something hard go across my butt or down my leg. It really made me feel very uncomfortable while sitting on their laps. All I know is that was the summer when it began!

Even though I was young I didn't like sitting on other people's laps because to me I could feel it wasn't right and that those laps were trouble. You see as I mentioned before my body did not look like a little girl. I started hearing remarks such as I know this not Little Lovely? They will make the statement as if they were asking a question but in reality they were thinking dirty in the mind. Their sick remarks continue. They would say things like, "Girl you kind of bloomed out there! You're starting to look like a lady." Little did they know I was already feeling bad and insecure about my body because

I didn't look like a kid. Therefore, they made me feel even more bad and insecure about my body. I was only nine years old and I looked as if I were much older.

They started throwing my name around to each other. Old nasty niggas I thought to myself! They were saying things like, they bet I'm being sucked and not by no young dude neither. Then they would look at me as if their mouth were hanging opening while talking about how upright and firm my breast were. Those lousy niggas continue to say hurting remarks to me like they know some old man is playing around with my young stuff. One of them said he could tell because my butt was well rounded. The day wouldn't go on before a few of my soon to be attackers grabbed me by my breasts; they started to squeeze them, and dared me to say something. I being afraid, and very self-conscious about my body, didn't say anything. I now know that's where I made my mistake. Prior to this I told my grandparents that they were fondling me, what good did that do; they teamed up against me. I didn't win. They started labeling me as a liar and I got punished for telling the truth. According to my grandparents and my attackers my truth telling was lying to them. What sense does that make?

Everyday my grandparents would go into town for three to four hours. So you see I had no other choice but to be quiet because no one believed anything I said. I knew then I was on my own and had to come up with a plan to take care of myself! One reason I got attacked was a result of being left in the house alone a lot! Therefore, once my grandparents (God rest their soul) started getting in the truck, I used to run and find a place to hide. I spent many days under the hot sun in the cotton or cornfields all day long until I heard my grandparent's truck coming up the road. I would jump up and run as fast as I could to beat my grandparents' back to the farm. What good that did me because I still got punished every time; due to the fact I knew I wasn't supposed to be in the sun in the first place.

You see I have this sensitive skin that blisters easily in the hot sun. Even if I wanted to I wouldn't be able to go outside to play with the other kids anyway. God knows I would rather put up with the pain from the sunburns, than have to deal with the aches, pains, and the sorrow my mind, body, and heart had to go through with my attackers. I got tired of getting whippings for being out in the sun. I had to come up with another hiding spot. I started hiding in the chicken coups, but the chickens made so much racket, which gave me away.

I then start hiding in a few old refrigerators that was in the yard on my grandparents' farm. That was a nice spot because my attackers never found me. The only bad thing about that spot was the refrigerator would get too hot. I knew I had to fine me another spot that was a little cooler. After then I started crawling under the porch to avoid my attackers. I didn't care what was under there. I didn't care if there were snakes, crickets, frogs, and dogs under the porch. I just didn't care! The creature of the creep could have gotten me or any other creature that walk on more than two legs. I just didn't want to be back in those sick minded attackers' hands again. I would lie under the porch praying that they would never find me because it would be sad for me once they did.

I would scream, kick, and holler for dear life when they would find me! All they used to tell the other kids was, "Get back, ya'll know she crazy." In fact everybody use to say this about me. Then they would tell the other kids not to pay me any attention we'll take care of her." God knows how I hated those words. I can still hear it now; all the other kids laughing at me and calling me crazy. They would all say at the same time, "Crazy! Look at her, Lovely. She really is crazy! Look how she's acting." I can remember those words so well; even now they're echoing in my head. No one tried to do anything to help me as they dragged me across the yard into the house. I try to tell the other kids that they were going to hurt me as they dragged me pass them. My attackers just laughed at me and continue to tell the other kids I was crazy.

They would take me and throw me in the room, slap me around, pull off my clothes, and fondle with my private parts. I can remember hearing one of them saying, "Don't go too far in her." They used to rub their private up and down me, across my breasts, and motioning it in and out between the cheeks of my butt. They used to grab on my breasts so much that I can still feel their hands touching on my breast. I'm kind of reliving those hands squeezing my young firm breasts while they were sucking on them till they became sore. Those ugly and disguising feelings are not the easiest thing to mentally relive. If I had the power, I would have killed them all including those that wouldn't try to help me. Man, my attackers are starting to release an ugly person out of me!

Since I stayed in the kitchen so much, one day I was looking out the window and noticed stacks and stacks of tractor tires at the back of the farm. The tires seemed to be in a lot of shade. I begin to look around even more to see what else could be a nice cool hiding place. Later that day I was helping my grandmother with the laundry. Once most of the lines were filled with clothes I made my way to the stacks of tires. I looked around them for awhile, trying to make sure there weren't any snakes, any other creepy bugs, and/or animals seeking shelter in them. I said to myself, "Yes, I think I found the right place!" For those of you who may be saying, "How can anyone hide in a tractor tire?" Well let me tell you, a tractor tire is so big that four or five grown people can get in one, from head to toe to form the inner circle of the tractor tire.

So the next day came and my grandparents had to go to town. This time I didn't wait for the truck to leave; I hurried up and ran as fast as I could to the stack of tires in the back of the yard. Afterwards my attackers started wondering about me and where I might be. I use to hear them walking around looking for me, saying things like, "We know you're on the farm somewhere and when we fine you, Lovely, you is going to regret ever hiding from us." I hated my attackers so much that I was wishing death on them! I can remember them making remarks such as, "Look how they (referring to my breasts) stand and stick straight out." I can remember it like it was just yesterday all the cure things my so call family members did to me. It's all still so clear in my head.

As I reflect back upon such terror and horror I went through it feels like, that is as if something is trying to get out of me; a different type of anger and pain. This anger and pain is very much unlike what I felt in the past; it is a feeling I not yet able to describe but its definitely unlike the anger and pain that contribute to my "silent cry." Yet these feelings are too afraid to surface and reveal its true face. It is like a horrible feeling, a battle, that is going on in my mind right now; a good vs. evil battle. I am not a bad person! I am not a bad person! My mind knows that! Once again it feels as if I am silently crying inside. The anger and pain can not and will not surface. I can't let it; it will be too much of a traumatic ordeal for me to allow this anger and pain relive through the lens of an angry adult. It is so hard to fight it. I'm developing a bad headache; feeling tension up, and down my neck and spine. My heart is starting to beat extremely fast. It feels like my head is going to burst. "Oh dear GOD, why me? Why did I have to be the one that had to go through this life of nightmares? When all I ever wanted out of life was to be a happy little girl!" I am so angry! My hate and anger is starting to take control of me, I must stop and rethink things through, myself, my mind and most of all my train of thoughts. Why me???

It's another day; let's try to continue. I tried to tell my grandparents over and over again. I would cry, and yell out, "Why doesn't anyone believe me? Why?" Then more tears of pain poured out of me as I yelled, "I'll be glad when my mama comes and I'll never see ya'll again as long as I live!" I can remember crying and stomping so much till I would get a whipping for trying to help myself. A few of my attackers stood by watching with that gleam in their eyes and smiling. Lord knows I hated everyone down there. I was sad because I knew they, my attackers, were gonna get me cause I told. I had no where to go or no one to turn too. My so call family members down here, down south that is, think that I have a mental problem and they marked me as being a liar.

My family down here, oh, how it's so hard to say those two words, really felt that I was crazy. No one believed a word I said. It seemed I made my attackers madder by trying to tell someone about what was happening to me. My attackers laughed at me and said, "What were you trying to do; get us in trouble?" As my grandparents walked pass my attackers spoke under their breath so only I can hear them say, "You are going to pay for opening your big mouth." I started feeling like I'm dammed if I did and I knew I was dammed if I do. I thought to myself, I should had just kept my mouth closed and never said anything.

From that day forward I became silent. I cried inside so hard and so much till I hurt as if my insides were knotting up. I kept saying, "I couldn't wait until my parents came down here to get me." I felt I was now in a place where no one loved me, believed me, and I was walking flesh that didn't want to be alive anymore. My attackers had destroyed any will of life that I may have had at one time. Once again, I kept thinking about how I had no one down there to turn to. I was alone! Alone in a world of evil wrong doers, and people too blind to open their eyes to face the truth!

Down in Arkansas, my grandparents had no running water. We had to make sure we saved a bucket of water over night to prime the pump every morning. If we didn't, we would have to go all day without water until my grandparents came back from town with a jug of water to prime the pump. Not only wasn't there no running water but my grandmother still also cooked on an old wood burning pop belly stove; it made some of the fluffiest cakes, pies, and bread that you ever wanted to eat. This meant the males had to make sure there was enough wood chopped to keep the food cooking. The farm life wasn't easy, but it was how my grandparents during this time were use to living. I remember hearing my parents, my aunt, and my uncle talked about wanting to get the farm up dated, but my grandma was so against that thought.

My grandparents had finally gotten electricity to the house. I was glad because before that we had to finish cleaning, washing, and whatever else had to be done to ourselves and around the farm before the sunset. Their bathroom was an old out house. Man, did I hate going out there! We had to use candles to see our way to the out house when it was dark outside. I didn't care to use candles; I would go out in total darkness. I'd rather for fire ants or anything else deadly to get me in the dark instead of my attackers. I knew if they had seen me walking with a candle in the dark they would come out and mess with me.

However, that only lasted for so long. Once a few of my attackers realized I was gone, they would sometimes come out with a candle and find me. During the late night assaults my attackers were not as hard on me as they are when my grandparents went to town. I believe it was because my grandparents were at home. Yet still that didn't really stop my attackers from doing what they did best; making my life a living hell. My attackers would reveal their private part to me and stick it up against my body. Every time I would yell at them to stop, and to please leave me alone. As I was trying to make my way back to the house, my attackers would pull and squeeze at my breast and my butt.

Each time I hollered they would say, "I saw a snake or something else and me being stupid wouldn't say anything because I felt no one was going to believe me any way. Oh dear God right about now I'm reliving how much I really hated myself, and I can feel the pain I felt back than of how bad I wish I was dead! Once again I entered the house silently crying to myself; sad, wondering, lost, and very confused. Life meant nothing to me. All I wanted to happen was for this nightmare to end. All I wanted was for my mama to come and get me from this house of hell! Most of all I wanted somebody to believe me!

We use to gather around this crazy looking radio and listen to different talk programs that were five to fifteen minutes long. Honestly it was not bad at all listening to the talk shows on the radio. I really enjoyed listening to the talk shows. The only disadvantage to listening to the talk shows on the radio was you had to create pictures in your mind about the information being interpreted. My grandparents transition from the radio to a blue tube television (TV). The blue tube was what we now call a floor model television set, but it had a little picture in the middle of it. Before you could see the picture, the tube had to warm up for awhile. My family had to place large blankets over the windows to keep the light out of the room. They also closed the doors to the other rooms.

It was like being in a movie theatre which only consists of total darkness just before the movie came on. It was kind of fun and a chance to be able to see a picture on TV while I was down south but then again the God honest truth was I wish my grandparents would never have gotten a dam blue tube. The funniest thing about the blue tube was we had to sit directly in front of it in order to see the pictures clearly. Unfortunately, the blue tube was not like our TV's today, which allows you to sit at various angles. The televisions today you can sit on either side of the TV, lay down on your back, or stomach and you're still able to clearly see the pictures. With the blue tube you had to sit in front of the TV and if it wasn't enough room that's when the lapping started again. God, I hated that! It wasn't anything but trouble for me. It was as if once the blue tube came, it was the continuation of hell day for me. I can remember how my attackers uses to take me out one or two of them at a time and do what they wanted to do to me and after they were done I would just go and sit in the corner and cry for my mama.

Some of my attackers would say, "Come on Lovely, you can sit on my lap," while patting their hands on their lap. How sickening, I thought to myself while watching them slob at the mouth. Each time I will stare them straight in their wicket and evil eyes and say, "I don't want to sit on nobody's lap." They always respond with a stupid comment such as "Do something Lovely! You're in our way." They really acted as if they wanted to watch the blue tube; however, their eyes watched me the whole time. My grandparents would always force me to sit on one of my attackers' lap. Each one of them used to argue with each other about whose lap I was going to sit on. In fact, they start arguing over me each day before TV time started. This is when I started hating the blue tube TV time. This use to be a time I thought I could relax and enjoy the TV but instead it became a moment of less enjoyment for me and more stress. The blue tube time had gotten worse for me then the mornings.

My attackers saw it wasn't doing me any kind of good by opening my mouth and trying to tell anyone about what they were doing to me that they became more abusive. They even had gotten so good with their little stories and lies that my grandparents would believe them every time over me. I hated them so much; they had me feeling like a scared helpless chicken at the age of nine. When I went into a room for something, I'd leave the door open and quickly run through the room to get what I need so they don't catch me in there. But there have been a couple of times when I wasn't fast enough.

Once my attackers would catch me in the house, they will say, "You know what time it is! Don't you?" Even till this day their voices hunt me in my mind. The dirty, rude, nasty, and cruel words they use to say to me rings in my ears. I can hear them even now saying, "You know what time it is? Don't you!" I use to just look at them with fearfully because I knew what was about to happen! I can remember hearing one of my attackers in the background saying, "She ain't gonna say nothing. She knows what will happen." Then one of them would push me and say, "Ain't that right!" I wouldn't say a word because I knew inside what they meant. I would just sit there and silently cry to myself while they assault me. To myself I will say, "God, I want to go home," as my heart hurt with pain.

Now I liked no one and didn't trust a soul on my grandparents' farm. I remember I had started standing up in back of everyone; up against the wall during TV time. I will take a whipping before I sat on anybody's lap. I had made my mind up not to sit on no one else's lap while we was watching the blue tube. I can remember one time everyone was centered in front of the blue tube, before I knew it, it had happen. One of my attackers had grabbed me around my mouth and pulled me out of the room so fast that I didn't realize what was happening. I guess you're saying, "Why not yell?" I did many times. I would tell them to stop and to let me go, but they, my grandparents, would tell me to be quiet. Every time I opened my mouth the abuse got worse.

So, now I'm just a child, lost, confused, insecure about my womanly looking body, afraid, feeling that no one truly loved or cared about me. All I knew was that I wanted my mama to hurry up and come back and get me. I can still remember sometimes when I did yell, holler, and kick my attackers would turn the situation around. They will tell my grandparents I something such as I slipped, or fell, or they accidentally stepped on my finger. Each time my grandparents believed what they would say. When I tried to tell what really happen they would say I'm lying. It was horrible to be down there.

There use to be a time before all this hell came down on me, I can remember when I would cry and have a fit when my parents use to tell me we couldn't go down south for the summer. My parents use to say, "Faye, you know you can't go down south because you're not gonna stay out the sun, and you know what happens to you every time you go out in the hot sun." I remember crying to them promising them I would not be in the sun, just so I could go down south. I use to hate myself because of my sensitive skin to heat. I didn't care about my skin when it came to going down south. I use to like down south so much that I use to tell my mom, "I won't be outside in the sun mama. Please! I'll stay in and help grandma cook."

As I sit here thinking and reliving my past life experiences, I really felt at one time I really was going to die if I didn't go down south for the summer. That was how much I use to love down south; however, the sick minded individuals I call family robbed me of my love and made me silently cry. I can't understand how the minds of people change from a good way of thinking to a bad way of thinking once maturity sets in. Now I can't stand being down south to save my life and God knows it's my life, my mind, and my peace of heart that I'm trying to save. The only words that I repeated over and over again while I was going through hell down south were, "God, I wanted to go home!"

I can still remember and can feel the hurt, the pain, the sadness I felt while asking God to please let my mother hurry up and come get me, "Please, God, Please. I need my mama. I wanted to go home," and then I'd start crying! That summer down south was a living hell for me. I felt hated by everyone down there. All I wanted was for this trip of horror to hurry up and end. There were a few days left before my parents were to arrive; I couldn't wait. I was a walking lifeless person; I cared nothing about living, I was half-crazy, and wanted to die. It seemed as if I was standing all alone in the world. No one wanted me around except my attackers. I asked God to forgive me because I was thinking of ways to kill them; my attackers and everyone else on the farm. I was also thinking about, if only I can just stay out of my attackers' hands for a few days then I'll be gone and I can leave this nightmare behind me. I promise I would never come back down here again.

Oh I was so glad, my parents had finally come. Once my grandparents got through with them, I wished my parents had never come to get me because I felt I could have killed myself and no one would have cared. My father yelled at me so loud that he could have busted my eardrums. I can still hear his voice echoing through my mind saying, "Mama is not going to lie on you!" I knew then that the only piece of hope I thought I had has just die. I also knew my mom would go alone with whatever my dad said and thought. Consequently, I didn't even try to win her over. I made up my mind to just cling to my mom, like a second layer of skin. I mean I didn't let her get out of my sight. When my mom sat then I sat. When my mom walked, I ran beside her and became her shadow.

I was glued to my mother like white on rice. If I could form, spell, and say the words for my mom when she talks, I would have. I didn't let my mom make a move without me. I can remember my dad and grandparents telling my mom, she should make me go and play with the other kids, and that I didn't need to be sitting under her all the time. I was praying to myself, "God, please don't let them pull me away from my mama again. Please God help me!"

I use to cry and scream because I did not want to be taken away from my mom. I even took a beating as I cried, "Please, mama don't make me go," while running back to her, grabbing her leg and hearing everyone calling me crazy. I could hear my so call family in the back ground saying, "Look at her, she acting like she done lost her mind." Little did they all know I really felt like I had lost my mind! After repeatedly tying to get me away from my mom, she told my dad to leave me alone and told me to go into one of the bedrooms.

You can bet I went into the bedroom my parents slept in and I left the door open so I could see my mother. As long as I could see her I felt safe and that's all I wanted. The window was up and my attackers would walk by the window telling me, "You know we gonna get you before you leave. You know they are all going into town and you can't go with them." They would laugh as they walked away. I became even more afraid because I knew they were right. Now the fear was all coming back again. I prayed out to God, "How I hoped my parents wouldn't go into town with my grandparents that next day." I cried silently to myself as I went to sleep.

TV time came later that day. I sat by my mom that day. I felt good! The blue tube even looked good to me this time. For once in a long time I could enjoy a program that was on the blue tube. I felt really relaxed while hoping tomorrow would never come. The blue tube went off and it was time to go to bed. Man how I hated that because I heard my parents and grandparents talking about going into town in the morning. Therefore, I couldn't sleep all night.

I was wondering and trying to figure out away I can go with my mom or where the hell I was going to hide until my mom came back. I begged to God. I said repeatedly, "Please don't let tomorrow come." Oh, but tomorrow did come and they all went. I cried and begged to them to let me go! I might as well been talking to myself because they didn't want to hear it. So I ran. I ran trying to run and hide for my life, but as usual it didn't do me any good. I was still being found by my attackers. They weren't anywhere near nice this time. I sometime felt as if I should just stop fighting with them and maybe they'd be a little easier on me.

I can remember hearing my attackers saying things like, "We got to make up for lost time, and Lovely you know that wasn't right by trying to tell on us." When one of my attackers said, "I'm going to teach you a lesson," I remember seeing all kinds of evil building up in his face. This time my clothes had gotten torn. I felt maybe this time I could get some one to believe me. Yeah, right! And I'm a man from mars. I tried to tell my parents when they came back, but my grandparents continued to convince my father that I was lying as usual. I tried to tell them about how my clothes gotten torn again.

But my attackers, who were supposed to be saints, came up with this crazy story which made me look like a complete liar.

For a minute there I started to believe their lie too. They said that I was playing on the stack of tracker tires and they, my attackers that is, were trying to get me down and make me go into the house. They claimed they were trying to keep me from getting in trouble for being outside in the sun. You know that could have really been true, especially since I am not supposed to be in the sun. Consequently, again my attackers have been looked at as being the good guys and I was labeled a trouble maker. Once again I began to silently cry inside.

I'm now feeling lost and gone all over again. I didn't want to live anymore. They say your parents were supposed to believe in you even if no one else did. However, I guess my parents had little fate in me because of my grandparents. My grandparents were suppose to be very deep into church and were elders of the church. These two advantages within the church caused them to gain superiority and respect over others. Therefore, many people looked up to them as if they were kings and queens and felt they did not lie. No one dear challenge there superiority or their decisions about anything. Everybody felt my grandparents were always right and my attackers were supposed to be saved. They are gonna kick holes through hell.

I really hate the fact that no one believed me. I started to think about what I could do to get at least my mom to have some kind of belief in me! I could think of anything. I hit a dead end; worthless! Just plain old worthless, I kept saying. Then I start feeling as if maybe I shouldn't even be here. "That's it," I thought to myself. Those were the key words to my master plan; maybe I shouldn't even be here. Then maybe they would believe me when I am gone and it will be too late. What an idea!

I kind of smiled a little inside behind that thought. It's funny because of that thought, I wasn't crying inside for a change. Now all

I had to do is come up with a master minded scheme to pull it off. I really started feeling suicidal but I couldn't bring myself to take my life in a painful way. I just wanted to roll over and die instantly. I try to drink some insect spray but that only made me sick. I even try going without eating, but my parents started forcing me to eat. After I ate the food I'd stick my finger down my throat until I brought all my food back up.

That was nasty and doing it didn't kill me. I was even more confused! Here I was willing to take my life, yet, still too afraid to make it happen! Another thing that also confused me was I couldn't understand why my mother out of all people didn't believe me. That hurt me even more. In some ways I think she maybe did not believe me because looked up to my grandparents. They, my grandparents, tried to portray themselves as being good and honest individuals. They try their best to keep their reputation too; especially due to their lifestyle and living situation. They were down home southern farmers and many people received products from them. For my readers that might want to know what I mean by down home southern farmers; well let me kind of explain it to you. They, my grandparents that is, didn't have electricity, running water, they used pot bully stoves, and there were not any nearby stores.

My grandmother, God rest her soul, was very old fashioned. My grandmother could cook any and everything on that pot bully stove. She believed in making her and anybody else clothing. Man, what I really didn't like was when my grandmother use to grab those chickens around their necks to kill them. She would hold a chicken by his head, spin the chicken body real fast in circles and then snap his neck off. I use to feel so sorry for the poor little chickens because I knew they were suffering and in pain. After the chickens' heads popped off their body would run around without their heads until they fell out and died. Finally, we had to pluck and clean the headless bloody chicken. My grandmother grew all her vegetables and most of her fruits; only the fruits that could grow in Arkansas weather. My grandmother use to tend to her garden two or three time a day. I also live by some of her values and beliefs as they pertain to being old fashion today.

There is not much I could remember about my grandfather because I was not around him much on the farm. I was mostly around my grandmother helping around the farm. I do remember my grandfather, God rest his soul too, uses to hit cows in the head with a hammer to make the cows dizzy. Then he would grab the cows around their necks and twist it. My grandfather would prepare the cows meat for selling or for our dinner that night. All the meat, vegetables, and fruit my grandparents prepared our meals with were always fresh. There you have it my readers a quick idea of real southern farmers.

Now let's get back to my story.....

Sad and confused, I couldn't understand why no one believed me! I felt in some ways I couldn't blame my grandparents for what was happening because my attackers had me labeled as a problem child. My attackers would always act as if they were trying to help me when I cry, yelled, scream, or tore my clothing. God, I really wanted to die! They had me so mixed up in the head, which lead me to start acting like I was crazy. I use to make crazy and silly sounds to myself. My life sucked a great deal and I honestly wanted to die! I use to take the razor out of my grandfather's shaver and hold it to my wrist while uttering to myself. I would say, "You know you can end it all right now. There will be no more pain, no more torture, no more living in fear and no more silent crying."

As I continue to talk to myself saying things such as, "Lovely, just think, you won't have to worry no more, no more wondering when, or who was gonna get you next." Yet I was afraid of doing it. I started remembering the biblical talks conducted by my grandparents. They use to tell us, younger children, bible stories and they spoke about the Ten Commandments a lot. I remembered what they said about how God, felt about self murder and that God will send murders to hell. I felt I was suffering enough; I didn't want to go to hell. So I threw the razor down and cried.

Suddenly one day it hit me. I came up with a clever brainstorm ideal. I remembered my grandmother was funny about rusty old nails lying around the farm. I remember she use to say, "If you get stuck with a rusty old nail, it could kill you. Man, if someone cried when they got stuck with a nail, the first thing my grandmother use to say, "Was it rusty and where is it?" With these thoughts in mind put me on a mad hunt around the farm for a rusty nail. I looked all over the farm for a few days looking for a rusty nail. I was about to give up until there it was; a blessed old rusty nail. Once I found it I thought to myself, "My way out of horror." It looked like "a nail of gold" to me, and it was sticking straight out a board.

I took my golden nail into the house and hid it. I didn't use it right away because when I stick myself with it I wanted to make sure it looked like an accident. Later on that day or the next day I slowly stepped on the nail allowing it to ease up through my feet but it hurt. I stopped trying and took the board with my golden nail in it and put it away to hopefully try again another day. A few days had gone by and my five attackers have not bothered me. I started to think that maybe I didn't have to use my "golden nail" after all and maybe I can go home and put these nightmares behind me.

Wishful thinking! It happened. My attackers made their move on me and sexually assaulted me again. Once they let me go I took off running with the wind under my feet. Nothing could stop me now from doing what I had to do. I ran so fast and crying at the same time. I knew no one was going to believe me. Therefore, I had to end this. Compared to all the pain I just went through and have been going though, that rusty old nail wouldn't hurt me at all. I did it; blood was rushing out my foot like a stream floating into the ocean. I was bleeding everywhere. Oh, what a relief, I thought to myself. I finally did it. I crawled up in a tracker tire to die. All I felted and remember saying was, "It will all be over real soon, you don't have to worry about no one hurting you any more."

After I did it I felt a sense of peace within me. It was a sense of peace, which set my mind free from worrying about my attackers and not understanding why no one believed me about my attackers. God knows I wasn't making those horrible things up. I wasn't an attention seeking child. I didn't do things and say things to get attention. I liked to be alone all the time. I truly liked being a loner! I guess me being upset from the attack; the lost of blood, the feeling of peace, and hoping that I will die all caused me to cry myself to sleep. It was like reliving the nightmare! I woke up and discovered I was still alive. I cried out, "God, why didn't you let me die? Why? I don't want to be here! I don't want to live anymore!" I knew after the rusty nail didn't kill me, I was going to always be a victim of abuse. In my mind I felt like I was reliving all those nightmares over again.

The sun had set and it had start getting dark. I climbed down and out of the tracker tire to go into the house. I remember getting holler at but what really hurt the most was got a whipping because my parents had been looking all over for me. I didn't care. I just took the punishment, like the abuse I've been taking and went into the room where my parents slept and silently cried to myself. My mom came into the room. She held me and was trying to talk to me. I remember just laying up in her arms lifeless. I felt a little bad because my mom was so worried about me while I was in the tracker tire. She thought I had fell out and died from being in the hot sun.

I felt bad at first but I change my mind quick once I thought about how my mom whipped me. Negative thoughts took over my mind and I start thinking with confidence that maybe my mom didn't really care about me. Right now I didn't want no one around me; not even my mom. Besides no one still has not noticed that I had a hole in my foot; this shows how much they really care about me. They, that is my so call family, don't care about me! A day or two went by and I started getting sick; keeping a fever way over 108.0. Each time I was given some medicine I would get rid of it. If it was a pill I'd hold it under my tongue and then throw it under the bed when my parents or grandmother left the room. I didn't want anything to help me get better. I wanted to die! I felt no one care about me. All I was concerned about was my "sweet golden old nail" was starting to do its job. I was gonna let what ever the nail did to finish taking control of me; take my life and let me have my peace!

I felt a sense of joy in my heart knowing that I was going to finally die. No one would never hurt me again or think about hurting me. The best medicine a doctor could order for me was to just let me die. I want all this horror I am experience to come to an end. I want to set my mind free and let my cries become cries of happiness and not pain. Life was hell for me and I don't want to go through it anymore.

I heard voices from many directions in the room I was in. I remember hearing my grandparents and parents arguing about what was going on with me. They start searching around the house for other home remedies to cure my illness. I was laughing inside hearing them run around the house like chickens with their heads cut off, confused, lost and not knowing what was going on with me. They really act as if they were concerned and cared about me. Well, if not believing an innocent child is how they show love I don't want any part of them or this life. Yeah, they honestly acted as if they were really so damn concerned about me.

Hearing them run around the house was the one time in a long time I felt good. Instead of crying inside I was laughing and enjoying every minute of their terror and fear. I believe the way they were all acting, they were more worried that I had gotten something that they would catch. My illness took total control of my body and I passed out. All I could remember was my body becoming extremely hot and I couldn't focus on anything anymore. I also remember my body felt relax as if it knew it was on its way to rest in peace. I was not worry at all about what was going on. I was very happy and I smiled. After feeling so happy and smiling I closed my eyes. No body actually knows what our bodies go through while we are sleeping. However, I could say if I had a choice to be sleep for the rest of my life or live to see another day, I'll choose to stay asleep for the rest of my life. To me anything was better than living in the crazy world surrounding me.

I could imagine the happy dreams I was having knowing that I didn't have to suffer anymore. I can picture myself as I smiled in my dreams. I never wanted to awake from my dreams. I knew when I wake up out of my fairy tale dream I will be back into my nightmare and all kind of hell will brake out. I saw my mother when I woke up, sitting on the side of my bed crying. I was told that I had been asleep for three days, but they were hoping for the best while praying. The doctor said, "If my parents wouldn't have gotten me to the hospital when they did then it would had been too late for me." I didn't care; I wished it were too late. I got even more upset when I heard that, because I wanted to die. Now I can remember saying to myself how I hated my parents for taking me to the hospital too soon. If it wasn't for them I would have been dead.

The doctor told my parents that my blood stream had so much infection in it that it took many different kinds of antibiotics before they found the right one to work on the unknown poison, which I had put into my body. Once I talked to the doctor and told him it was a rusty old nail. The doctors were surprised! I remember telling one of the doctors I tried to kill myself. I told him why and what had been happening to me over the summer and that no one believed me. I told the doctor how every one felt I was a liar and a big troublemaker. I remember crying and begging him to please help me. I remember crying out to him saying, "Lock me up because I am crazy, suicidal, and a danger to myself." I begged him telling him to please don't make me go back to that farm; please! I don't know what convince the doctor to believe in me. Then again I really didn't care. I guess it was the baby begging and the crocodile tears that did it because the doctor agreed to talk to my parents about the problem. He said to the other doctor the way I was acting was not normal. Thank God I said to myself!

The doctors talked to my mother. She agreed for them to do some tests on me. At first I was afraid but once they told me this one test was a must, I grinned and bared with them pocking around in me. I can remember them saying something to the fact that my hymen was still in tack. I being young didn't know what the hell they were talking about. I remember the doctor told my mother that it was some kind of truth to my story. I smiled feeling now maybe there is a God, who loved me. My mom got me together and we went back to the farm only to get our things and leave. Thank God, I was finally going home, hoping I'll never see that damn farm or those people again as long as I live.

Chapter Three
"A childhood life completely striped."

THE RIDE HOME was long as usual but more enjoyable, because I didn't have to sit on no one else lap. I was feeling maybe now I can live a little more relaxed and normal life. Chicago was an extremely bad city but I was so glad to see it. The Windy City is what many people call Chicago. I was home and it felt good to be home. I was finally home and away from my attackers. Only God and I knew how glad I was to be home. Like the little girl said that was lost in the storm, I started to say the same thing to myself, "There's no place like home." Deep inside, I wondered if home would probably hold some very unhappy times to come. With that thought in mind my smile slowly turn into a frown. We made it back home a few weeks before school started. My frown became deeper as I thought about it even more; I had only a few more good relaxing days left before I had to start facing the hell that await me at school.

Since my parents picked us up a little early this summer, we needed a baby sitter because they both had to work. There was a sweet lady who was considered our godmother and she had three boys. My parents asked her to baby sit us while they were at work. Oh, God, what did they do that for? I don't know why, but for some reason I felt it spelled trouble for me. Just call it my sense of smell. I couldn't understand why, but it seem like this was the year to get Lovely and make her life a living hell! Just when I felt all hell had stopped, and I could live a normal childhood life, it started all over again like it did when I was down south.

It was as if I was going through the fear, the emotional confusion; afraid all over again by just knowing I was about to experience the pain and suffering I felt down south. The best problem that added to my pain and suffering was most of my attackers were someone I knew, once loved, and trusted.

It was time for my parents to go to work. As a result they sent my brothers and I to my godmother house. I remember my godmother oldest son started making uncomfortable statements to me such as, "You went down south as a plump little girl. Now look at you; you're a vision for the eyes to hold; a young lady." All kinds of feelings started coming over me and running through my head. I silently cried out, "God, no, please not again." Before I knew it tears started running out my eyes. While I was crying my godmother oldest son was staring at me and said "You know you've been touched before." Then his sick minded, nasty self asked me was it and if I liked it. I wanted to jump up and dig his eyes out, but I was too afraid. I started feeling like I was going half crazy because I really didn't know when, or if he was going to try something. At the same time I started to wonder if he did try something would I be strong enough to tell someone about it.

So, in order to stay out of his eye site, I would hide in my godmother's room and pretend I was asleep until my mom came to get me. I really didn't care about playing outside because I couldn't go out in the hot sun anyway. It wasn't my fault that I inherited this crazy sensitive skin. As I think about it I felt my skin also contribute to me being a victim of life molestation. I was an easy target because I was always left alone and young. However, problems began all over again for me when my godmother started working. Guess who had to watch me? Of course, my godmother three sons.

All over again I became a victim because of my overly developed body and I was a loner. I did not trust them or males period. I would go into my godmother's room and lock myself in. Therefore, no one else could enter. The three boys use to knock at my godmother's door as if they were the police. I didn't care what they wanted out of her room; I use to say, "You just have to wait until she comes home because you are not getting in here." I knew it was just a matter of time they were going to figure out a way to get into her room! I was so afraid I didn't know whether or not one of them was going to attack me.

I would sit waiting with the TV turned down so I could hear anyone's foot step walking through the hallway. I felt like a sitting duck waiting there and not knowing when and if I was going to be attacked. It was just as horrible sitting there wondering if I was going to be attack as actually getting attack. One boy starts constantly knocking at the door; it sounded like the older brother. I could hear him some days messing with the door knob. I knew sooner or later he was going to get into my godmother's door and he was going to try and make a move on me.

Unfortunately, for me it was sooner than I thought. Being so afraid caused my mind to tangle while trying to figure out how I could avoid him and keep him away from me. I went to sleep only to be awakened by one of my part-time sitter; the oldest one. I didn't know at that time how he had gotten into the room. My only concern now was trying to figure out what he wanted? I remember asking him where the other kids were. He said he sent them to the store. I knew right then he had planned to make a move on me. "Oh God!" I thought to myself. He began to touch me. I started crying! He told me over and over again, "You're a young lady for a young man right now." Then he wiped away my tears with his hand and said, "I'm not going to hurt you."

I remember him pulling me closer to him and saying, "I'm going to make you feel good; like a real lady." I cried and begged him to please leave me alone. He said, "When I get through with you, you gonna want more." I start screaming louder as he tried to take my clothes off. I yelled at him saying, "Please no! Please no! Please no! Not again. Oh dear God not again!" My part time sitter began going under my clothes. I grabbed his hands and we start wrestling. We fell off the bed and onto the floor.

I end up on the bottom when we fell! He used his body to pin me down as he struggle to pull down my shorts. He placed his penis between my legs and start having sex with me. I could feel his hot smelly breath blowing hard on my innocent body while he rode me like I was a grown lady. He hurt me really bad. I felt like dirt all over as I laid on the floor crying. Continuously I screamed out loud, "Please make him stop." I wish I could have just have died that day.

If it wasn't for the kids knocking on the door, I don't think he would have gotten his nasty butt off of me. He jumped up and told me to fix my clothes. Then he said, "I better not say nothing to no one; or else," as he turned and walked out the door. He looked backed in the room so I could see his face and said, "Oh, and by the way, I'm not finished." I couldn't understand why and what it was about my body, which attracted mean, dirty, sick minded males. All they did was hurt me, and made me feel bad about myself. Like a scared fool I was I shook my head as if I was saying okay to him. He closed the bedroom door as he went out. After he left I start thinking to myself what I was saying ok to; for him to get me again, or not to tell anyone what happen!

I remember hearing him yelling at the kids for kicking and banging on the door. I also hear the other kids yelling back at him questioning him about why the door was lock. I didn't know weather or not I could use the other kids to help me with my story. I thought about down south! I went through a horrible experience down there physically, emotionally, and mentally, and most of all no one believed me! So once again I figure no one will believe me about what just happened to me. I decided to wipe my tears and say nothing. I told no one. After all, school was about to start and I felt I wouldn't have to see him again.

Therefore, I slipped into my own little world to deal with my pain and suffering as I silently cried to myself. I told no one. I began to put this horrible experience into the back of my mind. I felt as long as I wasn't around him I could deal with this nightmare and in time I'll soon forget. Talk about bad luck. It was just my bad luck; when it rains it pours. School started back and my mom started a new job which made her come home a few hours later. So instead of us being home alone until my mom got home, my little sister and I had to go over to our godmother's house for a few hours after school. I remember begging my mom to let me sit outside until she came home from work, or let me go by one of the other neighbors' house. But of course that didn't work.

My mom kept asking me why I didn't want to go over my godmother's house. I remember I just froze up and said nothing. Now I guess you are saying, why I didn't say something because that moment, would have been the perfect time to tell why I didn't really want to go over my godmother's house. I believe at the time, I was remembering all the pain he caused me and put me through. I figure he would hurt me more the next time for opening my mouth. I still had that fear of how my attackers down south use to do me when I only tried to tell my grandparents.So no doubt you could imagine what I was thinking at that time. I was only a child, who was only nine and a half years old at the time. I had a nice home, I could have been in the street, hungry, and with no nice clothes to wear. Now, I guess you are wondering what I meant by that statement! Well, it was like this.

I can still hear, see, and remember my parents saying, over and over again, if they didn't work we wouldn't have food, clothes, or a nice house. I remember my parents saying how hard a time they were having, trying to keep up with all the bills and the kids were continuing to grow. I really added to the clothing bill, being a child with a womanly developed body. My parents had to shop at the small lady store for my clothes. I can remember them talking a about how much more it cost to clothe me than the other kids. I heard this often as they talked between themselves. So, I knew my mother couldn't quit working to stay at home with me. You see, I was kind of forced to keep silent about the incident that happen to me at my part time baby sitter's house. I had to go over there because as my mom would say, she didn't trust anybody watching her girls. I was saying to myself, "Mom if you only knew." I don't know how long he went on with his abuse; but I didn't' know I had to put a stop to it! I didn't want to let it go on anymore.

I remembered the doctor down south saying to me, "stand up for yourself regardless; don't give up! One day you will ring the right person's ear and somebody, my child, is gonna listen and believe you're telling the truth."Yes, I had to remember those words to make me strong enough to un-bite my tongue, and swallow all those tears I was crying, and forget about my shame because I didn't do anything. I was going to make somebody listen to me. I did stand up, I told my mother. She didn't want to believe me at first. I truly believe when it came to details on how he did those things to me, and this time I had me some little witnesses to confirm the locked doors, and how he continued to send the kids to the store. The kids were wondering why he was constantly sending them to the store. They were all I needed to back my story up on how he would lock them out the house and I would look like I've been crying when they'd get in. That was enough that was all I needed. I cried tears of joy because I was finally being heard, and my mom really believed me.

I was taken to the doctor and you know what that hymen thing the doctor down south found was not there when the doctor look this time. I guess I should of felt kind of bad; but I didn't. As a matter of fact, I remember smiling when I heard that. The doctor said, "Yes, most definitely someone has been messing around with your daughter." Now I could stand a little taller because I had done something to help myself. No more running around with my head down, because I was feeling too ashamed to show my face. No more being afraid to face people because I felt they might have know or been able to tell what I've been through and would pick and tease me about it. This was another ordeal I wasn't ready to try to go through at the time. I mean this was too much for me to handle! Nothing happened to him because he was a minor, except he had gotten whippings by my parents and his mother.

It was suggested I receive counseling for the whole ordeal I had gone through. I didn't want to go. I felt if they didn't do something to him, how they could help me with anything. Since he wasn't punished by the law I felt like I should have kept my mouth closed. I thought, this person took something from me I would never get back and I hated him. The law says its rape, that is a crime but the only thing he gets is a slap on the back because he is a minor and he was too young to be charged for the crime. The courts only place the incident on his record, some punishment. So much for the damn law when you need them. I felt bad because so many people knew what had happened to me. My mom started coming home early to let me in the house. Oh yeah, remember I do have two brothers, but they belonged to the boy scouts club, which they went to everyday after school, so I couldn't go with them to their club. That's why I had to go to a babysitter's house but now my babysitter days are over, thank God!

To my readers:

If you have to work and need a babysitter, please make sure

you leave your kids with a very close relative or a very dependable trustworthy friend. As you have read in my case, the person you trust with your child may have to run for a minute and leave your child with someone else. That someone else could be a sick-minded person of some kind, an abuser, just waiting for a victim to prey on. Your child could be the one he or she may decide to pick to attack. Some kind of way, regardless how close you and your child maybe, it's possible the abuser will put so much fear in your child until he or she would be too afraid to say anything. I was so afraid because of all the pain my abusers had put on me. I started thinking that maybe if I keep my mouth close they wouldn't hurt me as much. The assaults slowly stop but they did not completely stop. Therefore, I seen I was wrong because my silence caused me more pain and made me an emotional wreck.

The fear of the attacker could be so strong that the child may feel it was best to keep silent. Like in my case as a child I knew I would have to be alone one day again with my attacker because of my living situation so I was scared the pain would be worst next time. I feel the emotional abuse I went through from being attack was a forever lasting assault on me and it was just as worst as being physically assaulted. I tried to go to school like a normal child but it wasn't easy because I knew what had happened to me inside. I knew I didn't have to live like that, but the fear of wondering who was about to attack me next wouldn't let me get on with my life. It seems once I try to put it all behind me; shit happens again. The rest of the school year was going along just fine; I was really surprised. Would you believe I had no problems! I decided to meet new friends.

Because of my overly developed body, I chose to hang around the much older crowd at school. I guess you can say I was finally able to fit in and wasn't uncomfortable with my body. The only thing about fitting where you really don't belong is I soon found out they were doing things I was trying to willingly run away from. Oh God, maybe they weren't the friends for me. Being with my new friends was fun, but hearing their sex talks brought up too many bad feelings and memories I was trying to bury inside and hoping I would forget. The memories hurt me so bad till I wished I were dead than going through that kind of pain. If that's what grown people do to show their love to each other and have kids, I promise you I wish I never grow up and have a baby.

What I couldn't understand was how they would talk about sex so calmly as if it's an enjoyment. These were kids talking about sex not grownups. I thought they were sick in the head. I didn't want to be a part of their little sex acts; I was now being called a chicken, a virgin, and a square. I didn't care! All I knew was I didn't want anybody to ever touching my body again. They did all that talking about me, but little did they know my virginity was forcefully taken away from me. I look at sex as being nothing nice, it was the worst and ugliest thing in the world two people could do to each other. I hated every minute of it and to hear my so call new friends talk about it turned my stomach. Now, I'm feeling like I don't want no parts of these friends of mines lifestyle, especially after school. School and my new friends seemed to be coming along ok! I can remember when I went back into the class some of my other students would ask me why wasn't I there for lunch or recess? I'd tell them some kind of crazy old lie every time they asked.

You see, I knew I had to eat lunch in the cafeteria with the older students in order for them to think I was an older person so I could become their friend! The funny thing about hanging with the older crowd was they would sometimes ask me why wasn't I in some of their classes! Yes, you're right, I told them different crazy old lies as well. Well, I soon found out that I didn't have to worry about getting caught up in my lying, because we were going to be moving soon. I didn't like that because I knew it was going to involve a lot of new people and I was going to have to try to fit in to keep from being attacked. We moved and did I hate it. We went to a school that went from kindergarten to the 12th grade. It wasn't as bad as I through it was going to be considering I only had a few problems at the school.

I recall my main problem was with a much older girl. Somehow, she found out who my brother was and I was going to be her connection. She liked my older brother, but he couldn't stand the ground she walked on. God, I believe I hated her as much as my older brother felt. Of course, she didn't care what my older brother felt because she was soon to be my new attacker. This older girl forced her friendship on me as she said, "To be my friend and protector." I really didn't mind too much at the time considering I was at the school and was trying to make some new friends. Believe me with a friend like her I didn't need any enemies. I can say she was cool up until the time my brother rejected her. She started kicking my ass around. This older girl that liked my brother, used to tell me every day if my brother didn't talk to her it was going to cost me. I couldn't understand why!

I knew I couldn't make him go with that girl. She was too ugly and she started to become mean to me. I wondered how I could get out of this mess! I couldn't ask my brother to do something he didn't want to do. I remember doing things I didn't want to do and it hurt me badly. I didn't want this older girl to hurt my brother because I wanted no one to feel those kinds of pains I've gone through. They were everything but nice! I used to go home with my clothes dirty, sometimes torn, and crying. Then when I get home I'd get a whipping because I was too afraid to tell who was beating up on me. My mom got tired of me coming home like that, so one day she tried to see if she could catch my attacker. Oh something I forgot to explain, I use to get my clothes torn by going through the bushes to avoid the older girl. One day my mom was walking to see me coming home because the school was only about one block from our house. You see my mom was wondering how I could be such a mess by the time I got home from school when I only had a block to go. This time I got caught.

My mom was looking down the street, I was hoping she would have gone in the house but she came down the block and there I was caught in one of the neighbor's bushes. Of course, I got a whipping because I didn't tell why I was in the bushes. You see the block we lived on just about every house had these high bushes in front of them. I use to sneak home climbing in and out my neighbors' bushes. And no, the neighbors or that big ass older girl did not catch me as I moved through the bushes. My clothes sometimes became torn while I was getting hung up in the bushes. My brother didn't like this older girl and I couldn't make him go with her for nothing in the world. I'd tell her I tried but she'd still tell me, "Unless I get them together she was gonna continue to kick my ass." Now this so call cool new friend of mine was now my new abuser.

My mom came home one day early. She got smart on me. I went to school that day to take pictures and I'll never forget this day. Remember I was always a big size girl for my age. I shouldn't have been afraid of anyone. Maybe the fear came from me trying to fight back my attackers, and trying to talk back to speak up for myself! This only made matters worse for me. I had developed a fear when it came to helping myself, and thinking I wouldn't win even if I tried. I had a fear of trying to defend myself and as I look back now that was a bad feeling to have. Now back to the day I got caught up. I was easing home through the bushes. I was climbing, running, and jumping in and out of the bushes. Now the funniest part was when I came to the end of my bush jump. I knew I had to look to make sure that big ass older girl wasn't around. Once I came to the end of the bushes, I knew I had to make a quick run for my house.

This time I didn't make it! Remember that big ass older girl liked my brother? Well, she spotted me in one of the neighbor's bushes. She tried to get me while I was in the bushes but I had gotten use to traveling through them. This man came out of his house yelling at her. I was inside the bushes laughing my butt off as I still moved to the next neighbor's bushes.I knew then I had to move a little faster because the old girl was show nuff steamed, because she was trying to get me and the man came out and caught her big ass messing with his bushes. Meanwhile, I'm still moving through the bushes. Damn, I made it! I was laughing for joy because I beat her to the end of the bushes. I broke and took off running for my life, only to get stopped at the end of the path.

No, it wasn't old girl, it was my mother. She was standing there on the porch with a big belt. Let me describe this belt to you! It was a cowhide three individual layered leather razor stip. I don't know how many of you can remember back in the older days when they had these leather traps to sharpen their razor before they would have the males at the barber shop. Well, that's what my mom had at the top of the stairs waiting for me when I turned the corner. My mom stopped me and said, "Now just turn your ass around and go out there and kick whoever you're running from ass, or I'm gonna whip your ass until you can't sit down." That was a whipping nobody wanted. I begged my mom saying, "mom this girl is big, this girl is real big, please don't make me go out there and fight her!" I can see her finger now as my nose followed to the end of it as she said, "Get!" That was all my mom had to say and I got the hell out there. I can remember that because my family even now sometimes teases me about it until this day.

As the big girl came from around the bushes I walked down the stairs off the porch crying. I stood there shaking and said, "I don't want to fight you but my mom said if I don't she's going to whip me with that strap she has in her hand." The big girl then said, "Good, now I'm going to beat you down in front of your mother." She kicked me down and the fight was on. I started biting, kicking, hitting the big girl, and at the same time crying. I felt I had no win, she had me down and she was beating me. I can remember hearing my brothers in the background asking my mother if they could get the big girl? My mom being the boss said, "No! Let her do this by herself. You can't always fight for her." Right then I started feeling like my mom didn't love me. This big girl was kicking my butt, and she was just standing there and wouldn't let my brothers help me. I just wanted to die!

I was trying to fight back but this girl was just too big, and she had me pinned down. All at once a light bulb flashed in my head. I remember something my mom use to tell us. She would say, "If you're fighting somebody bigger than you, pick up a stick, brick, or a bottle, and knock the hell out of them." By that time I focused on a brick. I grabbed it and bricked the hell out of her. I kept on bricking this big ass older girl remembering all those ass whippings she uses to give me because my brother didn't want to go with her. I bricked her for all those ass whippings I got when I got home from school. No one could tell me shit; I knew I was "Miss Stuff." I beat her seriously bloody. Old girl was bleeding; it kind of scared me for a minute. I thought I was killing her, so I stopped. My brother teased me after I explained the reason I had to beat that big ass girl up. My brother laughed while at the same time calling me crazy, and saying, "You now had your first knockdown, drag out, ghetto fight." It may have been dirty fighting but it worked for me. I became so big headed after beating old girl down like I did; I felt I could have taken on the world at that moment.

It felt kind of good to get the attention I was getting. It felt like I was being rewarded for beating somebody up. I still was soft hearted and started feeling kind of sorry afterwards for bricking old girl like I did. Call me crazy because everybody else did, but I was wishing I was strong enough to tell old girl I was sorry. But I was afraid she might wanted to fight some more and I was tired. So I went into the house as a hero. It's funny because after that fight old girl became my best friend for real. She was already the school bully, everyone was afraid of her, and I beat her down real good. I now had what they called a reputation; I was looked up as somebody special now. Now I had new friends coming out of the woodwork. I guess you can say I now live a normal life for about a few years. I never knew there was so much peace on this world we call earth. Yes, I had really started to enjoy my normal peaceful life. I didn't have to go down south for the summer and I was at a school where I could hide my true age even with my overly developed body; I fitted in really well.

Chapter Four
"I Just Want A Normal Life"

TO LIVE A proud and relaxing life was all that I ever wanted; worry free, no teasing, and picking, no insecurity about my body no more! But most of all no more grabbing, pulling, abusing, and hurting my body. Yes, I have started to live a normal life. Now I could learn things like I'm suppose to on a daily basis. Yeah, I changed my mind, I'm glad I didn't kill myself when I tried to. I had new friends who liked me for whom I was and not for how I looked. I started feeling secure about my body, proud, and walking tall. What else could a child ask for in life? I had the enjoyments of fun, a world that I never knew existed. Look at me now I can smile and it feels damn good; thank you God, because you do love me. As far as my best new friend, the older girl that was stuck on my older brother, whom I beat down, well we walk to school together every day. She even takes me to the store and I buy what I want on her. Yes, as I think about it, it felt real good to kind of have the shoes on the other foot. Thinking back to my earlier school years abuser and remembering how I used to have to buy him to leave me alone, old girl was the one who really surprised me! She had lost her crush on my older brother and I was so glad about that. Don't get me wrong, she still liked him, but now she would only speak and smile at him, and I don't get my ass kicked because he rejects her.

Yes, all was fine in life for me until a big major problem just exploded in my face and I was too blind to see the fuse burning while it was constantly being lighted. Remember that happy and loving home I had? Well, it was being torn apart and I couldn't understand why. As a child I really didn't know what had happened in my parent's life! I truly did not know why they were splitting up, but being grown now I know that in a relationship sometimes you will have problems. Sometimes it's best to separate because of those problems but being young, I couldn't figure out for the world what the hell was going on in my parent's life. All I knew was I used to hate hearing my parents arguing. I would be so confused till I will start crying and go to my room. I'll run and jump in my bed, hollering as I buried my face deep into my pillow on the bed. Crying, screaming, and talking to myself, "I thought they loved each other?" No more, as I continued screaming to myself. I don't need any more pain! Now, I have another kind of abuse and I don't know what to do about it! What am I suppose to do, as I continue throwing a tantrum like a small child, yelling, "I wish I was dead." My mind was so confused, God, maybe if I weren't born they would be happier. Why me? And I continue yelling, "Why, why God, why?" I pulled the covers over my head and before I realized it I had cried myself to sleep.

I remember I use to be afraid to come home from school because I didn't want to hear my parents' mouths as they argued. When I came home from school if I'd see my dad's car, I would go around the back, and climb in my bedroom window or sometime. Then I would run and hide until he left because I didn't want my parents to ask me to choose between them. I loved both of my parents so much; I could never choose. They were my life. God knows I'd rather die than to have to live without one of them in my life; a choice I hoped never to have to face! Remembering how I use to sneak in the house to avoid my parents, I'd come in and go straight to my room, and cry because I was so unhappy. One of my parents would always come into my room and ask me to come and eat my supper. I remember I would always lie and tell them my stomach hurt or I didn't feel good. I would sometimes replied, "I wasn't hungry," while at the same time my stomach was balling up in knots for some food. But I'd just turn over and lie down and cry myself to sleep with my face buried deep in one of my pillows and other one on top of my head.

This went on for awhile, the not eating I mean. My parents got tired of me lying because they knew I loved eating, so they started forcing my food down my throat but I would force it back up and out. I kept doing that for a while until I got caught! You know that ass whipping your parents always say they would give you and after wards you won't be able to sit down? Well, I couldn't sit down. I remember how I use to twist to the side of my hip to sit down. Even then my butt could still feel those stinging pains. Oh, let me tell you, that whipping that you can't sit down afterwards, wasn't nothing nice, it hurt. I was so confused till my mind started to hurt me bad. Talk about a sister with a headache, I kept them. Good thing I was a young girl because if I were grown my husband would have thought something was wrong about me getting headaches all the time. I was keeping headaches all the time from worrying so much. I use to cry silently to myself every night. I was afraid of what was going to happen to us if my parents got a divorce. I use to worry about who we were going to live with or were they going to lock us up in one of those homes? I cried so much because I couldn't understand life.

Now here I had everything I always wanted. I didn't have problems with people wanting to misuse and abuse my body. My home use to be so happy, what happened to it? There was so much sadness, unhappiness, and depression at my home. I really felt bad when I heard my parents argue about how one or the other was confusing my mind, when all the time it was the both of them. What I couldn't understand was here they were telling me life was gonna be better for me. They had even helped me build myself-esteem up with high hopes. I felt damn good about myself, only to find out life is like a roller coaster. It'll let you down just as fast as it'll bring you up. I started coming in even later after school because I began having these real funny feelings about something wasn't right, but I just couldn't for the life of me figure it out. Then the reason for those feelings surfaced. It was sad but my parents had worked their situation out among the results that weren't too good!

Chapter Five
"Torn Apart"

MY PARENTS HAD decided to go their own separated ways. God, I wanted to die, because we had to decide if we wanted to stay in Chicago, with my mom, or go back to Wisconsin with my dad. I had hoped that they would have worked their problem out so they wouldn't have to involve us in it, but I guess it was something we couldn't avoid. My parents started asking my older brothers, who they wanted to live with? It was clearly understood whom they were going to live with considering I use to hear them say all the time, "how tired they was of Chicago." Plus, even thou my older brother were a mama's child he was really a daddy's boy. It was obvious that my mom was gonna keep my little sister because she definitely was a mama's little shadow. The problem came in with me. My father felt I was stressed out with Chicago, with all the people I've been through, and needed a new start. That thought of his was fine, but the fact was I didn't want to leave my mama. My mom felt that if he was gonna take the boys, at least let her keep the girls together. That thought of hers was all good, but I still didn't want my daddy to leave me and take my brothers. So my parents went back and forth about why I should stay in Chicago, and why I should go to Wisconsin. Then something made the two of them realize I was standing there.

One of them said, "Lets let Lind decide whom she wants to live with." I was hoping that question would never get around to me. I was standing there as if I didn't hear them. Crying, hoping they'll just say, "I love you, let's stay together," and we could all live happily ever after. That's where my problems came in at, I was always living a fairy tale life, but now I had to face the facts of reality. This wasn't a story book, it was for real, and I had to decide which parent I was gonna stay with. I still just stood there crying because I was afraid that if I picked one over the other the other would probably feel bad and think I didn't love them. As my parents continued to pressure the question no me, I just started crying out real loud, "Why don't you two just stay together!" Unfortunately my parents weren't hearing anything I said. All they wanted was an answer from me and they didn't want to hear anything else. I was too upset, I had been crying for a long time. It felt as if I had lots of people in my stomach destroying me for the rest of life. I can remember, it was as if I was in daze; but I could barely hear my parents continuing to ask me, "Faye," as my dad use to call me, "what you gonna do? We don't have all day." I remember replying to him, "I want to stay with the both of you." Over and over again I kept repeating it!

Then I started screaming out as I cried inside out, "How can you all make me try to choose between the two of you, I can't!" I was a very difficult child that day. I can remember even yelling at my parents and saying, "If I can't live with the both of you. I'm running away to kill myself!" Oh, my dad didn't like that remark. It seemed as if it made him even madder at me. I guess because his stuff was already packed to go and that's what he wanted to do, but I was holding him up. My dad started hollering at me, "Why can't you make this easy and quit being so difficult!" Then when I heard him say, "I'll take you with me," man I really started acting a fool. I fell out on the floor, crying, kicking, and screaming, "No, no, I don't want to leave my mommy!" Well, I got my wish, my dad told me to stay with my mother, because they were leaving. What did he say that for? I wasn't hearing it. I broke the hold I had around my mom, ran and grabbed my dad around the legs, yelling and screaming, "Daddy, please don't leave me, please daddy stay, don't go daddy." Then before I knew it he had put my clothes in the car. I started crying even louder. I kept on crying then when it came time for him to try to put me in the car, that's when I began fighting, kicking, screaming, and falling out. I really felt like my mind had snapped because I didn't want to leave my mother and little sister.

To see my mother begging my dad and saying, "Herbert, please don't take them away from me, please leave my kids Herbert!" I hated seeing her, my mother in so much pain. I really started showing out, I began clowning bad, screaming, crying, and calling out, "Mama, I don't want to go please mama, don't let him take me." Before I knew it I was in the car crying, kicking, screaming, and even more crying with my head turned one way, looking out the window, wishing I was dead, and wondering if I'll ever see my mom and sister again. I started feeling light but heavy headed kind of woozy as if I was trying to pass out. It was as if I was watching my whole world coming to an end, flashing, and passing by me as my father drove up the highway. All I could think about was my mom. I kept thinking about how much I missed her, till I just started crying real hard, silently deep inside, sniffing, hurting in pain, until I felt knots forming in my stomach. I did a good job too because I cried so hard without saying a word until I made myself sick, my dad wasn't too happy about that, he started yelling and screaming at me. Telling me, "It's too late; you couldn't make your mind up, so I made it up for you."

Man, did I feel like a real sad, unloved, complete fool, and had no one to blame but myself. I really hated myself! Continually feeding my head the thought and reminding myself that my mom may never want to see me again, even thou I didn't want to go. I kept crying and saying, "God it's not my fault I'm young and very confused." I always felt your mom and dad were supposed to stay together until the kids grow up. Then after the kids get grown the parents were to live together until they get old and die. Or was that just myself living in a fairytale story again. I believe I was so much into those happy ending stories because my life was so sad. I use to imagine one of the characters in the book was my life until I realize that I was living a lie, and a make believe life I had created in my own mixed up confused world. As usual I must have cried myself to sleep because I remember nothing until I woke up and we finally made it to Wisconsin.

Chapter Six
"Misery Wisconsin/ Trying To Fit In"

EVEN THOU I miss my mama a whole lot, I guess when I look at it, Wisconsin doesn't seem so bad. I knew I was gonna have to deal with a bunch of strange new people. My main concerned was if the people were as rude and evil as the people in Chicago! Why me? Why? All kinds of fear and old wounds were reopening in my mind. I hated to have to start over and trying to fit in. So far it was all good because I didn't have to go anywhere. Now, I'm so afraid that when I do go some place what's gonna and/or could happen to me. The houses here in Wisconsin look a lot different from the buildings in Chicago. In comparison, at that time Wisconsin had nothing but little houses but Chicago had lots of sky scrapers. Even the smallest buildings in Chicago put Wisconsin houses to shame when it came to height. My dad had gotten a nice, kind of big and roomy house. It was pretty and he had furnished it already. It had me to believe that he was planning on leaving my mom anyway because I've never seen a house fully furniture as soon as you move in. I guessed! I never seen the furniture in this house before, it all looked newly bought. As I look at the house I had nothing but devilment thoughts in my head. I had a nice room but I hated it. I wanted my old room back in

Chicago with my mom.

Remember me saying I believe my dad had this all planned? Well, he did! He'd picked a girl on the block to be my friend before I even came up to Wisconsin. She seem like she was a nice person. I later found out that she was only a few years older than me. She was a lot taller and bigger than me but her body was developed like mine. So, I thought maybe we could be friends, since I didn't know anyone else. I didn't care if my dad said the president of the United States was cool, I still didn't trust him, the president, that is. So this-soon-to-be new friend of mine had nothing coming. We started slowly hanging out together. We would do girls things like play rope, jacks, hopscotch, and sometimes a little ball. I started kind of liking my new friend. She has gotten to the point where she had begun to wear out her welcomes. It was like every morning, noon, and night, there she was. I didn't mind so much hanging with her but it was getting out of hand. I remember how she would sometimes come into my bedroom and wake me up with this half funny ass touch that felt like a caressing type of hug! She claims she was trying to wake me up by tickling me. I don't care what she said it was suppose to have been all know is it made me very uncomfortable. My mind was already doubtfully wondering about everyone that came around me. So now I was show nuff closely watching her.

I went off on my brother for letting her into my bedroom and telling her to wake me up. He claimed it was time for me to get my butt up out of the bed. You see I slept late because while everybody else was sleeping at night, I was walking around somewhere at night. It was my way of kind of getting to know my new neighborhood. I guess you my readers are saying why would you walk around at night? Well, it's because that's when Wisconsin seemed more peaceful to me and usually was. There were no more than one or two people out at night. So I felt more comfortable as I walked, looked around the neighborhood, cried as I thought about my mother, and how much I really missed her. I would sometimes go and sit in this little park about a block from my house so no one can see me. I would watch the animals run around in the park and listen to the birds as they sing over my head and on the ground. You can call it wishful thinking, but I remember how I would always wish I was like those birds, free as if they didn't have a worry or care in the world; happy. Happy, a word that life just seems as if it didn't want me to live by. While walking around most of the night crying, thinking about my mother and sister, sometimes would cause me to get caught by the daylight sitting on the stairs in the back of my house. So I slept later and my so call new friend knew this. Not only did my so call new friend knew I slept late but she also knew I didn't come out until the sun started setting. Kind of sounds like a vampire to me, but I wasn't. I just couldn't be in the hot sun or it'll burn, blister, and peel my skin.

So now my whole thought is why she was coming over when she knew I was sleep? After I gotten myself together, I sat and watched TV. I was a big kid, I loved cartoons. I remember hearing a lot of noise outside as if someone was fighting. So I jumped up and ran to the door. It was just some of the neighborhood kids playing. You know I did get tired of staying in the house while everyone else played. I would stand in the door watching the other kids in the neighborhood enjoy themselves during the rest of the summer and wishing I could be out there. I couldn't go outside because I was different from the others; it was a sad life I lived. I noticed that once my new friend had realized I really couldn't be in the sun she started hanging with a larger and older crowd. She once brought them to my house and I asked her not to do that again. I told her to keep her friends away from my house because I didn't like them. You couldn't guess what she told me, but I'll tell you anyway. She had the nerves to say, "You just jealous." I looked at my new friend and told her, "You can stay the fuck away from my house too," and closed the door. So she left and the only time I would see her was when I was sitting on the porch; she and her friends would pass my house.

I remember one time one of her so call half-grown friends asked her who was I because of the way I rolled my eyes at her. Now, let's call her my ex new friend because she said some stupid shit like, "I just looked at everybody crazy," I thought nothing else about it. So here I was only a few weeks into a new city and I was back to my same old self; alone! God, I wish I was back in Chicago with my mama and sister. Oh my days were so lonely now. I became more and more sad and depress. I really missed my mom. One night I really couldn't sleep so I went for another one of my walks. Not really caring about the time I started walking back home; it was the wrong timing. As I raised my head up once I had gotten closer by my house I saw someone standing on my front porch. As I gotten closer to my house I seen that it was my dad. He had come home from work early and caught me walking up the street, man was he mad! I tried to explain to my dad that I walked the streets at night all the time, but he didn't want to hear it. I don't really know what it was but it seemed as if my dad had started to talk to me with this funny tone in his voice. Especially when he said, "You keep walking your ass out there somebody is gonna sash your ass up, this isn't Chicago." My dad just didn't know how bad I wished and wanted to go back to good old Chicago, with my mom, sister, and friends. I don't know why he said that because it really hurt my feelings, so I went on to my room and went to sleep.

A new day! Well the sun is up bright and hot as usual. Mc, I guess I'll do my daily routine, which was nothing! Once the shade comes on my side of the street, I'll go out and sit on the porch for awhile. Then when the streets are clear I'll go on my nightly walk. Sitting watching every one play and having fun had really started to get on my nerves. I started noting I was developing a hate inside me for those that could go out and enjoy the sun. Sometimes I would be so mad until I'll just say forget it and go out in the sun. Knowing that moment of enjoyment was going to cause me a few days or weeks of pain. The girls next door were playing rope; man when I was in Chicago no one couldn't beat me jumping. I haven't jumped rope since I've been in Wisconsin. They were having fun too. I mean they were enjoying themselves a whole lot. One girl was supposed to be "the stuff," as they say. She was really talking big time mess because couldn't no one beat her. I just looked and listened. I guess you can say when she claimed she was the best in the neighborhood that's when the dare came to me. You see, I already knew I could beat her jumping on one leg, that's how cold I was in jump rope.

Old girl kept talking and it seemed as if now she was directing her comments at me. Maybe it could have been because when she was standing down there talking all that garbage, I was talking and shaking my head to myself because I knew I could smoke her out something bad when it came to jumping rope. I'm saying to myself, "Look at her she thinks she's doing something but she ain't shit." I guess old girl must have been reading my mind because she said something and I replied, "You talking to me?" She said "Yeah." I then told her "You're sure you're talking to me?" You see, I wanted to make sure myself because in Chicago, we didn't just jump rope for the fun of it, we got paid. So I felt why not. I knew old girl had money because her dad was a police officer ad I use to sit and watch her tease the other girls with her money. So I said to myself, "Why not." I came down off the porch and stood under the big tree in front of her house. We began talking. I'm telling her, "You know you're o.k. but I'm better. Let's say we make the game a lot more exciting, and interesting." She replied by saying, "How?" Then I said, "You so sure of yourself, let's make a bet." The girl looked at me for a moment. I could tell she was hesitating! I had to do some serious talking, but she took bait. The bet was on, and I knew all the time her money was already in my pockets. I told her I had to warm up, that's so she could see and think I was a sloppy jumper.

She said, "Let her have a couple of turns, she look like she needs it." So I'm just jumping, saying to myself, "You stupid fool you, you the one who needs a lot of practice." So old girl decided to go first. You see we were to get two turns each. She started jumping. Oh she really thought she was doing something. Then came my first turn. I jumped well enough to make sure I didn't get close to her score. She laughed now; telling me I might as well give up because it isn't any way I could catch up with her. What she didn't know was I had it all planned so she could think like that. She took her second turn, which was to continue from where she left off. All old girl was doing was just talking stuff and I was laughing on the inside to myself. She messed up and it was my turn. I started jumping, talking, saying, "Man I got a long way to go," but all the time I knew I was going to smoke her ass. I'm still jumping; I even did one of those messed up tired moves on her just to keep her hype. She was so stupid and I just made me some easy money. I did another slick move on her. She really enjoyed that one. She messed up when she started talking big time shit to me. Man, I started jumping and playing around in the rope. Her eyes got big and her mouth shut the fuck up as her lip dropped to the ground. I was on that ass now. I got cold on her, I started doing criss-crosses with my legs and spinning around. My moves really fucked her up. I started jumping on one leg for a long time and she looked like she was ready to cry. Now her ass is not only smoked but she was smoking under the collar. It didn't make the situation no better because her friends were now teasing her. Even thou I beat her, I kept on jumping, until she got so mad about that whipping I was giving her, she stuck her hand in the rope and said, "You already beat me. I quit and give me my rope." I told her to take the damn thing and she better be glad it didn't hit me in the face when she snatched it. So she gathered her little old rope together and you know I had to stop her because she hadn't given me my money. Well, I got paid but I made an enemy too. I didn't care, but old girl wouldn't let me play rope with her anymore either. So I went and sat back on my porch with hers and my money in my pocket.

Dark finally came, man was I glad. I jumped up and off the porch I went to start my nightly walk. Up the block I went. As I began my walk, I don't know but for some reason the streets seemed as if they were quieter that night. Oh, I remember it well. I know I just didn't really feel right about being out there. Something was telling me in my own mind to take my butt back home. But did I listen; no! I had to continue up a few more blocks. It was nice and warm that night. I had on one of my favorite sizzler outfits and as my mom always say. "I be popping that gum and at the same time my ass," meaning it was short. My mom use to tease me the entire time saying, my gum and my dress is popping to a rhythm as I walk. She always no what to say to make you laugh or put a smile on your face. So I'm walking and popping to a rhythm as my mom use to say, heading on my way back home. I don't know what it was but I started getting a crazy butterfly feeling in my stomach. The same one I use to get when I was attacked. Talk about guts instinct. Here I am walking a little faster, constantly turning around, looking at every shadow, and noise I heard. Now I am very nervous. It's as if I can feel my blood plumbing through my veins. I'm starting to get now even more afraid but there wasn't anyone out there but me. A car goes by; I watch it until I couldn't see it no more.

So I turn back around proceed walking even faster up the street. It seems as if the closer I gotten to my house, the faster I'll start walking. I'm now only a few blocks from my house, God was I ever glad. I crossed the street. Now I'm a block and a half away from my house. As I walk pass the alley I heard a noise. I jumped but I didn't see anybody or anything. So right away I began speeding up my walking into a faster but yet still a lighter pace. I was now moving so fast and quiet it was as if I was walking on the tips of my toes. I'm walking fast looking back because I knew I heard something in that alley. While doing that I turned my head around only to walk right in the arms of my soon to be attacker. Damn it! I said to him right away, "Please let me go, I'm only eleven; please, I just stay right there," pointing at anybody's house. He said, "I've been watching you for about a week, and I knew one day I was going to catch you coming back this way and get you." By that time I was in tears, crying, begging him to please let me go, I just want to go home. I started pleading with him. Please, sir please don't hurt me; let me go, so I can go home! Please! My crying and begging didn't do any good. He took my arm and twisted it way back to the back of my head. Telling me the more I move the more it was going to hurt. I didn't care if it did hurt; I just wanted him to let me go. I started screaming for help but no one was out on the street that night but me and my soon to be attacker. He took his other arm and grabbed me from behind around my stomach; at the same time he was lifting me off the ground and carrying me back into the alley. I continued screaming but there was no one around to help me. So, I knew now that all I could do was pray. Pray that he didn't kill me because I saw his face.

He started kissing me down the back and side of my neck with his lock hold on me and my arm still twisted to the back of my head. I started twisting and wiggling my body, hoping I can break my attackers hold. As I remember now. It seemed as if it made my attacker madder and he put an even tighter grip around me. My attacker then kind of picked me up because I was trying to give him dead weight by trying to fall to the ground. That didn't do me any good because he just pushed me up against the building. Telling me all I'm doing is making it harder on myself. I begin crying, "Please let me go!" With all his weight pressing up against my body, I remember he wrapped one of his legs in between mine and began rubbing and squeezing my breast. By this time I was too afraid to even breathe! All I could do was have flashbacks of my previous attacks. God , I was so afraid, I knew my attacker was going to kill me, and no one was going to know. The way I was feeling at that time, if he didn't kill me after he was finish and let me go, I just might go and kill myself! This is becoming too emotional for me. It's as if I'm now losing my mind. I started begging my attacker to please, please don't do this! Just let me go I promise I won't tell no one. Please let me go mister!

He threw me down on the ground with my arms still twisted up behind my back. With his free hand he opened my blouse and began sucking on my breasts while lying on top of me. My attacker removed his hand from around my breast. He put his hand in my clothes and begins funneling with my private. I kept crying and begging him to please stop and let me go and don't do this to me. I now can remember hearing him unzip his pants. I really started crying louder and louder. I was so afraid because I knew what was about to happen. I was trying to kick and wrestle with my attacker to keep him from putting his penis in me. It did me no good, all it did was made my attacker madder and he was very ruff with me. All I could do was scream as his penetration hurt me. He continued raping me and did what he wanted to do. I really got scared because now he was laying on top of me breathing and saying, "What am I going to do with you now?" I really started begging my attacker then, saying, "Please mister, please just let me go, I won't tell no one, I won't!" At that time to get him to let me go on with my fuck up life, I would have been willing to jump off a building, and take my chance of surviving. I just begged and kept on begging until my attacker finally just let me go. I jumped up off the ground and started running home so fast crying my eyes out wondering if anyone was going to believe me? When I made it home my dad did not make it home from work yet. Not only did I have dirt all over me but I also I felt so nasty and dirty; I ran into the bathroom and turned on the shower. I begin to scrub my body with lots of soap faster and faster.

I knew taking a shower wouldn't wash away the dirt from inside of me but at the time all I could think about was maybe if I washed his scent off of me it would be a fresh start for me. After I showered I went and lay in my bed quietly, listening to the darkness, and crying my heart out. Like every night I cried myself to sleep and I never remember anything else until I woke up the next morning. My dad still wasn't home yet; I really started to worry. I got up and took me a nice relaxing hot bath. I can remember how my parent's use to tease me about the smoking hot bath I would take. I remember I would tell them when I first got into the tube I had to lay still in the water until it cool off. As I lay back in the tub, I started crying remember what had happened to me last night. The water felt good to my body but I still felt dirty and nasty all over. Good, I wish I could wash away what my attacker did to me.

The water was so relaxing until I just cried myself to sleep. I must have stayed in the bathtub too long because the next thing I knew my dad was yelling and banging on the bathroom door. Even though my dad scared me with that noise, I was glad to hear his voice. When I came out the bathroom, my dad started shouting at me for hogging up the bathroom. I was trying to tell him what had happened to me last night but he started talking about he was tried and didn't want to hear it. I knew then that history was repeating itself with me again. I was alone in this evil world; lost, hurt, and confused because I had no one to turn to. God, I want my mom. After seeing my dad didn't want to hear what I had to say, I made up my mind to try and forget what happened to me last night never happened. It was just a nightmare and I had to keep on living regardless.

I was so confused, at first I only though people you know did those types of things to you. I know now that anybody, even strangers does mean things to you too. The strangers would hurt you worst because they don't know you; believe me that was my meanest attacker. My attacker really hurt me bad. I convinced myself to try to adjust surroundings and hopefully move on with my life since I didn't know my attacker. For a few weeks I refused to go outside because I didn't know what to expect. I went no further than my house front door. From that night on until school started I stopped living, no more walks, no more nothing, I stayed in the house, sitting, and crying to myself. Once everyone left I'll lock all the doors and closed the windows. I felt as if I was going crazy, I would start screaming out loud, "Why me? God, why me? When is this hurt going to stop?" I had hoped I didn't have to go through this again for the rest of my life.

I remember how sometimes I would cry myself to sleep and my brother would be knocking on the door to get in. I can remember my older brother use to tease me and called me crazy for being closed up in the house like I was. I didn't say anything; I would just look at him and stared into my spaced out own world as if I really wasn't hearing him. I'll then go into my room and close my door. I was so lost and bitterer about myself, to me my life was a world of living hell. It seemed as if my presence here on this earth was enough to continue causing me more and more hell. I don't know what to do no more.

Chapter Seven
"Evil Over Coming Good"

I WAS HOPING when school started maybe my life would be back to normal. The first day of school wasn't as bad as I thought it would be. The kids there were much nicer than the kids at every other new school I first went to while I was staying in Chicago. I didn't feel like a freak of nature at my new school. There were girls and boys who were taller than me and the good thing about my new school was there were many girls who were bigger than I was in both the breast and butt. Yes, I really believe I am going to like it here at this new school. I fitted right in with no problems. I didn't have to sneak in the older kid's lunchroom or on the older side half of the playground. I think I finally found somewhere I just fitted right in as if I always belonged here. The first few months was great, I really enjoyed going to school. I couldn't wait until night came so I could go to bed and wake up in the morning for school. I wanted to go to school and hang out with my new friends.

My new friends at school were my type of girls because they loved to jump rope and they could jump really well. There was this one girl I became friends with by competing against her in jump roping. We use to compete to see who could jump the best in the school. She already had the title and I was trying to get it from her. I mean we use to jump the whole recess period and we use to continue jumping the next school day too. I remember the other girls had gotten tried of turning the rope for us till they just stop turning and would say, "You both won, neither one of you is a loser." Every time we played rope at school we were partners and we never had to pick up the rope to turn; we were undefeatable. School was going along super, I kind of forgotten about what had happen to me a few months ago.

One day I had stayed after school for the school's social center program they have a few days out of the week for the students. The program was design to give the kids something else to do after school to help keep them out of trouble. The program had all different kinds of board games, basketball, and of course jump rope. The social center program after school was fun. Sometimes we meet new people and I really started to enjoy myself. I started to think that everyone was not all bad like I had labeled them to be. I was having big fun at the center, it was unfortunate it had to end. Everyone had to go home. As I was walking home I kept saying to myself, "I couldn't wait until tomorrow come because I know I was going to have a lot of fun at school and after school.

For the first time in my life I really started enjoying myself till I began saying, "I didn't ever want to go back to Chicago." I still loved my mom very much and I missed her even more. I do want to see my mom and my little sister but I hope they would come up here to see me. Yes, it did feel good to be alive. I'm walking home, cheerful, full of happiness like I had never had a problem in the world. I was carefree and it felt damn good. The school was about four blocks from my house. How safe can a person be! Even though I didn't have far to walk to get home my nightmare had came back to life. I was about a block and a half from my house. It wasn't really that dark outside, so I felt like I was just as safe as if I was in my mother's arm. Then all of a sudden he came out of the middle of nowhere and grabbed me. I started hollering but my soon to be attacker grabbed me around my mouth. Once my soon to be attacker turned me around so I could see his face I said, "You! It's You!" Even now as I remember that day I could still hear my attacker voice as he say, "I thought you forgotten about me, and when I didn't see you taking those walks no more at night, I thought you left town or moved." All I could do was just pray he didn't hurt me again. God, why me? It happed liked to me again, every time I think my life is going to become normal something always happens.

While my attacker covered my mouth with one of his hands, he grabbed me up under my arms with his other arm and dragged me into this alley a block behind my house. I was kicking and trying to scream but my attacker told me if I didn't close my mouth he would close it for me permanently. I began to beg my attacker, "Please not again. Please mister don't do that to me! Please let me go!" I remember how I tried to explain to him how I kept my word and promised to tell no one. My attacker replied while rubbing his arm over my breast and still holding me, "Yeah." Then he paused and said, "You were a good girl and smart by keeping your mouth closed. If you want to live you won't say nothing this time too." Big tears started running down my eyes. I began pleading with my attacker because even though I was trying to forget I still remember how bad my attacker had hurt me the first time.

I can even now hear his rumbling voice in my head as he blew his hot breathe on me. I can see his ugly face as he said, "I'm going to make it better than the last time." I didn't understand what my attacker thought was so good about rapping and hurting a child. As I write frowns are appearing all over my face and the anger of trying to relieve that moment continue to remain with me. I'm sitting here thinking what did I do to deserve all the abuse in my life? Back to that day. I can remember my attacker asking me how do I want it. If he was listening the whole time, I wanted him to let me go. He started licking me on my neck saying, "I'm going to make it feel so good to you this time little girl, the next time you would come looking for me. I began to scream but it didn't so me any good because my freaky attacker started kissing me in my mouth to keep me quiet. After I bit him on the lip, I can remember and see my attacker now, how he drew his arm back and hit me hard in my mouth.

God I hated my attacker more because now my mouth was bleeding and I knew this time he was going to kill me. I remember he called me a stupid bitch as he said, "I'll teach you about biting me." My attacker started throwing me around wild and ruff. I was crying as he was swinging me around, I hit my head up against a building and fell to the ground. I couldn't do anything as he madly tore my blouse opened and started squeezing and sucking my breast. He was lying on top of me and then he did it. My attacker had once again penetrated my vagina with his nasty penis. I felt like shit again. Once my attacker finished doing what he wanted to do with my body he got up and said, "If you tell the next time I won't be so nice." I was saying to myself, "If that was nice I'm going to make sure it won't be a next time. My attacker began hollering at me. He said, "You hear me, don't you?" I was hurting and still bleeding at the mouth; all I was wondering was if he was going to let me go home. As my attacker reached to close my blouse I jumped because I thought he was trying to grab my breast again. Plus I didn't want that nasty dog to touch me no more. He told me to hurry up and get my clothes together. Then he said, "Remember you better not say nothing." When my attacker ran between a building, I stated walking home crying and feeling so confuse. I really didn't care who seen me because I felt space out like I had really went crazy. I felt like I had really lost my mind. I could had died or killed myself.

As I walked into the house with my head down and crying, I raised my head when I heard my father's voice. My dad right away yelled, "What happened to you?" I told my dad what had just happen to me and he called the police. The thought that the police might be a man had me more afraid as my mind began to wonder while I waited for them to come. As I lay balled up in my bed I could feel my stomach knotting up on me as if I was going into a shock. Once the police finally came I remember being awakened by hearing my dad yelling at them for taking so long. I had developed this fear and hate for men now. I didn't want to talk to the first officer that came in my bedroom because the officer was a man. The first police officer seen I was very uncomfortable with him, so he went out to get the other officer that was in the front room talking to my dad. Thank God the officer was a woman. The female officer was very kind understanding and considerate. I thought she was going to drill me with questions that asked every little ugly detail of my attack. It was kind of strange because this officer wasn't as nasty and mean like the officers in Chicago.

As I remember the female officer was more concerned about how I was feeling and thinking at that moment. She wanted me to leave with her, I felt very uncomfortable leaving with her. I went to the hospital, I can remember hearing the female officer telling the doctors what had happened to me so they won't have to question me. The doctor came in and did all kinds of tests on me. I believe I really got scared when the doctor was telling my dad that there was always a chance I could have got pregnant from my attack. That was something I really didn't need at all. I was released from the hospital to go to the police station to look at some pictures. It was so nerve racking but I went through the process any way. However, it was unfortunate I couldn't find my twice attacker's picture in their book for local rapists. So we were told when and if I see him again to call the police department right away.

I went home as a walking dead because I didn't care about living or about myself. I was wishing I was dead during the entire ride home. I was wishing I was dead during the entire ride home. I wouldn't feel so bad if only my two time attacker's picture was in one of those books. I remember staying out of school for about two to three months, around that time it had started to get cold outside. I knew my life wasn't going to never be the same again after that attack. The day would come one day when I could relax and not think about that attack but at that time it was hard to move on with my life. Especially, since the police didn't catch my two time attacker; I am only living to see that day. I sat and sat in the house. I didn't go out the door for nothing at all. I didn't even look out the window. I didn't want to be or have anything to do with the cruel world outside of my house. I was not allowed in my own world so I didn't and wasn't letting no one else in because I seen now that life meant me no good and was out to get me.

Anything and everything wrong a person felt they wanted to take out on somebody, they did it all to me as if I was the best candidate for the abusiveness. Now, I have to live a life afraid to go out my door. I never know if my two time attacker was out there waiting for me to show my face outside again so he can grab me. God it's nothing nice living my life. I guess you can say I sat in the house like an old maid day after day and night after night. The wondering of not knowing what was really going on with my case was really getting to me. I remember I use to pay my brother or one of their friends to go to the store for me because I was so scared to go out the house. I went out the house for nothing at all. I learned how to play all kinds of card games just by playing by myself.

I believe I was like a TV guide for the daily programs because I knew what came on for everyday of the week and could give you the time for a particular program you might be looking for. Even though I became very bored being in the house, I didn't care because I wasn't going outside and besides it was cold out there. The coldness gives more reasons for me to live like a hermit in my own house. The snow looked pretty clean, nice, and white but I wasn't going out there in it for nothing in the world and I did mean nothing in the world. Wild animals couldn't run me out the house. I went back and sat in my lonely room just looking at the walls and wishing something to do. Guess who came by? I don't know if you guessed right or not but it was my friend, or should I say my ex-friend from across the street. While knocking on my bedroom door my ex-friend was asking if it's ok for her to come in and sit with me for a little while. At first I was against it but I really wanted somebody to talk to.

I remember telling my ex-friend to please close my door as she entered into my room. My ex-friend came in and sat on my bed. She pulled some jacks out her pocket and we began to play with them. I should have known my ex-friend had her suspicious reasons for coming over considering she hasn't been over to y house in months. As we were playing jacks my ex-friend began talking about she is so sorry for what had happen to me and if there was anything she can do for me. She said she would like to be there for me as a true friend. I looked at her and said, "Who told you?" I can remember her saying something like, "I promised them I wouldn't tell you they told me." I just looked at my ex-friend and I can remember striking at her in an ugly tone of voice and shouted, "Some so call friend you are if you can't tell me who's talking about me behind my back!" We went on and on with the tell me who told you game back and forth but I still couldn't get my ex-friend to tell me so I just said, "Fuck it then," and decided to leave it alone for now.

Oh but that wasn't the good part of our little reunion. She began telling me this story about her mother boyfriend and how he use to come into her bedroom while her mom was sleeping and force her to have sex with him. My ex-friend also told me about how more than two or three of her mother boyfriend's friends had came over to their house with her mother's boyfriend all drunk and had intercourse with her many of times. For a while I stopped thinking about myself and started feeling sorry for my ex-friend. I remember asking my ex-friend why she didn't tell her mother. She said her mom stay drunk all the time and didn't believe anything she said. I thought about my mom and said to myself, "God, I'm glad my mom wasn't like her mother," because I wouldn't know what I would had did. Considering I had been through a seminar of situations. I understood how my ex-friend was feeling and what she was going through.

My ex-friend had started coming back over on a daily basis. We would sit and share our feelings and emotions about the things that had happen to us in the past. I started thinking to myself about how I never knew we had so much in common; maybe she can be a true friend after all. We would laugh about some things and get sad and depress about other things. Man, I thought I had a hard life. My ex-friend would tell me stories that made my head spin. It felt good to hear that someone else was going through some of the same things I hated but unfortunately I was experiencing at the time. My ex-friend had much more and horrible stories to tell than myself. It seemed as if every day she had a different story to tell me. My ex-friend and I became a lot closer. I started to feel more comfortable with my ex-friend because I felt she understood what I was going through while other didn't. Old girl was a good person. I mean my ex-friend was real good.

Let me tell you readers why she was so good. Old girl and I had become real good buddies again. My ex-friend had won me over completely till I had started going across the street over to her house. Remember now I've been closed up in the house for months. I was afraid to go out the door because I feared my two time attacker would get me again. My ex-friend makes me feel relaxed with her and I felt I didn't have to worry about a thing. Even over the months I would stay nights over her house. I remember how my ex-friend use to tell me, "As long as I stayed the night over her house she didn't have to worry about no one coming into her room and making her have sex with them." I can remember several times when someone started to open my ex-friend's bedroom door but they would look in and close it back.

Except for one night when I stayed over to my ex-friend's house, this one man came in. That night my ex-friend was in the shower and her mother came home with a few men. They were all drunk and talking loud just like my ex-friend said. I was in her room laying down watching TV and the man just open the door and came in. When he seen me he said, "Who are you?" I told the man I was a friend of hers and he turned away and went back out the room. I couldn't wait for my ex-friend to come back into the room so I could tell her what had just happened. We had us a good laugh and she said, "You see I told you, if you wouldn't have been here the man would had stayed in here until I came back into the room and he would have had made me have sex with him." I felt good because it seem as long as we were together no one would mess with us sexually. It was kind of like my ex-friend was now watching my back and I was watching my ex-friend's back.

My ex-friend and I began sitting outside at night because the weather was changing; it seem as if Spring was on its way. I can remember my ex-friend telling me from now on it was going to be just me and her. Not really understanding what my ex-friend meant by that, me being a big dummy I would say, "Yeah, that's right girlfriend, just me and you." We kicked it real good. Every day and at night but I was only allowed to spend the night over her house on the weekends. Yes, my readers my ex-friend and I had became real true friends. Especially, considering that our friendship had put my fears to rest. I think I would now call my ex-friend my best friend. My best friend and I would go for night walks together; like the ones I use to take before I got attacked. But you know what? Didn't no one or anything mess with us!I felt a whole lot better about myself and life but I still didn't trust no one but my best friend, whom was now my buddy.

Remember this is my life and nothing good stay or happen to me for long before something pull me back into the dirt. Things were going along just fine until this one night that's when it happened. Talk about my whole world got turned around and put upside down. Let me take you back to a statement my ex-friend said in an earlier chapter when I first moved to Wisconsin. Remember when my best friend and I had broken off our friendship the first time? I spoke about this one day her and a couple of new neighbors were walking pass my house while I was sitting on the porch and one of her friends asked who I was? My ex-friend replied, "Oh that's just one of my ex-girl friends?" Keep that statement in mind let's get on with my story. It was a Friday night; I can remember the day well because I could only sleep over to my best friend house on the weekends. Plus I remember being very sad the Monday before I returned to school every time. The evening was going good. We did our usual girl things. My best friend and I had even gone for a longer walk that night. Once we decided to turn in for the night, she took her shower first then I took mine. My best friend suggested we play some cards and we had fun but it was time for us to go to sleep.

My best friend lay in one twin bed and I lay in another twin bed in her room. I remember us talking like we always did; we laughed ourselves silly and talked ourselves to sleep. Now I knew I was asleep but at first I thought I was having one of those what they call a sexual intercourse wet dream. It was feeling good to me for a moment at first but then it started feeling a little too good. I realized I wasn't having a dream. First thing that went through my mind was what my best friend said about how her mother boyfriend and his friends would sometimes come into her bedroom while she was sleeping and started having sexual intercourse with her. My best friend said that by the time she would wake up and realized what was going on they would be all over her and doing their business. Once I really began waking up out my sleep I realize that someone was really sucking on my private part below.

I woke up and started pulling the cover off of me saying, "Who is that? Stop! What are you doing to me?" There weren't any lights on in the room; it was totally pitch black dark. All I knew was I was now squeezing somebody head down between my thighs and he was still trying to suck my private. No matter how much I was twisting, squeezing, and resisting my attacker of the darkest night he wouldn't let go of the hold on my leg or loosen up the mouth suction on my vagina. I started screaming and yelling for my friend to wake up but she didn't. Being afraid, I started kicking my attacker and telling my best friend to please wake up and help me but she didn't. I continued kicking my attacker trying to free myself of this ugly assault in the totally darkness. My attacker of the darkest night stopped fighting with me, jumped up on top of me and started wrapping my face with the bed covers. Once I got out the covers I jumped out of the bed and turn on the lights to wake my best friend up but she wasn't in her bed. I closed the door and pushed the dresser behind it so no one could get back into the bedroom unless I let him or her in.

I sat crying, afraid, and with the lights on wondering who my attacker of the darkest night could have been and thinking where was my best friend. Some one started pushing on the door but I just sat there staring at the door and I did not say a word. I didn't even ask who was at the door. I just sat there crying softly and silently to myself. Then he or she started knocking on the door, shortly after I heard a soft voice I recognized. I was my best friend. I was so glad to hear her voice; I jumped down off the bed and moved the dresser from behind the door to open it so she could come in. Once she started coming through the bedroom door I pulled her in quickly and closed the door with the dresser pushed back behind it. She looked at me and asked, "What's wrong with you?" I started crying. I can remember my best friend taking me in her arms and holding me tight. She said something like it isn't that bad, she's here now, and everything is going to be all right.

I broke down and told her what had happened to me while I was sleeping. I told my best friend how at first I thought I was having a dream. I can remember her asking me if I seen who it was? I told her no, I didn't see him, I don't know who it was. More afraid and confused because I didn't know who had attacked me, I asked my best friend, "Where was You? Why weren't you in the room with me?" I remember her saying she couldn't sleep, so she went and took her another shower." I told her the next time she wanted to take a shower to wake me up and let me know. She replied by saying, "You look like you was resting so good and I didn't want to wake you." As I was crying and screaming at my best friend I told her, "I don't care, wake me up! Because I was so afraid I didn't know if they were going to kill me or what. When you didn't answer I thought they had killed you!" My best friend grabbed me to comfort me. I felt safer not but yet I was still confused because I didn't know who had just attacked me.

I asked my best friend what I should do. She told me since I didn't see their face the police wasn't going to do nothing because it happened to her a couple of times before like that too. After listening to what my best friend had to say, I then started thinking about what had happen to me around earlier fall of last year. Just because I couldn't find my attacker's picture in the books downtown, there wasn't anything the police could do about my attack. I decided to forget about what had happened here with me tonight and I went back to sleep with the dresser behind the door.

Chapter Eight
"Shocking Over Nighter"

THE NEXT DAY when I woke up, I wanted to believe nothing had happen. I was hoping it was all just a crazy nightmare, but I could still feel my heart beating scared to death with fear wondering if they was going to kill me or hurt me so bad till I'll just kill myself. The crazy thing about it is I don't have an ideal of who attacked me last night. Now I'm going to walk around being suspicious of everyone in my best friend's house including her brother. I got up and ate breakfast, while watching how everyone looked at me. I thought to myself, that maybe I could figure out who attacked me last night by the way they lusted for me. The sad thing about my attack was all he did was sucked on my vagina and I knew there was someone with my private taste on his breath. The thought of that made me feel even nastier than him, who ever he was.

After I ate I went straight back into my best friend's bedroom. I really didn't want to be around no one, especially considering everyone in the house was a suspect to me due to the nasty attack on me last night. My best friend came into the room and tried to get me to go outside with her. I told her the only time I was going out the door was when I was going home tomorrow. For the whole day I just sat in her room and only came out to eat and to go to the bathroom. It wasn't all that bad in her room because my best friend and I played lots of different games; we also played cards. We still found time to laugh some, even thou I wasn't feeling too happy; my best friend was just a funny kind of person. My best friend would sometimes do all these crazy stuff and make all kinds of different types of noises. When you got someone around you who would go all out his or her way to cheer you up, how could you not have a good time!

Anyway I really appreciated her being there for me; I gave her a friendly friendship hug. I told her how much safer I felt being around her and I was so lucky to have a true friend like her. I can see that time and moment in my mind now and I remember I squeezed my best friend a little bit too hard when I hugged her. The time had come for us to get ready for bed, but this time we watched the television set until we fell to sleep. I can't say what time it was when we did crashed out. All I know is it was very late into the night or you can say early in the morning. I was very tired from not sleeping to well from that night before, so when I went to sleep I was really out of it. As I laid there sleeping while wrapped tightly in the cover it happened again; two nights straight. Now as I'm sitting here remembering those nights, I am wondering to myself, how could I have been thinking I was having wet dreams when I don't even have them as an adult! Now back to the story.

It happened! I thought my little old dirty mind was off into dreamland again. Only this time it was feeling real good. I couldn't understand why I was receiving this tingle that was very satisfying and pleasing to me. Now as I sit back and relive that night I do remember I was enjoying what was going on with my body that night. I was really enjoying this dream that night and it was wet. To me my dream I was participating with this faceless person while he was sucking me out. Oh but then it gotten really good because his hands started moving up to my breast and was squeezing them. I can say at that moment I was riding in the clouds of enjoyment and didn't want it to stop.

I guess with me responding like it felt good made it got really good to my attacker of the darkest night. Things had gotten a little too wild because he squeezed my breast a little too hard and as I stared screaming, "stop you're hurting me," a few times over and over again and he wouldn't stop. Then, I started resisting him by starting to fight him and by pushing him way. I believe when I started to fight him it made me slowly wake up. I felt like a big fool because of everything that was going on and I though I was dreaming. I really begun trying to fight and get away from my attacker of the darkest night but he was still sucking on me and he started to suck harder on my private. I began to call for my best friend to wake up and help me but she didn't. The room was totally dark like the night before but I knew when I went to sleep the TV was on. The funniest thing about this attack like the last one was every time I called for my best friend she would never answer. So, I continue to wrestle with this unknown attacker.

He was trying to pull the covers over my head like before but I wasn't going to let him get away; no way not this time. While all this is going on I'm still wondering why my best friend isn't waking up? My attacker and I both fell out the bed and I grab him around the ankles as he tried to get up and run for the door. The strangest thing was I remembered while we were on the floor struggling one of my arms hit the dresser, which was still by the door. Now I'm thinking to myself, no wonder my best friend wouldn't answer me because she had something to do with what was happening to me. She let my attacker in on me and she was supposed to be my best friend. I knew I really had to see who my attacker of the darkest night was. I knew my best friend's brother liked me but I didn't think they would go as far as wetting me up to be assaulted while I was sleeping. What could they have been thinking? I believe they thought I would wake up, summit, and to willingly continue to be apart of what was going on! Where were their minds at?

I began to wonder what kind of person was my so call best friend really was. Now, I was really mad, I knew I couldn't let him get away because I needed to know why and what part, if any did my best friend had to do with these attacks on me. I had to know! I knew two things had to happened: one was either my attacker of the darkest night will over power me, get to the door open it and get away, or two either while my attacker of the darkest night was trying to move the dresser I had to get to the light switch and turn the lights on. If I succeeded with option two then I would be able to put a face and a name to my attacker of the darkest night. I was pulling my attacker by the legs and crying, but I was going to see who my attacker was. I was going straight to the police as soon as I found out. He was going to suffer for what pleasure he had gotten from me. I began pulling my attacker across the floor so this way I will have a little more time to run for the lights as he was trying to run and push the dresser from against the door. I was praying, "God be with me, I hope I gave myself enough space to make my move. I just love when a good quick planned out plan comes together. It was just like I thought. As I let my attacker of the darkest night go he ran for the door and at the same time I jumped across the bed and ran for the light switch. I made it! I beat him! My attacker was to slow, the light was on, and he was caught. I've seen my attacker finally. I can now put a name and a face to my attacker of the darkest night.

Yes, I hollered, "Stop," as I turn on the light but he could have still gotten out the door and I again wouldn't know who my attacker was. What my attacker didn't know was I didn't turn around yet after I turned on the lights. I still didn't see him when I hollered, "Stop!" He could have still gotten out and again I would have never known who he was. When I did get myself up right and turned around, man was I shocked beyond surprised! I could have died to see whom I seen was trying hard to get the hell out the damn bedroom. First thing I said was, "No! Not you. Why?" At that moment as angry as

I was I didn't know if I wanted to jump my attacker or break down and cry like a baby. That's when the confusion really settled in on me even harder. Considering what had just happen to me, I still couldn't understand why. I sat back on the bed and asked my attacker of the darkest night that question again, "Why? Why, you were supposed to have been my best and only friend." Why did you do this to me? Why?" I jumped and ran at my so call best friend with rage, wanting to kill her because she is my attacker in the darkest night.

I started beating my attacker in the chest, while yelling, "Do you know what you have done to me? I trusted you with my life. I've told you things that I never told anyone. I shared with you my deepest feelings, heartaches, and thoughts. You knew me just as well as I knew myself. Why? Why? Why you? You was supposed to be my friend. But you like a thief in the night who just took advantage of my body and stole my security and my trust. Dammit, why did you do this to me?" I felt like I was the biggest fool living, damn I felt very bad, sad, nasty, stupid, and real low. Here it was all the time I thought I was spending the night with someone I trusted with my life. I felt we were going to be the best of friends, while all the time she was only out to get into my clothes like those other attackers of my past. The only differences were she was my best friend and a female like me, whom won me over to be comfortable with being around her. My attacker of the darkest night has won my trust and just to think I use to change my clothes in front of her. God, I feel so nasty now because I can image what her dirty, evil, ass mind was thinking each time I undressed. Now I was show nuff confused, how can I say another girl raped me while I was sleeping? I started getting my clothes together and I put them over my gown.

My ex-best friend again started asking me what I was going to do. I told her I was going to tell my father what she had done to me and I never wanted to see her again as long as I live. Old girl started getting kind of defensive. She told me, "They can't do nothing to me because I didn't enter into you." By this time we were at each other throats real good. I started calling her every name except the child of God. I didn't care because my ex-best friend now couldn't do another damn thing to hurt me more than what she has already done. All I was thinking about was getting the hell out of her house and to never return again but only with the police. She began throwing remarks around like, "If you go to the police the first thing they are going to want to know is why you didn't report it the first time it happened." I started throwing remarks back at her, telling her to shut the fuck up because I didn't want to hear her voice or nothing she had to say. I told my ex-best friend to get from in front of the door because one way or another I was leaving an she wasn't going to stop me.

My ex-best friend was still trying to plead her case with me but it wouldn't work. I told her, "I thought you was cool but all the time you wanted to get close to me just to have some freaky sex with me. I never would have thought you were that nasty and sick in the mind. Just leave me alone." I reached for the door knob so I could open the door but she just stood there against the door and wouldn't move. I asked her again to move from in front of the door so I could leave. But my ex-best friend didn't move out the way, for some reason she felt I had to stay and listen to what she had to say. I started yelling for her mom but my ex-best friend said, "They can't hear you. You should know that by now, they are all dead drunk!" All I wanted to do was go home but she said one statement that made me stop and started to think.

My ex-best friend whom was my attacker in the darkest night said, "You claim you were sleep, but can you prove it? You acted like you was enjoying what I was doing to you as much as I did. If you tell anyone I'm going to tell them you submitted to it and let me do it to you." Will you believe old girl really iced the cake when she said that she was going to tell everyone I liked girls. Man did I get mad. I really snapped then. I pushed the bitch out the way and left. I knew my ex-best friend was sick in the head from the first time I met her. Oh yeah, back to that statement she made to her friends, I now knew what she meant by it. Her plans all the time was to try and make me her girlfriend for real. No wonder people would look at us funny. Me not really knowing what she was talking about she had me saying I was bisexual. I thought she was talking about the twin Gemini signs when she was saying we are two of the kind. Stupid, stupid, crazy me!

Once I got home my dad wanted to know where I was coming from so early in the morning. I didn't know how to tell him what had happened to me the past two days. As I started to tell him I thought about what my ex-best friend had said before I left her house. Maybe she's right, I thought to myself. I didn't want her to spread false rumors about me, so I decided to keep my mouth closed while I felt like shit.

I really couldn't understand, maybe it was me, and what I was doing so wrong to keep people wanting to attack me. I started to hate the world. Now I loved no one, liked no one, and trusted no one. My life, mind, body whole heart, and soul was made up, I am going to live to get revenge on the world.

Chapter Nine
"Sick Minded: Something Just Wasn't Right"

I DIDN'T KNOW what to do anymore, so I made a very strong decision to live a lonely life behind what old girl did to me. Now here I was lost, confused, and turned the fuck out, and it was not by choice but by sick minded males and a female. Life wasn't easy! I can remember everyone use to always ask me what was wrong with me? As they say, I've been acting real funny and weird lately but I knew nobody would understand what I was going through because I didn't. It made me think about when I did fine how some sick-minded person would only be out to get some of me and it wouldn't be by will. I really hated my ex-best friend; I will never forget what she had done to me. Now I am alone! Tell me who I can run to in this sick, mean, and old dirty world! Even thou Monday was just a day away, I couldn't wait until it got here so I could go back to school. I felt I had some true friends at school even if it was just for a moment but I could keep my mind off the horror I had went through this weekend.

Morning finally came I was to happy to see the school because being at home just fucked up my mind even worst. After all that I have been through I always snapped back some where in my life but not in the total fullness of my mind. School looked so good to me. I was so glad to be back. Some of the students were even happier to see me than I was to see them. I felt the good times were back and I had to work on forgetting those nightmares out of my life. My friends at school acted the same except a few of them were acting strange and they change. I couldn't figure out for nothing in the world what the changes in a few of them were. Like the old people use to say, " Whatever you do in the dark will come out into the light," believe me that is one statement that will tell the truth on you every time.

This one day I hung with a few of my school friends after school. We all went by one of the girl's house we were hanging out with to kick it. It seems as if they were having a party because there were a lot of other kids from school over that day too. Talk about the truth coming to the light. Everybody was doing it. All you could smell when you walk into the house was weed. Then once you got good into the house all you could see is boys and girls hugging and kissing. I told the one girl that we rode with over to the house that I was ready to go. They assured me that I had nothing to worry about and if I didn't want to do anything I didn't have to. So I agree to stay for a little while. It wasn't all that bad after all. I seen sex in another way for a change; people were willingly and enjoying sex. I started to feel that maybe this younger generation knew how to be happy. I could image what was going on when they went into one of the rooms.

My mistake was that I sat a little to close to one of those rooms with a closed door. When I heard what was going on in that room it scared me because of the noise they were making. I don't see how they was enjoying themselves by making those weird noises. I remember this one guy seen the expression on my face and asked me if I was alright. I told him I'll be ok, I just need to get out of here for a minute. Dude seemed as if he was cool but I still didn't trust him. I just wanted to pick him up and throw him far away from me. He walked me outside and we sat on the porch and talked. Well, I should say I didn't do too much talking because I did learn from opening my mouth to let people get to know me. What was going through my mind as I did a log of listening, was that dude is kind of good looking! I must admit I was watching him out the side of my eyes but a boyfriend was the last thing on my mind. Then time after time I would catch him checking me out. What he did that for because now I'm putting him on my shit list. I don't really recall how long I stay outside with dude but I know I was ready to go.

I can remember that every time someone comes up on the porch they would say things like, 'man girl got it going on and or is that you?" They just didn't know I was like a time bomb with a very short fuse waiting to go off. My friends finally brought their happy go fucking ass out. I just looked at them and then one of them had the nerve to ask me if I scored. I wanted to hit old girl dead in her mouth. The tripping part about it was once we got into the car they started going on about how I was out there with the finest boy at the school and I didn't give him a play. I looked at them as if they had lost their rabbit mother fucken minds. I didn't care at that time if he was the only finest boy in the whole world: he did the right thing by keeping his distant from me and only tried feeding me a conversation. After all the evening wasn't that bad at all. I meet new people and found out things about almost all my classmates. Just about everybody were smoking, drinking, and having sex, what a life.

You wouldn't even thought they were doing all of that stuff just by the way they acted and carry themselves at school. Now I looked at every one of them a little bit differently now. I knew who was screwing who and who had the most trains as they said ran in their tracks. Ok, the train which I found out was when three, four or a lot of times more than five guys just take turns on sticking the same girl, in other words sex with the same girl. I would think that your ass would be super sore after all those guys got finish with you. That still didn't stop my friends at school from living their wild and happy go fucking life. I can't remember ever seeing anyone of them looking the way I was feeling on the inside. If they were sad they didn't show it at all. Wait as I think about it except for one girl; she seemed to always be very down in the weather. I felt her pain, I even felt sorry for her.

This one girl kind of reminded me of myself. She stayed to herself, was quiet, and dressed different, but deep inside I could tell something was really bothering her. I kind of slowly moved away from my other friends to hang with this one girl who seemed like she was more my speed. Talk about lightning striking in a small place; this girl had been through more changes than a little bit and I truly feel her hurts as she talks with tears in her eyes. This one girl so much like myself was new to Wisconsin and has been a victim of sexual abuse by male and females too. I said to myself, yeah, maybe this is the true friend I really needed. The one thing that uses to worry me about her was she looked like she could be in her twenties. It was so puzzling why this girl looked so old, I found out she was only one year older than I was. This new girl at school and I had even started hanging out some after and outside of school, which was how I learn that she had a guy friend that was old enough to be her daddy. She never told me if he was her man or not. I remember him well because he would pick her up after school and they would sometime drop me off at home.

This one day he didn't pick her up after school, so we walked over to my house. What she do that for because dude was tripping for real with this new girl at school who I was now hanging with. This guy didn't care who was around he was knocking and pushing my friend around. I was trying to stop him and he started talking crazy to me, about what he would do to me if I didn't mind my own business. By this time my dad and uncle had came to the front of the house and it wasn't anything nice for him. I remember my dad and uncle had beat him up a little. My friend girl still got in the car with him, talking about I didn't understand. What was it that I didn't understand? Hell, the man was beating her up, I only tried to help, and she still got in the car with him. You tell me what is it you don't understand about that? I really didn't feel good about that at all. I really started to worry if my friend was alright or not when she hasn't came to school for a week. I didn't know if I should go by her house or not!

Knowing what had happen and what she had been through in her life, all I wanted to know was if she was okay. After about a week and a half she finally showed up at school with shades on her face. She took the shades off and showed me how dude had beaten her face black and blue. I really started to hate him. It was kind of strange because my firend acted like she was proud of her black eyes. The way she talked about it I can tell this wasn't the first time he had beaten her up. She came to school as usual. Friday came and my other friends told me they were going to another one f their parties and practically begged me to go. I couldn't understand why my friends wanted me to come to the party with them so bad. Then, they finally confessed to me. Remember the real good looking guy I talked about earlier at the first party I went to? Well, the party was at his house and he wanted me to come.

Later, at school my friends told me that this good-looking guy has been asking questions about me. I don't know what for and in a way I wanted and I really didn't want to know. So, I told them I would think about it and let them know after lunch if I decided to go or not. I remember pulsing and asking them if I do go would it be okay for my friend to come along? They said sure the more the better. So, we all meet after school and carpooled to this good-looking guy house for the party. What I seen made the last party look like a kiddie party. It was so much weed and alcohol at the party; you would have thought they had their own weed farm and liquor store. There was boys and girls just doing their thing right in front of everybody, they didn't care who seen them. It was kind of surprising to me because I didn't think people were so open with things that were supposedly be private.

I remember one of the other guys at the party went and told the good-looking guy that we were there as he pointed in our direction. He came and took us to this house in the back. As we were walking to the back, the good-looking guy told us he was sorry for what we had just seen and he tried to explain that those were some of his older brothers' friends. That was a relief because I knew I didn't want to stay at that kind of party; they were a lot too wild for me. Plus I was beginning to get a different picture of the kind of person I thought he was. Well, the party in the back wasn't too much different. They had their sex acts behind close doors while the rest of the group was dancing and having fun even thou they was kind of high and drunk. My new friend girl from school and I just sat there looking and talking. I was surprised in her when I seen her take a drink, then again who could really blame her considering the life she was living. As for me, well, I tried to be Miss Goody two shoes, I didn't drink or smoke.

You heard the saying, "Birds of a feather flops together?" Well, I found out what they mean by that statement. I was introduced to my first joint of weed and it was by the good-looking guy. This good-looking guy and my friend girl from school was saying, 'Go ahead just smoke it like you smoke a cigarette!" The two of them laugh when I told them that I didn't know how to smoke a cigarette. So, they continue to push the joint of weed on me, telling me to just inhale and hold the smoke. I try the joint of weed with instructions and coaching from the good-looking guy and my one new friend from school. You know what? I'm not going to say its right to smoke weed but it did make me feel good. A matter of fact I liked it. I started feeling so good and relaxed till I got out there on the floor dancing no more Miss Shy Girl!!

I started complaining about how the work out on the floor had made me hot and dried out at the mouth. The good-looking guy told me the reason I had a dried mouth was because of the weed I had just smoked and then he handed me a glass with some wine in it. He told me to drink it; it will make me feel a whole lot better. I started drinking the wine. After about the second glass of wine, no one could tell me nothing. I was in a whole new world and you know what, I liked it. I believed my head really gotten big when the good-looking guy kept telling me how good I looked. My head and body really started spinning when he said, "I had a body like a Goddess!" Now you know I had to be in another world because usually when someone makes a comment about my body I freak out. I can remember it so well and what he had said to me didn't bother me at that moment. So I continued dancing, drinking my wine, and smoking a few more joints of weed with this very good-looking guy. Man, I was enjoying myself and having lots of fun. If all the parties are going to be like this I will start going every weekend with the girls.

I believe everyone had gotten tired of dancing that fast pacing music, so they decided to slow the music down some. I remember that was when I sat my ass down because I wasn't about to have no one hold my body close and tight to theirs. That didn't stop the very good-looking guy. He kept on trying to get me to dance with him but I wouldn't. So, the two of us just sat, talk, drunk our wine and smoked more weed. By the time two or three of those slow songs had played, they was sounding so good to me that I finally asked the good-looking guy to dance, considering he wasn't dancing with no one else all night. I do remember dancing a few records with him but by then I was so spaced out I didn't know if I was coming backward or going forward. I knew I was really enjoying myself and having fun. All I do know is that I was the attraction of the party because I heard about it the next day at school from my friends. Now lets get back to the night of the party.

No I didn't remember anything, but something happen to wake my ass up. I can't tell you how or what lead me to be in another room with the very good-looking guy. From what they told me at school I was all over him and he was all over me. Now let me tel you what I do know. I came back to earth when I realized that this very good-looking guy was trying to have sex with me. He had my clothes almost off, please don't ask me but I know now what they meant when they say, "A drunk ain't shit!" I started wrestling with him trying to get my clothes together but he just kept pushing my drunken butt back onto the bed. I started asking him why he was trying to do this to me and he said, "I thought you wanted it because the way you was all over me! No girl plays with my feelings and don't give up anything!" Now this very good-looking guy didn't look all that good to me anymore. I was fighting with him. I remember he had hit me a few times. I started crying asking him to please stop, not to do this to me. It didn't do any good because as he said, "You gonna give me some pussy!" I began screaming and he told me, "To go ahead and scream your lungs out because can't no one hear you and ain't no one going to try to help you!"

So, regardless to what I did, said, and fought, I was still fucked. This good-looking guy had entered me and I wasn't drunk or high anymore. I felt super nasty and very stupid! As this not so good-looking guy turns and went out the room, he told me to get dress. I got my clothes together but I was too afraid and shame to come out the room because I didn't want to face no one after what had just happened. He then came back into the room and asked me what was I doing? I just looked at him and thought to myself, this nice, good-looking guy had now shown his true color. He had started talking to me all mean and nasty as if he was a different person. I remember this not so good-looking guy told me if I said he raped me he had a whole house full of people that can say I was all over him asking, playing, around with him and grinning on him as we danced.

I was so confused because I really didn't remember what I had done after I had started drinking and smoking those joints of weed. He then looked at me as if he was confused. He then asked me if I wanted him to take me home? I told him no, I'll ride with my friends. He then replied, "Your friends had left a long time ago." I thought to myself, how could they have been my friends and leave me here by myself with people I didn't really know! I came out the room and you know what he was right. There was no one there but this not too good-looking guy and I. I asked him where everyone had gone? He told me, everyone had left hours ago. I then asked him, what time was it? He told me it was three a.m. I remember crying out that my daddy is going to kill me!So I had him take me home but I told him to drop me off at the corner from my house.

Once I gotten home I was afraid my dad was going to be waiting for me at the door with a belt to war my ass out. Then again I was hoping that he wasn't considering I was aching all over. I thought to myself, "Oh God why can't I remember what I did tonight." Every muscle in my body hurt me badly. If my dad would hit me now the way my body felt, I believe I would just confess to anything, everything I ever did and didn't do, and then die. I guess some good came out of tonight because when I got home I didn't see my dad car. I didn't want anyone to tell my dad what time I got in the house. So I climbed into my bedroom window to keep from wakening anybody else in the house. I sat up in my bed until daylight came because I knew if I went to sleep I wouldn't be able to get up and go to school. Plus I knew I wouldn't be able to explain to my dad why I was so tired. So I got dress and went to school a tired and sleepy sister.

Once I got to school all I heard before I could get on the playground good, all my friends were asking me, "What was he like?" They were talking about the good-looking guy that wasn't so good-looking to me anymore. I looked at my friends very mean and told them not ask me anything about last night! As I was talking to my friends, telling them how I just want to forget the whole night, guess who walked up behind me? Yes, if you were thinking that good-looking guy, you are right. He just walked his ass up to me as if nothing had happen and asked if he could talk to me for a minute! I could have die but I just looked at him with the ugliest look on my face and asked him, "What the fuck for?" He then said, "Please," and what he say that for because all ears was opened and the "woo's" came out of all my friends mouth at the same time.

I went on with the good-looking guy to see what he had to say because I didn't want him to talk about what had happen last night in front of all my friends. Even thou we walked away from the crowd their eyes were still stuck on us like glue, and they were watching our every move. They were making me feel even more uncomfortable being with this good-looking guy that had force his self on me last night. The good-looking guy had started talking. He started telling me how sorry he was for what he had did last night and if he wasn't as high as he was it wouldn't had went that far. I asked him why he didn't stop when I asked him to. He told me, that usually the girls will start saying no but once he start having intercourse with the girl she be all into it and there has never been a girl that he couldn't go to bed with. When he said that I knew he felt he could knock any girl that he wanted to because he was the most popular and good-looking guy in the school. I just looked at him and said nothing; I just listened to him.

Dude gave me this real sad story about how bad he felt this morning when he woke up. I looked at him with disbelieve and asked him, "How do you think I felt?" He told me that is why he is trying to apologize to me. This good-looking guy went on with a serious and begging apology. He started talking about how he knows he can't take back what had happen last night. However, he was trying to assure me of how sorry he was and hoping I will forgive him because he knows he hurt me and made a mistake. Then he reached and grabbed my hand and I snatched it away from him and asked him not to ever touch me again. The good-looking guy ended our conversation by putting the frosting on the cake by saying, "Lovely, I really like you. I'm hoping we can be more than friends, and I am very sorry if I hurt you in any kind of way. Please accept my apology!" After saying that he reached over and had the nerve to kiss me on my jaw. I wiped my face, wiping the kiss off and walked away from him. I did turn around just to see what he was doing as I walked away from him. Will you believe he was just standing there watching me.

I rejoined my friends as if nothing had ever happen. I knew then that he wasn't going to tell anyone about what happen between us that night. I also knew I wasn't going to say a word about that painful night because inside I was feeling that maybe I did leaded him on. I went on through school the rest of the day very tired but for some reason I still was thinking about what the good-looking guy had told me. Wondering that maybe there was some truth to what he was saying, or then again he could be trying to pull my legs. Anyway, at the moment I really didn't care and wasn't going to try and find out if he was serious or not. I was looking for my one friend but I didn't see her at school all day. Man, I really wanted to talk to her to find out what had really happened last night! I needed to know what all did I do and I feel she will tell me the truth. I needed her to tell me how I really was acting because she and I were together most of the night. Most of all, I needed to know why did she leave me there in the condition I was in! The whole school day had gone by and she still didn't come. You see most of the time the new girl at school who was my new friend would come to school in the afternoon. I always wondered why? I believed I will ask her when I do see her.

Well, the school day had come to an end and the new girl at school that was my friend hadn't shown up. I went home hoping she would come to school tomorrow so we could talk about what happened last night. The evening for me that night wasn't to good, I guess you can say I was back to my normal self; lost, no one to turn to, crying inside, confused, and very unhappy again with big crocodile tears in my eyes. I was the only one who knew why they were there. I really needed some on e to talk to but I was more afraid of what they might thing about me because I was drinking and smoking weed. Over and over again I kept asking myself what am I going to do! How am I going to tell my dad what I did and what had happen to me? Man, what am I to do? Too worried and confused I felt it was best if I just kept my mouth closed. Plus I knew my dad was going to kill me if I told him what I did. So, I put what had happen that night into the memories of my mind and heart. I just considered what had happen to me as an assault that maybe it was somewhat my fault and maybe I did lead that good-looking guy on. Something that I will prepare myself to live with in my mind for the rest of my life. God, I wish my mom was here with me; she'll know what to do!

Please understand how I am feeling. I'm torn up in the inside; my mind is on the edge of snapping. I really don't want to live but I am just a little too afraid to try and kill myself. So as I do every night, I cry myself to sleep hoping tomorrow will be a better day.

Chapter Ten
How and When I Got My Introduction To Dancing

A NEW DAY but I still have to live the same old depressing ass life I had gotten myself into. Why me? I went on and got myself ready for school, hoping when I get there my friend girl will be there so we can talk. I left out a little early this day so we won't be late for class once we started talking. I don't know but I think maybe my friend girl was reading my mind this day. Because when I got to school, she was already on the playground. I hurry to her; we met each other in the middle of the playground and began walking off to the side alone. I asked her why she was at school so early. She said, "I was hoping to meet you here early because I really needed to talk to you." I started laughing and I remember my friend girl asking me what was so funny. I told her and she begin laughing too. She was so right when she said, "Ain't we two a mess in life." My friend girl and I then ran to the other side of the school building where there was no one else around but the two of us. We sat down with our backs against the building and she said, "Ok, what you want to know."

I begin telling my friend girl my story about what had happen to me after she left and I asked her why did she leave me? She looked really surprised and yelled, "I knew it, I knew something wasn't right when he took you into that room." She further stated that when she had came into the room I seem like I was ok and told her it was alright for her to go. I felt kind of bad when I seen how bad my friend girl felt as she was talking about how she would had never left me but I had assured her I was going to be alright, so then she left. I told my friend my mind was blank and I knew you were the only one I could really trust to tell me the truth. When you didn't come to school yesterday I was hoping you would be here today. I asked her to tell me what I did that night because I didn't remember anything until that had happened. My friend girl started off by saying, "Girl friend, you know how the two of us think a like!" I asked her to just tell me everything and don't leave out anything. Man when she begin talking I wished I had never asked her to. My friend told me things that had my head spinning fast.

She said, "Lovely, girl, I'm glad you was my friend because if I didn't know better I would had thought you was a tramp." I looked at her and said, "Whatyou mean? Did I clown that bad?" She said, "Did you ever! You started dancing all over that good looking guy as if the two of you were sleeping together." She started telling me how I was dancing and swinging my butt all between the good looking guy's legs and how he was enjoying every second of my performance. My eyes really got big when my friend said the two of us were doing this dance called the "bump." She also said the good looking guy and I was really bumping. I really didn't want to hear nothing else but I needed to know why the good looking guy said, "I acted like I wanted it," and believe me I am now finding out the truth. To force yourself on someone isn't right and to lead a person on with sexual acting behavior isn't right either. Now I'm starting to see a different picture about why things happened like it did. It seems as if I had no one to blame for what had happened but myself. How could I have been so foolish! My friend continued on by telling me how I was kissing all on the good looking guy and he was all over me. I couldn't believe I had carried on that way.

She also told me that after a while, even on the fast records I wanted to dance slowly with the good looking guy. I now had started looking at the good looking guy and I started to understand the situation I had put him in. I guess if I was a dude and a girl carried on with me the way I did, I would perhaps think she wanted to have sex with me too. What really got me was when she said I started talking about I was hot and I started stripping. She pulsed and asked me, "Did you dance in a bar before?" I told her, "Girl no! I'm too young to even go in a bar. So what you talking about dancing and taking off my clothes!" That is when she told me she have been a professional go-go dancer for the last past three years. I couldn't believe she was a dancer. I asked her how she got away with it and she said, "I have a fake ID." I really had this crazy surprised look on my face and said, "How do you get a fake ID?" My friend girl then went into her book bag, took out her ID, and showed it to me. I couldn't believe what I was seeing. Her picture was actually on the ID and it said she was grown. My friend girl then started showing me some of her little biddy outfits she would wear before she take them off on stage. I looked with my mouth wide open and said while in shock, "You mean you dance with no clothes on?" She said, "Yeah," like as if it was nothing to be ashamed of. Then she said, "You get more money and bigger tips but you don't have to take all your clothes off if you don't want to."

I then started thinking about how I could get paid just by letting niggas watch my body. Maybe this is what I need to do to get back at life. Especially considering what people thought about how my body looks so damn good that they could just take my shit and do as they please with it. I said, "How do I get me one of those fake ID's?" That question was the beginning of my new life at the age of 12 years old. I had became interested in this dancing career that I forgot a moment about the other questions that were bothering me. Then I asked my friend girl the two part question that has been eating at my mind for the past few days. I remember starting off by saying, "Now I know how half of my clothes had gotten off. Girl friend please tell me how did I not only get into the bedroom but how I also got in the bed with good looking guy?" I tripped and started laughing when she told me. My friend looked at me and started laughing too. She said, "Girl you're a fool but you are cool with me." So we sat there talking about that night some more, continue to laugh as my friend said, "I kind of guess you had a little too much to drink , which is why I didn't really want to leave you that night." When my friend girl continued by telling me how I was dancing, taking my blouse off, wildly swinging it around my head, and then throwing it I could had fell out and died. She also said, "Good looking guy was trying to stop you from stripping and he was trying to cover you up with his jacket but you wouldn't let him." It was kind of funny because my friend asked me, "Why every time you were pushing the good looking guy away from you, but you would grab him back when he was trying to leave and you were telling him you sorry?" But no that wasn't the good part.

I remember I kept telling my friend, "Girl you lying! You're lying! No, that couldn't have been me! I didn't act like that!" My best friend and I were like two little kids in a toy store laughing and acting crazy. I don't care how high and drunk I was, I couldn't believe that I had acted like that. Readers tell me this doesn't sound like me. My friend started talking about how I was dancing all nasty with the good looking guy, I kept repeating over and over again to him, "You want me, don't you? They all want me! They all are thinking I have a body like a Goddess." I was saying to my friend, "No, not me! I know I didn't say that?" I really froze up when my friend said, "I started spinning around and dancing on the table and the good looking guy was trying to get me down." She also said that it was kind of funny because all of a sudden I stopped and said, "Woo the room is spinning around and around. Some body please make it stop!" She said I threw my cup up in the air and passed out but the good looking guy was there to catch me as I was falling. He told my friend I needed to sleep the alcohol off some. I asked, "Well when did he come back into the room?" She said that he only came in to check on me off and on and he wouldn't let anyone go in the room I was in. Now I am thinking to myself what his reason for showing concern was. My friend again started talking about how bad she felt for leaving me. She said before she left her and the good looking guy kept checking on me. She then, eventually left after several hours of waiting. Plus it had gotten late and every one had started to go home she claim.

The good looking guy told her he was going to check and see if I had wakened. Both of them came into the room and my friend girl said she shook me so I would wake up. My friend said I woke up looking around for the good looking guy. I then grab him by the hand and asked him where he has been because I missed him. I told her to go home because I would be alright. So, she turned and walked out the room saying, "By girl, I'll see you at school in a few days." My friend girl said I told her bye, and get the fuck out! She said I was also acting like I wanted her to hurry up and get the hell out the room. Once she started walking out the door she said I pulled the good looking guy down on the bed. I just shook my head because I couldn't believe what she was telling me but I knew she wouldn't have lie on me. I remember saying, "Oh My God, I acted like that," and put my face into my hands. I had got quiet and start thinking to myself for about a minute or two. My friend asked me if I was all right. I look at my friend and said, "You know what? I don't know why but I believe you because I felt with the relationship we had you would tell me the truth." Then a storm rushed through my head and I start yelling, "Did everyone see me acting like that? Please tell me they was all gone when I started taking off my clothes?" She motioned her head as if she was saying no. I screamed, "Ah! I'm going to die, no wonder those boys at school was looking at me yesterday and smiling." If I would had known I carried on like that I wouldn't had came back to school.

Oh, what my friend girl wanted to talk to me about was regarding to what had happen to me after she left last night. She said she knew these people who wanted to hire some dancer, which is where I came in at. She felt that after the way I was acting the night of the party that I would be good for the job. The bell rung my friend and I had finished our little private talk just in time. We were still talking as we started walking back on to the playground to get in line so we could go into the building for our class. The morning had gone by just fine, even thou I was doing a lot of thinking that didn't have to do with class work. I had been thinking about this new kind of life I could live and wondering if it was what I wanted. I just don't know?" Then again I was leaning more heavy towards the maybe I should. I smiled with the thought as I continue on with my school work. For some reason it seemed as if the day went by much faster than usual too. It was all ready time for us to go home. I could not have been gladder to get away from those lusting eyes guys in my class. It was as if I could feel the guys understanding what I was thinking with their nasty minded eyes. When the bell rung, I hurried up and flew out the door. Once we all were outside I walked with my friend girl to the end of the fence. We saw her ride waiting for her. I told my friend girl I would see her tomorrow and let her know what I decided to do about that little situation we discussed.

As I was walking home I kept thinking about what my friend had told me. I just couldn't believe it. Well, I guess I will put what had happen that night deep back in my mind as a memory I will never forget. If drugs and alcohol makes you forget what you done the night before then I don't want to get high again. Then again, I do remember the feeling I somewhat had after getting high; I felt so dam good and relaxed. I think the next time maybe I should not drink or smoke as much. The evening was fine. I felt a little different about myself but yet I still felt kind of embarrass to know how bad I carried on that night at the party. Talk about a double killing if, my dad found out he would kill me and then bring me back to life just to kill me again. I was sitting on the porch some today thinking and watching some new neighbors move in across the street. It was kind of funny because the whole family was moving their things in the house with no shoes on their feet. Right away I said to myself, "I could tell that they were from down south somewhere but I didn't know what part." I remember saying in a soft voice, "You'al gonna wish you'al had on a few pair of shoes after you'al finish stepping on all that damn glass."

You want to hear something else funny? The mother of the new neighbors had stepped on a piece of glass. I started laughing but then I closed my mouth after she pulled the glass out of her foot and said, "Oh, it's just glass," pulled it out her foot and continue moving. I shook my head and said, "Her feet must be made of metal or something." There was a bunch of ruff looking kids over there too. The girls were all hard looking just like the boys, except the boys were a real nightmare to look at. So you can get a picture of what the girls looked like. Afterwards I found out that they were cool. No, but wait a minute, guess who were on them the first week they moved in? I'm not sure if you guessed but it was old girl that lived across the street; remember my ex-friend, she wouldn't let them breath good. She was worst than a dude, she tried to turn the table around on me. I remember telling one of the country girls if they keep hanging around with her they would find out whose lying. My book isn't about them it is about me but I could tell you some crazy stories about that family from the south. You would burst your sides open laughing about them. Oh yeah, my new country neighbor's sister did fine out who really liked girls and who really didn't. My ex-friend tried to eat some of her private and I was rolling as she was telling me. All I kept saying was, "I tried to warn you but you didn't want to listen to me. Well, I now had new friends and it felt good having someone you could use. I meant, if I asked them to jump off a bridge they would do it without no questions. I knew that was wrong of me but in their parents' eyes I was the perfect friend.

I remember I was on my way coming home one day from the bar where my friend girl from school dances at, everyone was running up to me. They were coming to tell me how my new country friends' older sister had hit my baby brother with a stick. What she do that for? The neighborhood kids had wired me up and when I seen the knot on my baby brother's head I knew I had to whop her for him. I had this outfit on I was dancing in. I didn't want to get my dress mess up so I took it off. I had on a bikini swimming suit under my dress. I believe I would have let the older country girl off with a warning, but she was talking strong shit about me. She was saying things such as I'm not shit and how she was not afraid of me. I started beating the older country girl up like a crazy mad woman and her brothers and sisters ran in the house and locked the door. They just left her out there for me to cream and I was enjoying every minute of it. Then the funny thing about it was the other country girl whom was my friend came running out the house. She said, "I don't want to fight you but my mother said I better help whop who ever out there fighting my sister." I told her to bring her ass on. I hit her a few times and the boys got to yelling. You know how the boys are when there are females fighting. They always hollering "Take off her clothes," and I just start throwing off her clothes.

By that time the country girl's mother came out and started whipping her and telling her, "You don't be fighting with Lovely." The country girl that was my friend tried to explain to her mother the whole time that I was the one fighting her sister. She started yelling at her mother while she was whipping her. She was yelling, "That was what I was trying to tell you the first time when I was in the house. The person who was fighting my sister was Lovely!" I later found out that the country girl's mother thought I was the prettiest thing that she had ever seen. The reason she didn't want them to fight with me was because she was going to make me part of their family. She was going to make me her monster looking son girlfriend. I could have died when I found that out. Now let's get back to after the fight. While my country friend was being beaten into the house, I got my dress, put it on, and left because I knew whatever I did tonight I had to beat my dad back home. So, I was as they say, "off the scene of the crime." I made it down to the bar, it was ok but I still didn't try to dance that night. I kind of hung down there just checking out everyone. You know what, not once did any one ask me for an ID while I was in the bar. Cool, I thought this might be all right. Even if they would have asked for an ID, I had a few of them I couldn't wait to show.

Yes my reader I now had identification that said I was old enough to go into any bar I wanted too. I stayed for about a few more hours but I was ready to go because I was getting tired. I told my friend girl from school bye and as I was on my way out the door this one guy was coming in. He grabbed me by my arm and I remember him saying, "Excuse me but you're not leaving?" This guy stepped back outside the door with me to talk and insisted that I stay only long enough for him to buy me a drink. I said sure and went back into the bar with him. I didn't know he was talking about a drink as in alcohol. Once I came back into the bar my friend girl from school leaned down from the stage to tease me and said, "I thought you were gone?" I just laughed, smiled, and went to the bathroom to touch up my makeup. When I came out the bathroom I was looking around the bar for the guy I came back in the bar with. I spotted him and went to join him at the booth where he was sitting at. I remember the guy that I had came back into the bar with said, "I didn't know what you were drinking. So I hope it was ok I order one for you." This guy had a gentleman charm, was to damn pretty, and he had long jet-black hair. I didn't want to be rude by saying I would have a juice or a soda pop after he already got a drink for me. I didn't want this guy to think I was too young to be in the bar, so I took the glass which was suppose to be my drink and smelled it. It didn't smell too bad, a matter of fact I remember it had a sweet smell to it. I asked the guy what was the name of the drink and he told me, "Metexa." This drink was a smooth, sweet, relaxing, and flavored drink; this became my favorite drink and even now I still drink it.

Oh, but honey after drinking a few too many glasses of that Metexa and listening to this guy continue to talk about how my body looks better then any of those girls up there dancing started to make me thinking crazy. He started saying if I was up there dancing he would sit and watch me all night nonstop. I kept drinking on my drink while talking with this guy and becoming very big headed because I knew I looked good and had a very well constructed hourglass figure body. My friend girl from school came over and sat with us for few minutes. I asked her since some of the other dancers had two girls on the stage at one time, if I could dance with her on one of her records? She hurried up and said, "I tell you what you can pick the song you want to dance off." So to the jukebox we went and before I knew it I was up on the stage dancing and having fun doing it. My plan was to do only one record with my friend girl from school. The customers wanted us to do a few more songs together. I mean I was really enjoying myself and the guys in the bar loved me, not like I thought that they wouldn't. I started getting big tips, which made the dancing more enjoyable. I was feeling as if I was all that and some more. This was something I felt I didn't mind doing and plus I was getting free money from nigga's looking at me dance around in my swimsuit. I thought to myself, "What a life." I guess it was something about being in those lights that made me feel like a star as I danced around on the stage, saying to myself, "Yeah, eat your hearts out niggas. I love it, all eyes on me." The attention I was getting from both males and females was all good. I really started to enjoy dancing so much that night till I did a set of five records by myself and got paid damn good. So, I spent the rest of the night drinking, talking with this guy, and doing a little dancing.

Again, I said what a life; partying and getting money. The next day I woke up feeling kind of sick because I had drunk I don't know how much of that Metexa. My head was still spinning and hurting me so bad that I said to myself, "I'll never do that again as long as I live." I didn't go to school that day either. I slept the whole day trying and hoping this headache will go away. I don't see how my friend girl from school did it, but I now know why she only came to school most of the time in the afternoon. Honestly, it took me even the whole morning to try and get up out of bed. Later that afternoon my nose started picking up the smell of food cooking, so I gotten up and started moving around a little bit. Just so happen this was the one-day my dad didn't drive the cab in the morning. He was cooking a meal that smelled so dam good that I couldn't wait to eat it. I believe I got hungrier just smelling the food cooking. Man when I did start to eat, I got sick. I jumped up ran to the bathroom to finish bringing up the food. I remember my dad saying, "If I didn't know better I'll say you either got a hang over or pregnant." Hearing what my dad had just said made me even sicker. I was saying to myself, "Dad if you only knew!"

When I came out the bathroom I looked at my dad and I tried to clean my actions up some. I said, "Daddy now you know good well I am not messing around with no body because I don't want to have a baby and I am too young to get into the taverns." Well I really didn't lie about the hang over, I just said I was too young to get in the taverns so my dad wouldn't think I have been drinking because

I knew he would kill me. I played my hang over off real good but I still felt bad. I went back to bed and tried to sleep the rest of the day away. I woke up a few times off and on that afternoon. Before I knew it, it was evening time and my headache was still there. I hope it may be gone by next morning. I couldn't wait until tomorrow come because I hope I will be back to my same regular self. So I tried to go back to sleep with my empty stomach and sleep the rest of the night away.

Chapter Eleven
"Relief of Frustration"

MORNING FINALLY CAME and I couldn't wait to go to school because I need to ask my friend how in the world did she do it. The other night made me think about not dancing especially if the enjoyment makes you so tired the next day. You know as I think about it I can't remember the first time I had me something to drink, it maybe because of all the weed I use to smoke that made me so forgetful. Anyway, I knew I didn't want to deal with another one of those hang over as my dad called them. I jumped up and got myself together and to school I went. Once I got to school I looked for my friend. When I found her we started talking about the night before and when she told me the owner wanted to hire me, I was so surprised. I said, "You're kidding me right?" She looked at me and said, "Lovely, I kid you not. He said if you want to dance you got you a job." I really got surprised when my friend told me some of their regular customers were asking about me last night too. I looked at her and said, "No way! I couldn't even get up the next day and come to school because I was so tired and had a hangover."

I remember telling her that I don't see how she do it. I completely understand now why she came to school in the afternoon most of the time. My friend told me to at least think about it. I did think about the dancing job but I also through about how tired I was from dancing and that damn hang over I had the next day. I guess you can say I chose not to go back down there no more because it would be too much pressure put on me. A few weeks had went by and I only seen my girl friend at school. I give her credit because it was too hard for me to do one day of dancing but she is still hanging in there with her dancing job and schooling. We only had a few months left in school before our summer break. Man I couldn't wait.

I found out my family and I was going to be moving. I hate that because I would have to start all over making new friends and trying to fit in not only with the new school but with the neighbors too. I made my mind up that when we move I am not going to be anybody's friend. It seems like every time I made new friends we had to move and I was tired of the moving around. I remember saying to myself, "When I get grown I am not gonna move as much as my parents did?"

There was this one day in particular; I remember it because it was on the weekend. I was so board this one day I didn't know what to do. So, I decided to go for my last little walk in the neighborhood since we were going to be leaving soon. I was walking around and thinking about the memories I used to have of the last time I felt comfortable to be walking in the hood. It also brought back those bad memories too. I started remembering how twice I got grabbed up and assaulted by the same man. Now, I am wondering if the police will ever catch him before he hurt someone else. Walking and thinking brought up all kinds of sad and mix emotions, which stated to make me cry as I walked down the street. I went and sat in the little kiddie park area for a moment watching the kids play and while I was trying to get my sensitivities together.

As I got up off the swing to leave I kind of re-looked down the street because this person caught me eye. I kind of stood behind this one big tree which I was standing by so he wouldn't notice me trying to check him out. I had to dry my eyes up because I wanted to be for sure I was seeing who I thought I was looking at.

He was about a few blocks down the street but where we stayed. The blocks were very opened blocks, meaning they weren't as many trees and brushes around like you see on other blocks. Thank God for that! Just to think I believe I finally gotten my prayer answered. It was something about the way this man walked that had caught my attention, even though my glossy, wet, red eyes I felt I knew him. I said to myself, "I know I knew that man!" I would have bet my life on how for sure I was that it was him and as he started getting a little closer I began to focus more on him. Guess what? I was right! It was my two time attacker and I said in a soft voice, "Yeah, now I got you. This time I see you and you don't see me!" All kinds of anger were rushing through my head and body. I knew I had to think fast. My attacker was a lot closer now; I knew if I came from behind the tree he would recognize me. So I kept saying, "think fast Lovely, think fast."

Instead of running right away to get help I knew I had wasted a lot of time trying to figure out if that was my attacker coming down the street or not. I took a while figuring out if that was him or not because I almost caused an innocent man to get beat up. God I would have never for gave myself if that would had happened. One day I had decided to go to the store because there wasn't no one around to go for me. That is when I thought I saw my attacker. As I was walking to the store I had seen this man who scared me so bad because from the distance he looked like my two time attacker. I turned around and ran to get my dad. When I got to the house I was so upset; all I could say was he going to get me again. My dad looked at me and start shaking me and saying, "Faye what are you talking about?" I told him, "That man, he coming up the street!" I told my dad what the man had on and then I ran to my room. I remember my uncle girlfriend saying, "Lovely, you better go and make sure it is the right man." At first I was not going to go because I was to afraid. I went on down the street in the direction where I seen the man coming from. Once I made it to the corner I was so glad I did come because they had the poor man on the ground. I remember my uncle saying that someone was just about to come and get me to identify the man who was on the ground. I remember my uncle who loved to fight telling the man as I was walking up, "Once she ID you nigga we going to kick your ass and then hold you here until the police come!"

It is kind of funny now but it wasn't funny then because I was scared as hell when I thought that was my attacker. I remember looking at him and saying, "That's not him." My uncle and older brother both yelled, "What!" I remember how the two of them then picked the man up off the ground and helped him brushed off some of the dirt on his clothes. They started telling the man they were sorry and it was a mistaken of identify. The man was upset but became very understanding once my uncle explained to him why they did what they did to him. I remember the man saying he was sorry too and he went on his way. Man, did I get it from everybody that day. They hollered and yelled at me until I started crying all over again. I felt so bad that I went into my bedroom and didn't come out at all for the rest of that day. Now, you see why I had to take a little time out to be for sure that was my attacker coming up the street that I was focusing on. Now, lets go back to that day I think I was looking at my attacker. I was nerves and very shook up. I was more confused than a little bit. I knew I had to do something because I didn't want him to get away and climb over this fence. I needed to go and get help quick. I ran through the alley so fast till I almost killed myself running so hard. I surprised myself because I didn't know I could run so fast.

Once I got home I was so out of breath till I had to crawl up the stairs while calling my dad. Everybody ran to the door to see what was wrong because if you were in the house at that time it sound like

I was being drugged up the stairs crying for help. I didn't care, I just wanted my dad and them to catch my attacker before he gotten too far way. My dad started yelling, "Faye what's wrong with you?" All I could say was, "It's him, I'm sure this time it's him! Hurry before he get away!" My dad yelled, "You're sure, you remember what happen the last time!" I told him, "Yeah dad I remember but this time I watch him. I'm sure, please go and get him before he gets away!" My father seen the expression on my face and they all ran off the porch in the direction I told them where I saw my attacker going; this time I was behind them. It was all perfect timing because once my dad and all the rest of the gang made it to the corner my attacker broke and ran. But he still got caught. I was so glad; I was crying for joy.

My dad and some of my uncle's gang held my soon to be identified attacker down to the ground until I got there. They all at once said, "Is this him?" Breathing hard, I looked at the man my dad and the gang was holding down on the ground and began crying loudly and yelling, "That's him! That's that dog!" Then I just started wildly hitting and kicking my finally caught two time attacker like I was crazy. I remember my uncle girlfriend grabbing me and saying, "They got his no good ass now Lovely, let them take care of him!" She then held me as I cried. My uncle girlfriend kept her arm around me as I cried while we walked back to the house. No one could really understand how much of a relief I was feeling or the pain of happiness I was going through. It was all because I knew that was my two time attacker. I was walking saying, "Yes, I knew that was him. I knew it!"

I said to my uncle girlfriend, "They got him, don't they?" I remember my uncle girlfriend holding me a little tighter and said, "Its okay, everything is going to be okay now." We then went into the house and called the police. By the time the police had came my dad and the gang had brought my two time attacker to the alley by our house; he was bloody. I remember my two time attacker yelling to the police he wanted to press charges against my dad and the gang for beating him up. I am starting to really worry even more because now I feel that my dad and the gang could go to jail because they were trying to help me. Life isn't fair at all but leave it to my uncle to yell out, "We had to man handle the nigga to get him here and keep him here until you got here and it wasn't easy." I kind of laugh inside because if you would have seen the way my uncle was acting you had been laughing too. I remember my uncle started talking about how big my two time attacker was in comparison to him and he said, "He fell several times trying to get away from us and we did not touch that lying nigga." I told the officer not to ask me because I did not know what had happen after I left.

All I know is I am glad my nightmare was finally over, they had my two time attacker. The police said, "He won't be seeing the streets for a long time." Once before I was for sure I seen my two time attacker but by the time my dad and the gang got to the corner he was nowhere in sight. You couldn't guess why! I thought that was kind of strange for him to disappear like that so quickly. Now, I know why and how he vanished so fast. My two time attacker lived in the alley directly in the back of our house. When he seen me running to my house that day he hurried up and got in his house. This is the main reason my attacker had disappear so quickly when I seen him. The police now had him and that's all that really matter to me now. The police then took him away and I felt today was the start of a new life for me. I finally felt I could live a life of freedom from fear. I didn't have to worry no more if he was going to try to grab me a third time or not. My pray was answered.

That following week we moved into our new house but lucky me, I was still in my same school zone area. I was so glad I didn't have to try and make new friends. It didn't take us long to get settled in our new place. My bedroom was a lot bigger than the other one. The only thing I didn't like about our new house was that it was upstairs. You know me I had to get to know the neighborhood. So, I decided to take me a walk. Once I started walking around to check out the neighborhood, guess who lived around the corner from me? That good looking guy that I spoke about in my earlier chapters; I was surprised. I knew our new neighborhood looked kind of familiar but you see the last time I came over to the good looking guy's house it was dark and plus I was riding in the back seat of the car. I couldn't tell where I was at from the man in the moon that night. This is one reason why I had the good looking guy take me home the night of his party.

Now let's get back to how I found out the good looking guy lived around the corner from me. While I was walking around I sat on the court to watch these guys play basketball. Let me tell you it was a lot of good looking ball players out there that day. I was so focusing on the game that someone came up from behind of me and said, "Lovely!" As if it was a question asking is that really you! The voice kind of startled me at first because I didn't know no one around my new neighborhood. Unaware of who this man could have been that was calling my name had me so afraid that I couldn't breathe. I then jumped up and was I surprised when I did turned around. He was just standing there looking at me. Little did he, he was like a breath of fresh air to me; I could now breathe again. I was that good looking guy I thought to myself. He asked me what I was doing in his hood! I then told him, "Well it's now our hood because I just moved around the corner about two weeks ago. I remember him asking me what was I doing sitting on the basketball court?

I told him I was just watching the guys play ball. The good looking guy then laugh at me while saying, "I don't see how you can see anything sitting way over here." I told him that I didn't want to get to close because I might distract them while they were playing. But the truth was I didn't want to attract the wrong person; I was hoping the wrong person would not see me. You know one of those individuals who might be kind of sick in his mind and might want to grab me. I was always very concern up about any new neighborhood we moved into. I learned from being in my old neighborhood that whenever I set myself out not to be seen by anybody I usually don't have many problems with sick mind people trying to grab me. When I allow myself to be seen by others I have problems. If they see me they would seem to seek me out for their sick fantasies and take advantage of my young over developed body. I usually stand back in a shadow, which is why the good looking guy saw me sitting in my shade far back from the court.

In my new neighborhood I had started dressing kind of like a boy when I hung out in the hood. I still wore my little clothes for the rest of the weeks we had left in school. I remember the good looking guy telling me, "I wouldn't have never known who were because of the way you are dressed. But you have one of those faces that could never change." Even to this day I am always seeing someone from my past and they say the same thing to me now. They always say how my face looks like I did twenty years ago and that the only thing different is I picked up some weight. Now let's get back to the day on the basketball court. The good looking guy and I started talking about what we were going to do for the summer. I remember him telling me about all the parties they have every weekend while they were out of school for the summer. He then stated that maybe if I wanted to I should attend one of their parties. I remember telling him I would have to think about it. I then change the subject and asked the good looking guy what they do all through the week around here. He kind of laughed and said, "I, well we play ball most of the day."

The reason he laughed was because he had a basketball in his hand, so I guess that was kind of a crazy question for me to have asked him. It is really a crazy question for me to ask when all he does at school is play ball and do he have a crowd. I can remember when the good looking guy and some of the other guys at school would be playing ball, it seemed like every girl in the school and the neighbors' girls would be standing around as if they were watching professional ballplayers. The good looking guy could play ball real good and when he got the ball and dunk it, man do the girls go crazy. I knew he like the way the girls be tripping over him, it rises his ego till you can't tell him anything and you couldn't top him. Dude was too damn good looking and had it going on; the females just made a big mess over him. He better been glad I was in my sick state of mind about males or I probably would have been all over him too. Then again he would have been nothing but trouble because of his high ass ego.

Anyway the good looking guy was ok with me even after what he had did to me because I seen where I had something to do with it at the time too. He asked me to come over and watch him play ball and that I didn't have to be afraid. I went over and sat on the other side of the fence under a tree. The game was very interesting. You would have thought you were watching a professional game because the good looking guy and his friends were playing a lot of grown men and they all were good players. There was this one young man was on the court who was very good too. I mean really good. He was giving the other guys a run to the ball. The only strange thing about this young man was he was a lot shorter than the other guys that were playing ball. He was handling his self and the ball well. Watching the guys play ball and considering everyone was having fun gave me a thought of something for me to do. Maybe I could come back up here when the girls were playing and get to know the game a little better. These guys played for hours and when they stopped I started talking to the good looking guy from school, which was now my neighbor. I asked him when the girls play. He told me there were only four or five girls that play with the guys regularly. I looked at the good looking guy and said, "You're lying, right!" He said, 'No, I'm not lying." I couldn't believe him, so I asked, "How can the girls play with those men? Especially, the way they be bumping, running, knocking down, and hitting each other!" The good looking guy kind of laughed and said, "Lovely, when you out there on the court, male or female you're just one of the guys." I left that topic alone and didn't ask no more questions about how.

Now, I was asking the good looking guy how I can play ball up here. He asked me if I could play. I told him a little bit because I played around with the ball by myself and I've played with my brothers a few times. He then said, "That wasn't good enough and if I really wanted to play for me to start coming to practice. They have practice every day after school." I agreed to come and the good looking guy said he would come and pick me up if it was okay! I can remember him asking me if it was ok for him to walk me home. I told him it was. I guess I started feeling a little bad because he was going all out of his way trying to be so nice to me and plus I felt kind of guilty for never telling him I was sorry for how I lead him on that night at the party. Every time I seen the good looking guy at school I was too afraid to say anything to him so I would just walk off with my mix feelings inside. Maybe I should tell him now I thought to myself; then again, I kind of like the good attention I was getting for a change.

For the few weeks we had left in school, the good looking guy and I had started walking to school together too. Man you should had seen us together. I really didn't care what people thought, a matter of fact I was kind of enjoying the way people were talking about us and he was too. He would tell me us being together kept a lot of girls off his back. After I gotten to really know the good looking guy, he became a more like a little gentleman. He would wait for me by the fence after school and he would walk me home. I was really surprised when he came around to my house after dinner to see if I wanted to go with him to practice. He told me if I didn't want to try out I could watch until I became comfortable to play. I was surprise and very nervous to see so many people on the court at practice.

There were people of all ages and different races playing ball. It was like the good looking guy said, "The most important thing about the game is that everybody always enjoyed themselves when they play."

There were many partner groups practicing; male and male, female and female, and co-ed groups, which means opposite sex partner. I really enjoyed myself at the center and the good looking guy said he will make sure he stops by to pick me up next time too. It seems as if the evening had gone by quickly, it was already time for me to get ready for school tomorrow and bedtime. It took me a while to get my school clothes ready for tomorrow because I was unsure of what I should wear. Usually on the last day of school from the way everyone was talking they fight and throw water on each other. Well, I knew no one wanted to fight me but I wasn't to for sure about this water throwing things. From the way those boys has become dreaming eyed about me after that night at the party, I don't know what could happen! I decided to wear one of my sizzler outfits. You remember my mom use to say, "I was popping and slapping!" Well, I decided to wear one of those outfits that were really slapping me on the crease of my butt according to my mom. Of course, my mom used more verbal language than, I just put it mildly wrote my mom's way of saying it. Either way it was all in the name of fun because my mom uses to say I remind her or herself and to me that was a damn good honor to here. With those thoughts in mind let me take my butt to bed and we will continue this conversation in the morning.

Well here I am bright in the next day. I can't wait to get to school so I can see how crazy everyone is going to be acting. While I was getting dress for school my doorbell rung. I holler down the stairs and asked who it was. It was the good looking guy from school who is now trying to prove to me that he is a gentleman. I told him to hold up for a minute and that I will be right down. I continue putting my clothes on quickly. Once I gotten downstairs I told him I was sorry for having him wait for so long. The good looking guy gave me this look that kind of made me nervous and worrisome. He then said, "Looking at you was worth the wait! What did you do to yourself?" I was half hesitating about answering him. I said slowly, "Nothing?" He then replied, "I don't know but you look like that outfit is you, it shows your entire figure well!" I looked at him and asked him what he meant about that, because now this good looking guy was making me very uncomfortable. I remember him saying he was sorry, it was just he never seen me dressed like that before. Then he said, "Lovely girl you can get mad at me if you want to but damn girl you look good. I wish you were my girl. Come on, let's go to school now." Then he grabbed me around the neck. That made me blush because every girl in school wanted his fine ass. Even if they just wanted to sleep with him, the girls all wanted him and he telling me he wish I was his girl.

As we started walking down the street to school the good looking guy told me to get on the inside of the sidewalk because I was going to cause a whole lot of accidents with my outfit on.I just looked at him and smile while saying, "Yeah right!" Well, he was somewhat right because dudes were calling out to me from their cars window. The looks I gotten from some of the dudes that were walking, their eyes alone could have burned my little outfit off of me. I just kept on walking as if I didn't care what they were thinking. I was saying to myself, "Lust on mother fucker's because I know I look good and had a knock out body!" It felt even better that all the females were looking at dude too. I must admit the good looking guy and I did look good together and something inside of me was kind of hoping that I was his girl too.

I knew I wasn't ready to call myself going with someone, at least not now. Plus I was much too young, even thou I didn't look nowhere near young. We finally made it to school and all I kept hearing was my outfit was the bomb and I was wearing it! You know there had to be some ass hoes in a group who had something slick to say. For example, some of the other boys were saying things like, "I can't wait to see how it looks on you wet!" I knew now I was going to be one of their water victims and I had no way out. As the day went on I was hoping my friend would at least come to school so we can give each other a way to stay in touch with each other this summer, but she never came to school. I felt kind of down because I thought I wasn't going to see her anymore. Especially, since we were going to different schools next year. So leaving that topic alone I went on with the school day. It was so funny because we didn't do any work; all we did was play games and ate treats. After lunch is when all hell broke loose!

Everything was going along just fine until this one teacher came back from break. I should have known she was up to something because this one teacher took about five or six boys with her in the teacher lounge and student were not allowed in there. I am not for sure but I believe they must had to stay in there for about a half hour to forty minutes. When those boys came out of the teacher lounge they came out shooting like crazy. They each had their own garbage cans full of nothing but water balloons. It was fun because we tore the school up. Everyone was running up and down the halls, in and out of whatever room we got to first, trying to get away from the balloon throwers. The teacher unfairly set us up because she gave the boys water balloons and left the girls out there to get wet. I remember a few girls and I were carrying anything we can put water in, into the girls' bathroom so we could wet the boys up.

By the time the end of the school day ended nobody had to throw water on nobody. All you had to do was lay on the floors because there was so much water on the floors. I guarantee you once you get up off the floor you would be dripping with water. It was so funny because I can remember it now and smile as I think back to those good old days. This one janitor was said he hated the first and the last day of school because the kids go wild with water balloons every year. Then one of the boys came up from behind the janitor and poured a big bucket of water on him. I thought the janitor was going to get mad and kill the boy but he and the other teachers all joined along with the water fight. I never have seen so many people having fun and just enjoying themselves. Everybody was walking up to each other and throwing water on them. If you were dry they would throw water on you and sometimes say things like, "Ain't no sense you thinking you're better than everybody else, you're wet," and then they would throw water on them. After the boys wet somebody up they had the nerve to say, "Now you're like part of the family," and then run to wet up their next victim.

Like some of the students would say, "This was the one time you can do things to the teacher and they can't suspend you for it." So the students took a big advantage of this day and it was fun. Well, we had lots of fun on this last day of school and I wished it would not end. Some of us would see each other over the summer, and some of us would have to wait until school starts back up to see which of our friends would be at our new school. Anyway I really enjoyed myself today and I am going to miss some of my friends I enjoyed being with. Most of all I was wondering where my friend was and I was hoping she was okay. Well, another good thing about today was there weren't any fights after all. It's kind of sad to say but we all must go home soon. Now I wonder what this summer was going to hold for me! How was I going to spend it? And with whom?

Chapter Twelve
"Caught Up In the Wrong Game"

WELL I'M JUMPING around for a few days basically all I did was sit out on the back or hung out in the house until the good looking guy from around the corner came over early evening and got me to practice at the center. The practice at the center was coming along just fine. I had started working out with them and I really enjoyed basketball because it was more fun playing it than watching it. No wonder people can play the game for hours at a time. From that point on whatever chance I got I was around the corner and down the street playing me some ball and I had gotten a little good at it too. One day they were having a game for the church and needed a few more players. Lets start calling this good-looking guy my friend boy because even thou we liked each other and we were still good friends and really enjoyed each other company. My friend boy asked me to play with them so they wouldn't be disqualified and plus, "he felt I was good enough and they could beat the pants off of them" as he put it. So this one other girl and I agreed to play even thou we sat on the side for the biggest time of the game. I didn't really care about the sitting because I was too afraid I would mess up and cause them to loose the game. Plus I didn't want the team to get mad at me. They were good, actually they were damn good as usual. They did beat the other team but the other team still had their pants on and I was gladder to see that.

Yet still in all both teams showed good sportsmanship and that as my friend boy said, "What really counts in the game!" Afterward everyone went back down into the center and had some refreshments. I remember the other team telling our team, "You just wait till next week; we are going to kill yall!" Me being stupid with my mouth open and eyes bucked just looked and listened. I guess I wasn't use to this different language they used. The language was very violent but it didn't call for you to loose your life. If you were in Chicago and told someone wait until next week, you was going to kill them! You better try and run for your life because they would tell you something like, "Why wait," and kill you jonnie on the spot. That was something else I had to get use to, the way people dress and talk up here. I felt kind of good about myself; it was as if the world and my life were going my way. I started going out on the courts and playing ball with the fellows as my friend boy had suggested. Everyone there was really nice. It was a daily routine I couldn't wait until the next day to come so I could hang out with the fellows on the courts. The fellows on the courts looked at me as another player, as being one of the others and having fun.

Oh let me tell you something about my friend boy. He had a big family and they all stuck together. One day the court was fuller than usual. I thought there was a usual game going on but this was a special game. I found out it was a game of cousins against cousins. I meet really good looking niggas in my life and in one place. These were the type of niggas that would take a lady's breath away and would leave her in a daze with just their looks alone. I am too young now but they had some of those as I call them now, grab me, hold me, pick me up, and shock it to me bodies! They looked damn good! These cousins had girls from around the corner, down the street, across the street, and even girls that didn't live in the neighborhood being their personal cheerleaders. I just sat back in the shade and watched the game. Once the game was over instead of everyone going down into the center, they went and all hung out at these two houses across the street from the courts. My friend guy seen me and asked me to come along but I told him I don't think so. We sat on the courts and talked for a little while but I still chose to go home. I remember him saying, "I can't get you to change your mind?" before I could say anything this one dude came up and said hi. He was good looking too and seemed to be polite and told my friend guy to bring your good looking friend with you. That made me feel kind of tingly. He acted like he understood what I was feeling from head to toe as he stared at me with his eyes; I didn't think he was so good looking anymore.

It's strange because I have been watching that dude while he was playing ball. Plus my little dream bubble got busted when this girl came up and locked on to his arm. She was trying to get him to go with her but he just acted as if he didn't want to be bothered. I told my friend guy to go ahead with his friend and I'll talk to him later. As I turned and walked away I was kind of hoping that this one dude was looking as I walked away because I did have my eyes on him. I turned around and he was looking, I smiled and thought to myself, "If only I was a few years older." So I walked home and spent the rest of my day alone listening to my music and kind of wondering about what my friend girl from school was doing. I wish she would have came to school so we could have stayed in touched because we did have some fun times. It was only a thought but I did miss her. As the summer started to move along I had no problems. However, I believe some problems started when this man open this pool hall sweet shop downstairs from us, was my dad hot about that. The hall had started gathering a lot of niggas and most of them were from around the corner playing ball. That was right up my alley because now I gotten the chance to see this one dude more. One day I was trying to go to the back to go upstairs and he came out the door to speak to me. My poor heart started beating faster; I could had just melted and died. Me with my scary butt just said, "Hi," and I kept on walking and hurried upstairs.

Once I got up there I ran out on the top side porch and heard him talking to my friend guy about me and I started smiling. This dude asked my friend guy, what kind of relationship do we have and my friend guy answer really surprised me. He said, "We are just friends." I remember this dude saying, "You mean to say you not boning her? Everybody saying you is." My friend guy cut him off and said, "I have more respect for her than boning her. She's a good person and if we only going to be friends, I'm gonna make sure she don't get involve with none of the crazy, just want to fuck her, no good niggas." I felt a little guilty standing up there listening to my friend guy talk about me like that. I didn't know he cared so much about me. My friend guy then went on to say, "you understand what I'm talking about my brother, don't you?" I really started feeling bad for ez-dropping so I turned away and walked back into the house because I knew my friend guy was what you call a real friend rather I was around him or not. With that thought I smiled opened the door and went in the house. I went to bed that night feeling a little good about myself because what my friend guy had said. Maybe he really does care. I know I am going to look at my friend guy a lot different now, especially since I can't tell him I heard what he said about me. I remember all that night my friend guy's words. They kept going around in my head and I went to sleep with a smile on my face.

The next day I woke up I couldn't wait till the evening came so I could see my friend guy and talk to him. I did my work around the house quicker than usually so time could hurry up and I can go to the courts. This time I dressed a little beside myself. I putted on one of my not so revealing sizzler outfits but it was also something I could still play ball in. I was kind of nervous at first when I went around to the courts but I received the reactions I knew I was going to get from the people on the courts. Once I seen everyone's face on the court I knew I was a well put together female. They were all trying to get over the shock of seeing that I had a beautiful body under all those baggy clothes I be wearing. I then said in a smart but modish way, "What yall act like you never seen a girl before. Come on lets play ball!" I don't know why I dressed like I did. I guess you can say I wanted to be looked at differently that day. You know like they say it is always one in the crowd. This one guy that plays ball all the time at the courts had to say something all the way to the left. Talking about a hard up nigga, he said, "I'll play ball with you alright, but it'll be in bed!" Well I just looked at him like he didn't say anything but my friend guy stepped out the crowd and said, "Man don't be talking to her like that!" I can remember how this one guy then said, "Excuse me, I didn't know she was your girl. I'm sorry man. I just always looked at her as one of the guys and I see now that she is a real girl."

Well, I felt that this one guy was sincere and didn't mean any disrespect about what he had said, he turned right around and said, "Man, I would have never knew she was built like that. You better hold on to her bother!" My friend guy looked at this one guy and said, "No problem," and we started playing ball. After a few games of hustle I decided to sit off to the side and watch them play. My friend guy played a few more games and then came over and sat on the window ledge with me. We began to talk. He started telling me what this dude was asking him about me last night. He also told me that I shouldn't dress like that when I come around the courts for now on. I looked at my friend guy and told him, "You or no one else can tell me how I can and can't dress!" I was mad at him. I started remembering everything he had ever said to me and what he had said to the dude last night. As I think about it, I was kind of mean to my friend guy. I remember telling him, "Wait a minute! Do I sense a little jealousy?" Understanding where his feelings were at, he then told me as I can remember back to that day, "It has nothing to do with being jealous. I know these guys and some of them ain't no damn good!" My friend guy was trying to convince me how most of the guys we play ball with at the courts were no good. I had gotten quiet while my friend guy was talking because I had really got tired of hearing him put down most of the guys.I looked at him with one of those yeah right looks. He said, "Lovely, I'm only thinking about your welfare, be careful!" Who would have thought that those words of my friend guy would one day come back to haunt me?

Here is that story. Remember I told you about my friend guy saying that they have parties every weekend. The parties were actually going on every weekend and none stop. Everybody be there doing their own thing. By mid-summer I had never missed a weekend party, I was at both Friday and Saturday parties. I was at one of their parties jamming my butt off, except now I had become the queen weed smoker and drunk nothing but MD20/20, which was the shit to drink at the time. It seems as if each party brought more new faces. I believe I had started tripping because all the girls were all over this one dude. You remember that one good looking dude that was asking my friend guy questions about me? Well, it was him. I don't know why but it just seem like the more I had seen him the more I wanted to be with him. But I couldn't because he was much older than me. Plus I knew he was doing the wild thing as we called it, having sex and I wasn't. So we just talked and danced a lot together. All that holding just was making me want to really hold that body of his but without any clothes on. I knew I wasn't ready for a sexual relationship and if he knew how old I really was he wouldn't even look my way. I was as they called it back then, "jail bait." Jailbait was a minor girl in a grown woman body and if an 18 year or older person had sex with her, your ass will go to jail.

So I had came up with a solution to keep his eyes only on me when I was around and once I leave he can go and do whoever he wanted to do up. I noticed that he was like all men, always talking about how females are dressing and how he likes for his girl to dress nice for him. You know me; I started reading between the lines and thoughts. I knew how I could get him now!" The parties were great as usual and me I was as high as I could be like always. But you know what I had nothing to worry about because my second daddy was around. I'm talking about my friend guy. He would tell me, Lovely, don't you think you had too much to drink! And things like, "I wish I never gave you that first joint!" Me being Ms. Too Damn Good Looking for myself now paid him no attention. I continue to get stone as usual because I knew my good looking friend was going to make sure I got home ok. I always thought that was so sweet of him. I partied and partied until the party started to end and just like I said, "My good looking friend see me home and waited until I gotten in the house before he would leave to walk back home." The next morning came and man did I have a hangover but I knew dude was going to be at the courts and I had to see him before tonight. So now I had to work with this hang over to make it through the rest of the day.

Once I got to the courts there he was, I don't care, I still say that my friend guy was jealous because I can remember him saying that day, "Why you looking at him like that?" I turned around and told my friend guy off real good. My friend guy then said, "I'm surprised you got out the bed the way you was drinking last night." That wasn't all, my friend guy then had the nerve to tell me I need to go home and change my clothes! I told him, "Dog you're supposed to be my hommie not my daddy!" He didn't like that because he said to me in a nasty voice, "Remember I told you so. You're around here playing with fire Lovely and don't even know it." I turned around and walked away without saying anything to him. I went on and played a half a game of hustle. I stopped and went home because I had gotten depressed after my friend guy and I got into a little disagreement. As I was leaving I heard a voice say, "I hope I see you at the party tonight Lovely." I turned around to look back and it was that good looking dude I've been having my eyes on and had my arms around while we danced last night. I went home and tried to get me some rest. I say this trying to be older game is wearing my ass out, I am tired as hell. So I lay down to try and go to sleep before the time came for me to go to the party. I finally went to sleep with him on my mind. I thought about what I would have to do to make him my boyfriend but most of all I was not ready for such a big step? I must have been really off into dude because I slept like a baby. I woke up and seen what time it was. I jumped up and said, "Damn I'm late!" Like I had a job to go to but in a way I did because it was a job trying to keep all of dude's attention on me.

This night I really dressed to impress. I wore my three piece sizzler outfits and did it get lots of attention from every male and female. You know, I can get real big headed from wearing this outfit. To tell you the truth I was really bigger headed than ever. I knew I looked damn good because I looked too good to myself. I not only showed it but this was one time I acted like it too. I twisted as my skirt slapped me on the ass. Now check this out, it was already short as hell but I still had it unbutton. I had my skirt unbutton up to the top of my thighs; all you could see was nothing but thick legs. I went and got me a glass of wine and that was when dude came over to me. You see when I first came into the party he was talking to this other girl, so he didn't see me. I got jealous and said to myself, "Fuck him." Seriously, how can he be for real about me when every time I see him he got a different girl pulling on him? So I was going to party without him this time.

You know how every time you make your mind up by saying "fuck a person," they always seem to know this. Like always they seem to come around and make you change your mind. Well, that is what dude did to me. He came up to me and said with that voice of his that made me melt in my shoes, "I thought you wasn't going to make it tonight?" I remember saying something half smart such as, "Oh because you thought I wasn't going to make it, so that gives you the right to be all over and locked up in another female's face." Dude looked at me and said, "I'm not about to trip with you Lovely!" As he turned to walk away, me being stuck on stupid grabbed him by the arm and told him, "Wait, don't walk away from me like that. I'm sorry. You know as I think about it even to this day I don't know what the hell I was telling him I was sorry for because I hadn't done nothing wrong. Now back to the party. We really party that night. I had big fun and yes, my second daddy was there. He had gotten on my nerves so damn bad that night. When I look back at the way I acted I made myself look like a food and I should have been the one embarrassed.

I was talking about my friend guy. I kept telling him he was only having guilty feelings, which is why he became my protector. If he wouldn't have ever had sex with me when I was drunk and high he wouldn't feel he needed to watch over me. I remember telling him all he wanted to do was to get back in my panties again. That's why he was so defensive of me and was only jealous because I had my eyes on someone else. I felt bad about the way I was talking to my friend guy but I didn't know how to tell him I was sorry. I drowned myself in the bottles of liquor. I was drinking so tuff that night till I remember I grabbed one of the bottles off the table and started drinking right out of the bottle. By this time I was wasted but there was always another daddy at the party for me. Now, dude I kind of had my eyes on was trying to be my third daddy. I went off on him and I can remember I was falling all over the place. Who would have known someone else was watching me at the party. I remember I got so mad that I left the party and started walking home by myself. My house wasn't far; I was only two blocks from my house or a block and a half if I took the alley. Yes, me being stuck on stupid had decided to take the alley way.

I was walking down the street trying to keep my eyes focused. It seemed as if it was taking me forever to get home. All I know is I had to hurry up and get in the bed because I was feeling real sick. I stopped by the alley behind my house because I felt the alcohol wanted to come back up the way it went down. Again, I still would say, "A drunk ain't shit," because if I wasn't as pissy drunk I could remember things and could defend myself. Now, I'm leaning on this pole because I can't hold myself up right. My insides were not right; man, did I feel ill. I remember trying to stand on my own because my house was just across the way right in front of me from the "T" shaped alley. As I try to get my eyes focused right so I could continue t make it home, everything all of a sudden gotten totally dark. At first, I thought I had passed out because I could feel myself trying to. But I realized that someone put something over my head. Right away I started grabbing whatever was covering my face but the more I struggle the tighter it seemed to have gotten around my neck. I could now feel myself passing out. I started trying to tell them I couldn't breathe. Then a voice said, "If you quit trying to fight maybe you would get out of this alive."

I started crying begging them to please don't do this to me. I said, "I'm only a child. I'm only twelve." I remember I tried screaming but every time I would try to scream they would tighten up whatever they had over my head and around my neck. They would keep tighten up whatever they had around my neck so I couldn't make a sound. They then pulled where as I was kicking and begging them please, "Please, no please let me go! Don't do this to me!" I stopped trying to scream and fight especially since I seen it wasn't doing me any good. As I'm writing this I trying to see if I can recognize any of their voices but I was too fucking drunk that night, so everyone sounded like an echo. God that was one time I wish my friend guy would have been there but I knew I had no one to blame but myself because of the way he talked to me. It wasn't much I could do. All I knew was that there were at least three or four attackers that had me down. All I could do now at this point was cry because they were hurting me and I wanted to die. I can remember how they not only took turns doing what they wanted to do to me but each time the next attacker would change the cloth around my neck and he would make it tighter. I was now really crying wondering why is this always happening to me. What about my body did people feel they could hurt me whenever they wanted to by rapping and abusing my body?

Everything had happened so fast. But it seemed like it took them a long time before they got finished taking turns doing what they wanted to do to me and then they let me go. It was so upsetting even for me now to think about what I went through thcat night. I know I got to try to write and remember what I can in order to continue on with my book. I know how I'm feeling now and I know all I really wanted them to do was to let me go. If I choose not to live afterwards, I would like to be the one to take my own life. I don't want to die by the hands of some sick minded ass niggas that wanted to get their kicks off on fucking a twelve year old kid. Sitting here trying to relive that day back in my life, seemed as if I can still hear their voices echoing through my head as one of my attackers told the others to hurry up and make sure the jacket is tight enough around my head so I can't see who they were.

I knew now I put myself in that situation, but my God, everyone had the right to dress as they like and they should be able to walk the streets anytime they got good and ready. I still felt regardless of how I looked or dressed, they still had no right to do the things they were doing to me. You want me to tell you some more real fucked up ass parts about it all? I was too damn drunk till I couldn't hardly stand up and I couldn't even try to defend myself. The bad thing about it all was I didn't know who they were. All I knew was it was horrible being ganged raped by some niggas I knew but was too drunk to really focus on their voices. I was a kid with so many problems that caused me to start drinking at a young age. I use to drink so much that I would get to the point of passing out and now my drinking has gotten me in trouble. Once they let me go I do remember hearing one of my attackers saying, "Hurry and go because I'm going to take the jacket off her head!" I was thinking that maybe now I could come back to earth just in enough time to see the one attacker or at least something about him I can remember. I thought maybe I'll be able to see his face or anything that would help me to identify him but that didn't do me any good.

As my attacker pulls the jacket away from around my neck, he pushes me and knocked me down into some bushes between the garbage cans and I didn't even get the chance to see his face. You know what was even more hurting? Once I had gotten up and realized where I was at I could have died. You wouldn't believe that they had raped me by this empty house next door to my backyard. I really felt like an ass then. I went into the house and everyone was at home except for my dad. I said to myself I knew they heard me in the back when I was trying to scream because they were all woke. Then I started thinking that maybe they didn't care about me. I just looked at everyone in the kitchen as I walked by them and went into my room and started crying. I started telling God I didn't understand why I was here on earth. I asked him, "Why was I born? Was it just so people could take advantage of my body?" That hurt and hurts me like hell! I couldn't believe people on the earth were still so cruel. Now you know where this all is leading me to? I had to start all over again with trying to get my head back on straight. After another one of those thoughts of thinking I guess my only purpose on earth was to only be attacked and assaulted put me to sleep.

I woke up the next morning just feeling like real shit. I didn't come out my room for nothing at all except to go to the bathroom. Before I came out my room I would listen for noises throughout the house to make sure nobody was in the house. I didn't want to look at or see anyone and eating food was the last thing on my mind. I didn't care if I live or die; therefore, you have an idea of what I thought about eating. I believe I stayed in my room for three or four days before anyone really notice that something was wrong with me. Like I said before I knew they heard me in the back and didn't try to find out what was wrong. When I was finally asked, "What was my problem," I felt they really didn't want to know. I felt they only asked to pick at me and tease me. Now I knew I was all alone in this mean would with no one I could turn to. You know for some strange reason all I kept thinking about was my girl friend from school. You remember the one that danced in the tavern.

I wish I could talk to her but I had no way of getting in touch with her. I wasn't for sure if she still danced down at this one bar or not. That was only a thought; something I was too afraid of was going out the house to find out. I became like a hermit. I only came out for food when no one was home but me. I also took a bath and shower when I was home alone. If you came to my house when I was there alone, I didn't answer the door or the telephone. When anyone came by looking for me, I told whoever answered the door to tell them I was sleep. A few weeks had gone by and I still haven't been out the house. I never wanted to show my face around the neighborhood as long as I lived. I was now cutting myself off from the whole world and even my family. This is a short poem of how I felt about my life. I called it, "My Life,"

My life is so blue till there's no one in this world but me.
My heart is so empty and hurt, till there is no love for this earth
    for anyone to see.
With those dark clouds always over my head and lady luck is
    never holding me,
I hate the whole damn world, everyone except my mother who

birth me.

So now I am an avenger, full of spitefulness, malice, hostility, bitterness, and malevolence waiting to explode.

Now they all will know me and one day my story will be told, everyone will be punished for what they have done to me because male life I will and out to destroy!!

For the next few days I couldn't think about no one but my girl friend from school who danced at the tavern. I started remembering how good it felt to have all of those nasty niggas slobbing all over me, begging, all hard up because they wanted to be with me. It was a real kick of super ego to see and knowing how they were suffering because they wanted them some Lovely. To me every male wasn't no good. They were only out for one thing and will take it in order to get what they want. Now I had came up with an idea to make all males and females undergo the infliction for what life had done to me. The evening finally came and dark was shortly to followed. All I could think about was to get down to the bar where my girl friend from school dances. I was hoping they needed more dancers at the bar because here I come; I'm ready! My mind was made up now. I had come up with my own little style I was going to put on them. If I performed the way I should, I would have the whole bar wanting me but all they can do is kiss my ass, give me some money, and buy me something to drink. My stage name should have been Ms. Tease, because I plan on making whoever cum all over themselves and then laugh at their ass afterward.

Once I gotten down to the bar I didn't see my friend girl from school but that didn't stop me from putting my plan to work. I went down there dressed and looking like Miss Good-Body; showing it, throwing it, and rubbing it all in their nose. I felt like I was Miss Mother Fucken It, you couldn't tell me shit. At a month pass twelve years old, I was five feet eight inches tall, and built like a pleasing healthy hourglass. I had long black hair, nice up right size breast, a little tiny waist, a big ass, and big hairy legs. Yes, I had one of those perfect figures that every female wanted. I guess that was why everyone was taking it from me. I had the prettiest light golden brown sugar looking skin and it was soft too. I was a very natural looking woman with little make up. Something I remember even now, they use to tell me I had those perfect shaped lips that a lot of women were trying to draw on their face. Seriously, I knew I looked good and a lot of other people did too. I made up my mind that since they wanted to take my body and abused it, I'm going to use what God and my mother gave me to hurt them. I was talking to few guys in the bar; they too felt that I had what it took to be a great dancer. I can remember how they use to always say, "All I had to do is just stand there and don't do nothing. I didn't have to take off no clothes and they would look at me all night."

Big headed I was. Yes! Yes! A zillion times yes. It was all I needed to keep my blown out of proportion ego blown up even more bigger. By this time I've had more than a few drinks and well you know how that goes. When I'm drinking I know I am the finest bitch on the earth and all I wanted to do is shake my ass. I'm just sitting here enjoying all these hard up ass niggas, if only they knew what was going through my mind. They'll take off running. I was thinking the worst about them all, calling them all kinds of motherfuckers, and every other dirty name I could think of. I looked at them with the prettiest simile, as they would always say but behind that smile was an anger that wanted to kill. I was really feeling good about myself because I had them focus where I wanted them. Now I wanted some of their money they were holding in their hands and pockets. Those other girls were ok but they weren't holding the attention of their customers like they should have. I know I was and I loved every minute of it. By this time the owner of the bar came in. He wasn't to please with his dancers because I had their best spending customers focused all on me.

Let me tell you why. Once he gotten down to the end of the bar I noticed the owner was talking to one of his dancers and looking down in my direction. Would believe as soon as he walked away from the dancer, she got up and brought her stupid ass over to our table. I remember she asked one of the gentlemen I was sitting with if she could join us? One of the other guys said, "We have all we need right here," as he grabbed me around my shoulder and squeezed me kind of tight up against him. He just didn't know I wanted to straight snap on him but it was all part of my plan to tease and destroy. So old girl walked her unmarried ass away not to please of course but you know what? I didn't give a hot fuck. She did the right thing. She danced her ass back to the end of the bar and drunk her ice water. The gentlemen I was sitting with ere all buddies and I was still trying to milk the hell out of their pockets. I wanted it all, if I could get it, every dime they had I wanted it. Then I would send them home to their wives fucked up, broke, and confused. They really thought I was all into them; they were a bunch of horny ass drunks. They just didn't know what I thought about them; I could throw up in their faces.

We all just sat, drank, and I pretended to be enjoying myself while also in m case lying through my teeth. You should have seen them, they were all so happy because I was sitting with them. Little did they know I wanted to cut every last one of their throats quicker than they could blink their eyes. It gave me so much pleasure rejecting these hard up gentlemen as they begged me until I finally danced for them. I knew I had them right where I wanted them. I got my overly glad ass up on the stage and started dancing. At first I had to talk to the owner about let me dance on the stage. He said, "Yeah get up there and let me see what you can do!" I went over to the jukebox and picked out a few "lay me down relaxing" songs. Again, remember it's all about the teasing so that was why I choose those kinds of songs.

I got up on the stage and it felt so good to see all those eyes focused on me. I had everyone's attention including the owner's brother. As the music stated to play I for a short moment had to think about how I was going to start dancing. Right away the little voice came and it hit me. It said, "Go out there the way you feel and the role you're now playing. Miss It, teasing can't no one get any or touch this was how I was feeling. I knew I was too good for myself. I began dancing like I was the queen of all dancers and couldn't no one do it like I can. I had all kinds of heads turning my direction. Everyone wanted to see and fantasized on what and how they could get with and some Lovely.

Lovely, yes that was my name but it just didn't seem to fit me on the stage. So from that day on I became "Luscious Lynn!" Everything you wanted and all that you'll ever need was in Luscious Lynn. Of course, I was better than great and on the stage I was super. Even the horny owner started to want some of what he was seeing moving across the stage. I received so many applauses and when my last record was over the customers at the bar were yelling, "Don't stop now." I remember how I would tell them the music had stop playing and I didn't have any money to play the jukebox. Then I would a little smart remark like, "If you all want to see me dance some more then you better play the box!" All that statement usually did was have my ass on the stage dancing a few extra songs than before. The customers would reply back by saying things like, "Don't worry about that." It was so funny to see them all run to the jukebox. All those horny nasty mother fuckers were running to the jukebox to play me some music and they were asking me, "What song do you want to hear?" I would laugh and say, "Play something nice and slow but romantic. Something that I could really shake my ass too."

Then I would yell out, "These lights are too hot up here. I need something to drink," and the drinks came rolling in. I felt like what a life! The music stated back up playing again. I had already peep what the owner was looking for in his go-go dancers. Now it was time to put my plan into action by being the best I can be at work and I let it flow. I had this smooth sailing snake movement about myself. Man did that style look good because I looked damn good to myself till I would say, "I see why everybody wants you; you're gorgeous!" All the time while I was on the stage I was hustling those crazy fool ass customers for big drinks and tall tips. I made my money and the owner did too. The owner really liked that up till when I got off the stage. The owner brought me plenty of drinks while we discussed business. I felt damn good, I mean real damn good to know I turned all of those horny customers on and when I got ready I turned their asses off. Yes! They were telling the owner, he should hire me and maybe he would see them down at the bar more regular. With those words from some of his best spending customers, I just smiled and said to myself, "You did it!" If you want something I found out, you can get it. I didn't say that the tasks would be easy but if it was meant to be, then fight for it. Don't give up and I guarantee you would succeed.

Chapter Thirteen
"The Misleadings: Who Am I"

I WOKE UP the next day realizing what I had did last night but you know what? I didn't feel bad about it and it really made me forget about all my problems I was having! Who knows maybe I will take him up on his offer to dance! My day was basically the same as usual; in fact for the next few days things have been as usual. All I did was sitting in my room and went no where, which is how my day has been for the past few days. I was kind of really surprised that my friend guy hasn't came around and checked on me. I guess I couldn't blame him considering the way I talked to him the last time I seen him. You know what? I sometimes sit and wonder if he knew what had happen to me and just didn't want to face me with the , "I told you so's," statement. What I do know is that it was definitely some of those guys from the party, which is why they covered my head. I also remember the one guy telling the others to hurry up and move around so I wouldn't see their faces when he takes the jacket off my heard. It hurts really bad not knowing who had gang raped me, so I just sat there crying, wondering why me! Why always me? I know one day the truth about that night will come to the light and I will be able to face my cowardly attackers.

After that night all my attackers have done was made life a planet of hell because I was out to destroy everyone. I really started thinking about what had happen to me. As usual I have to make up my mind to try and go on with my life. It's most definitely wasn't easy but now since I have a master plan in mind I know I should be able to get through this. With my master plan, I see nothing but smooth sailing down the road for me from here on. I did get up and fixed me a sandwich a few times. I noticed how time had just really flown pass and I knew I had to make up my mind about the dancing job. So, I decided to get up and start getting myself together because it is going to be dark and I am going to hit it as soon as my dad leaves to drive the cab.

Let me tell you how I manage to dance in the taverns at the age of 12 years old without anyone knowing until I turned 15 years old. Remember my dad was a hard worker who kept two jobs; at night he drove the cab. You see I knew my dad work schedule just as good as he did. I could time him to the second when he was going to leave up to the time he would come into the door for the rest of the day. Therefore, it wasn't hard for me to get away with murder if I choose to because every time my dad leaves I was at home and when my dad came back home I was still at home. My dad would come in from one job and if dinner wasn't cooked he would cook for us. Usually after dinner he would lie down for a few hours and asked me to wake him up so he doesn't over sleep. I would go back to my room and sit up, lie down, or sometimes just read to help me keep from sitting around all the time crying and feeling sorry for myself.

I kept my bedroom door closed at all times and by the time my dad got ready to leave to drive the cab, I would be ready too. I would be dress to leave right behind him. I guess you might be thinking how did I get away with it? Well, it got easier. You see you always have to have a well put together plan and my plan was the best for three years. My dad really didn't notice me at all; he only cared that I was at home at all times. At one while my dad had started to get suspicious about where I was all of a sudden getting a lot of new clothes from. I would tell him that the clothes belong to one of my so-called friends he never gotten the chance to meet. You see I use to also do people hair so sometimes I would tell him I made some money doing XYZ hair and bought me an outfit. My dad believed anything I said because he looked at it as long as he seen I wasn't out there getting in trouble than it was fine. Oh God, but if my dad only really knew the trouble I have been in!

I was still too afraid to tell my dad because I didn't know what he would do or think about his sweet innocent Faye for waiting so long before I told him. It was my decision to keep every thing that had happened to me to myself. As I think about it now, the only thing I did was staying closely to myself. I wonder why my dad didn't think about that when I started telling him those lies about the clothes I was wearing. Now since I covered up some of my tracks, I learned to become even better at not letting anyone know nothing I didn't want them to know. My dad would usually peak into my bedroom and tell me he was leaving. I knew I would be pushing for time to get down to the bar if I waited around for my dad to leave before I got dress. I started getting dress at the same time he did. I would have on one of my big walk around the housedresses on to throw my dad off. My dancing clothes would be under my walk around the housedress. I did this so he would think I wasn't going out the house and so he didn't have to worry about me.

I'll go into the bathroom and do whatever I had to but I made sure I was out the bathroom in time to keep my dad room asking questions. Once I have done all I had to do in the bathroom, I would go into my bedroom and get dressed. My dad knew I couldn't deal with a whole lot of heat. So when I would tell him I'm going to bed or was in bed early because the heat had made me kind of sick and I didn't feel to well he believed me. However, if he would have ever decided to come in my room and pull my covers back, he would have seen I was fully clothed from head to toe. No soon as my dad would leave out the door, I would jump up as if I had springs on my body and look out the top window as I watch my dad drive off; I usually peak through the curtains so he couldn't see me. He would sometimes look back up at the house as if he didn't want to leave me there alone all sick. My dad just didn't know that all the time I was praying that he hurry up and go.

Oh but when his car made that left turn at the lights on the corner, I'll then watch his car go down 17th street until I couldn't see it anymore. Then, down the stairs I would go; walking up the street trying to get to the bar so I can shake my ass. It was good; I really enjoyed making those nasty, no good, money spending, tongue handing nigga's suffer. I couldn't make the people that turned me the way I am now suffer, so everyone else will pay for the crime and do the time my way. Teasing you with something that you want but you can't have or get is my way. After dancing down to the bar for about a couple of weeks I became the highest paying dancer. Was I the shit or what? I knew I was all that and some more! I kind of started being the all in one employee; I was running the bar some what. I became good and fast in seating, serving, and mixing drinks but most of all what I was down there for and that was to dance.

I had become so great with my dancing till I would stand on my head, move real smooth, and nasty for the customers. Of course, doing these things got me paid with the bigger and better tips. I also had the biggest opportunity to really fuck with the fantasies of the customers' mind. I made sure that the head standing had become a part of my daily act and those horny mother fuckers loved it even the boss. He would even sometimes tell the customers if you buy her enough drinks to get her lose, you should see what she can do when she stand on her head. Some more of my boss's favorite words when I stood on my head were, "get your tongue back in your mouth!" He also made the job kind of fun. I was enjoying the job, including every second of my performance on and off the stage. Yes, my reader I had became a real hustler and I was damn good at it. There wasn't a night I didn't leave out the bar with at least two hundred dollars or more in tips. We could also get pay from the boss nightly or weekly; so I always went home with a personal bank.

I made my money nightly; therefore, I would let my money add up for the week before I spent it. The owner was very pleased with me because I made him just as much money and sometimes more. You see, I was a well paid dancer; I was getting paid more than the other dancers. I can remember how many of the customers came into the bar with five or ten one dollar bills in there hand. I would in a playing mood just take their money out their hands and say, "Since you were going to give this money to me anyway, you might as well just give it all to me at one time." These fools will come into the bar and buy me sixty dollar bottles of champagne like it was nothing. Some of the good spending customers will sometimes come into the bar and see me talking to another customer and say, "Luscious when you finish at that table we got a bottle on ice for you over here." I would just smile and say, "I'll be right over." I never kept my customers waiting to long; I would excuse myself for a minute from the table I am sitting at so I can greet my customers at the other table. I would laugh and talk with the customers I'm servicing for the moment and then I will promise them I will be back.

It felt good to have so many people trying to compete with each other while trying to rent my attention for only a short moment. While all the time I was cursing the ground they walked on and were poisoning the air they were breathing. Luscious Lynn had become a monster. I had it going on so tuff at the bar till rumors had started going around saying I was sleeping with one of the owners but I wasn't. To be honest with you didn't care what anyone said because I was making my money and I wasn't giving it to no damn so called wanted to be half slick ass pimp. I knew what I was doing and I had become a master with my plan; I was working it out to my benefit. It has been all most a month now since I have been dancing. I started to wonder why I haven't seen my friend from school that uses to dance at the bar too in a while! Then, just so happen who comes through the door and I couldn't have been more than too glad to see her. I finally felt I had somebody I could trust and watch my back.

We talked about what had happen to me that one night when I had left the party and now that I'm dancing and enjoying every second of it. I then, asked my friend from school, "Why haven't she been dancing?" When she told me that she never stopped, I thought to myself, "Ok, now you got me confuse!" I told her how long I've been dancing down here and she said, "I only dance down here when I'm in town." She also told me that they get paid big money up north dancing. I asked her what your mother said about you leaving out of town like that! Will you believe that she told me her mom doesn't care if she comes home or not. I understood once she went into details so we just left that subject alone and kicked it at the bar. You see when the bar closed I knew I had to get my ass in the house and fast. She had started telling me about the money I could make by dancing at the after hours. My girl friend from school then explained to me that I could dance as many sets and records I wanted to.

Some girls only dance off of two records, get paid, and hit it. I thought about it and decided to go with her considering that she have to make sure I got home before my dad. I went with my friend girl up north and I was having so much fun. You would have never thought that deep down inside I was hiding some ugly dark hunting secret that was continuously running around in my head. I realized what time it was and told my girl friend that I have to go. She got some crazy dude to drop us off at my house. Talk about good timing. No soon as my girl friend and I got out of the car and was walking through the game way to the back door, I noticed my dad car pulling up in front of the house. I just knew he seen me and was going to kill me when he got in the house. I hurry up to open the door and told my girl friend to run up the stairs. I knew I was so use to taking off my clothes but this time sister girl really broke the record. I didn't know I could undress so quickly. I had pulled my shoes off as I was running up the stairs. Once I made it in my room I began taking off my clothes as I let them fall to the floor and put on my big housedress that my dad seen me in before he left to drive the cab.

I started messing up my bed like I had been sleeping in it. I ran to the bathroom, put big toothpaste, and about four sticks of gum in my mouth to kill the alcohol smell. Then I went to the refrigerator and took stuff out to make my friend girl and I a sandwich. My friend girl and I sat at the kitchen table and made our sandwich while we talk about our shake dancing career and the customers we be dealing with. I did all of this before my dad made it up the stairs. It was kind of funny but at the time I knew I had to make it look like I've been home all the time. Of course, we all know the truth, which is I had just gotten in the door. Once my dad came in the house he did ask, where I was coming from because as he drove up the street he thought he seen me walking away from a car. I told him, "I've been home all night. I went downstairs to let my friend girl in and she was introducing me to her father. Her dad wanted to be sure she was going where she said she was and not by no boys house."

Then I finished cleaning up my tracks by saying, "That's probably why it looked like I was walking away from the car." I introduced my friend girl to my dad. I could tell my dad kind of liked her because he said she seemed like a real sweet girl. My dad then went to his room to go to bed. This section of my book is really to my dad, here are all your answers to all the questions you use to ask me. So, dad if you are this far into my book, now you know why I use to have all those big old balls of gum in the refrigerator. As you have read, I needed to throw a big ball of gum in my mouth to kill my alcohol smell from drinking. They always say the truth will always finally come to the light.

After my friend girl and I ate our sandwich we went into my bedroom to go to sleep. I can say that this job does wear you out because we slept the whole day away. When we woke up it was dark outside. I now knew what it was like to work a study job and let's not talk about trying to hold down tow jobs. I see why my dad be so tired all the time because I'm feeling every second of the time I worked now through my aching tired body. My friend girl told me I would get use to it after a while. I really wasn't having problems with the bar hours, it was those after hours that were killing me. It's true the quick money was easy and good but to see those mother fuckers nut all over themselves made getting the money double great. Like my friend girl said, "I'll get use to it and believe me I did and I really enjoyed every second of the getting use to it. I was having so much fun until the whole summer vacation had pass by.

School was in a week and I hadn't decided if I was going to go back to school or what! Then, I thought about it, I might as well go and forget about the "ifs" and the "or what" parts because my daddy will kick my ass just for me even thinking the thought. So now the question was how do I juggle my dancing job with going to school full time? I knew I didn't want to quit dancing, plus I had become addicted to my own vengeance plans and enjoying every second of it. The high I got from the thrills, the satisfactions, and the results of a good plan coming together, but now most of all the money I loved. So, I said, "I'll just cross that thought of school bridge in another week when I get to it, because in the mean time I am going to continue dancing.

This one day when I was getting ready to go to work, I had the downstairs door open because my friend girl was coming back to pick me up. I heard someone knocking at the door; I just yelled out, "come in!" I right away just assumed that it was my friend girl. Man did I get a surprise! I'm just walking my too good-looking ass around the house singing and dancing to myself. Then I could tell that the footsteps had gotten closer so I yelled, "I'm in the bathroom. I'll be out in a minute. Have a seat." I bring my wild, fast, crazy ass out of the back talking big shit saying, "girl friend I'm going to make those horny mother fuckers come all over their mama with this outfit!" As I turned around to ask her what does she think by saying, "I look good, don't I?" I froze in my own tracks while spinning once I seen that it wasn't my girl friend that I was talking all that shit to. I pulled the ends of my blouse and closed my arms around front of me. I couldn't do nothing now but stand there with my mouth hanging opened as if I was in a state of shock to see that it was my friend guy from around the corner. He had his mouth opened; eyes bucked, and said in a surprising voice, "I've never seen you looking better!"

He then said, "I came to see how you was doing," as he looks me up and down with amazement in his eyes. He asked me why I hadn't been around to the courts and before I could say anything he turn around and answer his own question. My friend guy stood up and said, "I see by the looks of you, you've been doing bigger and better things!" I guess you can say that I was speechless for a moment and a little embarrassed too. I didn't want to tell my friend guy that I've been dancing by taking my clothes off in front of a tavern full of niggas since the last time I had seen him. I guess deep inside I still felt like I wanted his respect because he did try to look out for my well being at all times. I though if he knew I was a striper dancer than he would think less of me and especially since there was this statement going around, "If you were a dancer then you was also out there selling your booty." I knew that the statement did not applied to me and there have been times in my life that I had to prove it.

You see there have been times when I would leave with one of those tricks from sown at the tavern and hook them up with someone else I knew. Once I had gotten known in the street life many of the tricks would say, "Luscious or Lynn is a dancer not a hoe!" I had to prove who I was to keep my name clean and earned the respect of the streets. I know my friend guy should have known me by now but he hasn't seen me in awhile, and I had a new appearance and attitude; I really didn't know what to say to him. All I knew was I had to explain to my friend guy what I meant by the statement I made about making all those horny niggas come all over their mothers. The thought didn't go completely through my mind about what to say to him until he asked me what I meant about that statement. At first all I could do was just look at him. I knew then I had to tell him the truth and hopefully he would understand. It wasn't easy but I sat down with my friend guy and told him what I was now doing for a living. He looked even more shocked and said, "You didn't look to be that kind of girl and anyway you are too young to be in the bar!" I told him I didn't have too much time to go into detail about everything but I promise to explain it all to him later. I remember him telling me to make sure it's soon because he didn't want to think bad thoughts about me especially since we were once so cool.

As I can remember that day I know I was rushing around because I had to be ready when my friend girl came to pick me up. I can remember telling him I didn't want to be rude but I was in a hurry and I will make sure we talk before the week is out. As I walked with my friend guy to the door, he stopped and said, "Oh yeah, the reason I came over was to invite you to our back to school party we are having this weekend." I told him cool, I'd just stop through there for a minute before, I go to work. I remembered he said, "Ok, make sure you do that," and left. It wasn't long before my friend girl came. I locked the house up and left. I started telling her about how my friend guy had came around and the way he acted when I told him I was a striper dancer. She told me, "Don't worry about it he'll be alright," and my night was alright too. I made like close to four hundred dollars that night and then went to the after hours just to enjoy myself this time. I guess I kind of disappointed everyone because they all had started teaming up on me saying, "Come on just do one record!"

Me, already feeling like I was on top of the world couldn't let my loyal customers down. So, this time I danced a few records for free but I still gotten big tips. Dude that ran the after hours was glad I danced free because I usually charge him $50.00 a song but this one time I told him was on the house. My girl friend was cracking up laughing. I could remember her telling me, "Fool, you're crazy, everybody like you, even that female pimp. Just keep on enjoying yourself that's all that really counts." After I finished the second record my friend girl and I sat down at the bar and start talking. The first thing that came out my mouth was, "What do you mean about this female pimp shit?" She started laughing and said, "Here take this," as she handed me a drink. Then my friend girl said, "Because you are going to need it." When she told me that dude was really a lady I almost mess all over myself. The reason was I kind of had a little liking for dude; he was damn good looking and had two to five hoes on his arms every time I seen him or should I now say her. I didn't say anything to him because I knew he was a pimp and I didn't want one. That was another one of my main reasons for coming to the after hours to look at him but now my friend girl is saying that his is a she.

I had my friend girl rolling when I said, "She got one of those you know what!" My friend girl wasn't making it no easier because she kept saying, "What? I don't know what you mean about a you know what?" So I just said, "Girl you know one of those things that a man got. A dick! He can't be a woman!" That's when I found out that she had one of those you know what a man got that wasn't real. God, I could have died. It didn't end there he-she came over and brought me a drink. Now, I did say thank you. Then I remember how he-she said that my style of dancing was unique and he-she thought I was the best he-she had ever seen. When he-she talked he-she even sounded like a real dude. I still couldn't believe it and I wasn't about to ask him, or her if it was true or not. I mean dude, old girl had some pretty hoes and not trying to be funny but he-she had some of the best dressing and best looking hoes at the after hours. I couldn't understand what they wanted with another woman. Oh but then I remember what I had went through with that one girl that had lived across the street from me. I guess there's a lot of them type of people out here in Wisconsin.

Old girl had started talking and she said, "Where is your man?" When I told he-she I didn't have a pimp I can remember he-she saying, oh, you're an out cast! I'm stuck on stupid I said, "No I 'm a dancer only and all I do is dance." He-she kind of laughs and said, "I see you really don't know what I am talking about." Then he-she started to explain what he-she meant by an out cast. He-she said, "An out cast is a hoe working without a pimp but still making her money." I stopped him, her and said, "Wait a minute; I'm not a hoe so that means I'm not an out cast!" He-she laughed and said, "I still like the way you dance and if it's ok with you I would like to come and watch you at your job?" I just looked for a second and then thought to myself hell her money spends just as good as the next man's money. With that thought in mind, I told her, "Sure," and then he-she went on about his-her business with his-her hoes. I just looked and shook my head and said to myself, "Why?" Except for the shocking news about dude really being a girl the rest of the night went fine. My friend girl knows she kept rubbing it in on me and teasing me because I didn't know and couldn't tell I was eyeing a girl. It was all in fun and we were having lots of it. My friend girl and I hung out for a few hours longer and then decided to leave to go over to my house. This time I got caught coming in. By the time my friend girl and I made it to my house we were laughing about what had happen at the after hour. You know when drunks talks, they be talking louder than they think. So even now I'm sitting here picturing my friend girl and me going through the gangway walking to the back door. We were very loud, hitting, and pushing each other. I really busted out laughing when my friend girl said, "A lot of hoes wanted to be in her family. They say that she treat her hoes better than these male pimples do theirs." I didn't care how she treated her hoes I wasn't about to be part of no family, not even my own. Plus if the thing wasn't real than what was it made of and how does she use it.

Old girl was known to take a hoe from a pimp with no problems. You see back in the day they use to say, if another player pulls one of your hoes then the other pimp have to let her go if the hoe chooses the other pimp. With all do respect to the saying, a better man win but in this case the better woman won each time; what a life. I remember saying, "No way," as I reached to stick my key in the door but the door opened for me. As I slowly raised my head up, the thought the whole time was running through my mind was, I was about to get my ass beat down into the ground. I started looking at the feet first saying, "Oh my God," then someone grabbed me by my arm and said, "You thought I was your daddy, didn't you?" What he do that for because man it was a shame to say I had to pee and I did standing at the door. That was somewhat of a release but I didn't mean to do it on myself. He started laughing at me and told me I smell like a brewery. I remember burping and saying, "So, I smell like pee too!" He changed my attitude real quickly by saying, "I bet you won't be saying that if I told Hubbard how you've been coming into the house right before he does!"

I remember telling him, "You won't do your favorite niece like that?" My uncle then told me, "Well, I'll make a deal with you." Now it seems as if I am going to have another problem so I told him, "What? Anything, just don't tell daddy!" He then said, "If you hook me up with your pretty girl friend, I won't say nothing to Hubbard," I told him cool. I knew she liked older guys anyway and he would be right up her alley plus my uncle wasn't bad looking. However, once

I did hook them up I regretted every second of it. Honestly, I just don't know what I did that for? Readers let me tell you something, whatever you do, don't never match make your friend with a member of your family. It seems as if your friend would start tripping and he or she will soon push your ass to the curve. When I told my friend my uncle wanted to be with her, she hurry up and jumped in the bed with him. I was really surprised in my friend girl when she said, "I was going to ask you to hook me up with him anyway," and that same night my friend girl and my uncle slept with each other.

The next afternoon I looked at her and said, "How can you just sleep with someone you just meet?" I remember the old tramp said, "You're just jealous because I'm doing it and you're afraid to." She had delivered a low blow and it hurt, I just looked at my friend girl because I thought we were better than that. I just took it and said nothing else to her for the rest of the evening. Even at work that night I kept brushing my friend girl off but man I could had straight killed her when I seen my uncle and some of his friends coming through that door. I looked at my friend girls and said, "Why did you tell him? How am I supposed to take off my clothes in front of my uncle and his friends?" Believe me when it came for me to dance, I took off as little as possible. My performance was somewhat the same except I had on more clothes than usual.

The tripping part about the night was that my uncle brought all these horny ass friends of his that had been trying to get in my panties from the first day I came up here. I didn't hear the last of it because once I went over to their table one of my uncle friends said, "Little Lovely is a lot bigger than I thought she was," as he grabbed me pulling me down on to his lap. Good thing for him I was at work and the boss was there because I wanted to bust him in his head. I remember that night so clear because I went and sat with some of the other customers and will you believe my boss called me to the end of the bar. I knew this was going to be one of those talks about go get that customer talk. My boss said, "You see that gentleman sitting over there? I tried to look as if I didn't know who he was talking about. Then he said, "A customer is a customer and he said that you didn't want to drink with him." After I explained to my boss that he was with my uncle and his friends and I don't really care for them. My boss said, "Just sit and have a glass or two then leave." He added, "Plus I don't want to give his money back because he bought a $100.00 bottle of champagne for you if you just sit with him for a moment."

I said fuck it, I did, I sat with my uncle and his horny ass friends. I threw three glasses of champagne down my throat so fast you would had thought I was drinking soda to kill my thirst and then I took the rest with me. My boss really didn't know why I didn't want to be bother with them at the time but then again he really didn't care, especially when they're buying a hundred dollar bottle of champagne. I really didn't mind too much myself but one of the reasons I was drinking those expensive bottles of champagne was because I'll receive a third of what ever a customer spends on me for drinks. So, I knew sitting with him just got me a quick $33.00 already in my pockets. You can say that it was about $11.00 a glass; therefore, I made that $33.00 real quick in a matter of only a few minutes. You see I really enjoyed my job because I made real easy money all night long. I could get paid nightly for dancing, plus I made even more money with my daily tips. The only reason I drink like a fish when I am at the bar is so I could make more money. Yes, I really liked the life I was now secretly living. I got money, enjoyed taking my clothes off, but most of all I was getting revenge for those nasty mother fuckers who had hurt me. To see those niggas, no let me rephrase that, to see these males and females lust for my body when all the time I knew I was only teasing them made me feel better.

You remember me telling you about that good looking girl that I thought was a damn good looking dude? Well he-she came up in the tavern that same night. I guess you can say that this was my night for everybody I really didn't want to see. It was also really strange how everybody all decided to come in on the same night. However, old girl that I thought was a dude came in while I was on the stage dancing. She stood right in front of the stage watching me without blinking. I tried to pay her no attention at first, until she pulled out a bankroll of money that would have killed a cow if he tried to shallow it. I said to myself, "Fuck it! Hell her money was like everybody else." I came closer to the front of the stage and started messing with her mind. I knew I couldn't make her dick hard like a man because she did not have one. But if she did she would have soak her pants because she had her mouth wide open and drooling. I remember her tipping damn good.

She then asked me if I could dance off this one record she liked. I told her I could dance off anything she plays. I remember she said, "Bet those." As old girl who I thought was a damn good looking dude turned away from the stage and walked over to the jukebox all I could do was look at her and say to my self, "Damn why couldn't you had been a guy for real?" Sad to say but I kind of liked old girl! Anyway I knew we would never have a true man and woman relationship, because she just did not have a real dick. Therefore, I just looked at her as being another good tipping customer and treated her as if she was one of these horny niggas. As a dancer my customers would usually ask for a special dedication. A special dedication is when a customer wants a dancer to dance to his or her favorite song. When I dance I always left one song to dance to for a special dedication request. So when old girl asked I told her that I had one song left on the box and to play her song.

I was tipsy, bubbly, high, and was feeling good. Old girl asked me, "Are you sure you can dance off this song?" Me being me said something like, "I could dance off whatever you play!" I was kind of tired and was thinking to myself, "I hope she doesn't play a fast song because I really wasn't in the mood for fast sweating." What I mean by fast sweating is when I have to tire myself out in by getting hot, sweaty, and wet by dancing harder and faster than before. This was something I wasn't ready to do. The music started playing. "Bless her heart I," said to myself. She played the song <u>Under the Sheets</u> by Tee's Brothers. While I was dancing to her song I really felt like lying down on my ass because I was extremely tired. Anyway that song was right on time or as I use to say, "On and about the money."

As I danced to her song I started to reflect back during the time when she first walked in the door. She stood for a minute. Then she went and got a chair and sat right in front of the stage. At that time she told me, "I want you to dance to this song especially for me." I remember just looking at her and smiling but in my mind I was saying, "How in the hell am I suppose to dance for a bitch?" Of course, reality hit me and I said, "Fuck it! I'll just act like she's a dude, since at once I thought she was. Hell, she looked like a dude; she talked and acted like a dude; plus she had big money. I was dancing to her song and really thought about the money. So I put my normal plan in to play to get my money. I got closer to old girl and start teasing her with my body.

After I was finish she gave me another big ass tip and said, "If I was all man you would have just made me come all over myself." I just looked at her and gave her one of those fake smiles. As I was backing away from her I thought to myself, "You really don't want to know what I am thinking about you and want to do to you!" Once I came down off the stage she asked me to join her for a drink. I told her, "Sure but let me go to the bathroom first." You see another thing about me the customers' say they notice I do that the other dancer don't do is a keep a fresh smelling good body.

Every time I got finish dancing I would walk off stage and freshen up. My towel, my soap, my deodorant, a clean outfit with a cover up, and myself would go straight to the bathroom to wash up. Then when I am done I would come out to socialize with the customers and make more money. One thing I couldn't stand was to have a stinky body. Some of those dancers were fired up with funk when they came off the stage. Dancing was and is a fun job but its hard work. Believe me, you will sweat on the stage under those hot ass lights. I enjoyed every minute of the bright spots on the stage.

I came out and joined old girl that looked like a dude at her table. I can remember that night as if it happened yesterday. I had no problem sitting with her and a few of her women she brought to the tavern with her. Besides that it was all part of my job to entertain my customers regardless of who they are and with. Once I sat down I can remember the female pimp telling her girls; "Don't you all have some place to go?" They just got up and left with out saying anything. I said, "Don't make them leave on account of me because I can't sit to long anyway." Old girl said, "They wasn't, they have to go out and get my money." I knew then she was talking about something I didn't know nothing about; however, I left that subject alone too. After the female pimp's, that is old girl's, women left she asked me what would I like to drink? Before I could get the words out of my mouth she stopped me and said, "No! Let me order for you if you don't mine?"

She put her hand up in the air; calling the bartender over. When the bartender came over he brought over a hundred-dollar bottle of champagne. Old girl told me, "You deserve the best." At that time only the big wheelers bought the hundred dollar bottles. I sat and talked with old girl for a minute. As I was talking to her I realize as a female pimp she wasn't a bad person at all. The only problem was she liked women and she wanted me, which creates a problem for her; I didn't like women the same way she did. Now if old girl was a real man, I would have given her some pussy with the quickness. I stayed and talked with old girl for a moment but then I had to move around because she wasn't giving up the bread. She was determined to get her some of "Luscious," as she said. Old girl was nice in all but she was pressuring me to get with her. She was really nice and I didn't want to hurt her feelings. I told her I had to go and her time was up.

I got up and start moving around in the tavern for a moment; kind of socializing with some of the other customers before I had to go back on the stage to do my next set. A set is what we (dancers) call our group of four records we played when it was our turn to dance. The night didn't turn out as bad as I thought it was. Taking for granted that people I didn't want to be bother with was in the tavern that night. But my uncle's friend got on my last nerves. I tried my best to stay away from my uncle's and his friends table. Even when my uncle or one of his friends would call me I still stayed away from their table. Their money was worthless to me and I could do without it.

As for old girl, the female pimp, she became my biggest and best tipper. I didn't care and she could keep on liking me as long as she kept on tipping me like she was doing. The night came to an end. This time I was beyond tired out. My female friend was trying to get me to go to the after hours with her and her friends. I would have gone with them but I really didn't want to be bothered with my uncle's friends. So guess who I had to drop me off at home?

Yeah, you probably guessed right! I had old girl, the female pimp, take me home and she was a perfect gentleman. She opened and closed the door for me when I got in and out of her car. As I was approaching the car to open the door she, the female pimp that is, ran to the door and said, "No! Let me get that for you." At first that moment kind of tripped me out because she was so generous like a woman's dream man. Once I got in the car she closed the door behind me. I knew I was on drugs but she even carried my bags to and from the car. When we drove up in front of my house we sat in the car for a minute talking and filling our noses up with that white powder shit (cocaine). She walked me to the door and made sure I had got in the house before she left. Man, I must say I was tripping and saying to myself, "A girl can get spoil to this kind of treatment.

I see what they mean when they said, "Old girl treats her women right!" I then took my tired, drugged up, and drunken high yellow ass up the stairs and crashed. I remember these days because it was my crazy life that I was living, enjoying, and suffering through every minute of it. Usually when I feel that everything is going along just good for me, it never fails, something bad always happens to me and disturbs the peace of mind I was having. I woke up the next morning wondering if my friend girl had made it home or not. She usually spends the night at my house since her and my uncle hooked up. However, this morning she wasn't at my house when I woke up. Then the evening had come and I still haven't seen her. Even when I got dress for work I still didn't hear from her.

Remember my friend guy that lived around the corner was having a back to school party and I promised him to I would come around there for a minute. Well, I had got dress to go to his party. I planned on leaving a few hours before the party ended. As I finished getting myself together I heard my friend girl voice. I told her that I was going around to my friend guy party before I went to work. I asked her if she wanted to go but she was all stuck on my uncle and seen nothing pass him but her job. The two of them had started getting on my nerves too. I grabbed my bags and left. At first I was kind of afraid to go but then I thought about the fact that my friend guy was going to be there so I had nothing to worry about.

When I first got to the party I had seen that my friend guy wasn't there. So, I asked his brother where he was. His brother told me that my friend guy had said, "If I came to tell me to wait because he will be right back." I got me a glass of wine sat back to listen and enjoy the music. I wasn't going to drink too much because I wanted to talk to my friend guy sober. Plus I didn't want to get to bubbly before

I got to work because I knew I had a long night at the tavern. You remember this one good-looking dude from court I had my eyes on and talked about bad in front of my friend guy? Well, he was at the party too. He was looking better than ever before. I start thinking to myself, "If he only knew what was going through my mind about him and that body of his."

We talked for awhile and he was trying to get me to smoke some weed with him, but I wouldn't. It wasn't because I didn't want to but I only smoked weed when I was trying to bring my high down from that white powder shit. You see dancing had given me another bad habit and I loved every minute of it (weed and cocaine). However, I decided to smoke some weed with the good-looking guy after all but I didn't want to smoke his stuff. I reached in my bag and pulled out a sandwich bag full of weed and told the good-looking guy to roll a nice joint. Yes, I guess you can say that I was trying to be a big shot. What the hell; I only live once. I remember dancing a few songs with him. We only danced to the slow jams because I didn't want to get myself all sweaty up before I go to work.

He wanted to get with me but I told him I was not interest at that time. He still looked good to me but it was just I was into this other kind of life style now. I didn't know if he would approve of his lady friend dancing in a tavern taking off her clothes? I remember him asking me where I've been and what I've been doing. I had become so wrapped up in my plan till I started using it on him and he was falling for it. I mean I knew what it felt like to have a man grow a half of a third leg while dancing with him. This good looking dude started telling me about how I have changed. He said, "Damn Lovely, you have grown up and you move more like an experience lady!"

"Experience lady," I said to my self, "What do he mean by that?" It wasn't too long before I found out! After our last nasty dance, he busted a nut in his pants he said. Of course, that was part of my plan. I said to myself before I started dancing with him that I was going to see if I was really good at what I do at work, which was making niggas cum. I can remember the last time we danced the good looking dude said he wanted me but there wasn't any erection. I really didn't care because I didn't want to have sex no way; I just wanted to play around. Oh but this time I said to myself, "I was going to put one on him, a tease dance that is, and make his shit shoot out of his pants!" Of course, it worked and my plan was a big success.

When the song stopped I can remember the good-looking dude pulling me back up against him saying, "Lovely don't leave me standing out like this." I laughed as if I didn't know what he was talking about. He then motioned his lower part of his body moving it as he rubbed his private male jewel across my leg. I learned from being out there dancing that a lot of females were quick to say, "it was that time of the month," when they really didn't want to be bother with a guy in any kind of sexual way. Yes, I did use that line because I didn't want to tell the good-looking dude I didn't want to have sex with him. I do remember him responding back by saying, "If I ever get him all hard up like that again he didn't care if I was bleeding or not he was going to take him some pussy." Oh, did that statement make me think!

You should have seen how the expression on my face changed real quickly when he said, "Take him some pussy." What he say that for? All kinds of thoughts were going through my head. I also began to wonder if he was one of the guys that had raped me before! Behind that uncomfortable statement dude made to me I knew it was time for me to leave. I told the good looking dude that I had to go to work. As I was leaving I noticed that my pretty eyed guy friend still hasn't come yet. I went over to where my pretty eyed guy friend brother was spinning records at and asked him to tell my friend guy to come around by my house in the morning.

My pretty eyed guy friend's brother still tried to get me to stay. I explained to him that I had to be at work soon and I didn't want to be late. I really didn't know what to say when he asked me, "what kind of job do you have that allow you to dress like that?" Then I thought to myself, "hell he didn't mean shit to me!" So I told my pretty eyed friend's bother, "I'm a dancer." First he looked at me in silence. Then he said, "I believe it. You got the body for it and I bet you're damn good!" I said, "Yeah, I know," and walked towards the door. When I first came out the house I looked down the street to see, which route would be the best route to take to work. I was also trying to see, which direction had the most traffic. Therefore, I knew I would be able to get a ride to work. So I started walking north up Seventeen Street.

There was something really wired about that night. I thought I heard all kinds of strange and crazy sounds and voices, but the streets were deserted. It felt as if I was the only one out walking those dark streets with strange voices and noises talking to me. It felt as if the silent night was trying to tell me something but I didn't understand what was being said. As I was walking that night the voices and strange noises started to get louder. I just had a strange feeling about that night, which gave me scariest chills. I started thinking about the statement the good looking dude made at the party to me, which didn't help my situation at all.

All I wanted was to hurry up and get to a busy main street. I started worrying more and began to panic. I had made myself very upset, pissed off, and nervous. It felt as if every bush, crack, house, and even signs had its own little noises. I start saying to myself, I needed some cocaine now to relax me. However, I was too afraid to even take those few seconds to take a sniff of that white shit. I got so scared that I started to freak myself out of my own skin. I said softly, "Fuck it! I can't take it no more." I stop to take me a relaxing one on one. For those of you who may not know what an one on one is I'm not talking about basketball. It is when you inhale a powder drug in each side of your nose, one side at a time; in my case my drug was cocaine. I was feeling a little bit more relaxed.

Now all I wanted to do was to get my ass to work where I had no worries and no fears. I was safe at work but unfortunately for me I never made it to work. I was about four or five blocks from the party. It was very dark only a few street lights were on that night. It was one area I approach seem as if it was a black out. There weren't no lights on in this one particular area. My vision was already impaired from the drug I took and by the streets being so dark didn't help my situation much at all. I started to hear a different kind of sound within the dark night. It sounded as if someone was running but every time I turned around I seen no one. So, I would continue walking but this time a little faster; however, I guess I wasn't walking fast enough.

I continue to hear noises as if someone was running through yards and in the alley behind the houses. Every time I turned around I didn't see anyone. Straight ahead of me I could see I was approaching a boarded up house I didn't want to go by. I guess you can say something inside of me was telling me not to. Then something else inside of me was telling me I just had the creeps that night because it was so dark. I started walking a little bit fast almost like a medium running walk but I still couldn't shake the scary chills I had. Now I begin saying to myself in a soft voice, "girl you need to quick it!" I had scared my self almost shitless.

Talk about a bitch falling for the oldest trick in the book! I heard this noise that came from these bushes and jumped out of my skin and back into it again in just that fast second. The noise had scared me so bad. The noise sounded as if some one had fallen or was moving around in the bushes near this boarded up house. I really started moving faster only to become careless. As I moved faster up the street my crazy butt kept looking back at where the bushes were.

I knew if someone would have came out of the bushes I would have a good running jump start on his ass. Once I realized that I had a good head start on whoever could have been in the bushes I turned around and began walking even faster.

I had made it pass the boarded up house that was giving me the creeps. I wish I would have paid more attention to where I was going. I was standing along side of a burned up building near an alley and two open empty lots were in front of me. However, it was too late for me to try and turn back. The two empty lots in front of me I thought was kind of good because I could see anybody if they was trying to come my way. The mistake was the large open alley I was now standing in front of. The burned up building next to the alley had its surprises waiting for me too. I felt like I was doing everything my soon to be attackers wanted me to do, that is, walking towards the burned up building near the alley. Now, I started to remember the whole incident in my head from the time I left the party. It was as if they had planned where they were going to grab me at, which explains why they were running through the yards and in the alley behind the houses so I couldn't see them. This was all part of their plan to keep up with me and make their move at the right time, which was near the burned up building.

Once I realized I was seeing something moving towards me I turned to run but I didn't move fast enough. This person that was moving towards me came from the side of the burned up building with a face mask hat pulled over his head. He grabbed me and we began to wrestle. I can remember hearing him telling somebody to hurry up. I knew then he wasn't by his self. I had to try and get away from him before whom ever he was calling to hurry up got here. I was kicking, hitting, and biting him. The biting kind of did it because he let me go and I fell to the ground but it wasn't soon enough.

I jumped up and started to run but because I fell trying to get away so fast from the attacker with the facemask hat pulled over his head, the short time I used to get up off the ground caused me some valuable time. The other guys he was calling for had caught me and gotten control of me. I remember the other two attackers had on ski hats with masks attached to them. It wasn't anything else I could remember about them but they all had dark clothing on, which didn't help me identify who these guys were. I was kicking, screaming, and hollering. I had placed in my mind to really hate and make all people suffer for my pain. Especially, after seeing people were walking by on the other side of the street was just looking at me while my attackers were struggling to pull me back into the alley next to the burned up house. No one thought about or even try to help me. I didn't think people could be so unconcerned about another human being's life. I knew then that my life and I was again at the mercy of my mental, sick-minded attackers. I thought to my self, "God what kind of world is this that we live in?" Unfortunately for me my attackers did get me into the alley.

However, this time, even thou they covered my face, I was determine to be able to identify one of my attackers if I couldn't identify all of them. I cursed everyone including God because he didn't help me. I can remember pretending like I had passed out when one of my attackers was choking me so hard to keep me from screaming out for help. I lay there and just let my attackers do what they wanted to do until I could figure out a way to try and get my self out of this mess. Then all of a suddenly an idea hit me and it worked. My stupid attackers thought that I was really out of it. One of them started to slap me in my face to see if I would respond but I didn't. I just accepted the slapping and laid there. You see I needed my attackers to feel I was out cold; therefore, they would let my hands free. I had figured out how I was going to mark the first attacker I could get my hands on. Remember I said, "I always had long pretty finger nails?" Well my nails were my big bright idea and this is one time that I didn't care about breaking all of them off! They fell for it. My attackers let my hands go and what they did that for?

If only they knew that they played into my plan which was what I wanted them to do. If they knew it was all part of my plan they would had knocked me out for real. One of my attackers had gotten on top of me thinking he was about to easily fuck him some knocked out pussy. Little did he know I had a plan to stop that shit! I put speed and all the strength of pride I had left. I stabbed my fingernails into both of my attacker's ears while holding on to his ears. This time my attacker was doing the screaming and the hollering for help while trying to keep his mask from coming up. I maintained a grip on the sides of his face and torn away skin from his face and ears.

As the warm blood started running down my hands I knew I stuck my nails far into the sides of my attacker face. I continue to dig at his face with my nails until I felt them break deep in to my fingers. I was saying to my self, "I know I'll be able to ID your ass now!" I know I marked that one attacker face up real good. It didn't matter nor did him any good that his partners in crime were trying to free him because I had a death lock on the sides of his face; I wasn't going to let go. I left tracks from the back of my attacker's ears down to his lips as if I was trying to cut his ears off with a knife. While a few of my attackers friends was trying to release my grip, I continued with the digging scratch marks along the side of my attacker's face. I made tracks on his face leading all the way to the bottom of his lips, which I then tried to rip his lips from his face. I may sure I got him good. I bet he'll think twice before he use his lips to suck another one of his victim's breast! I quickly let go of my attacker's face and lip to only lock around his neck with the little nails I had left. I could feel my grip weakening as his friends kept trying to pull my fingers lose. This time I was more determined not letting my attackers get away so easy with their assaults on me!

I was blindfolded but I knew for a fact I scared that one attacker up. So he would be marked for life; I fucked him up! It would be easy for me to I.D. him. To this day, I can still hear the echoes of my attacker hollering as I dug my nails into his skins. My attackers roughed me up even more while I was trying to mark one of my attackers but I didn't care. I may not be able to identify all my attackers but just as long as I knew I would be able to identify the track face attacker that was good enough for me. My attackers were so much in a hurry to get their friend away from me that they allow me to walk away with the sweater they had wrapped around my head. This was the second time I was attacked after leaving one of my pretty eyed friend guy's parties.

I felt and knew my attackers were related to those parties but I couldn't prove it. Only this time I made sure I was able to identify one of my attackers. Therefore, they would all be as good as caught. Plus I wanted to be able to look these cowards in their face when they realized they had just raped a twelve-year-old child! Once I got away from the scene of my assault I just sat on the stairs of the burned up building for a minute and cry. I couldn't understand why me! Why always me! This time the police and I would be looking for a man with scares on his face like tracks running from his ears to his lips. I got up off the stairs and start walking. I did not pay attention to my surroundings at all. I just got up and started to walk through the alley. I almost made it to the end of the alley but I fell back up against a garage to keep from getting hit by this car. Afraid, crying, feeling like the lowest person walking the earth, a man and lady got out the car to check on me because they almost hit me with their car. Therefore they wanted to make sure I was alright.

Right away these people looked at me and could tell what must have just happened to me. My heart felt a little better! I started to think maybe there are still some good people on this earth that do care about others. I remember the nice caring lady asking her husband to get a blanket out of the car as she held me in her arms telling me, "Baby don't worry! Everything is going to be alright. I promise I won't let no one hurt you." Just hearing those words for the first time sounded so sweet and good to my ears! I didn't know this woman but at that moment I honestly believed every word she said. However, I started to think about how terrifying my life has been so far and said to myself, "I wished life was easily said and then done for me. I have been a victim most of my life of sexual abuse and assault. Believe me it's nothing nice, that shit hurts. To add to the abuses and assaults, I felt that no one truly cares about me and I was just a mistake in life for whatever reason God only knows.

"I promise I'm not going to let no one hurt you," oh, how those words even now echoes through my ears and heart. As I type now I could remember feeling the pain and hurt during the horrible assault I experienced that night. All over again I could feel the hurt, suffering, tears, and pain I felt during the time of my assault surfacing upon my body. The worst part of my abusive attack that night was when I had to just lay there like I was unconscious and let my attackers touch me in those nasty sexual ways. While I was laying there the hurt and pain I felt allowed my mind and heart to build up enough anger to lead my arms and hands to the right place. The misery I went through that night still rest as scares I carry upon my mind and branded in my heart.

For the first time in many years I truly felt that someone cared about me. The most surprising thing about the whole situation was these people didn't even know me but they cared. This made me cry out even more. I felt seriousness and goodness coming from the lady who helped me feel a little better. The lady tried to gain my trust by constantly re-ensuring me that everything was going to be okay. This stranger held me and started to cry with me as if she understood what I was going through.

I can remember the nice lady saying, "Baby, what animals did such a vicious thing like this to you?" The tone of her voice didn't only sound as if she was asking me a question but I could also hear a tone of anger and hurt from her. At the same time I was thinking to myself, "How can I feel a sense of care and concern from this woman when she doesn't even know me?" Her husband had finally brought over the blanket from the car. She wrapped the blanket around my shoulders and kept her arms around me as she walked and helped me into their car.

When we got in the car I can remember her husband asked if I had told the lady where I stayed. She told her husband, "Baby right now that's not important! Let's just get her to the hospital!" With no questions asked that is what they did. Even today as I re-live that moment tears are rolling down my eyes as I remember words coming from that nice lady. I am still touched by the level of concern the nice lady had for me. Once they got me to the hospital it was like a mad house. The way the doctors and the nurses were running around kind of scared me. I didn't want any one to touch me. Oh my God, when the police came into the room I could have died. I just knew they were coming to take me to jail.

Now, I guess you are saying to yourself, "Why would the police be coming to take you to jail?" Well, I was sitting there even more afraid wondering if the police had searched my bag and founded my drugs or not. I was praying that they didn't. I softly asked the nice lady if the police had my bag. I felt a little better when she told me her husband had my bag and the police haven't searched it yet. I asked her to please get it for me. The nice lady came back into the room and handed me my bag. As I started looking in it I noticed that a few items were gone. I wasn't for sure what happen to them but I believe they may have wasted out my bag while I was wrestling with my attackers. Well, I wasn't to upset about losing them. I was just wondering where the items could have been!

The nice lady asked me, "What are you looking for?" I really hated lying to her but I told her my money was missing and I believe my attackers may have taken my money. I wondered to myself what would she have thought of me if she knew I was looking for some drugs I had in my bag? In so many ways I did and didn't want to be at the hospital. Deep thoughts of not being too sure how my dad was going to react when he seen me. I was not sure if he would be more upset about what happen to me or the fact I was in the streets and not in the house. Either way I knew I was in big trouble because I was supposed to be at home and not in the streets. I just sat there afraid, looking into space, wondering what was going to happen next, and if some one had gotten in touch with my dad! The two police officers finally came back in with a doctor and a few nurses. One of the officers asked the nice lady to step out side the room with him for a minute because he would like to talk to her. She got up and said, "If I needed her she'll be right outside the door." The doctor began to ask me lots of questions. I was afraid of what they were going to say to me regarding the incident. However, I told them what had happened. After I told them my story, one of the police officers said, "That was a smart move you did with your fingernails." I felt a little better after speaking with the police officers because I believe my plan for scratching my attacker's face up may have worked out alright.

While the nurse was taken blood from my arm, the doctor explained was explaining to me the reason why they were drawing my blood. He said, "We need to draw your blood because we need to make sure we can tell the difference between your blood type and the attacker scratched." He also assured me that once the police do catch the guy who did this to me they will be able to identify my attacker by matching up his blood type with the blood and tissue they took from what was left of my fingernails. They did so many tests on me but what really scared me was when the doctor said, "If you don't come on your period then you should come back in a few weeks to retake a pregnancy test." I responded, "You mean to tell me that there is a chance that I could be pregnant?" He looked at me as if he didn't want to answer the question and said in a soft voice, "Yes!" My mind had become even more lost, upset, and confused. I was thinking to myself, "If I was pregnant how am I to love my baby who father has viciously beat and rapped me?" I remember saying; "I don't want to keep it if I am!" The doctor saw how upset I had became so he began talking to me trying to calm me down and to assure me of the odds. He started telling me that there is a very strong possibility I really wasn't pregnant and that the pregnancy test was just part of the natural procedures for this type of incident.

After I gave the doctor, nurse, and the police officers all the information they needed, I was free to go home. One of the officers said, "We will be looking in the neighborhood for a guy with scratches that look like tracks running across his face and with the samples the doctor took from you we will be able to identify your attacker. I heard a voice and right away I knew who it was. The police officers had got in touch with my father and man, was he mad. I could here the doctor outside of my room trying to calm him down and assuring him I was doing okay considering what I have just been through. After a few minutes they then let my dad come into the room where I was. As my dad quietly came into the room, he looked at me with a caring and sad look. I remember him saying, "Baby is you alright?" I looked at my dad, hunched my shoulders up and down one deep time; as if I was saying, "No daddy, I really don't know!" At that point I began to cry because I didn't expect him to say something like that. I guess I was expecting him to give me that, "I told you so lecture," like he usually does when I get in trouble.

My dad said really loudly, "I hope the police fine that no good ass nigga before he did because they wouldn't have to worry about locking him up." As I looked at the hurt and anger expressed on my dad face, I thought to my self, "Oh, my God what's going to happen now?" My dad started pasting the floor in the room as if he was trying to calm himself down. He kept repeating over and over again in a soft voice, "I'm going to kill him!" For a second I stopped thinking about my problem and started feeling sorry for my attackers if my dad caught them first. Plus I didn't want him to go to jail for murdering someone that wasn't worth the waste you flushed down the toilet. My dad was a person you didn't want to cross or make mad! I honestly wanted the police to catch my attackers and lock them up before my dad found out who they were. Now I had to go home and get myself together because I knew as soon as I could I was going to try and help the police look for my track face attacker.

Chapter Fourteen
"A rapist caught"

AFTER WAKING UP the next morning I had so much on my mind. I just sat in my room all day and only came out when I had to go to the bathroom. I guess it was because I was too a shame to face anybody. Mainly, because of what had happen to me and I really didn't want anyone to see how my face looked. Besides I didn't want nobody feeling sorry for me. Looking at me all funny; especially, when I don't know what they are thinking! I was under enough pressure and also worrying about my dad. I knew he wasn't going to be able to sleep in peace until he got his hands around the neck of my attacker with the tracks running across his face.

It seems as if I am always putting stress on my poor dad and some sick-minded person is always out to hurt me. Then, I thought about the owner of the bar where I danced. He knew I usually call and tell him if I was going to be late for work. I know he was wondering why I didn't come into work last night. Considering what happened to me last night, I know he will understand? All of a sudden another thought had come into my head! I totally forgot that I had told my pretty eyed friend's brother to tell him to come around to my house today! God, I hope he doesn't show! How am I to face him looking like this? I feel bad enough and I am too a shame to look anyone in the face right now.

I have such a hurting feeling inside of me feeling because I am still confused and puzzled about what am I doing wrong to continue to draw these sick minded typed of people to me? I have a bad headache right now! I'm always developing headaches because my mind is always working over time from thinking so much and hard! Most of the time I don't know what I am thinking about! I feel as if I am going crazy! As if I have lost my little mother fucken rabbit mind! No one understands and really knows what I am going though. All I want is to be able to live a normal life with out so much pressure and abuse.

Why couldn't I have been on an island alone; by my self, with no one else around but me and the beauty nature have to share with the world. Of course, the people of this world don't know how to appreciate the beauty of nature. God, if I had my mom here with me maybe I wouldn't be going though all this crazy shit! I balled up and cried out, "Mama if you can hear me, I really need you so bad!" I lay down in my bed and cried like a big baby wanting my mama.

I can remember my younger sister telling my younger brother that I was in an accident. I kind of smile because I knew then they really didn't know what had happened to me. Then again they were too young to really understand. I'm glad they didn't know because I didn't want to hear it coming out of my younger sister and brother mouth that I got rapped. Rape! That word was, is, and sounds so ugly! What I couldn't understand is why people have too rape another person when there is so many hoe's on the streets that is trying to give their stuff away? Maybe everybody second think and wondering about the stuff that is too easy to get? Maybe if I had said something about this the first time, I wouldn't be going thought this again?

The thought of just "maybe" if I would have done this or that kept going in and out of my mind. The deepest "maybe" was if I wasn't alive I wouldn't have to worry about going through all these mixed up, horrifying, and hurt aching emotions. With this thought in mind, I knew I could end all the pain, the hurt, the suffering my family and I are going through. I would be at peace with myself because I wouldn't have to face this terrible and mean Old World. Most of all I would eliminate all the embarrassment that is killing me inside from being a shame, which I'm having the hardest time trying to deal with. Life itself is not too nice to me and I don't see where life would ever get better for me. I was tired of living in this crazy mixed up world; I wish I was dead.

Then I thought about how my family might feel if I killed myself. However, I wonder if they would truly understand the reason why I took my life? Oh God what am I thinking, I would add more pressure and stress to my family's life if I took my life. What am I to do? I just wanted to get away from this life I'm living and surrounded by. If Jesus can touch the dead and give them life back, then why can't I have wings like a bird and fly? If I could fly I would glide across the skies, free from all pain, heartaches, and worries. Free, so as no one can lock up my life any more. In the big beautiful skies just the clouds and I. I would watch this nasty dirty world from up high. Thanking God that I feel so good I can fly. I'll keep my wings extended so wide and free, letting no one in my world as I fly above the trees.

I'm smiling now with the thought of being free; no more frowns because I plan on never coming back down. Yes, how I wish I could fly because I would live a peaceful life; just the skies, the clouds, and I. For all of those I did not like, I would drop them down a hot black, gray, and white present. How I wish I could fly because I didn't want to be on this earth anymore alive! I sat thinking in my room all the time; thinking and wondering if anyone would ever understand what I am going through. Is there anyone that can stand to feel my pain? If somebody, anybody could just take these pains away from me for a second; it'll feel like a lifetime of suffering have been released off of me.

I have no life worth living for! I don't want any part of this life! For now my life will only exist in a world here in this four corner room of mines. As long as I am in this room I don't have to ever worry about anyone doing anything to me anymore. I sit playing and picking with my lips, rubbing my arms as I moan softly to myself; I'm so confused and I wanted to die. I feel like I honestly lost my mind and I'm going crazy. I started crying harder than before until I cried myself to sleep. I was awakened by my girl friend I dance with coming in to my room. She was yelling and screaming with her big mouth, "Girl you better get up! What you doing? You want to be late for work or something?" Little did she know I was not going to work; of course she was about to find out why! She came closer to my bed and pulled the covers from over my head. What did she do that for? She was surprised to see me and the reason I was laying in bed totally covered up! I was hoping she would have taken her happy ass back to wherever the fuck she just came from. I guess you can say I knew I was going to see her eventually, but why now?

When the covers came off I try to hide my face. I didn't know how bad my face had swollen from the beating and hard crying I had done! All I knew was I could barely open my eyes and my face felt very tight. My girl friend started pulling at my arm as if she was teasing me in a little game of tug a war. She start saying, "Oh girl what dude got a little to rough with you or did you have a hard night? Come on, let me see!" How I remember the look on my girl friend face when she first saw me. Even now that moment still touches me deeply and brings tears to my eyes. But now I can cry a little as I smile because I made it through that horrible time! She grabbed me as she began to cry. Holding me in her arms as she rocked with me like a baby saying, "Damn girl who did this to you?" I guess what really got to me was when she said, "I don't need to know no details because I'll end up killing him for you! Whatever it was you didn't deserve this!"

My girl friend kept holding me and crying telling me, "Girl friend I'm here for you. I'm not gonna leave you!" I guess she was serious because she called down to the bar where we danced at and asked too speak to the owner. She sat by my side with one arm securely wrapped around me as she talked on the phone to the owner. She told the owner she will not be at work for a few days because I was in an accident last night and I really needed her. Listening to my girl saying, "She's okay considering what she had been through," made me start thinking that the owner was really concerned about me. Then she got quiet for a moment and said, "Yeah, she's at home. Okay, I will. I will. I'll tell her," and hung up the phone.

It felt kind of nice having her by my side to talk with. After all I shared many of my problems from the past with her, which made it a little easier confessing to her about what had happen to me. I spoke to my girl friend about what had happened to me last night and how I felt my attackers were from the party. She asked me why I felt that way. Then I told her about the first time I was attacked and told no one. I explained to her how I felt both attacks were the same people and how each attack had happened right after I left the parties. I really felt she was starting to see my point and believing my attackers were connected to those parties. Just when the conversation was really going good some one came into the house. It was my uncle and he was calling for my girl friend. Man I really didn't want to see him. I knew he was going to ask me all kinds of questions that I wasn't ready to answer. I asked her to go out and explain to him what had happened because I was too embarrassed to face or talk to him right now. My girl friend jumped up off the bed and told me she will be right back. She went out the room and pulled my bedroom door up tight behind her. I could hear my girl friend answering my uncle, "what?" From the sound and the direction their voices were coming from she must had caught him in the kitchen.

I could hear my girl friend talking and the next thing I knew I was hearing what sounded like chairs being thrown or kick down. Then, I heard my uncle yelling, "Low life ass dogs!" After he had calmed down some, I heard him asking her if I was ok. She slowly opened my door and asked if it was ok for my uncle to come in because he wanted to see for himself that I was alright. In an unsure voice I told her, "Yeah, come on in." The two of them then came into my bedroom. The first thing my uncle asked me was "Are you okay niece?" I responded back, "Yeah!" He then said, "You got him good?" I showed him my hands and said, "I broke all my nails digging in his face!" Everyone knew how fond I was of my nails.

He then put his hands on my shoulders and said, "You marked him good! I'll find him and take care of him. I promise you that." I knew my uncle was very serious about what he had just said because he uses to always tell me don't make a promise that you can't keep and won't keep. I just looked at my uncle with tears in my eyes. He held me and said, "You don't have to worry about a thing." I began to think about the first time I was attacked in back of the house next door and when I came in the house everybody was woke. No body in my house including my uncle noticed that something was wrong with me. I just felt they didn't care. Therefore, I didn't tell anybody what had happen to me. I just went to my room and cried. Maybe I was wrong for thinking that my uncle really didn't care? Maybe if I would had told him what had happen to me the first time perhaps he wouldn't had stopped looking until he found who rapped me. And just maybe the second time may not have ever happened!

My uncle stood up and left my room. He stopped for a moment and turned back around to look at me. From his body action and what I seen tonight, I now knew my uncle really does care about what happens to me. My uncle stood there shaking his head while clashing his fist into his other hand saying, "Believe me, I'm going to kill the punks who did this to you niece!" I started to worry more about my uncle now than my dad. Even though my dad was working a lot I knew when he drove the cab at night he was looking out for my attacker with track marks across his face. You know what? I do pity my attacker when my dad catches up with him but when my uncle catches him it's a different story.

Now I am thinking to myself, "Old my God. I have another big problem. My uncle usually doesn't think before he does anything!" Deep inside my uncle is a very good hearted person but at times I too wonder what kind of heart do he have beating in his chest? He just does things in front of anyone; then goes on about his business as if nothing had happen and faces the outcome good or bad later. This is what I didn't want to happen after he founded one of my attackers or all of them. I kept thinking, "What if someone saw my uncle kill my attacker with the tracks across his face and tells?" I wouldn't be able to live with myself knowing my uncle was in jail for the rest of his life because of some sick mind ass nigga! I just don't know what to do to make this horrible time a little easier for my family and me?

I just laid back down when my uncle and my girl friend left to go to the store. I don't know why but I guess they must had left the door unlock not knowing it. I went to the bathroom and heard some footsteps coming up the stairs. I thought nothing of it because I just assume it was someone who lived here. Since my assault I always peek out the door of any room I'm in first before I came out because I didn't want anyone to see me looking like this. I knew I heard someone coming up the stairs but I didn't remember hearing him or her come into the house.

As I was coming out of the bathroom someone called my name. Right away I just figured my uncle had locked himself out the house again. If you close the top door too hard when leaving out of it, the door would lock on an accident and whoever went out the door would be locked out. There was an old lock on the door, which we tried to keep pushed in but if somebody slams the door the lock would jump. So, this is what I thought had happen to my uncle. I went to open the door. Once I unlocked the door I just turn around and walked away from the door. However, as I was walking away from the door I heard a familiar voice warning me about opening doors to strangers. He said "You got to be more careful who you unlock your door for." The voice kind of startled me for a moment because it wasn't my uncle.

The first thing that came to my mind was the voice belonged to one of my attackers. I was really afraid. Especially, since my attackers knew who I was. Therefore, I thought right away they must have known where I stayed. For those quiet seconds I was praying that someone would come back to the house that lived here. As the door started too open wider, I nervously and slowly turned around to see who had made that statement. At the same time I could hear voices coming along side of the house. It was like a prayer instantly coming true for me. It was my uncle and my girl friend.

I guess I made them move faster because they ran up the stairs when they heard me at the top of the stairs sounding as if I was upset. Once I turned around I was kind of relieved from fright that it wasn't one of my attackers. Yet I was still surprise and upset because I didn't want anyone to see me looking this way. Even thou it was my pretty eyed guy friend I still yelled at him in an angry voice. I yelled at him for scaring me like that and I questioned him about how he got in the door downstairs. I can remember him asking me in a loud voice, "What the fuck happened to you?" Then all I seen was an arm reach around from the corner of the door grabbing my pretty eyed guy friend.

I pulled the door open wider to see who had grabbed him just that quick. My uncle had made it up to the top of the stairs and put some kind of crazy halt hold on my pretty eyed guy friend before I could even think about giving him an answer to his question. I began yelling at my uncle, telling him to let him go! My uncle started dragging my guy friend out the house. I rushed over and start pulling at my uncle arms to try to release my pretty eyed friend out of the choke hold my uncle had him in. My uncle started questioning him about how he gotten up the stairs to the top door. My guy friend was upset and confused about what had happened to me; however, he explained to my uncle how the downstairs door came open while he was knocking on it. Assuming someone was at home he came up the stairs calling my name not expecting me to be looking like I was! We all then went into the house after I told my uncle I mistake my guy friend for him. I thought he was calling me because he had gotten locked out again. My uncle and friend girl stayed in the kitchen while my guy friend and I went in to my bedroom.

Once my guy friend set down I explained to him what had happen to me from the time I got to the party up until the time when the nice lady and her husband had helped me. He was very upset about my assault. I didn't think he was going to take it as hard as he did. My guy friend said, "He was going to be looking for this dude with the tracks running across his face and nine out of ten whomever hangs with dude had something to do with my attack too. My guy friend said this would be his way of helping me find those punks and besides that no one will be suspicion of him. He assured us if it was some niggas from the party who attacked me he was going to find out who they were.

I remember my uncle saying to my guy friend, "You know what? You're an all right guy," and then hit my good looking guy friend on the shoulders. My uncle and friend girl went to his room. My guy friend and I sat in my bedroom and talked for a long time. He made me feel a little better about myself and I became comfortable around him. I really enjoyed my guy friend's company because he was a friend in deed when I needed him. I see what they mean when they say, how time flies when you're having fun. Before I knew it I heard my dad voice coming through the house. I was afraid because

I thought we had talked until the next morning. I knew there was no way I will be able to explain what my guy friend was doing in my bedroom this early in the morning.

I knew my dad was going to have a fit to see a boy had stayed in my room all night. Plus I didn't have enough time to have my guy friend run into another room because my dad would have caught him. I just prayed that my dad would understand considering nothing happened? Right away I started explaining to my dad who my guy friend was because when he first seen my friend he was very upset. After my dad calmed down he said, "Your bedroom is no place to sit and talk with your male friends." I can remember how my guy friend was very well mannered towards my dad. He told my dad that it was his fault for being in her room and that he was only concerned about what had happen to me. He also apologized for staying so late and told me he would check on me tomorrow if it was ok with my dad.

I just looked at my dad because I thought he was going to curse my friend out. However, I was really surprise when he said, "Yeah, it's all right." I walked my friend to the door downstairs and made sure the door was locked this time. Once I had got back upstairs I remember my dad saying, "He seems like he's a nice boy." I said, "Okay dad, he's just a friend." Then, I changed the subject quickly by saying, "Besides, what are you doing home so early?" He responded, "I only came by for a minute to check on how you were doing." He also said he was worried about me being at home alone. I told him that his brother and my friend girl were here.

I told my dad that I was alright. Some what tired but I was okay. After talking with my friend I felt like I could get me some rest. My dad then went back to work and I went to my room to go to sleep. I remember hearing my dad telling my uncle to keep an eye on me. My uncle being the person he was said, "Oh don't worry, you know I am!" I believe my dad felt a little better knowing that I wasn't going to be home alone. I also think he kind of liked my guy friend because he was so concern and supportive of me. I got me some juice that my uncle and friend girl had gone to the store to buy for me. I crawled into my bed and softly said to myself, "When is this hurt gonna ever end?" The next week was pretty much the same old routine; everyone was checking and waiting on me. I know one thing I would be glad when they do get the sick mind niggas that attacked me! All this sitting around and wondering was really beginning to drive me crazy. I believe it was about a week and a half since my attack. I remember this because my sister and brothers were in their second week of school. I was getting restless, tired, and worried from just sitting in the house all the time.

Suddenly one morning I heard someone knocking on the door and calling my name. It was my pretty eyed guy friend. He had stop by with some good news before he went to school. I went downstairs to let him in. As we were walking back up the stairs I remember my guy friend saying, "You're looking a whole lot better." I replied, "Yeah! Most of the outer bruises on my face are gone. I still had a little darkness around my eyes. I guess that's really not the problem now." Flash backs of that night ran through my mind, I had to pause for a moment from talking to keep from crying.

My good looking guy friend then said, "Lovely, is you okay?" I said, "I'm alright. I'm just trying to deal with these lifetime scars inside of me that I have to live with. I'll never get over all this pain!" He put his arms tightly around my neck pulling my head to his shoulder as he offer security and comfort. Seeing how upset I had got, my guy friend said, "I might have some good news that will cheer you up." Right away a whole different expression had come across my face. I couldn't wait to hear what the news was. I remember scrambling these words out my mouth, "What? What is it?" My friend took me by the hand and told me to calm down as he led me to the couch in a romantic way, which kind of confused me. I really start wondering what the news could be; especially, since I knew he still liked me as in a girlfriend and boyfriend relationship.

I asked him to quit keeping me in suspense. Then in a calm but serious voice I said, "Dammit will you tell me!" He went through the whole thing about how he had promise me he was going to do everything he could to help me. Not only that but my guy friend also told me how he start hanging out with his older brothers and some of their friends. In the mean while I'm on pins and needles wanting to twist his neck because he was not telling me the news quick enough. I was saying to him, "Yeah, ok, tell me, and get to the news!" In my head I was saying, "My guy friend doesn't like his older brothers' friends so what in the hell does this news have to do with them."

Then a light bulb lit up in my head; he knows. He knows who my attacker with the tracks across his face is! Talk about a person with no kind of sense, I quickly forgot about myself for a moment. I start feeling a little more depress and very sad as I thought to myself, "God, I hope my pretty eyed guy friend older brother had nothing to do with my attack?" Now in a way I didn't want to know the news that he had came to tell me. Then again as I thought about it he didn't seem as if he was at all too upset and I remember he said the news might cheer me up. So I asked my guy friend to please tell me because the wondering is starting to run me crazy. Then he said, "I think I know who your track face attacker is!" The news was like a pretty song too my ears when he told me.

I became quiet for a few seconds, and then I asked him, "Are you sure? How do you know it is him?" That is when he told me the answers and story to my long wondering question, that is, who was one of my attackers! He started off by telling me that last night he went with his older brothers to one of their friend's house because they were suppose to go play basketball. He also said that once they got over to this one guy's house and left with him in a van. So now I'm saying to myself, "Will you hurry up and get to who is my track face attacker!" He then goes into detail about how they all were riding in the van. He said, "Now image a vanload of guys driving up the streets with the music blasted, talking loud, drinking and smoking on their weed sticks. I said to the driver, I thought we were going to play some ball?"

My guy friend said the driver told him to be cool we have to go pick up some buddies of my. Therefore, my pretty eyed guy friend said he just sat back and enjoyed the ride. He further said that they picked up all dude's buddies from their houses; however, at the last house we stopped at we went inside. This is where my guy friend said he saw this one guy coming out a room half dress with scratch marks across his face. My guy friend said, "Once I seen dude face I knew he had to be the one you scratched! So I asked him, man damn what cat got a hold of you?" The track face dude try to play it off by saying his girl caught him with another girl and snapped. In other words the scratched face dude claimed his girlfriend jumped on him.

My guy friend told me that as the track face dude was talking he was paying attention to everyone's facial expression in the room. He said he notice that a couple of the guys in the room had a look on their face as if they knew the track face dude was lying. Then the track face dude laughed the lie off with them so he wouldn't have to further explained himself. My guy friend also said when he and his older brothers returned home that night he asked one of his older brothers to tell him what really happen to dude face. His older brother said, "I don't know what to believe because dude told me a different story about how his face got fucked up. Dog really need to get his lies together." Then, my guy friend went into details about the story his brother told him about dude's face. My guy friend said "It was said that the dude with the tracks across his face had gotten into a fight with some other nigga's. The nigga he was fighting girl jumped on his back and start scratching him in the face as if she was trying to pull his ear off."

The one thing I really didn't like was when my guy friend told me that he had told his older brother how dude really got his face scratched up. He said that his older brother was shocked that it was me but not surprise that dude with the tracks across his face did something like that. However, his brother said he was sorry for what had happen to me. I scrammed at my guy friend and said, "I can't believe you told your brother what had happen to me!" My guy friend said, "Lovely, I had to tell him because he was wondering why i was asking so many questions. Plus it was the only way I could get the track face dude real name from him." With that piece of information I grabbed my guy friend and gave him a big kiss. I was so excited. While wiping his face off I told him to make sure you give your older brother a great big kiss for me. My guy friend said, "I ain't gonna kiss that ugly nigga!" Both I and my guy friend started to laugh extremely hard. I thought to myself, "I actually laughed." It felt so good for the first time in a few weeks to finally feel good enough inside to laugh and smile again. I remember my guy friend said, "Now that's My Lovely," and I kind of smiled again. I told my guy friend, "Thank you. Thank you for everything you've done to help me!"

I made us some sandwiches while we finish talking. He stayed for about twenty more minutes after he ate his sandwich because I didn't want to be alone and then he left. Before he left he assured me that he will be over later to check on me. He also doubled check to make sure I locked the door once he left. As I walked back up the stairs I thought to myself, "He is a sweetheart, maybe." Before I could finish the rest of my thoughts I hurry up and said, "Nah!" Then I went upstairs to my room. I couldn't wait until someone came home so I could tell them the news that my guy friend had told me. That day seemed as if it was very long and the evening seemed as if it would never come.

My feeling right away was I couldn't wait to watch my uncle kill my track face attacker by beating him to death and I was going to help! All day I thought about how much pleasure I was going to get out of seeing him suffer for all the pain he had put me through! I was thinking of mean evil ways of torturing my track face attacker. I wanted to cut his penis off. Therefore, if we choose to let him live I know for a fact that he wouldn't rape no one else! Then I smiled when I thought about how I was going to enjoy watching and hearing my track face attacker scream for help like I did while I pour boiling hot grits with honey in it on his body. I want to make him suffer by causing him as much pain as I could possibility think of!

Yes, I had it really in for dude and I knew everything I wanted to do to my track face attacker, my uncle would be all for it! Man, this sitting around, waiting, and thinking of how I wanted to make my track face attacker suffer were really running me crazy. It was as if I was feeling the pain I was going to put my track face attacker through. I couldn't wait to torture him. It seemed as if my uncle was taking forever to come home that day! Every time I heard a car outside of my house I would run to the window to see who it was. I was hoping it was my uncle. After waiting for such a long time for my uncle to come home, I didn't care who came home first anymore. I just wanted to hurry up and get this all over with. I had murder in my eyes and I wanted my revenge!

Have you ever wanted to do some thing so bad that you can taste it and/or feel it?" Well, that's what I was going through. It's as if I have knots and butterflies forming in my stomach. I had made myself so hyper and high on the thought of how I was going to physically abuse my track face attacker that I begin pacing the floor. I continue to run back and forth from one window to the other, but I never seen anyone coming. I had gotten so excited about my plans on how I was going to make my track face attacker suffer that I started to get mad because I couldn't do it quick enough. The waiting was nerve wracking for me. It was as if I was torturing myself due to eagerness to see my track face attacker go through pain and suffering from being torture. The thought of thinking about how much he is going to suffer triggered my nightmares of horror. I started thinking about the hell my track face attacker and his friends put me through that night. All at once I could feel nothing but evil, hate, super anger, the deep desire, and want to kill my track face attacker. That whole fuck up ass night of my rape just came back to me all over again! Damn I wish he were dead!

Most of all I wish my track face attacker could have his disturbed minded ass here right now with me, alone, so I can have the sweet pleasure of twisting his fucken head off! The thought of seeing my track face attacker die a painful death is causing me to feel the blood warming up as it rushes through my veins. He deserved whatever suffering he got coming to him and I wanted to be part of giving it to him too. Time just was not going by fast enough for me. After giving myself a headache and every other ache that I could think of I finally heard someone coming through the door downstairs. Yes, it was my crazy uncle! I began to holler, "Hurry up! I know who he is!" My uncle then rushed up the front porch stairs to hear what I had to say.

Once my uncle came into the house I told him the news my guy friend had told me. The first thing that came out my uncle mouth was "Is he sure it's him?" I then told my uncle, "Yeah, my guy friend is sure. He had seen the scratches on his face like I had described them with his own eyes." My uncle picked up the telephone and made a few phone calls. I got mad at him because I didn't want the whole world to know what had happened to me. I remember asking my uncle, "Why did you call them?" My uncle told me that they really don't know why he wanted to beat dude to death but they are willing to help with no questions asked. I was touched when I was reminded of how much my uncle really does love me.

He grabbed me by my shoulders and said, "Niece I love you and

I seen the pain you were going through. I wouldn't do that to you." I was silent for a moment because I felt like a dummy and didn't know what to say behind those words. It may have been about an hour since my uncle had made his phone calls. Then, I heard someone knocking at the door. It was my uncle friends all geared to go and ready to commit murder! The wait was too long for me; especially, since I've been waiting all day for someone to come home. I was just sitting back listening to how my uncle and his friends were planning on killing my track face attacker. Believe me they weren't talking about nothing nice either. I thought I was coming up with some crazy mean ways of torturing my track face attacker but their plans were more brutal than mines. I guess by them being men they knew what would really hurt another man the most.

I don't know? You can call me crazy but listening to my uncle and his friends talking made me start to feel kind of sorry for my track face attacker. Maybe I believe I began having second thoughts about doing anything to my track face attacker. I guess it was from me listening and hearing how evil it sounded to put a person though so much pain. Thinking of the pain I had been through, I felt that no one should have to go through something so awful, especially if they really didn't have too. Now this was where my confused mind and feelings were starting to really get the best of me. I started saying to myself, "Girl is you crazy! How can you feel sorry for him? Did you forget what he did to you?" I guess you can call me stupid but I still was feeling that no one deserve to go through any kind of horrible pain or suffering if it wasn't necessary; not even my track face attacker.

I couldn't understand why I was feeling the way I was. However, my uncle and his little hit squad had the uttermost level of torture in storage for my track face attacker. I know before I wanted my uncle to kill my track face attacker but come on, regardless of all I have been through, I do still have a conscious and feelings. Therefore, regardless of what he did, two wrongs isn't gonna make this situation I'm going through right. You can now say I'm going kind of soft because I start hoping that my dad will hurry up and come home. I was hoping that maybe my dad could stop my uncle and his little hit squad.

Perhaps my dad would be a little more understanding and let the law deal with my track face attacker. Time has finally ticked out because my uncle and his little hit squad were ready to go. Every time my uncle asked me was I ready, I would find any kind of excuse to keep from leaving. I was stalling time because I was trying to give my dad time to make it home. I end up running out of reasons for why I wasn't ready to go. I finally had to start walking down the stairs to do something I knew was wrong. Plus if it wasn't done the right way my uncle, his little hit squad, and I could go to jail for the rest of our life. Wondering if I might go to jail behind killing my track face attacker was the scariest part about the whole plan.

Once we got into the car I lied and said I left my keys. I remember my uncle making a statement like, "You don't need them I have my." I then said, "No, I want my own keys. What if something goes wrong or happens and we have to split up!" After saying that I took my uncle keys and ran back into the house to get my keys. I tried to take my time continuing while saying, "Daddy will you please hurry up! Help! I really don't want go, watch, or even have any parts of a murder!" My uncle and his little hit squad started blowing the car horn. I knew if I didn't come down the stairs soon they would end up going with out me, especially, since they really didn't want me to go in the first place.

I knew I had to go other wise I would be running myself crazy wondering what happen and if my uncle and his little hit squad were all right. As I stomped my foot on the floor I yelled, "Damn, this isn't fair!" So I started making my way to the door to go downstairs to leave with my uncle and his little hit squad. You know I kind of got this feeling inside as if I was walking down these stairs for the last time. As I slowly walked down the stairs and made it along side of the house outside my uncle yelled out the car window for me to hurry up. He just didn't know that at the same time I was praying to God that my dad would hurry up and make it home. I wanted him to put a stop to this plan before it happen. Just as I was about to get into the car a set of head lights from another car had pulled up behind us. They say that God answers prayers; it was my dad. I was glad to see him but from the look on my uncle face I don't think he was.

My dad got out of his car and walked over to the car we were sitting in. My dad asked where we were about to go? My uncle lied to my dad. Well, actually he really didn't lie; my uncle just didn't tell the whole truth. My uncle said, "We were going to make a run real quick Hubbard. We'll be right back." A small voice in the back of my head said to myself, "Yeah, ok right back. How do you know how long it takes to beat a person to death?" The way my uncle and his little hit squad were talking up stairs in the house, it was going to take a whole lot of time torturing my track face attacker, and then they were going to kill him.

So I kind of loudly whispered, "I think we should tell him. What if something goes wrong?" My dad then replied, "Tell me what? What are you talking about Faye?" I was glad that even though my dad was tired he still had good enough ears that he heard me. Now I knew we weren't going anywhere without talking to my dad about the plan first. My uncle and his little hit squad knew when push came to stub my dad was meaner and he didn't play. Therefore, we all had to get out of the car and go into the house to explain to my dad where we were going and what we were about to do. After I saw the displeased expression on my uncle face I became very quiet because I knew he was upset.

My uncle and his little hit squad were even more upset after they told my dad about their little torturing murder plan. I watched the angry facial expressions on everybody's face as they told my dad what they were about to do. Even thou my uncle knew the reason why they were going to commit murder and his hit squad didn't; they really wanted to get their hands on my track face attacker bad too. Every so often my uncle or one of his friends from his little hit squad would look at me and shake their head in a discouraged way. I sat quietly watching and listening to them trying to convince my dad to go along with their little murder plan. At the same time my uncle and his friends' eyes were staring at me as if they wanted to put their hands around my neck and choke my tongue out my mouth. In a way I was afraid but I really didn't care because I knew my dad could beat the living hell out of my uncle and his whole little hit squad.

So I just looked and didn't say a word because I knew I was going to hear my uncle month later on once my dad did leave. I really started looking at my dad face; his facial expression change from an angry expression to one of those surprising maybe stare. Even my dad's whole tone of voice changed; it went from a high are you crazy tone to a low maybe this can work tone. My dad also began talking as if he was willing to go along with the little torturing murder plan. He began asking my uncle all types of questions such as the step by step thought out master murder plan. He wanted to know in detail from the beginning to the end.

As I think about it, it seemed as if my dad was looking for a security blanket that no one was going to get caught up and go to jail behind what they were about to do. You should have seen the expression on my uncle face changing as he looked at me as if he was saying, "Yeah, niece, your little soil everything for us plan didn't work." Talk about a sister feeling heated around the collar. I slowly slid down in my chair as my uncle burned me with that I'm going to get you look. Now, it seems as if I had no one in the house that was thinking with a level head; everybody was out for murder and it was my entire fault. Why did I have to be so womanly developed at such a young age? As far as I was concerned I still had a few more years before I obtain my womanly spread as they called it. Don't get me wrong. I been taking an advantage of my development and enjoying every second of it since I've been dancing. However, I didn't want anybody to die behind the fact I am overdeveloped at a young age. To be honest with you I have been getting all kinds of lifetime thrills seeing males and females wanting me and my body. For the most point many of them couldn't have me or it.

I thought the past was the past and no one was able to touch or hurt me anymore. All kinds of thoughts were running through my mind on how to prevent this murder from happening. I was hoping that my dad will come back to his senses. I just sat there listening as he, my uncle, and his little hit squad continue discussing their little torturing murder plan. Then out of the clear air I said, "What if someone be looking out their window and see ya'll coming or leaving his house?" My uncle said, "Lovely don't worry we got everything under control!" No matter what I said I couldn't change their minds.

I kept saying to myself, "It's not right! I know it's not right!" Then I said out loud, "Daddy remember you use to tell us two wrongs don't make a right? Daddy please don't do this, it's not right!" I remember my uncle said, "Hubbard don't pay her no attention." My dad got quiet for a moment. I said to myself now is the time to try and get my point across. First, I gave him the sad story about how I wouldn't be able to live with myself if they were to go to jail or something were to happen to anyone of them. Then, I coated it with telling him about the guilt I would have to live with; knowing that the reason someone got hurt or went to jail was my fault. I begged my daddy for a long period of time. I kept saying, "Please, please daddy, for me let the police get him, and lock him up in jail!"

My dad uses to call me fat face. He uses to always say he was a sucker for my fat adorable face, smile, and cries. Therefore, I started to fake cry and the tears start pouring out my ears like a floating wild river. This story had a little happier ending for me because I didn't have to worry about my dad or my crazy uncle going to jail or getting hurt. For a moment there I thought my dad was thinking about going along with my uncle and his little hit squad plan. The police was called and when they came I told them everything my pretty eyed guy friend told me about my track face attacker. My uncle wasn't to please but I figure he would get over it. After all I felt it was the best and right thing to do.

Once the police left my uncle gave me a big tight hug and said, "Niece, I still love you." That was a relief for me because I just knew my uncle was going to twist my neck from soiling his little torturing murder plan. I knew once I was for sure the police had my track face attacker then I figure maybe I could get on with my life again. I missed school but most of all I wanted to go back to dancing at the strip club. I knew that was the atmosphere I needed to get over all this hell I have been through and living in. Plus my friend girl had told me that my boss said, "I'll have a job at his club whenever I decided to come back to work." I thought that was rather nice of him, besides they, that is the people at the tavern, make me feel like part of their family.

Three or four days had gone by and we still haven't heard anything from the police about whether or not that was my track face attacker. The suspense was starting to kill me. I hope it was and then maybe he would tell who the other guys were that was with him at the time of my attack. I had started to go out on the back top porch just to get me some air. As I open the door I could hear some voices coming from the side of the house that seem to be getting closer and closer to the downstairs back door. I stood there quietly to see if I could recognize any of the voices but there were some kind of interference such as a walkie-talkie or some thing. Then hard and strong knocks were coming from the door downstairs. I didn't know if I was to answer it or say nothing because I was scared and I didn't know who it was.

My heart started beating extremely fast. I start thinking the police might have arrested my track face attacker, but released him for some reason. My heart started to beat even faster as I thought to myself that maybe my attackers had return and were knocking at the door to get me for telling. I didn't know for sure who it was at the door and it was even scarier wondering. I slowly and softly open the top porch door and tip toed to the edge of the porch to see who was downstairs banging on our door. If nothing else I thought maybe I could get a look at them as they walked away from the door.

Whoever it was they banged on the door again; maybe four or five times. Then I heard a man voice say, "Looks like no one is home." I also heard a scrambled voice as if the man who was talking was changing the dial on a radio real fast. Now I'm wondering who it really was and why did they bring a radio. Do they think I'm that crazy to just come downstairs to the door and open it? I wonder what they are planning to do with the radio. My only thought is maybe they are planning to turn the radio up real loud once they grab me down by the door so the neighbors wouldn't hear me scream. Whatever their plan was I'm making sure I am not a part of it! I'm staying up on top of this porch where I know it is safe. Now let me see how bad they wanted to get me. I just stood there waiting for them too leave.

My wait wasn't too much longer because a voice said, "Let's go, I'll leave a note for them to get in touch with us." Now I'm thinking why if they were my attackers are they leaving to get in touch with them; I thought that was really stupid. I move even more softly to the side rail of the top porch to get a look at the faces that belong to the voices I was hearing. Man was I surprised! Here I was afraid but not once did I think about calling the police. Well, I guess you can say it is because if I did I wouldn't have got quick service. I now know what they mean by saying, "Where is a police when you really need them, they are no where around?"

I should have known that it was the police banging on my downstairs door like they had lost their mind. As they were walking away I asked, "Excuse me but are you looking for somebody?" As one of the officers step back so I could see him I recognized him from being over at our house earlier in the week. He said, "Hi Lovely, can we talk to you for a minute?" I told them to hold on I'll be down. As I walked back to the top porch door the whole time I was thinking what the police want to tell me. Yes, my reader you kind of have an ideal of how my mind gets to wondering about little things.

Before I got down the stairs to open the door I had thought about everything negative the police could end up telling me about my track face attacker. I figure they may tell me anything within the boundary of "that was the wrong guy" to "maybe my track face attacker had changed the story around to make it seem like I wanted to have sex with them." I even thought that perhaps the police had found out about the first attack I didn't tell them about. As if I was asking a question I open the door and said, "Yes?" The officers began to explain why they were here. I just stood there with my mouth open, in shock not knowing what to say about the good and bad news I was hearing! I really had gotten my wig blew back as they use to say. I didn't know if I was to pass out, brake down and cry, jump for joy, scream, kiss the officers or what?

The news was good because the officers said my track face attacker blood type, sperm samples, and everything matched perfectly. They also said the reason it took so long to get back in touch with me was because they didn't catch him until a few days ago. Now the bad news was the way they caught my track face attacker. After numerous attempts of going back and forward to my alleged track face attacker's home they were unsuccessful in making an arrest. After the police officers told me the story about how they did catch my track face attacker, I felt sad that the police didn't catch him when they first went by his house.

For some reason I use to feel this strange gouty feeling in my stomach. Not sure why but I just didn't feel safe in my neighborhood. Sometimes I would feel as if I was over reacting because of my last attack. It was as if I could feel my track face attacker close by me and again my deepest inner thoughts was right. When the police officers told me that they had caught my track face attacker just a few blocks from my house I wanted to cry. First thing I said was, "I knew he was close by me! For some reason I felt his presence, as if he was watching my house!" One of the officers assured me that it wasn't like that. I was not trying to hear what the officer was trying to say. I began screaming in a worried and afraid voice, "What you mean it wasn't like that? He was just a few blocks from my house!"

Then one of the officers showed me a picture of my track face attacker. I really felt nasty and like a big fool because it was this one guy I use to play basketball with on the courts around the corner. He wasn't a bad looking man but I could tell that he was a lot older than the other guys who would be on the courts. I remember how I use to feel kind of nervous when he would call me "A young brick house." It was something about the way he talked and looked at me that I didn't like. My girly instances would keep me away from him on the courts. Now I know my girly instances were right about him; he was sick-minded. Yuk! He is the face that belongs to my unknown track face attacker. Like I said before, I was in shock. I believed it but I didn't want to believe it when the officers showed me who he was. Everything in my mind finally did come together.

Now I had a very good ideal of who a few of my other attackers were. Determined I was to make them pay the price for what they did to me. The officer continued talking while I was thinking to myself. He said, "Lovely, I know for a fact he couldn't have been watching your house because he was to busy assaulting a thirteen year old girl." All I could say was, "No!" I knew the horrible torture he was putting her through and I know she didn't deserve it.

My track face attacker had the thirteen year old girl in the alley but good for her that someone heard her screaming and decided to call the police. His ass was caught in the act. The officer said that with my statement and the matching of the blood type and sperm, and now these new charges they had a strong case against him. The officer told me that I would be notified when and if I had to come to court. he also said, "Believe me Lovely, he won't be seeing the streets for a long time." That's all I needed to know. Now maybe I could get on with my life and I didn't have to worry about him attacking me again. I closed the door once the police officers left and jumped, ran, and danced up the stairs. I couldn't wait until somebody came home so I could tell them the good news. I felt really good all over again. You know how you feel when you know you are on top of the world? Well I became a live again. I played me some music and even cleaned up the house. Yes, it did feel good to know that, that monster was locked up and was going to be locked up for a long time. I felt so much better. I put me on some more clothes and stood downstairs in front of the side of the house to get some fresh air. It felt so good to be able to stand outside and breathe again with out worrying about my unknown track face attacker.

We lived upstairs over a pool hall. Like most businesses that have an apartment over it. We didn't have a front door entrance. In order to get to and from the door to my house you would have to walk through this fenced walkway along the outside east wall of the building. Once I got downstairs I seen that the little pool hall was back open. So I kind of just pecked in it hoping not to be seen by anybody; just to see who was in there. A few seconds after I stepped back into the gangway on the side of my house, I heard the door to the pool hall open. Was I surprised? Unaware that someone in the pool hall had seen me, a guy came out to talk to me. While I was still standing on the bottom stairs to the pool hall he stuck his head around on the side of house where I was standing and said, "Hi, how are you?" The voice sounded familiar to me.

At first I wanted to just take off running to the back and go upstairs but then it was the way he spoke to me. I hesitated for a moment, and then I said in a wondering not too sure voice, "Ok?" Now I'm saying to myself, "You can at lease hear what he has to say. After all if it wasn't for him you wouldn't have known the name of your unknown track face attacker." Still very much insecure I stood on the side of my house as my pretty eyed guy friend good-looking brother talked to me. Another thing that made me decided to listen to him was when he said, "I'll understand if you don't want to be bothered."

I stopped and listened because he was really sweet; however, this person is known for his charm. My pretty eyed good looking guy friend brother could charm a rattle snake to stop and listen to him. For that reason, I really forgot who I was stopping to listen to for a minute. I knew right away after I came to my senses that I was going to receive some of his unusual charm. He was really nice, in a gentleman kind of manner, polite, very respectful. Well, I didn't trust anyone anymore, not even him. So, I guess you can say I was wondering why he was trying to be so nice to me and what did he really want from me? My pretty eyed guy friend's brother began telling me how sorry he was for what had happened to me. He didn't try to make excuses for what his friend had done. He also said he wanted to assure me that they all weren't like that.

He said once his brother had told him what his friend had done he rejected their friendship. He chose not to be his friend ever again. He went on telling me if I ever needed someone to talk to he is willing too lend me an ear or two. I was just standing there not moving, listening and not saying a word to him. He then said, "If you need a friend just check down in the pool hall. I'm here every day!" By the time my dad came home I was back up stairs. I told him what the police officers had told me and that my track face attacker will be off the streets for a long time. A few months had gone by, and then we received a phone call that said, "I did not have to come to court because my track face attacker had pleaded guilty."

That was another great day in my life. I really didn't want to sit in a courtroom in front of all those people and relive that ugly night of my attack. Let's just say that was another one of my deep held fear; sitting in a crowd courthouse telling my side of what happen to me that night and seeing my attacker's face. I was praying that I didn't have to see his face again. With that news I went on with my semi-usual life. As for my pretty eyed guy friend he was still giving his little weekend parties but I didn't go too them. He and I talked at school and every so often he would come by to check on me at home. He was still my friend even thou he didn't approve of me dancing and engaging in heavy drug usage.

Like I told my pretty eyed friend guy, "I have to try to live with my crazy fucked up, abused, and misused ass life. The drugs are what keep me going. Plus the drugs kept my mind leveled out so I wouldn't kill myself. I honestly felt like I lost my mind; there are some things in my life I would never be able to get back. My childhood life has been stolen and robbed from me." I live with the pain and agony of my life experiences everyday even though another day is a new day.

The only things that keep me straight and focus is my true friends, dancing, and drugs. As far as my pretty eyed guy friend's brother goes, well he's a whole different story. You will read about him a few more time as you continue going through the pages of my book. As for my family and me it was life as usual. They lived their life and I was secretly continuously living my double undercover life. I was still being a risk taker and taking beyond chances with the hope that my dad never fines out.

Chapter Fifteen
"Living A Secretive Double Life"

FOR THE NEXT year or so life wasn't all that bad for me. I was doing well in school when I went but when I didn't go I made sure I got my make up assignments. This way I wouldn't fail none of my classes. I knew as long as I was going to school regardless of how tired I was I knew my dad wouldn't thought I was the one moon lighting. When the winter time was here and the snow came down I can remember hearing my dad making statements such as "Who just came in the house?" He could see the fresh set of footprints in the snow. I would just lay there with the cover pulled up tight around my neck fully dressed with my eyes closed. Every minute I remain under the covers I was praying. I pray that my dad would only softly crack my bedroom door to look to make sure I was in the bed sleep and not come all the way in. I use to also fix my pillows as if a body was lying in my bed.

I remember a few times I had just made it in the house just in time before my dad did. One night I made it in the house almost too late. Talk about a sister holding her breathe as I lay on the floor until my dad made his nightly rounds. Afterward as I creep into bed, high as a kite, drunk, laughing and saying to myself, "Girl, you're starting to play it a little too close!" Still trying to be good in what I did on the side without my dad knowing, I made sure I never got caught creeping back into the house.

The only new thing that came about in my life was that I was now thirteen and was calling myself seeing a young man. Don't get me wrong my dad did notice the new change in me; I was becoming a lot wilder. I notice my dad started to be stricter on me. I was not completely sure why he became so strict but he did and I couldn't even breathe with out his permission. I was only allowed to leave home to go to school and back home again. I was not allowed to go anywhere else. I really didn't care because I was still going to do what I wanted to do anyway. I would say to myself each time my dad gave me a lecture about where I could go, "Oh don't think you stop my fun dad!" I would still do like he told me, you know, go to school, come home, do housework and homework but as soon as he left I was out the door on my way to the tavern to shake my ass.

Oh, but he did stop my ass shaking for a moment. I came home from school one day and my dad was there as usual. I did my housework and then sat in my room listening to my music as I did my homework. I was almost completely done with my homework; however, I noticed I didn't hear my dad moving around as if he was getting ready for work like usual. I was saying in a soft mannered voice, "Come on dad hurry up and leave. You gonna make me late for work!" After a few more minutes had went by I got up and looked into my dad's bedroom to see if maybe he had went back to sleep. I surprised to see him just lying in bed watching TV like he didn't have to go anywhere.

I asked, "Dad ain't you going to drive the cab tonight?" He blew my wig back when he said that he was taking a few weeks off. Yeah, I just wanted to die. Now I'm saying to myself as I walked back to my room, "Damn, how am I going to sneak out the house with my dad home?" So I called down to the tavern and told my boss that I was going to be a little late. Afterward I thought about it, I should have told him that I wasn't coming in. Waiting for my dad to go to sleep, I sat quietly in my room high and thinking. I got up several times and tipped toed through the house to see if my dad was still woke or not. When he finally went to sleep I was out of there like a bird set free from her cage. Whenever I was late I would tell my boss any kind of crazy lie.

I remember even using my uncle for an excuse so I could leave with him. My dad didn't mind that so much. He would just say something like, "Don't keep her out to late. She got to go to school in the morning." My uncle would reply, "I'm not Hubbard," and out the door I would go. Like all scams they're only good for a moment because guess what! My dad had another treat for my tricks! I decided to dance the afternoon shift to keep from getting my uncle involved to deep. I didn't want my dad finding out the truth about where I was going when I left with my uncle. If my dad knew the truth he will be mad at my uncle and I didn't want that to happen.

I didn't have any problems joggling my afternoon dancing job and school. Especially, since I'm accustomed to always doing all my assignments, plus some extra work to make up for the time that I was not in school. I must say I'm still good at what I did because I didn't get caught. However, I must say, I don't know you can call it what you want or perhaps help me to understand what's really going on? For some strange reason it seemed as if once I changed my schedule around so I can continue to dance with out my dad knowing, he changed his work schedule too! Even to this day I still can't really figure it out. All I knew was it seemed as if he was trying to catch me in the act of something or with a boy. Honestly, I was not really scared at all about my dad catching me in the act. I had my school, home, and dancing well planned and all together.

I knew when it came to trying to out slick my dad there should not be one second of anyone's daily activity not accounted for or uncover because he will catch it. Now, I had to make sure I covered my ass at all times while living with my dad. If I decided to go to work during school hours, I knew I had to cover up my evidence so my dad wouldn't know I been around cigarette smoke and drinking. To kill the cigarette and some of the alcohol odors I would spay some perfume on me as soon as I got to the bottom door of my house. I did this to make it seem as if I've already had the perfume on me and it won't smell as if the perfume was freshly sprayed in the hallway as to cover something up. By the time I made it upstairs to the second door of our house, I would have opened up at least four or five sticks of gum and chewed them up in my mouth.

There were times I did forget to get some gum on my way home, which meant as soon as I got in the house I had to run straight to the refrigerator. Again, I stored my big balls of gum stash in the refrigerator in case of an emergency. I would rush to the freezer because I knew once I got upstairs my dad was going to be on his way to see who was coming in the door. Yes, call me Miss Slick at the time. I had my speed together and I always made it to the freezer before my dad made it to the kitchen catching me coming in. When I did see my dad, I played everything off real quick because I knew he would be mad. Well, I would grab one of my old balls of gum out the freezer and put it in my mouth to kill some of the alcohol smell on my breath before I start talking to my dad. Usually, I was only talking to him to give him a long list of lies for why I was coming in the house too late after school. All while I'm talking to him I'll be chewing my gum all wild, talking fast to him, and making my way to my room. I honestly be trying to get my high ass out of my dad's way.

As I mentioned before I made sure my strategies to my plan were very well thought out and together. I knew what would happen if I made a mistake. So, that meant I had to continue telling him the same lie to support the other lies. I stuck to the same lies each time. I didn't change my lies because of my drug abuse and alcohol drinking. I didn't want to forget what I said just in case my dad decided to ask me about it later. I uses to tell my dad that the reason

I am coming home later is because I stayed after school for the after school activities. I would get home around seven something or eight. I remember my dad would ask me the same question every time but worded differently and make some silly comment. He would sometimes say something like, "I know it don't take you no hour and something for you to get home on the bus! Faye you only have to catch one bus!"

I would throw him off by saying that a few of my girlfriends and I walked after we missed the first bus. He would respond with this strange tone of voice and look at me with the evilest eyes as if he knew I was lying. Then, he would say, "Yeah, okay Faye." I always felt that my dad was the nicest, evilest, but hardest man to understand. However, he was my dad and I loved him even thou he made me mad by not allowing me to go anywhere. I don't know what was my dad's reason for putting me on such strict restrictions; they were harsh too. I had become a prisoner in my own home. All I know, his strictness made me wilder and wanting leave the house more; I became very deceitful and started to develop a strong disfavor for my dad.

I had to try and stay at lease a few steps or more in front of my dad, that is, if I wanted to continue dancing. I had to do what I had to do to keep from getting in more trouble with my dad so that I won't get caught. I had no problem with my new schedule. However, the real problem came about when my dad started sending my younger siblings to Chicago to stay with my mom for the summer. Now with my new life style I knew that wasn't going to work. I felt my dad usually wouldn't send me back to Chicago because he knew I didn't want to go. But now I think he might try to send me because he wanted a break from me. I remember him saying a couple of times that he was not going to be here to keep an eye on me like he wanted to because he was taking on a much heavier work load. I knew that was just a nice way of saying what he was really thinking. So, I didn't care I wasn't going to no Chicago. I learned my dad's work schedule and worked my dancing in it. Everything was going along ok, except over the summer we had moved into a bigger house. This time we were on the first floor instead of the second floor. I said to myself that this would be even better. Oh, but that thought got changed real quickly. I thought that since I was at home to help with the moving I could get first pick of my bedroom. Well, it didn't work out that way. We stayed in a four family united and my dad gave me one of the middle bedrooms, which didn't have a window.

Yeah, I said the same thing, "Just my luck." It wasn't all that bad because I was now allowed to go as far as the front porch. I couldn't understand why my dad was being so mean and hard on me. However, I came up with plan B. When my dad went to sleep, a deep sleep that is, I would creep off to dance. Another good thing about us moving was I now lived closer to the tavern where I danced. A few times I almost got caught but I played it off as if I was at this house in the back where some of my uncle's wife in laws stayed. My dad must have forgotten that I am a child of his and my mother's. Therefore, I learned all the tricks of the tray on being sneaky and good at it from them. Plus I stayed around them all the time until they separated. Not only did I have my own crazy gifted ways of thinking but I also had both their ways and method of doing things and getting my way.

One of the main things, I really hated about us moving was, it seems as if my dad whole attitude had changed for the worst when it came to me. He had started talking to me any kind of way, which I wasn't gonna accept it from him or no one else. When I try to defend and stand up for myself by telling my dad he was wrong for the way he treated me everybody would say I was being disobedient and I was talking back to him. When I try to talk to him respectfully about how he treats me, he would never give me a chance to talk. My dad use to try to beat me or hit me for no reason. Well, at least it seemed that way to me because I felt I wasn't being disrespectful or talking back to him. I was only trying to get my point across but my dad didn't want to hear it; in fact he never wanted to hear it.

How I remember how my dad didn't want to her anything I had to say! He used to make this statement to me all the time, "I'm going to beat you like your dad should have done!" I would become even more confused because I always believed that he was my daddy?" I started to feel as if I was such a bad child that even my biological daddy disowned me. I knew then that I was in this cruel, wrong world on my own and it wasn't fair! Then remembering what my friend girl had said to me started to dance around in my mind. She said, "Why don't you go back to live in Chicago with your mom!" If only she knew how I wish it was so easy. I thought about it, but I could never go back there. True enough I loved my mom more than life itself but I wanted and was hoping that she would come to Wisconsin to live. "Who am I to ask for anything," which was another one of my dads haunting put down statements.

I had this deep, painful, hurting fear of my mom telling me no and to hear her say it I believed would be the cause of my death. She was the only person I felt truly loved me but I couldn't understand why she wouldn't come to Wisconsin to be with me! Like my dad used too tell me, "Who am I to ask for anything." Then again, why should I ask when I knew I wasn't gonna get it anyway! For that reason, I lived a very flustered and lonely life journeying through this world with a confused mind with out my mom. My every other thoughts are wishes; wishing how I could find the solution to her problems so she can focus on me. I need her to help me understand and regain my mind.

If money can buy you happiness, then why can't it buy me love? If money can solve all men's problems, then why can't it fix my heart? If money is the controlling ruler in life, then why can't it take over my pains and give me back my mind? Money is only paper you can ball up, tear up, throw away, and burn it too. Well, to be honest with you I feel like money after all. I feel like I could be ball up, tear up, thrown away, and burn up because that is how life has been treating me! At this moment in my life I felt like my dad is balling me up and throwing my life away because all I could do was sit on our front porch and go to school.

My dad had become extremely hard on me until one day my uncle decided to talk to him about giving me a little freedom. My uncle talked my dad into letting me come over his house to stay the rest of the summer. At first I didn't think my dad was gonna let me go. When my uncle said, "Go pack you some clothes," you should had seen sister girl running. I bet you I broke the record for the fastest and the most stuff packed in less then seconds of time. In my own way I was hoping that I didn't have to come back to live with my dad. Even thou I knew it was impossible but it was a good thought for the moment. I said "bye," in one of those I really don't want to say anything to you tone of voice. Then, I hurry out the house and put my things in my uncle's car.

My uncle felt that I needed to get away for a minute because it was just too much hostility between my dad and me. When I first got to my uncle's house he told me that my room was in the back. I felt as if my uncle had planned this because I had my own bedroom with a complete bedroom set. I said to myself, "Freedom!" I'm gonna enjoy being over here with my uncle, and his family, plus. What I mean by the "plus" is that my uncle's fiancée older brother stayed with them too. My uncle's fiancée brother wasn't really trying to be a man; he was gay and very cool to be around. I could go on and tell you so many positives things my uncle's fiancée gay brother helped me to recognize in myself and life but that's a whole different story. Now back to the stay at my uncle house…

I too had my chores and responsibilities while staying with my uncle and his family. My uncle wasn't anywhere near as hard on me as my dad was. My uncle was always opened minded when it came to me. He talked to me a lot, which was something my dad and I didn't do. I was even honest with my uncle about me dancing, using drugs and drinking alcohol. Sure he didn't like it and he wasn't trying to accept it. I made a promise to him. I promised him that I would try stop using cocaine if he would always be there for me when I need him. The conversations and relationship I had with my uncle started to make me feel more confident about myself and I gained a little more self-esteem.

All the talks my uncle and I had were very educational; however, he schooled me on my dancing but I refuse to stop. I loved and still wanted to dance. I couldn't promise him that would stop dancing. So, we all, as a house whole, had an agreement to watch what we do and make sure we did things in a respectful way because there were younger kids in the house that look up to us. I loved staying with my uncle. I finally had a life again in his household. He treated me as if I was his own daughter. Therefore, I spent my summers with my uncle's family.

Yes, I became the summer sometimes live in babysitter. It wasn't that bad because I still was allowed to dance. One of the good things about it was that my uncle's fiancée gay brother hung out on Third Street where at the time I was dancing. I remember how he/she would come in to the tavern with one or two of his/her friends and tell them, "This is my niece, make sure you watch out for her!" Even thou the man was gay, he was like a big brother and sister in one to me. I couldn't have asked for a safer and better guardian angel than him; especially, while I was on the streets. Life has finally dealt and seems to have given me another chance to view the world differently. To tell you the truth I was taking advantage of it too.

As time slowly moved on I took a little too much advantage of life pleasures. I had gotten a little too serious about this one guy I was seeing. He became the comfort that I needed when I didn't want to go to my uncle. This guy made me feel safe and secure when I was with him. Whenever I was with him I felt as if I was in heaven; so beautiful and relaxed. He treated me so good. The feelings I had developed for him were so strong and I hope they would never end. Then a thought came into my mind that made me want to cry. I knew once I went back home my dad was not gonna allow me to see a boy. Especially, a young man that was much older than me. I knew I had to come up with a good plan so I could continue to see him with out my dad interfering.

I talked to my uncle to see if it would be ok for me to stay the weekend with him and his family. He said, "If my dad says its fine then he doesn't have any problem with it." Now, I knew once I went back home I had to try and stay on my dad's good side because my relationship, that is my first time puppy love, was depending on it. Remember I always thought my plans out to the fullest before executing them. Therefore, when I went home I put my plan in progress. Of course, yes, it worked I was now going over to my uncle house for the weekends. The only thing I don't like about a good plan that is spinning great is somebody always have to throw a monkey ranch in it to put a holt on the running. Let me explain what I mean about that.

My uncle was at first going along with the weekend stays as long as I stayed around the house. I remember how he uses to tell me to be careful because I was going a little to fast and he didn't want to see me get hurt. What he meant by moving to fast is my uncle knew I had really started liking this light skinned, charcoal gray eyed man, which was much older than I was. Considering and knowing some of my bad habits and situations that I had gone through and been in, he just didn't want me to be hurt and taken advantage of. Now, I could have male company as long as I didn't take him in my bedroom. The problem started when I changed my schedule for staying at my uncle house for the whole weekend. My dad would drop me off at my uncle house on Friday where he would pick me back up on Sunday. I would rush into the house to call my friend guy and tell him what time he was to pick me up from my uncle's house. However, my uncle and his fiancée started nagging at me about where I've been going when I get there. This is when the monkey ranch started getting thrown into my well thought out plan.

My uncle and his fiancée knew where I was going once I left his house during the weekends. It was not like they didn't really know at all but I honestly felt it wasn't any of their business anyway. They allowed me to see this guy at their house all night as long as I didn't take him into my bedroom but they change their minds about allowing me to go off with him. I don't understand how that works! Anyways how do they know we stay in front, the living room that is, all night when they went to sleep! I believe their true problem was they thought they had them a personal weekend babysitter, which wasn't part of my plan.

Seeing that I was now getting pressured from my uncle I knew that my weekend escape plan wasn't going to work out much longer. I continue coming over on the weekends. I obey some of my uncle rules and regulations until I came up with another great idea. School seems as if it was going by so fast. I now only danced the matinee because I had told my light skinned charcoal gray eyed friend guy I had stopped. A matinee was the mid-day early evening shift I danced, (from 11:00 a.m. to 4:00 p.m.) Considering that he only saw me on the weekends and talked to me after school hours in the late evenings my dance schedule worked out fine. So as far as my light skinned charcoal gray eyed male friend was concerned I wasn't dancing anymore.

I had to figure out how I was going to joggle my dancing career and see him during the summer without him knowing I still dance. That was another problem my devilish mind had to work on and I knew when that time came I would have to deal with it. Time really pass by quickly. Summer did come and I went over too my uncle's house to spend the summer. As far as my uncle's rules went I had to be in or at the house by the time it got dark. I agreed with his rules because my friend guy worked in the daytime and he usually didn't come over until after it had gotten dark. Besides, having him come over after dark was less work for me to do, that is, trying to sneak out my uncle's house after the kids went to sleep. Therefore, everything just fell right into place for me. I became the best babysitter there was. I took care of their kids so much I thought for a minute they were mine.

My uncle and his fiancée had started going out regular, which made it easy to set them on a time schedule. My clock was clocking every minute and move I knew they would make. Then I made my moves at the right time; however, I tend to their kids first. I held conversations and played with their kids. I use to take them over to the park to tire them out. After we left the park, the kids and I would make it in the house about nine or ten at night. I fed the kids, gave them a bath, and put them to bed. I always tried to have them in the bed before my friend guy came over because the kids would always be all in our face; we couldn't even get a kiss in when they were awake. Since, winter we were doing more than just kissing, if you know what I mean. I had to make time to get laid before my uncle and them came back home. I always did pretty well with my timing too. Usually by the time they did make it home, hell I was laying on the coach knocked out sleep. Yes, I wasn't worrying about a thing because I just knew all my tracks were being covered; at lease I thought. One night while in the deep mist of making love my uncle and his fiancée came home. It was too late to try and run out of my room and into the front room; my room was way in the back. I knew my uncle was going to kill dude. So my guy friend made his way out my bedroom window.

Another problem began to surface for me. I miss my menstruation that month. I told my friend guy but he was like, "Just because you miss one month doesn't mean you're pregnant!" Therefore, I continue dancing in the afternoons, watching kids in the evenings, and getting my groove on at night. A well put together life for a fourteen year old girl. Now we're talking into another month I still didn't see my period. I knew it was much too late to start worrying because the damage was done. I knew something was wrong last month because I never missed my period. I was afraid for real now! I knew my dad was going to kill me, the baby, the nigga, and fall out with my uncle, which I couldn't let happen. I went on with my life and kept quiet. I didn't say anything to no one. I was very confused and I really didn't know what to do.

I went to work the next day and my friend girl teased me by saying, "Girl you're picking up a few pounds." My first thought was to run into the dressing room and cry. I just went to the dressing room and balled up in a chair. As I sat there balled up my friend girl came into the dressing room. Right away she said, "Lovely what's wrong? You're not pregnant?" I responded, "I think I am and because I was afraid of what my dad will do I couldn't tell anyone." I sat there crying my eyes out, while saying, "I thought that having a baby is suppose to make you feel good and happy!" Then I asked my friend girl, "Why do I feel so sad?" She asked me if I had missed my period. I told her I missed two cycles so far. When we got off of work that night she went with me to my uncle's house and asked him if it was okay for me to spend a couple of days with her. She was indeed a true friend to me when I needed her.

It took her a few days but she got me in this clinic on North Avenue and sure enough I was now expecting my first baby at the age of fourteen. I was ready to go home because I knew my dad was going to kill me. As the months started going by my stomach was getting bigger. I started wearing big baggie clothes and one to three girdles so that no one could tell I was expecting. Like my girl friend said, "I could only hide it for so long." I was at school participating in gym, trying not to over work myself, and draw attention on the pain that I was feeling in my stomach; that didn't work. The next thing I remembered was I woke up in a hospital bed; every one knew now. A social worker got involved in my case because the doctor had a feeling I was having problems at home. The doctor especially felt this way because I went through such great extremes to try and hide my pregnancy. It seemed like once the girdles came off I started blowing up fast. I had hid my pregnancy so well that no one knew. Therefore, once I removed my girdles my pregnancy was a total shock to a lot of people. My stomach was out there and I could not hide it anymore.

The doctor placed me on total bed rest at about five months. All the junk food I was eating and not really taking care of myself like I should have been caused me problems! The doctor was going to admit me into the hospital until I gave birth. How I cried because I didn't want to be in no hospital and not for four month. Then my doctor came up with an alternative plan than staying in the hospital. Once I heard his alternative plan, I told him to give me a few days. I promised him that my mother will come take care of me. Talk about putting my fat foot in my mouth, I knew she wasn't. I was just lying to myself. My doctor made all the arrangement to have me admitted on my next appointment. He told me if I didn't find anyone to take care of me while I'm at home on bed rest, then during my next check up he was going to admit me to the hospital.

A few days went by and I still haven't call and asked my mother will she come up here. I knew I had to do something because I didn't want to be lock up in no hospital. I remember picking up the phone several times attempting to call my mother. I would sometimes dial all the numbers except for the last one and then hang up the phone. I was too scared to call my mom. I wasn't for sure if my mom knew I was pregnant or not. I was also afraid that she was going to hate me because I was pregnant. I was worrying myself sick but I knew I had to call her. I picked up the phone and did it. I was talking to my mom for awhile. I was surprise to hear her response to my pregnancy. I then start feeling bad because she said, "Baby I'm not disappointed in you for getting pregnant. I'm hurt because you felt you couldn't come to me with your problem."

I cried and told my mom what the doctor said and she said, "I'll be there in the morning." She actually came and she came without a problem. I remember the day she arrived well. She told my dad, "Hubbard, I'm only here because Lovely needs me. After she has the baby and get back on her feet I'm going back to Chicago." I was really glad my mom was here with me. When I saw her I squeezed and hugged her really tight and cried because it felt so good to see her. As she rubbed my stomach I remember her saying, "So you got yourself in a little mess here." Of course, that moment was the start of catching up on many missed mama and daughter talks.

My mom was an angel, I really love her, and she did everything for me; she even ran my bathwater. I remember while I was in the tub my mom would continue coming back and forth to check on me. She knew I'll get too relax and go to sleep in the water. She would say, "Baby we don't want to have no more crazy accidents. Ok!" I would answer her by saying, "Mom, I'm woke." Let me explain to you why she said that. Once I get in the tub, I would lay back in it, and let the hot water slowly run until the water is smoking hot around my neck. I mean the tub will be filled to the top of the rim. All I used to do is relax in it because the water would be so hot that if I move it'll burn me. Therefore, I would just lay back in the tub until the water cooled off. I'll slowly raise one of my legs till my big toe could touch the hot water handle and keep pushing it until the water turns off. Then I'll very slowly lower my leg back into the water.

This one time I went to sleep while I was in the tub and it didn't take me long before the water took control of my relaxed body. Heavy as I was, I guess I slowly sledded down in the bathtub and under the water. I woke up and came from under the water slashing and hollering for my mama. I was coughing and gushing for my breath in hope that I did not in the bathtub. I had the door lock, so my mom started beating and pushing on the bathroom door until she pushed it open. I was afraid but more embarrassed than anything; however, my baby and I were alright. Every since then my mom would always check on me to make sure I didn't go to sleep while I was in the tub.

I was only allowed to go to the bathroom; I laid back and got bigger and bigger as the months slowly went by. Believe me my mom made sure that lying on my back was all I did. In the daytime she would fix my cover and pillow on the large sofa right in her eye view. If my mom looked through the house and didn't see me lying there on the sofa she was coming to look for me. I kind of liked the attention but I was getting very bored just lying around the house. Well, another good thing came out of my bed rest was that my mom was home for some of the major holidays. My dad was a pretty good cook but there was nothing like the aroma that mom put in the house. I remember how everyone loved mom's pineapple upside down cake. I did too but lucky me I was allergic to pineapples. Therefore mom had to make sure she cooked another kind of cake I could eat. The Christmas she was in town taking care of me she cooked her famous pineapple upside down cake. I remembered that day clearly. She was very tired from taking care of me and she was trying to get Christmas dinner together, which lead me into having the wrong craving.

That night after my mom was done cooking and went to bed I stayed on the sofa because I couldn't sleep. When a female gets pregnant she gets all these crazy cravens for certain foods to eat. Well, I was having one of those craving attacks and I could not sleep until I got what I was craving. I was determined to fulfill my craving. Well, that night was not my lucky night to have one of my craving attacks. The smell of those pineapples in the air wouldn't let me sleep. I said to myself, "Maybe just one won't hurt?" That one lead to me eating the whole can of pineapples. After I finished the whole can, I tipped toed my big ass back on the sofa and went to sleep. Later that night I began feeling as if someone had stuck me in a hot oven filled with itching powder. I started scratching and pulling the cover off of me. The last thing I thought it would have been was from me eating those damn pineapples.

I ran me some bath water; I thought it would help but it made me feel worst. My mom came to the bathroom door and asked me why I didn't wake her up to make my bath water. I told her she needed the rest and besides running my own bath water wasn't that much work for me to do. As she left the door my mom told me, if I need her to call and not to stay in the tub to long. I responded, "I'm not," while rubbing my body hard and ruff. I also told her I needed to get in the water to just cool my body off some. If my mom knew why I really was in the tub she'll twist my neck. I continued with my bath and then went and lay on the sofa. I did manage to get some sleep but the burning and itching didn't stop. I remembered being awaken by my mom voice saying, "Alright now, which one of you night walkers ate a can of my pineapples?"

I just laid there with the cover over my head waiting to see who was going to admit to eating them but no one did. Everyone kept saying, "I didn't." I was under the cover scratching and laughing but it wasn't funny about how I was feeling. I was too afraid to tell that I was the guilty one, so I stayed under the covers suffering while those damn pineapples were doing a job on me. As the day went on I would peak out from under the cover to see if the coast was clear, so I could go to the bathroom with out being seen. My mom always fixed my food and brought it to me. Normally I would eat my food right away but this time I told her to just sit it down and I'll eat it in a minute. I stayed under the cover the whole time. What she really didn't know was that I didn't want her to see my face because it looked as if I had been beat by a whip. I had these red elevated whips all over my face and body from me scratching like crazy. I knew once my mom seen me she was going to freak out. Why couldn't she just kept on cooking and left me alone.

My mom kept asking me, "Lovely, is you okay?" I would answer her as if I was asleep and say something like, "Yeah, I'm just tired." Oh, but that wasn't good enough for my mom. She had to see for herself if I was actually okay or not. My mom later that evening started calling my name again. She said, "Lovely, is you sure you're okay? You have not been getting up too much today?" My mom was always a good analyzer; she notice when a change in a person occurs immediately. She then came over to the sofa where I was laying at and said, "You got to get up and walk some, even if it's only to the bathroom just to show me you're ok." As she started pulling on the cover I was saying, "Mom I'm ok." I was hoping she would have accepted my answer and go back into the kitchen, or anywhere as long as she wasn't messing with me. My mom started pulling at the covers even harder saying, "Come on Lovely! Get up. You gonna make that baby lazy."

So now my mom and I were playing tug a war with the covers. She wanted the covers off of me bad and I wanted them to stay on me. Mom being my mom got what she wanted and pulled the covers off of my red blistered itching body. First thing she yelled was "baby what's wrong with you?" She was worried because my mom knew I couldn't stand a lot of heat; the heat breaks my body out. Plus she remember that last night I told her I was getting in the tub to cool off, so right away she thought I had broken out because the house was to hot for me. Seeing how upset my mom was I sat up and said, "Mom, Mom, I'm ok. I ate your can of pineapples." After I explained everything to my mom she didn't get mad. She told me that I suffered enough and helped me get myself together to go to the doctor.

Well, I missed Christmas dinner with the family because I had to stay in the hospital for a few days. However, my mom had cook so much food till it was still some left when I came home. I learned from that experience to resist some of my pregnancy craven, especially the ones that I am allergic to. A new day has come and my due date wasn't too far a way. I know these next few months will just fly by. Then again, I'm really not ready to deal with the pain of childbirth! As big as I am I knew this baby was going to rip me open every which way but loose. I believe it's about that time too. All through my pregnancy I've been having all kinds of pains. I was in so much pain, that I use to say how was I'm going to know if I was in labor or not. My doctor and mom use to tell me, "Believe me, you'll know." For some reason it seemed as if this baby just loved having me in the hospital during the holidays. It was the week of Easter weekend and the house was rather warm so I had a hard time getting comfortable. I remember moving from room to room lying in everyone's bed in the house and balling up in it. I also moved from one sofa and chair to another I seen in the house. My mom would come find me and ask me if I was ok and like always I would tell her, "Yeah!" I didn't want to tell her I was hurting again considering we had numbers of false labors just because I've gotten some really bad pains.

This time I couldn't understand why these pains wouldn't stop, so I figure I'll get up and move around some hoping just maybe they will go away. My older brother had finally left so I went into his room to lie down. The prefect bed, only his room was too hot for me. I decided to close his bedroom door and let his window up some so I could get some cold air in the room. Yes, it did cool off my body some but it wasn't helping the pains. I laid there and rocked holding my stomach praying for the pains to stop. Wishful thinking, on my behalf the pains gotten worst. My mom found me again and asked me was I ok? This time I said, "I don't know? My stomach hurts and it won't stop!" She then sat beside me to feel how my baby was balling up in my stomach as I had a pain. My mom then told me to go to the bathroom to see if I had a bloody show. As I try to get up I got a really bad pain that made me ball and fall back down to the bed. My mom seen what she wanted to she told me I was gong to have my baby. The pain felt like some one was pulling all my insides out. The pains were coming back to back; I couldn't even stand up right to walk. Good thing my older brother came home because I don't know how my mom would have got me out his room. I was having really bad pains. As soon as they started lightening up I tried to move a little faster only to get a few feet before the pain got stronger again and made me ball back down.

After all the hard work of trying to get me out the room, my mom did finally get me to the hospital. Well, my job wasn't done yet. My blood pressure was at the boiling point; it was ready to explode, sending my baby and me over to another life. Plus I had toxemia, which was a lot of water that had me blew up like a jellyfish. It seemed like once I got to the hospital my pains began to get even worst. I just knew I wasn't going to be much longer before I had my baby. Remember you talking about me; once I feel that things are and might be smooth sailing for me a strong wind come out of no where and tangle up my sail.

Who said that labor was supposed to last three days? I went in on a Tuesday and had my baby on Good Friday. I gave birth to an 8-½ pound baby girl. She was a little doll; she was my little angel from heaven with cold black eyes. After all the pain she put me through I had to give her a special name. So I gave my baby girl a name that means a beautiful goddess, an angel from heaven, strong and full of life. I was to stay in the hospital for three more days after my baby was born but I changed the rules a little to fix my needs. I was glad I did finally have my baby. She is a blessing to me but then again I was even sadder.

I knew once I got out the hospital and back on my feet my mom was going to go back to Chicago and I didn't want that to happen. So I had to come up with a way to keep my mom here longer. I did come up with a plan that only worked for a moment. By the time I went home my baby was almost two weeks old. This is what I did to stay in the hospital longer, each time the doctor said I could go home I would make myself sick by crying all night, which caused my blood pressure to go up higher. Sometimes when the nurse turned her head I would take the temperature of my hand so I will have a high fever reading. Guess what? It worked! The only thing I didn't like about my little keep mama here longer plan was that the doctors would go digging all up in side of my vagina. The doctors will say they had to see if I was hemorrhaging and they were looking for blood clots.

The doctors' also mentioned they didn't understand why I was having high fevers and they didn't want to take no chances on sending me home. I was getting tired of the doctors digging all up in me with their hands so I went into a deep stage of depression. Now, I didn't really care about what happened no more because I knew I couldn't keep my mom here with me forever. Well, the doctor said I was good to go home. I really got sick and I didn't try any of my tricks. I had a really high fever; I remember the nurses packing me in ice to help my body cool down faster. This time I was afraid because it seem as if I wasn't was passing away; I was not aware of my surrounding and everything seemed unreal. I learned from that experience not to play no more pretend games because they may come true. After a few days I went home sad. My mom had gotten a call about her apartment in Chicago and had to go sooner then she had plan on. All I could do was cry. For many days and months, even now I sit and cry inside because I remember how my mom put her whole life to the side for me. Mom, I love you so dearly and you mean the world to me. I still treasure all the compassion and caring that my mom did for me. I would sometimes rock and cry while holding my baby tight, saying, "mama loves you," over and over again.

I guess I was reminding and telling myself my mama does love me. While at the same time I was telling my new born baby girl I love her too. I hope when my daughter grows up we have a special close mother and daughter relationship. I promise to always be there for her anytime she needs me.

Chapter Sixteen
"What A Load To Handle"

MOTHERHOOD WAS COMING along just fine but a more serious problem was being boiled for me, which I didn't know about. I had gotten back in school but not yet to go back to dancing. A few more months went by, I became a year older. I was going to school full time and taking care of a baby at fifteen; this was a full time job for me. My dad would watch my baby while I was at school but I had to be home as soon as school was over, or else I will hear his mouth and everybody else in the house at that time. I appreciated my dad watching my daughter so I could go back to school but I wished it was my mama instead. You see my dad's girlfriend and I didn't really see eye to eye, which was part of my problem. It was as if whatever she says goes and my dad went along with everything she said. My dad started nagging me about my baby's daddy. I would tell him, "What my baby daddy do or don't do for my baby is my business." Then he started talking about how hard it is for him to be trying to watch a little baby.

I started taking my daughter to her daddy so he could watch her while I was in school. Of course, that didn't work out to long because he started working first shift. That means I had to fall back on my dad to watch my baby for me again but I still wasn't going to kiss his or his girl friend ass either. As soon as school let out I would catch the bus over to my dad's girlfriend's house and get my baby. I remember how sometimes they'll ask me to let her stay and my dad will drop her off on his way to work. I wouldn't because I already knew how my dad felt about watching my daughter. He uses to say, "You lay up and had her, so you keep her." I knew it was my dad's girlfriend that was talking him into asking me to let my baby stay longer. I use to say, "NO! NO! NO!" I would get my baby things; wrap my little angel of love up, and out the door to catch the bus. With me nothing seems to last to long. My dad started to complaining even more about not getting enough rest and what all he was doing for my baby and me. I didn't want to hear that! I stop going to school as much as I use too. I would go to school sometimes, maybe two or three days out of the week because my dad needed to get him some rest so he could go to work at night.

I knew my daughter was my responsibility but my dad was trying to take over. Believe me my baby girl had her share of my problems too. It seems as if everyday my dad and I were arguing about my daughter. I use to tell him, "Daddy this is my daughter! I say what goes on with her!" It was like my dad was trying for some strange reason to take control of my daughter but I wasn't going to allow it. The bad thing about everything was he complained everyday about her keeping him from doing the things he had to do. The bomb exploded when my dad reminded me that I was still a minor and had to do like he said. Did I listen? NO! I felt he was trying to change from being the warden of this prison he created to being my lord and master controlling daddy?

At that time, I had so many rebellious emotions towards my dad that I use to ask God, to forgive me because I felt like killing him. Only God knew exactly what my dad was and what he had put me through. I only putted up with his shit because he was my dad and deep inside I still loved him regardless of the way he treated me. I really pissed him and his girlfriend off when I started getting money and doing for my baby and me. This way he couldn't throw that, "what he was doing for us mess in my face no more!" I figured out a way to joggle those few days I went to school and my dancing job, while also paying a baby sitter. I must admit I was bringing my baby in the house late hours but she wasn't missing any care or sleep that she needed. My dad didn't have any rights telling me I couldn't take my own baby out the house, especially when he had a problem with watching her. I use to say to myself, "He better be lucky that he is my dad. No wonder my mom couldn't deal with him no longer." Seeing that he couldn't control me my dad started talking about how much older my daughter's daddy was in comparison to my age. I was a minor and my baby's daddy was ten years older than me. My dad said to me and others, "That is considered rape!" My dad was seeking control over me and became very evil just to get it. He had my baby's daddy locked up for <u>statutory</u> rape.

I told the judge that my baby's daddy was under the impression I was nineteen and plus I had false identification to prove my false age. It was ordered that my baby's daddy had to stay away from me until I became eighteen. Also, he was not to have any contact with my baby unless it was approved by my dad because I was a minor in his custody and so was my baby. Well, that didn't work out to well because my dad said, every time he caught my baby's daddy around this house he was going to have him lock up! I couldn't understand why my dad was so hard on me? I went along with his little game but I still did what I wanted to do around his work schedule. Life went on and everything was going along just fine; I was going to school, seeing who I wanted to, dancing, and my daddy still didn't know yet.

As the year went by I was so proud of my daughter because she was trying to talk and walking. I guess you can say she was doing this all at the right time because I found out I was pregnant with my second child. I had no one to blame but myself. I handled this pregnancy a lot better; I didn't get sick like I did with the first one.

At the end of my ninth month I had another baby girl. She was a bigger baby girl, nine-lbs and 14-½ oz. She was my great big bundle of joy. She was given a name that means a special gift of joy from God. My two girls gave me life and a reason to live; they were my inspiration and strength that kept me going. I'm now sixteen with two beautiful little girls and was proud of it. Like they always say, "life is what you make out of it!" My life was stable for now. I did the same thing every day but most of my time I gave to my two girls. After the pleasure and enjoyment I got doing things with my girls I would feed them and get them ready for bed. Once they were asleep I knew that they weren't going to wake up until morning.

One of my older brothers' bedroom was just across the hall from mines. When I leave at night to go dancing I would leave my bedroom door crack so he could hear my girls if they should wake up or start crying. When my older brother changed his work shift I paid my younger brothers and sister to keep an eye on my girls as they slept. I then will come home, go to bed only to get a few hours of sleep before I had to get up for school and get my girls ready. It was a load on me but I brought it on my self. Now remember this is my life, we all know how great my luck has not been. My dad started creeping around in my room as if he was looking something. He did start asking my younger siblings if they knew where I was going at night. Now I'm thinking to myself what does my dad know? Has somebody been telling him something? Either way I knew I had to stay a few steps ahead of him because I didn't want him to take my girls away from me like he always have threaten to do. I was more confused because he hadn't been talking to me lately either. Well, one night I found out what the big mystery was. This one night on my way to work I stopped down to this one tavern where I use to dance at. However, I stopped a few days ago, lucky me. My former boss called me to the back and told me, "Some man has been coming in here asking about you but he called you Lovely."

Not knowing whom it could have been I asked my former boss what you told him. He said, "I told him I didn't have anyone by that name working for me. The man left but he kept coming back for a couple of night in a row. The last time he came he talked to one of the other dancers." I said, "I don't know who that is. Maybe it was just one of my old customers!" I told my former boss, "Next time just tell him I'll be back in a few weeks," and then I left to go to the tavern where I was now dancing. You see I was out there bad in the go-go dancing life that I didn't stay at one place for more then two weeks at a time. By me moving around like I did, some of my former bosses would tell me that customers were coming in asking specifically for me. If it's one of my good spending customers I'll tell them in advance or leave word where I was going to be dancing when I left one tavern.

So who this man was that was looking for me I can't say. That night at the tavern I was kind of slow, not many customers were out; this gave me more time to work on some of my schoolwork. I made a few dollars that night but nobody was gladder then I was when it was time to go home. I got in the bed and kissed my two little girls good night. Then I stretched my arm across them both to hug them and went to sleep. As the year came and was almost gone I was still living an abnormal life for a sixteen year old. Later that year I also found out that my second baby's daddy was a big hoe so he had to go. So I was a beautiful single girl looking for a good-looking man. I didn't have to look to far considering that it was lots of good-looking man coming down to the tavern where I danced. The only problem was I was afraid of them because they were calling themselves pimps and they had all these women on the street selling their bodies.

I was already in the fast lifestyle but being a street hoe was another lifestyle I choose not to have part of. I flirted with some of the guys but that was as far as it ever went. It was this one so call pimp that always seems to find where I was dancing at who would always let his present be known. This so call pimp was ok but I was afraid of him because he had so many women. He would talk that I want you for my lady shit to me all the time. I would look at him like he was crazy and ask him, "What do you want with me? Look like you got enough women to me?" He would tell me, "Those are my hoes. Every pimp needs a main lady and I choose you." I told him, "Thanks for the honor but I don't need a pimp. I have two female pimps at home that get all my money."

From that night on that so call pimp became a good customer of mine. Every time he came in he would order me this hundred-dollar bottle of champagne. Impressive! Yes, he start paying me more than ever before! This so call pimp went from bringing me stuff to bringing both me and my girls stuff; he bought my girls candy and pretty little outfits. Impressing I thought! Yes I was trying to win my heart! This so call pimp was trying hard to learn how to get to my heart. I must say he was doing a damn good job of it. Being always high on cocaine and sometimes speed I wasn't thinking straight one night. This so call pimp decided to make me an offer that I couldn't refuse and I accepted. Remember I was about teasing male and female I didn't care. Their money was the same color.

This time I got caught up in one of my own traps. I forgotten for a minute the charm this so call pimp uses to get his ladies. He had my nose spreading wide open and breathing into his trap. He bought me little gifts and took me out to eat all the time. I must say, "I see why he had all the hoes that he has."He really knew how to treat a woman; like a queen and I was enjoying every bit of this so call pimp's spoiling me treatments. He was giving me a whole different view about how I looked at a pimp. I started to think that maybe pimps are not bad after all. According, to the pimp his offers were just to show me how a real lady is suppose to be treated. Everything was great, superior, to good to be true. This so call pimp made me feel so good that I was almost willing to move in with him up until this one night.

He came down to the tavern like always and sat in his usual seat. I remember how I use to want to dance all up on this so call pimp but he would tell me, "not now. It's a time and place for everything. I just like looking at you." A real gentleman, I was even more impressed by him every day. Well, this one night after I came down off the stage he asked me if I would dance privately for him. Right a way without thinking about the answer I said, "Yeah!" This so call pimp bought me a bottle of champagne and told me he will be back to pick me up. I was kind of disappointed because he left. I don't know why but it was just something about his presence that made me feel so good that my joy showed in my dancing. I had this strong desire to have him. I use to image what he was like in bed. All that night I kept thinking about getting laid by him.

Well the tavern closed and it looked as if this so called pimp had finally let me down. After waiting and continuously looking out the door one of the other customers asked if he could give me a ride home so I accepted. As I was going to get in the other customer's car another car pulled up beside us and someone said, "Baby please don't do that. I'm so sorry that I'm late." I said to myself, "He came back," and smiled. I told the other customer who was going to take me home, thanks for looking out but my ride is here. Then I left his care and got in the car with this so call pimp. All while we were driving I never once thought to ask him where we were going.

This so call pimp took it upon his self to explain to me why he was late. I said nothing as he began telling me how he had to go and check his trap and get his money. Dirty thoughts were really deep in my mind when this so call pimp pulled up behind this hotel. As he came around the car to open my door I was thinking to myself, Yes! I'm glad you're thinking like me because I've been wanting to be somewhere along with you all night. Just as long as I make it home in the morning before my girls' wake up I knew our night at the hotel was going to be ok. It was a really nice hotel considering I have never been to a hotel before with a man. He was a real gentleman while we sat and talk. Then I sat my wild high ass on the bed and asked him to join me. What I open my big mouth for. Yes, he came and we began with the kissing, rubbing, and touching then to the bumping and grinning. When he started with the sucking and licking it was on. My body was feeling things that even I couldn't explain. It was as if my whole body was like butter melting in a hot pan over a fire and believe me this so call pimp was hot!

I must say this so call pimp knew how to turn the flames up high in your body. Everything felt all good. He had a strong dark solid and rock hard body that every female would want to enjoy but this time I met my match. Now while this so call pimp is bumping and grinning on me I'm saying to myself, "I hope that's his bank roll I'm feeling because damn, he's big!" Fearing that this so call pimp was packing a penis like a horse I had to see it because if I was feeling what I thought I was feeling, he wasn't going to put that in me! By the time it came down to the real part of our rolling around in the bed this so call pimp had practically undressed me. Yes, while he was rubbing and bumping against me he was taking my clothes a loose and off. I was half nude already.

I was asking him to get up so I could finish taking my clothes off. He told me just lay there and let him remove them. That wasn't the real reason I wanted him to get up, I wanted to see the size of this so call pimp's penis. The way he continued to lick, kiss, and suck all over me, my body melt with inner burning, desiring, pleasing, and uncontrollable feelings of wanting the body of this so call pimp more. It was too hard for me to tell him to stop. All the time I'm still feeling his big, long, hard, fat, and heavy pickle up against my body. I was wondering to myself if I'll be able to handle it? Then I started to think to myself, "If I can have a big ass baby come out of my vagina, I know I should be able to handle his oversized penis."

My sexual hormones was raising to the highest desirable point as I was getting very hot from this so call pimp sliding his private part in and out between my thighs. The rush I was getting I don't know if it was from the cocaine or the speed, maybe both or maybe it the so call pimp had me high on his love performance! Not wanting to truly accept the fact that this so called pimp was really turning my body and me on with some of the most unexplainable feelings. It was as if I was floating on clouds; my body seemed so light as if everything wasn't real. I could fadelessly hear his voice off and on asking me, "Can I put it in now?" I kept moaning in the heat of passion, "No, not yet!" While at the same time saying to myself, "Why am I trying to fool myself? If this so call pimp got what I think, he's going to rip my ass wide open!" Then out of the clear I said, "Now, give it to me now!" What the hell I say that for?

No soon the so call pimp try to put his private part in me I hit back down on earth to reality real quick and screamed, "Oh My God! Stop! Take it out! What the hell is that?" It seemed as if the more I tried to pull myself out of his grip he had around my body the stronger he got. The man private part was shamefully big. No wonder he has his women on the streets because they didn't want to have to deal with the torture of what he was packing in his pants. Of course, he didn't want to stop or get up. This so call pimp kept telling me, "I'll be gentle to make it easier for you to handle." I told that fool, "how in the hell can you make it easier? That thing is too big!" He having that special charm talked me into letting him continue trying to put that big ass thing in me. Believe me I paid anguishly that time for opening my mouth. I knew when I accepted that offer that I couldn't refuse it was going to get my ass in trouble.

No but I wanted to be miss hot ass so now my moans of heated passion has all turned into screams of tormenting pain. Every time he tried to push it in a little, off the bed I would slid but he would grab me and pull me back to him. God what I had gotten my self into? This so call pimp had my ass ready to jump out the window to get away from that thing he had that was suppose to be what they call a penis. Wrong, I think someone took one of those light poles and sew it in place of his private part! It was so big that it didn't even look real when I did see it! That was something you only see in those X-rated movies and I've never seen one that big! This so call pimp finally decided to give up after numerous times of trying to enter my vagina without success and me begging him to please stop! Not knowing what to say to him behind that experience I got dress so he could drop me off at home. While he was driving I remember him asking me, "I hope I can still see you?" I said to my self, "I hope I never see you again!"

I was so quiet during the ride home that you could have heard a piece of hay drop. He kept asking me was I ok? I was saying to myself, "Would you be ok after what you just try to put me through?" I was so glad to see my house because I was to embarrass to look, face, or even be around this so call pimp. All I wanted to do was get out his car and go in the house. I was about to open the door then the so call pimp said to me, "No, wait, I'll get that for you." Even after the torture he put me through this so call pimp was still trying to be a gentleman. Only this time I was to a shame to be impressed. I said thank you while he held the door for me as I got out the car and went into the house. I just lay in the bed and softly cried because as much as I liked this so call pimp I knew I couldn't see him again. Mainly, because I couldn't perform the womanly duties that he would be expecting out of me as his lady. All that day in school I thought about this so call pimp and what had happened last night. I knew when I went to work tonight he was going to be there and I wasn't ready to face him, at least not yet. I knew I had to come up with a good reason so I wouldn't have to go to work. That evening I called and told my boss my babysitter didn't show up so I wouldn't be in. I believe that was the saddest day of my life because I had for the first time can say I was in love and it was with a so call pimp.

Even thou he didn't have the kind of job I had expected my man to have, this so call pimp knew how to treat his woman; like a lady. What hurts is the only thing this so call pimp asked of me I couldn't do. The size of his private part makes him somebody I can't do anything with sexually. I really wanted to be with this so call pimp as his main lady but I knew I could loose him because I couldn't perform in bed as his lady. The man was just too big. So I just stayed at home with my girls trying to forget about him. Well, one day off of work turned in to a week because I was just to depress to go back down to the tavern. I guess it was because that was where I met this so call pimp and I really didn't want to be hurt by the happy memories he and I had shared. I went back dancing but at one of my boss's other taverns. I didn't tell him the reason why just I couldn't come back down there. This way I didn't have to worry about running into this so call pimp and going through those heartaches again from seeing him. True I missed him a lot but I knew I had to get over him. I must say it was some good looking guys at the other tavern that was helping me do just that.

After a few weeks dancing at the other tavern I thought I had start seeing some faces from the pass. Not for sure I just continue being me; Luscious. I flirted with all the customers because that was how I got my hustle on. Then one night a face that I knew came into my life again. Remember my good-looking guy friend's god brother I talked about earlier and he gave me the name of my track face attacker? Well, he came into the tavern while I was on the stage and was I shock; surprised and kind of glad to see him. When I got off the stage my good-looking guy friend's brother called me to his table. He ordered me a drink so I sat down with him and we began to talk. My good-looking guy friend's brother was telling me how his cousin and a few of his friends had told him I was dancing down here. He said he didn't believe it and had to come see for himself.

One thing lead to another. Then he asked if he could take me home later. I told him sure.

It was so good to see him; we talked about the past and what we were both doing with our life now. I really enjoyed talking to my good-looking guy friend's brother but most of all I was so glad he didn't bring up that night of my horrible attack. Even thou I knew my good-looking guy friend's brother thought about it but I was hoping he didn't bring it up. I guess he had feelings and didn't want to reopen that nightmare I went through. He took me home that night and we started to see more of each other. He was whom I needed to get my mind off of that so call pimp I was moaning over. I stopped dancing for a few months so I could spend more time with my kids. My good-looking guy friend's brother and I relationship was ok even thou my father didn't approve of it. I still found sometime for my good-looking guy friend's brother when I wanted to see him. We use to meet up at the parks or over to his brother's house. He was really nice but I wasn't trying to get to serious with him.

After that experienced with that so call pimp I promised myself not to let another man get the better part of my heart again! Only thing about seeing my good-looking guy friend's brother was he had a specific hour each day for us to meet. Just like a man I said but I went along with the program only to find out that the reason we meet other places was because he was living with a female. Oh yes, he got dump very fast so again it was just my kids and I. My good-looking guy friend's brother only made me realized I really couldn't put my trust in no man. Well life wasn't the greatest but I had much worst. I was raising my kids and was back in school regular. I was proud to be a mother of two, even thou it was a job but I joggled it around to try and make the best for my kids. I was now seventeen years old and my dad still was hard on me with his demanding restrictions. Like always I played along with his rules but I still did things the way I wanted to. After my dad found out that

I was sneaking around seeing my oldest daughter's daddy I wasn't allow to go anywhere. You know me, I had to come up with a plan because I didn't want to take a chance of loosing my kids. Remember my one friend girl I danced with? Well, she became a part of my well thought out mastered plan.

My dad always liked my friend girl because he said she was very respectable and nice. She had three kids of her own at that time so I would go over to her house sometimes and met my baby's daddy. When I seen that my dad was approving of me visiting with my friend girl I had her lying like I was staying the weekend with her so I could stay over my baby's daddy house, which he shared with his brother. My baby's daddy was much older then I was and I wasn't about to go through that locking him up stuff again with my dad. Nothing good seems to last forever in my life. My baby's daddy brother tried to get in the bed with me one night while I was sleep so that was the end of me staying over there.

Spring came around and I remember I was going to take the kids to the park. This one-day I guess wasn't a good day for my dad or me because all kinds of hell broke out. I remember walking through the house downstairs after getting off the phone. I had told my baby's daddy to meet me at the park. Now I'm not sure if my dad over heard my conversation or if he was just pissed at the world. My dad was telling me I wasn't going to take my kids no where. I told him, "Daddy, I'll be eighteen in a few more months then you can't tell me what I can or can't do with my kids no more!" What I say that for because then my dad started hollering, "Oh, you talking back!" I was trying to tell him I wasn't talking back to him but he didn't want to hear nothing I had to say. My dad began yelling and pushing on me. Remember that favorite phrase of his that I couldn't understand why he uses to say to me? Well, it came back this time even stronger.

He started yelling and pushing me around. Then he grab this three layer old time barber razor strap and said as he swing it hitting me anywhere on my body that he could, "I'm gonna beat you like your daddy should had!" Except what my dad didn't know this time I wasn't going to take anymore of his unexplained beatings. My dad and I wrestle a little then I pushed him really hard and he fell into the tub. I got away from my dad and ran upstairs and locked the door because I knew if I would had stayed downstairs with my dad as mad as I was I would have tried to hurt him. My dad didn't like the fact that I had over powered him. He got on the phone and called my aunts on me, as if I was so out of control but he had failed to tell them how he was trying to beat me. They tried to talk to me like I wasn't shit but I had made my mind up and I wasn't about to accept their attitude neither. My aunts really pissed me off when they started talking down on my mom. I just told them where they can get off at and if anyone of them even thought for a moment that they were bad enough to come and whop my butt to come on with it.

I let them know that I wasn't about to lay down for no ass whipping. If they raised their hands at me they were getting hands laid back on them. I hope they didn't think they weren't too old to get my hands raised back at them. My dad was talking big stuff but like I told him, "I'm not accepting no ass kicking from him, his sisters, and nobody else." I remember how my dad wouldn't hang up the phone downstairs so I couldn't call my mom and tell her what happened. I played his phone game for as long as he did it but remembered he had to go too work. I said, "I'll call my mama then." After my dad went to work I called my mom and told her everything. She mom told me some shocking news. As I was telling my mom what had happened she said, "oh my God. Baby I'm so sorry I put you in that situation!" I was trying to tell my mom that it wasn't her fault. She said, "Your daddy is taking our separation out on you because we look so much alike."

My mom said when she was younger my dad use to tell her his favorite phrase too. Of course she said he told her, "I'm gonna beat you like your daddy should had," when they use to sometimes get into it. So now the mystery of my dad haunting phrase was solved. The next day he tried to talk that stuff again and I told him, "I'm not my mama and I'm not gonna let you beat on me anymore." Every since that day my dad never raised anything at me to hit me again. I knew now what I had to do. I had to leave my dad's house but with my kids. I felt it was super because the years was going by quickly and I couldn't wait until I got eighteen so I could take my kids and get the hell out of my dad's house. It wasn't not that I didn't love him but my lifestyle wasn't going to stand for no one to tell me what to do. I knew May 30 would be here before I knew it so without my dad knowing I started looking for me an apartment. They were hard to find plus people didn't want to rent to me because of my age. I even went and filled out an application for the low-income housing.

After all that running around as the month came closer I still was unsuccessful in finding me an apartment but I didn't give up. My dad was a different person; he was kinder. He knew and seen how badly I wanted to leave his house. I remember when my dad found out I was pregnant with my third child and I was trying to find me a place to move, he suggested that I stayed until I had my baby and got back on my feet. I wasn't for sure if should take that chance then again I really wasn't trying to find out. I felt like maybe now I was getting too close to eighteen I didn't have to go by his rules anymore, plus he knew no one was going to keep up and take care of the house hold needs the way I did. Besides that I was my younger siblings' second mama and they wanted me to stay. I explained to them I'm going to leave but not just yet and anytime they needed me all they had to do was call. As summer slowly came close to an end I gave birth to a premature baby boy. My son was coming out with his shoulder in the way and if I tried to push him out he was going to break his little shoulder.

The doctor told me later what was going on and why they didn't want me to push my baby out. The horror came when the doctor said, "Ok, go." Let me explain a little. I knew it was something different about my delivery because I never had x-rays taken while I was in labor and they never strapped me down on the delivery table. Plus there were doctors, nurses, and a lot of other people with mask all around me. They brought in all kinds of machines that had me worrying. At first I thought my baby was dead so right away I said, "What's wrong with my baby?" The doctor would answer each time I asked that question, "Don't worry your baby is going to be alright." What did he mean by my baby is going to be alright? I knew then that there was something very wrong! My head was constantly going trying to watch as everyone was talking and moving fast around me. The way they were acting I didn't know what to expect out of them. Like I said, "I knew something was wrong and different about this delivery.

After the doctor that was standing down between my legs got back my x-rays I remember hearing him say, "It's what I thought." Again, I hollered as I was in pain, "What is it? What's wrong with my baby?" The one doctor started rubbing and pushing on my stomach as he said, "Don't worry Lovely, your baby is going to be alright," and behind those words he said, "Ok, go." Hands were coming from everywhere attacking me and they covered my face with a gas mask at the same time. The doctor that was standing between my legs took both of his hands and stuck them up in my vagina bracing my baby by the head and the shoulder pushing him. These other two doctors were pushing down on my baby butt and back as they turned my baby around completely while he was still in my uterus. I didn't know what they were trying to do to me. I was thinking real crazy. I thought maybe they were going to steal my baby away from me.

I began trying to fight my way out of those damn straps as I held my breath to keep from inhaling as less of that gas as I could. It worked for a moment but they got me strapped back down on the table. Half spaced out on that gas I did it again only to be re-strapped back down. As I tried to fight it, the gas was doing its job, and I had to accept the fact that I was slowly going to sleep. By this time I was almost totally out of it but the last thing I remember hearing before I went into my deep sleep was one of the doctors yelled, "He's not breathing!" As I went into a deep sleep I do know for a fact that I did delivered a baby boy and when I woke up the doctors told me that he was born dead. I finally did wake up out of that sleep in which the gas had put me under. The first thing I did was run to the nursery looking for my baby boy. I started getting upset because the last thing I remember hearing was my baby wasn't breathing. I even looked in the infant's intensive care unit for my newborn child but he wasn't there. I then wildly went to the nurse's station and asked the nurses where my baby was.

At first they try to give me a hard time. I'll never forget how even one nurse said, "Are you sure you had a baby?" Man did she press the wrong button! Angry, mad, worried, and upset, I screamed, "Bitch, I wouldn't be on this floor if I didn't have a baby!" That was when the head nurse came and took me to the side to calm me down. She saw how upset I was so she was really nice to me. I explained to the head nurse about what I remembered in the delivery room and she understood. She assured me that she will find out where and what happened to my baby. I asked her to please tell me if he was dead; I just wanted to see him. So I went back into my room waiting to hear from her. Fifteen or twenty minutes had gone by before the head nurse came into my room. I remember she had this sad expression on her face as if she didn't know how too tell me what she found out about my baby boy. I asked her, "He's dead isn't he?" She then sat down on my bed beside me and said, "Ms. Riley I did find your baby and he is not dead." I knew by the way she was talking it more to the whole situation. She told me everything.

The head nurse had told me that my baby was still alive for

the moment. She said, "Your baby boy died three times last night and they had to use the machine to kick his heart back in to start beating again." She also said, "Not only did his little heart give out on him but one of his little lungs had clasped because he was a seven month preemie and his lungs wasn't quite developed right or strong enough to work on their own." She told me that they have him on all these different types of machines; he was in one of those bubble incubators, and there were tubes running everywhere into him. She said I could go up to the intensive care unit to see my baby boy but I wasn't allowed to touch him.

The head nurse said she wanted to prepare me for what I was about to see because it wasn't a very pleasant sight. I told her to please take me to see my baby. I started to cry when I first seen him lying there in that bubble with all those tubs in his body. I asked God, "What did I do so badly for my baby to deserve this?" The nurse explained to me that there was a fifty-fifty chance of my son surviving. She said everything was left up to him and the Lord. She gave me a little more confidence when she said, "He was a big baby so maybe his weight will help keep him strong." I sat there crying, looking at my son, praying that he didn't die on me, not after what I went through to have him. Later that day I went downstairs to my room and called my mom crying my heart out about my sick baby boy. I told my mom another reason why I loved her was because she always knew something positive to say to make me feel better. My mom calmed me down and said, "Baby if God really wanted to take him away from you he had three chances have done so to last night. The boy is a fighter and he is strong, watch he gonna come out of this."

I didn't want to believe my mom at first because she didn't see him lying helplessly in that bubble. Again, mom knew best, my son did come home in three and a half months. He was on a heart and oxygen machine when he slept for about two more months after he came home but he got strong and the machines were gone.

Chapter Seventeen
"Heart Broken Struggles"

I WAS STILL looking for me an apartment so by the time spring came I could move. Well, this time a little luck ran in my favorite. I received a letter from the low-income housing authority stating that they had an apartment available for me if I chose to take it. I later went to the appointment that was scheduled for me to meet with the housing authority people. They said I qualified and was accepted for a low income home. Now I didn't tell my dad anything about the letter because I felt he would try to talk me out of moving again. Well, I was again in the earlier months of my pregnancy but this time I wasn't going to stay no longer than I had too in his house. The housing people had told me that it would be at least two to three months before I could move into the apartment. I was about to have my fourth child and I needed to be on my own. I was really happy; I was soon about too have my own apartment and didn't have to go by no one else rules. Everything seems to be pointing in my favor except I started noticing my dad and uncles were having these little private like talks. When one of them seen me coming they will always motion the other to be quiet.

Now I'm wondering if they were talking about me. Especially since everybody else did because I was nineteen and was pregnant with my fourth child. I didn't care what no one said about me because I was taking care of my kids. One day I was laying on the sofa downstairs sleep and over heard my dad on the phone talking. I couldn't make out what he was saying all I know he sounded very sad and depress. So, I started to become miss snoop. I was determined to find out what the big secret was and a few days after hearing my dad on the phone I found out. It hurt me so bad because like always everybody knew the big secret except for me. When I asked my dad why didn't they tell me he said, "I didn't think you could handle the news." He claimed he was thinking about the health of me and my unborn baby too. Even thou my grandmother thought I was different and a liar, she was still a part of my roots, life, and I still loved her. My dad had found out my grandmother was sick with cancer and it wasn't looking too good for her.

So my dad and all his brothers and sisters were planning to take a trip down south to see my grandmother before she die. I wanted to go because everybody was saying, "O she is going to be alright," but I didn't believe them. After ear hustling on my dad's talks and phone calls I felt they were lying to me. I needed to see for myself. Then I will know the truth once I seen for myself. For two or three weeks I've been trying to get members of my family to let me ride down with them to see my grandmother but they always said they didn't have enough room for me and my three kids. Sometimes my uncles will tease me and say, "You aren't having that baby while on the road with me?" No one! I couldn't get no one to let me pay him or her so I could ride down south with them. Then again I kind of understood why. I really wasn't their favorite pick of the family.

God did send me an angel and it was my uncle that I use to stay the summers with. I remember he said, "You can go under one condition." I said to my uncle, "any thing! I'll do any thing I just want to see if grandma was ok with my own eyes." Like I said earlier in my book, he always knew how to make me laugh. My uncle said, "If you promise me you are not going to have that baby before we get back, then you can go with me." I told my uncle, "I know my body this baby ain't coming no time soon." My uncle then told me to have my things ready by the weekend he'll be over early Saturday morning to pick me and my kids up. I got up very early so by the time my uncle came we would be ready for our long ride south. I remember my dad wasn't too happy with my uncle. Anyway, I didn't care. Hell he wouldn't take me. Plus I really wanted to see my grandmother since it has been so many years. Besides it was more then enough room because my uncle had one of those large mobile homes so it wasn't like my kids and I were keeping anyone else from going.

The way everyone else's schedule worked out my uncle was going to ride alone anyway if we didn't go. He was glad to have our company. The ride down south didn't seem as long as it did from what I can remember when I was a little girl. Maybe it could have been because we didn't have to pull over as many times for someone to use the bathroom and I didn't have to sit on some sick minded person's lap. Everything we needed was in my uncle's large mobile home; he even had a stove. When we made it down south my uncle drove directly to the hospital where my grandmother was. Talk about a person heart beating in their stomach. It seems as if my stomach had started knotting up and I was having light contractions. I thought to myself, "No not now! I promised him! You can't be in labor?" My uncle came up to me and said, "No matter how bad mama look be strong for her until you leave out the room." Of course, he had to put a little joke in afterward. He said, "Now I don't want to have to leave you down here because you got yourself upset and had that baby early." I hit my uncle on the shoulder in a playful way as I tried to cover my true facial expressions from the pains I was having. Then we went into my grandmother's hospital room.

As we all entered the room I could see my grandmother just laying there and not moving. My grandfather as usual was right by her side. For a minute I thought that maybe I was too late to see my grandmother alive for the last time. I slowly walked over to my grandmother's bed; I gave her a hug and a kiss on the jaw but what I seen in her eyes hurt me so. Have you ever seen death on a person's face? Well, I did and it didn't look to good, especially since I saw death in my grandmother eyes. My heart really hurt me, I felt something dreadful while tears of sadness, and pain was running over from my eyes as I cried silently to myself. Many thoughts clustered my mind. I was wishing I could have more time with my grandmother to show her I really do love her. I felt breathless and overwhelmed with sorrow inside of me as I watch my grandmother. A cramp started forming in my neck because of the tears of pain that I couldn't let come out my eyes to pour down my face showing my true emotions. I wish I could turn back the hands of time as far back as the year of 1962-65 when I was a little happy girl running around in my grandmother's kitchen trying to help her cook.

I never had gotten the chance or even the opportunity to fix our grandmother and granddaughter relationship and now I'll never be able too. As I looked at my grandmother I notice this pal, grayish, and peaceful glow on her face, and her eyes were a sad cold still shiny icy grayish black coloring. It was as if her eyes were saying, "Grandmother loves you but I'm dying baby and it's nothing that no one can do about it." When I first seen my grandmother I knew that everyone had been lying to me. My grandmother was dying and I'm glad my uncle brought me down here to see for myself. It was difficult for me to accept the truth that was right before my eyes but I was trying to do as my uncle asked me. I was trying hard to be strong because I didn't want to upset my grandmother no more then she already was. Believe me, it was very hard to do, especially, taking into consideration that I've become an exceedingly out spoken person.

I said to myself, "If my grandmother could be calm about her situation then I can too, even thou it was hurting me to see her in so much pain." As I attempted to leave her room, I was kind of surprised when my grandmother grabbed me by my arm and said, "Stay, don't go no where." Now I'm wondering what she heard or had to tell me? Whatever it was I knew I was going to stay right here to hear what she had to say. If I could answer any questions for her to ease her mind I will. It's been almost ten years since I last seen my grandmother. After that last awful experience down south I said I never wanted to see anyone down there again as long as I lived. I hope she don't want to discuss the ugly past? I guess in my heart my grandmother, regardless, always had that special unique part in my life. So now I'm standing on the side of my grandmother's bed confused. I said to myself, "An old lady on her dying bed was full of all kinds of surprises for me that day." My grandmother said, "Lovely, they tell me that you gave me some great grand babies." All I could do was answer her with a yes madam.

She then asked, "Well am I gonna get the chance to meet my greats?" Before I could say anything my uncle went out in the hall and brought my kids back into the room to meet their great grandmother. She was so pleased to see them while trying to smile. My grandmother kissed and hugged my kids one at a time as I introduced them to her. I'll never forget my grandmother last words to me. She said, "Lovely you got some fine kids. You take care of them for me. Don't let no one mess with them." I heard my grandmother's words very clearly. My eyes flooded with water as it took all the strength that I had to tried and hold back my tears, keeping them from streaming fast down my face, and upsetting my grandmother. In my mind I felt that in her own way my grandmother was saying that she was sorry for not believing in me. Just by the way my grandmother said those few words. Our grandmother and grand daughter relationship was bounded back together in my heart forever.

We stayed down south for two days and then returned back home. On the ride back all I could do was think about my grandmother. I really felt good going down south seeing her after all those years of anger that I held inside of me. I only wish it could have been on a happier occasion. I guess you can say I really wanted to get down south so if my grandmother was to die I would have made peace with her and myself. I said to myself, "Grandmamma I'll always love you." Well, they said God knows best because my grandmother died a few days after we left from seeing her. God! I was so glad and thankful that my uncle took me down south to see my grandmother barely alive for the last time. Now I have to go see her laying in a coffin to be put back into the ground. I remember it was around July 1st or 2nd, 1978 my family drove down south to buried my grandmother. Again, my kids and I rode down to Arkansas with my uncle in his large mobile home. This time my kids and I stayed with my older sister who lived in Missouri. I was so glad to see my older sister considering that it has been about ten years since I last saw her. My sister made my trip down south happier. She was glad to finally see my kids and myself since I became an adult. We spent most of that night and the biggest of the day before the funeral getting caught up on our lost years. I must say she is the best big sister a person could ever have because she treated me like a queen and my kids like royalty.

I was really enjoying my stay with my older sister but deep inside I knew it was only for a few days. Happiness doesn't last forever when it comes to my life. All while I was laughing I was saying to my self, "Damn, I'm gonna hate going to that funeral!" I felt I was self consciously trying to build my self up for when that day came by trying to laugh and enjoy my sister's company. I really had a hard time sleeping that night before the funeral. Not only was I nervous, worried, and upset but also another reason I didn't like going down south in the summer was because it be too hot. I went outside and sat on the porch to get some air but there was no wind blowing; only hot, stuffy, dry, stilled air. My older sister came outside and said, "I see you can't sleep neither hey sis?" I told her, "I'll be ok in a minute or two I just needed some air." My older sister laughed and said, "Don't look like you can get some air out here? Come on back in the house and I'll make you a big bowl of ice cream." I was always happy whenever I was with my older sister; however, during my grandmother's funeral will be the only time I won't be happy while I'm with her.

For what I can remember about the service and funeral isn't much. It was over so fast or should I say I was out of that place so fast. I remember being very nervous and having knots in my stomach, while I felt breathless as my throat felt like it was closing up. For a moment I was worried that maybe I was going to die too. It was hard trying to keep myself from getting upset about someone I loved laying up there dead in a coffin. I remember holding my stomach rocking back and forth while getting light headed as tears began rolling down my face. I cried so hard until my whole body started aching from the hurt I was feeling. Then with a blink of my eyes the service was over and they had buried my grandmother. I remember waking up in my uncle's large mobile home and then running back into the little church asking, "Where is she? I didn't get a change to see her!" My older sister came to me and told me they had buried my grandmother already. I began crying over and over again and yelling, "Why didn't they let me see her? Why?"

My older sister told me I had passed out during the funeral and they had to take me outside so I could get some air. I start remembering what my grandmother had told me at the hospital and right away I asked, "Where's my kids?" My older sister pointed over in the direction under some trees where my kids were playing with my mother. By that time my mom was pointing at me showing my kids where I was. My older sister and I started walking over to where my kids were. The first thing that came out of my kid's mouth was, "Mama is you alright?" I hugged, kissed, and told my kids, "Mama Fine. I just want to go see great grandmother's grave." My older daughter said, "I know where she at, they put her over here." So my kids, my older sister, and I walked over to my grandmother's grave. I sat down on my knees and started to think about our visited at the hospital. I kept thinking about the promise I made to her. I promised her I will take care of my kids and I am.

I just sat there on my knees think about how the funeral was over. My grandmother was buried and I didn't get the chance to say good-bye. I know our last moment together was great; at least I did get the chance to tell grandmother I loved her and she said, "I made her very happy by coming to see her." I took a flower from beside my grandmother's grave and the family and I went back to the farm. I had gotten me a few of her little wood knocks (figurines) as my keepsake in memories of my grandmother. My uncle didn't want to stay down south no longer then he had to so the day after my grandmother's funeral we left. In away I was glad to get back home because it was too hot but I also didn't want to leave my older sister. I had to get over it because my life had to go on.

A few days after we returned home I received a phone call from the low-income housing to let me know that my unit was ready. Some happy news for a change I thought to myself. That following month I was moving into my own apartment. I was so pleased with my new place and decided to live there for six years. During those six years my life changed so much. I stopped using drugs and started selling them. I went back to dancing. As a dancer many men asked me to sleep with them money and materialistic things but I didn't. I would always see if one of the other girls wanted to make the money instead. They'll go and turn their trick. When the girls came back they would always give me some of the money. This kept on for some time and then some of the girls talked me into becoming a female pimp; running a hoe house. The only different in my girls, we were a family and they were not allowed to bring any tricks of the street into our house.

I've never been shot at but I have shot at others. My life had been threatened so many times buy the male pimps on the street. A lot of them so call male pimps got their women by using drugs to pay them. Now I've smoked, toot, ate, and even mixed drugs in my drinks but I never used a needle. I lived a very wild and crazy life but never did I ever take anything from someone else without permission. I got what I wanted on my own and had the money to buy whatever my kids and I wanted and needed. My kids were very well mannered and I took damn good care of them.

Somebody was very jealous of me and tried to have my kids taken away from me. One day my kids and I came home and I found a note on my door from the department of social services. After reading it I became upset because I couldn't figure out what the hell the note was talking about. I said softly, "They must have the wrong person?" Everybody I knew and who knew me knew I took dam good care of my kids. So, now I'm confused because my kids were my life and I took care of them well. For about a week I didn't answer my telephone or my door. I couldn't understand why these white people were trying to take my kids. I finally decided to call my mom to tell her what was going on and what I was about to do. I told my mom my story and how much I loved her but I felt the less she knew about my where about the better off she would be.

Mom being mom said, "Lovely slow up! You can't run forever. Think about when they do catch you what do you think is going to happen to the kids?" Again mom was right. Her words made me re-think out my plan. I'm really glad I did because I was about to pack up my kids, leave Milwaukee, and never see my mom or family again. To be honest I really didn't know how I was going to live without my mom in my life. My mom talked me into calling the lady whose name was on the card and to meet with her. The lady came by my apartment and she was really impressed. I was really scared when she first came in because I only knew part of what was suppose to be going on. After the lady from the department of social services introduced herself she asked if it's ok for her to sit down. I told her, "Sure?" As if I was unsure if I should let her in my house in the first place. We start talking and I was really surprised.

This lady asked to go through my whole house checking to see if I was an unfit mother. So I walked her through all the rooms of my house. I remembered how she said, "You have beds for each one of your kids, nice," as if she was really surprised. After she went through the rest of the house she said, "I don't need to see no more. I don't see how you are supposed to be an unfit mother. You got a lovely home and every room is fully furnished. It's procedural for me to check to see if you have food for the kids though." She just didn't know I had a large deep freezer, refrigerator, and all cabinets were overly full with all kinds of food. This was the part I really liked the most because if I didn't buy my kids anything else I made sure they had plenty of food to eat.

I asked the lady from the department of social services where you want to begin. I went to the deep freezer and opened it as I talked to her then walked over to the cabinets and started opening one door after the other. She said, "You don't have to open nothing else. What I've seen so far can fill up a store. Every kitchen cabinet door you opened up had food on every shelf, top to bottom." We went and sat back in the front room to continue talking. She said, "Lovely, I came out here with a car to take your kids from you until we finished our investigation but I'm not." I looked at the lady and told her, "That's why my kids are not here because I wasn't going to give them up." She then told me; "Don't you know that you could go to jail for not turning your kids over to the state?" I told her, "I didn't care. No one was going to take my kids from me because I know I am a damn good mother and no one is going to take care of them like I do!" She said, "From your home I can see that. That's why I'm going to work with you so that you can keep your kids." Tears came to my eyes because I realized I almost made a big mistake by running with my kids.

I did exactly like the lady from the department of social services had told me. Every time someone from the department of social services came to visit, I let them in no matter what time of day or night it was. The first lady from the department of social services was working with me to keep my kids she also was coming by checking on me to see if there was something else she can do to help me. She was really supportive to me. I've told her I was interesting in going back to school to get my GED. She set me up an appointment at MATC. I went to MATC to take the test so they can figure out my weak and strong subject areas. I did a lot better then I thought. After the scores came back I received a phone call from MATC; the person asked me when would I be able to start my adult education classes? I remember telling the lady I would get back with her in a few days because I had to try and make arrangements for someone to watch my kids while I went to school.

I got on the phone to get in touch with the first lady from the department of social services. I explained to her how I was accepted into the program at MATC to get my GED but I had no one to watch my kids who weren't in school. She told me she'd get back with me to see what she can do to help me out. The next day I received a phone call from the first lady from the department of social services. She had arranged for my kids to be placed in a daycare that was in the same building where my classes were going to be held. I started my classes and successfully got my GED in May 1980; thanks to the lady from the department of social services that was supposed to have taken my kids from me. However, instead she led me in the right direction for bettering myself and helping me keep my kids.

I decided to further my education by signing up for some pre-college classes at MATC. Two classes I was able to take right away because they were only offered in the summer. I enjoyed school. I gotten the chance to meet new people but the first week is a week that I will always remember. I was going up the stairs on my way to one of my classes and I heard this voice from out of no where say, "Damn baby you're hairy all the way up your butt." Right away I turned around and said, "Too damn bad! Don't look if you don't like it or close your eyes!" I was silent for a few seconds and then I said, "You shouldn't been looking under my dress in the first fucken place!" Then I watched this body that belonged to this voice from out of nowhere said, "I'm sorry. I didn't mean you no harm but I was watching you downstairs as you were eating and I kept saying to my self, I can't let her get away without knowing something about you."

When I first turned around I wanted to say, "Damn baby, you sure is fine," but I didn't. Standing a few stairs down from me was this good looking, tall, slim, medium complexion, reddish-highlighted hair young man! I never would have thought he would be a chapter in my life that scared me with deep emotionally engraved painful memories. After this red head young man said he was sorry I told him, "Now you still don't know nothing about me," and turned around to finish walking up the stairs to my class. Only this time I gathered my dress in the front so I could pull the back close to my butt so he couldn't look up under it again. I don't know what it was about this red headed young man because he didn't give up. As I walked up the stairs he kept on talking about how he was going to make me his lady and he liked the fire in me. I started thinking that maybe this red head young man was one of those fatal attractions.

It seemed like no matter where I was in the school building he was there. I would come out my classes and he'll be coming down the hall. I went to the lady's bathroom hoping he didn't follow me in there. I didn't have to use it I was just trying to avoid the red head young man. I believed I stayed in there for at least ten minutes and when I came out he was sitting on the hall way floor. This red head young man got up off the floor to follow me saying, "You really had a load to let out." I turned around and screamed at him, "look the only damn reason I stayed in there was because I was hoping you was gone when I came out!" You would have thought he would have gotten the hint that I didn't want to be bothered. This red head young man told me, "Yeah, I thought that was what you were trying to do so I stayed out here waiting until you did come out." It was as if I had a different colored shadow every time I turned around he was always there and others started to notice his presence too.

One day a few of my friend girls at school and I were downstairs in the cafeteria going over some of our assignments. One of them said, "Do you know that guy?" I said, "What guy?" Then she said, "That red head guy that been watching you every since we been down here." I turned and looked and said, "He's always following me around." Girls being female they started talking about how quiet he was and how they wish he was following them around because they would let him catch them. My one of my friend girls did make me start thinking a little different about this red head young man. When my friend girls and I got up to go to our last class, the red head young man got up too. My friend girls started teasing me talking about "What you did to that man Lovely? He's not following you around for no reason?" I wanted to snap on them and him too but then again I was starting to get use to seeing him. He would sometimes motion his lips saying, "I'm still going to make you my lady." I would look at him and just shake my head no.

When we got to our class this red head young man had the nerve to tell my friend girls, "Go on in she'll be in later," and closed the door so I couldn't go in behind them. I told him, "Look, this is going too far!" The red head young man said, "No, I just wanted to see if you know where this class was at because I couldn't find it." Yes, stupid Lovely believed that fake line. I walked him to this room he was looking for and then went back to my own class. The next few days were different because I didn't see my red head shadow so I was kind of worried about him. Then I started thinking to myself that maybe he got tried of trying to make me his lady and found somebody else!

On the third day I had seen my red head shadow, only this time he was sitting outside the building waiting on me to come out. We began talking and that's when he told me the whole story about himself and how he still wanted me to be his lady. The red head young man said he had just came down from servicing time in penitentiary and was now staying in a half way house. He further started explaining to me that he was from Kenosha and would be having his probation transferred back down there when he was released in a few weeks. The only problem now was he said he really liked me but he didn't know how I would feel about being with a man coming out of jail. Oh but as far as the jail thing go I felt that wasn't nothing comparing to what made me stand up and try to chew his head off. My red head shadow told me he was a pimp and had several women. I told that fool, "Nigga you is crazy!

I may have been able to deal with the half way house situation but ain't no way in the world am I going to be with you and you got a woman for every day of the month!" He started explaining to me that these were his hoes and how he needed a main lady to have his kids. Even those words I remember sparked up some more anger from me as I screamed to him, "Do I look like I'm advertising to have a mother fucken baby?" He hurried up and said, "No, I just didn't want you to walk out of my life." Yeah, I fell for all of my red head shadow lines and when he got out of the half way house he moved in with me. Our relationship was fine. I dealt with his lifestyle and he dealt with mine. We both decided to give everything up and just be with each other; no more out side money. After being together for about two years I gave him a big fourteen pound fourteen and a half-oz baby boy.

Now my red head man got into a fight and because he broke

this one guy jaw he had to go back to jail for a little while. He finally got out and we were back together again. Only this time he had start lying and being gone a lot. I later found out he was cheating with his wife and according to him they were supposed to have been legally divorced. He told me that once he found out they weren't divorce he knew the only way he could talk her into divorcing him was by going by her house occasionally seeing her. I didn't believe that line of his. Well after then our relationship wasn't going to well. Matter of fact he had started going down to Kenosha and staying sometimes a week or two. In between those times while he was gone my depression sends me back to my drug habit and to the taverns but of course I wasn't out on the street to support it.

I started hanging in some of my old hangouts as they called them but the people had changed. I noticed that the men were much larger, friendlier, and not from the United States. These citizens from this other country were real gentlemen, they believed in spoiling their women and of course I fell for that kind of treatment. Let's say I played on the treatment because I was seeing three of these guys from this other country. The only way they didn't find out was because I didn't allow the other two the opportunity to come to another one of the neighborhood tavern I also hangout at. After I seen that this race of people were very close I knew I had to keep them apart to get what I wanted. So I put my charm into work. Everything was working out ok even when my reddish highlighted head male friend came into town he went a long with my plans. I guess that was another reason why I put up with his disappearing acts because when he was around he put up with my devilment.

As time slowly came and gone I was now supplied with all the cocaine I wanted and needed for my habit. I know some people say you can't be a good mother to your kids and on drugs too; but I was. I feel it all depends on the individual because looking at my kids, my house, and my self no one would had ever known that I had a bad drug problem. I still cared about my outer surrounding appearance. I remember how my reddish head male friend and I had these people I was getting my drugs from fool like we were brother and sister. Let's call them my fools from another country. Until one day I got mad and tripped on one of my fool from another country. This one fool from another country was trying to talk hard and strong to me. I had told my reddish head male friend that he was talking too much game with my fool from another country. So this one day this fool from another country decided that he was going to be like these crazy American males and talk that half-slick ass talk to me but it back fired on him. I told this one fool from another country that I was the slick one in this game! I remember he said, "What you talking about?" I told him that, "You see my so call brother look at him good. He's not my brother. Now look at my kids. He's their daddy!"

I'll never forget the rage that came up in my fool from the other country face when he said, "I'll kill you!" I wasn't afraid because my reddish head male friend was in the other room. Then I told this one fool from another country, "You know why your other buddy stopped hanging with you? I told him too because I see him too." This one fool from another country jumped up and pushed my table and said, "You gonna pay!" I told him, "Whatever. Get the fuck out my house!" This one fool from another country started kicking my kitchen chairs that's when my reddish head male friend came in and exhorted him out the house. Oh but it wasn't over!

A few days had gone by and my reddish head male friend had to go to Kenosha to see his probation officer. When I came back home I noticed that someone had been in my room. So I asked my kids and they said, "That when they came home from school this one fool from another country was coming out my room." First thing that went through my mind was to check my money. I ran back into my room and began throwing clothes out the dresser drawers.

Saying out loud, "Dammed, dammed where it is?" I knew then when this one fool from another country said I was going to pay I didn't know that he would sneak into my house and take my money. I told my kids to lock all the doors and don't let anybody in while I was gone. I remember it was rainy like hell that day but I still went over to this one fool from another country spot to get my money back. Once I got there someone kept telling me this fool from another country wasn't home. I knew they were lying because I seen his car go into the underground parking.

After a third attempt to try to get into the apartment, someone was still lying saying that this one fool from another country wasn't there. I knew then what I had to do. I went down into the underground parking structure with the extra set of keys to this fool from another country car and drove off with his car. Considering that this one fool from another country was in a very large and strong criminal gangster organization I knew I had to get myself safe until I could get in touch with the one that they called the godfather. I knew if anyone would listen to me and help straighten this mess out it would be the godfather. After I drove off with this fool from another country car I went directly to my brother's house. I told my brother that I didn't know how much time I had but I had to leave town for the safety of my kids. I explained to my brother how this one fool from another country had some how got into my house and took all my money.

Then I told my brother what I did and that I was going to Kenosha and then south but before I took off I gave my brother some money. The first thing he said was "Where you get this from?" I told my brother, "While I was in the back of your house I went through the car and found a small envelope of money and a half of brick of cocaine. You see this is the way I had to go because I knew when this fool from another country realize his car was gone he was going to make up more lies and have the organization after me about their stuff. I know the organization will come for my kids to get me and I knew I had no win with out the one they called the godfather and he was out of town.

Before I could say anything else my brother said, "go. Don't worry about the kids just call and let me know you made it." One of the hardest things in the world I ever had to do was to leave my kids but I knew it was best. I couldn't put my kids in anymore danger than they already were. This was one time my drug habit got my ass in some serious hot water and I had to figure a way out of it so I could go back home to my kids and keep them from getting hurt. My kids were all that I had and I cried all while I was driving. From dealing with the organization I knew if they came looking for me and couldn't find me they will try to use my kids to flush me out. So I figure I'll go on the run to lead them away from my kids. For three months I ran from state to state until the godfather came back into town. I would call off and on to keep in touch with my brother to see how my kids were doing and if the godfather had came back yet. I remember how I cried when my brother told me that the one fool from another country and some of his friends had tried a few time to get my kids.

First thing I said was, "I'm coming back home. I can't stay out of town like this knowing that they are still trying to get to my kids." My brother told me, "look you won't be no good to your kids dead! I'll handle this. You just call back and check up on us." A few days went by and I called to see how my kids were doing and my brother told me that he took care of the problems. From that day on when I called home my brother always said, "Everything was ok here at home. We got to work on getting you back home safe." I felt a lot better knowing that this one fool from another country had stop trying to get my kids. Now I didn't have to worry so much about my kids' well being. When I left my kids with my brother I knew they were in the best and safest hands next to mines. As days continue to go by I missed my kids so much but I knew if I went back home I would only put their life in danger. I knew I had to stay on the run for my life from state to state until I was able to talk to the godfather because he's the only person I could trust to help get this contract off my head.

I would call home three or four times a week to check on my kids. Then one day I call and my brother gave me some very good news. While talking to my brother he said the godfather had came over to my house and talked to him. That was the sweetest short song I ever heard anyone sang but then he said, "The godfather left a number for you to call." I got quiet for a moment and then I said, "Do you think he's trying to set me up?" I had to be reminded about the trust and faith that I'm supposes to have in the godfather. My brother said, "Lynn, all this time you been saying he was the only one you could trust. Call him and you'll be able to tell by the way he talk if it is a set up or not." I thought about what my brother had said and he was right. I told my brother either way I was going to call him back and let him know what I was going to do. I also told him to tell my kids that I loved them and hopefully I'll be home soon. Then I hung up the phone and kept looking at the number I had gotten from my brother over the phone. Trying to decide if I should call it or not.

All I knew was I was tired of running and wanted to go back home to be with my kids. Calling this number might solve the problem for me. I picked up the phone several times and dialed the phone number up until the last number and then I would hang up. I was afraid and unsure. Deep inside I knew I had to do it for my kids so I dialed the number again and it started ringing. When someone answered the phone I asked them, "Can I speak to the godfather?" The voice on the other end of the phone kept questioning me about who I was. Of course, I didn't tell the voice on the other end of the phone who I was. The only answer that voice kept getting from me was, "Get the godfather to the phone, he's expecting my call!" I understood his superiority and importance but I got up set and then told the voice on the other end of the phone, "Tell him you ask too many questions. I'll call him back later!" I hung up the phone quickly because I wasn't for sure if the voice on the other end of the phone knew who I was and was trying to trace my call.

The security of knowing the godfather would be waiting for my call I decided to wait a few days before I called him back. This time when I called the voice on the other end of the phone gave the godfather the phone. Once he got on the phone he said, "Is this Lynn?" I was afraid to talk to him. Then I remember him saying, "You need to talk to me. I need to hear your story." I said, "I'll call right back, just answer the phone when I do," and hung up the phone. When I called back the godfather picked up the phone. I told him, "I'm going to talk quickly because I don't want my call traced." I began explaining everything that had happened while the godfather was gone to him. He told me, "You know you have to come in?" I hung up the phone with out saying anything and call right back. I told him, "I am. I want to make sure my kids are safe. I'll call you back in a few days." Those were the longest days of my life because I couldn't sleep knowing what I was about to do.

It was now the second day and I told the godfather I was going to call him back. Believe me I was afraid but I was more tired of running and I really missed my kids. So I went to a pay phone and made that call for freedom and hopefully everything would work out like I had planned it. When he got on the phone the first thing he said was, "Are you ready to come in?" I told him yeah but he must meet me in an open place I picked. This way I can tell if he was alone or if he was trying to set me up to be killed. I went back to the hotel where my reddish highlighted hair male friend and I were staying. I waited until later that night after I had talked to the godfather and told my reddish highlighted hair male friend what I was going to do. Man was he upset but understanding too. I told him that I had to go back for the kids. Then he started yelling, "If they kill you then the kids still won't have a mother!" I looked at my reddish hair male friend and said, "That's the chance I had to take but they would still have a father." It took some convincing him to go alone with this plan of mine. So early evening the next day I had my reddish hair friend drive me back to Milwaukee to the spot I picked to have the meeting with the godfather.

We sat in the deep shadows of the trees in the park. This way we could see in all directions. Around 11:00pm I seen a car pull up along the street side of the park, it was the godfather. We sat for about an hour and just watch to see if anyone else was nearby. When I had seen that the coast was clear and I knew what I had to do next. I held my reddish head friend and said in a soft crying voice, "If anything happen to me take care of the kids." He didn't want to let me go. I felt a little better when he said, "Let me go. I'll tell them I took the car. The kids need their mother more then a daddy." I thought that was so sweet of him. I gave my reddish hair male friend a big good-bye kiss and then ran out into the opening. As I ran down the grass I was yelling, "Here I am." When I got to the car where the godfather was standing I seen there was someone else in the car. I said, "I thought I asked you to come alone?" The godfather replied, "He's only my driver." As I got into the car I looked back at the trees to get what I thought to be maybe my last look at my reddish hair male friend and father of my two kids.

Once we got on the highway the godfather said, "Lynn, you trust me?" I said, "Yeah," as if I wasn't for sure. Then he said, "I must cover your head, so you won't know where I'm taking you." As the godfather pull a black covering over my head he again said, "Just trust me." Well at the moment I really didn't have no other choice I was in a car, going God knows where and he asked me to trust him. All while we were riding I kept thinking to myself, "Is I'm going to ever see my kids again?" In total darkness I was silently crying for my life because I wanted to live. The ride had to be at lease a few hours because I was very restless but I became really afraid when the car came to a stop and I heard the driver say, "We're here." My heart started beating very fast when the car doors opened and the godfather said, "Just give me your hand." Of course, I was thinking to myself, "Give you my hand before you kill me?"

This is one time I can say I understand what that old saying, "If you use drugs you're asking for trouble," meant. All this time I thought I was doing something by playing my little games with my fools from another country and now I see it wasn't worth it. Now I know what the saying, "Playing games with people lives will get you hurt!" As the godfather still held my hand leading me blind folded I felt I was walking my unknown plate of darkness to my death. I always knew the mob was the one organization that didn't let you get away with anything. I knew when I took that damn car a contract would be out on my head. The hurting thing about it all is that my kids are so innocent of all my wrong doing and I won't ever see them again. Well, one good thing I did know would come out of this was, "I knew the organization will leave my kids alone now that they have taken my life." The godfather stopped me and said, "Watch your step." Scared to death already I was and I asked him, "Where are you taking me?" I remember hearing this different strong power tone in godfather voice as he said, "Lynn, from here on you only speak when you is asked too," and then he set me down in a chair. The blind fold was removed only to blind me with this really bright light.

As I was trying to block and see around the light I started asking, "What is you'al going to do?" Then a strong hard voice yelled out from behind the light, "Quiet, you weren't asked to talk!" Now I'm like really ready to shit in my clothes because I thought these things weren't real. Here I was in total darkness except for a bright ass light shinning directly in my face and a voice telling me to shut the fuck up. Oh but when those unknown voices started talking man did they knock my wig off my head! I remember the first question was "Where is our dope and money?" I answered, "What dope and money?" I believe I was making the voices upset because one of the voices said, "You don't ask no questions, you just answer them!" Now knowing I was going to die anyway but hoping what I might say wasn't going to get me kill quicker I replied, "I swear I don't know what dope and money you are talking about!" The voices kept yelling at me, telling me I was lying and if I wanted to ever see my kids again I would tell them where their stuff was. I'm still crazy to what the hell was going on I started crying, "Godfather I don't know what they talking about!"

Then a hand grabbed me around my shoulder as this voice that I recognized said, "Lynn, calm down, everything is going to be ok." This voice next to me said, "Lynn, tell us why you took the car?" I got quiet for a moment and then I explained why I took this one fool from another country car. The voices afterward asked me a few more questions and I answered with the truth that I knew of. You could hear a pin drop it had gotten so quiet in there and then I could fadelessly hear the voices talking among themselves. In the mean while I was sitting afraid for my life because this one fool from another country had told the organization that I had ran off with their shipment of dope and the money. This fool from another country and a few of his buddies said I was waiting in the underground garage, pulled a gun out on them, and made them get out of the car. Then I was suppose to have jumped in the car and drove off with all the dope, money, and guns in the trunk of the car. Now I know why the organization had this one fool from another country trying so hard to get to my kids.

I'm thinking to myself, "If these people behind those voices let me get out of here with my life spared I would personally kill this one fool from another country!" The voices stop talking. Then I heard one voice say, "Godfather go back to her." As I heard footsteps coming to me all I could think of was, "They going to have the godfather kill me!" Too afraid to even move my lips I softly said, "Godfather is that you?" A hand out of the darkness grabbed my hand and a voice sadly said, "Yes, Lynn it's me." I knew then that the organization had made their decision about what they were going to do with my life. As I reached and laid my other hand on top of godfather hand I said, "My life is in your hands." I'll always remember that sad, down, and depressing moment for me. Knowing that one word was now going to determine if I should live or die. A voice said, "Godfather we've talked among ourselves. We heard the story of some of our own people. We now heard her story. Still you have the final say."

All I could think about in my head was, "Godfather please don't let me die?" Then a voice from the darkness said, "Godfather do you believe her?" When the godfather didn't answer the question right away I felt as if he didn't really believe I was telling the truth. I knew then that I was good as dead. It was as if I had stop breathing and my heart had stopped beating for those few seconds wondering and awaiting the godfather's answer. The silence was so thick in the darkness that if I had a knife I could cut me a door to get out of that black room. Then the voice from the darkness said, "Godfather did you hear the question?" The godfather said, "Yeah, yeah, I heard." I knew the godfather cared a great deal about me but I didn't know how much. The way he said those words were as if the people who belonged to those voices were trying to pressure him into saying something he really didn't want to say. Then the godfather voice ranged out but this time proud and loud as he said, "Yes, I do. I believe her!" Talk about a person wanting to jump up and dance but first I had to figure out away to get my heart back where it belonged.

When the good father said those words it was as if the breath of life came back into me but my heart fell down to my feet. While at the same time I cried tears of joy as I thank God for my life. The next thing I said was, "Can I go home now?" Oh but I should have known it was a catch to that answer. Either way I didn't care because I knew it couldn't be worst then me being killed. I just wanted to get this over with and go home to my kids. The godfather explained to me about how the organization hasn't seen this one fool from another country in over a month. The organization also shared with me about how this one fool from another country they were dealing with has been coming up short a lot with his drop off and is debt with the organization. The godfather then explained how he felt that the one fool from another country had taken advantage of my stealing the car to cover up his wrong doing. They felt that this fool from another country had hided somewhere and they wanted me to help bring him out of his hiding place. I agreed to help.

Again the godfather blindfolded me and took me home. As I turned around to close and lock the downstairs door a voice said; "Just stay where you are." The light came on and it was my brother on guard watching over my kids. He said, "Did you take care of that problem?" I replied as I walked up the stairs, "Yes, my brother everything is alright." I told him I would explain everything to him but first I wanted to see my kids." I went into the front bedroom where my brother had all my kids. He said, "By having all the kids in one room I could keep a better watch on them. Three bedrooms out of the four were my kids' bedrooms. I was so glad to see my kids but I couldn't wake them up because they were sleeping so peacefully. As I kissed each one of my kids on the forehead I said softly, "Mama gonna make sure you always can sleep in peace," and left out the room to talk to my brother.

I started telling him about what had happened from the time I came into Milwaukee and sat in the trees at this one park until the decision was made that everything was okay. Then I told him about the blindfolded ride to no where land and how I was badgered with questions by unknown voices up until the decision that got me home. I told my brother about how this one fool from another country had lied all over me and what I had to do to prove I'm telling the truth about everything I said. My brother and I talked for awhile and then I went to sleep. Man, it felt so good to finally lie in my own bed again. I planned to get me a few hours of sleep and awaked my kids by cooking breakfast for them like I use too. I remember how I use to wake my kids up every morning by going into the kitchen and start cooking breakfast. It wakes them up every time.

Being on the run must have really tired my body out because my oldest daughter looked into my bedroom while I was asleep. All I knew was she screamed, "Mama back home!" I didn't realize how much I missed her big mouth. To hear her voice again was like being awakened to the prettiest song I ever heard song. It was kind of strange because my other kids didn't come running as if they were glad to see me offend. I felt a little hurt but then again I knew I had it coming after all I've been gone for a little more then three months from my kids. I never told them anything, all my kids knew was I was gone out of their life and they did know why. So I could kind of understand the anger my kids may have had at me. It really hurt me when I heard my second oldest daughter cry, "Quit telling a story. Mama left us and she's never coming back!" Then she ran back in to her bedroom and slammed the door. Even when my boys came and seen that I was home my second oldest daughter still didn't come to see me. I later found out why.

After getting all my hugs and kisses while at the same time I was getting the where you've been questions thrown at me and the I miss you mama I asked my kids why my second oldest daughter didn't want to see me! Everyone wanted to tell me at one time, they started to push and hit each other. From my understanding the pushing and hitting among them started up while I was gone and during the time I was gone. My kids told me how my second oldest daughter wouldn't eat for awhile and when she did start eating it wasn't enough to feed a bird as my one son said. My kids told me how my second oldest daughter use to keep them woke at night crying because she thought I was dead. Kids being kids played little games on her. They confessed that they uses to tease their sister and put on a big front like I was here and then when she came running they'll say, "April fool."

So it wasn't that my second oldest daughter really didn't want to see me, it was just she thought her sister and brothers were playing another trick on her. My kids and I went to my daughter's room; I'll never forget her facial expression she had when she saw me. It was like God had put two baby suns in her eyes when she seen me. My middle son was always the joker of the family. He was the first one in the bedroom where my daughter was. He started jumping in the bed and saying, "See I told you mama was here and there she go." I remember how she jumped up around my neck and gave me the biggest and tightest hug and cried. Not asking me where I've been or anything, all she kept saying was, "Mama don't leave me no more." Then her next words were, "Mama I'm hungry." I remember how my other kids started teasing her saying, "Looks who hungry. Oh, you hungry now?" I had to make my second oldest son stop since he was the ring leader of the laughs and jokes.

I kept my kids' home from school for a few days so we could catch up on the last three months. When the weekend came I knew what I had to do but it didn't bother me because I was back home with my kids. I knew this time I was going to stay. I went to all the places I knew this one fool from another country hanged out at so his friend would see me. I even went by a few of his buddies' houses so they would get the word out I was back in town and wanted to make everything up to him. After being home for about a few weeks I received a phone call from one of this fool from another country friend. The voice on the other end said this fool from another country wanted to see me and he would send someone over to pick me up later. I agreed to the meet. Now I was saying to myself, "He doesn't trust me. I got to build up his trust in order to do what the organization wanted me to do." So right away I came up with a plan. After what had happened before with me having to leave my kids I started explaining everything to them to keep them from worrying if I was going to come back home.

They understood but my two oldest daughters said, "They were going to stay up until I came back." A car came and I left only to be taken around through so many turns and dark alleys. My first thought when I seen this fool from another country was to blow his head off after all that shit he had put me through but I knew I couldn't. I knew now it was time to put the charm of Luscious Lynn back to work. This crazy fool from another country played right into my hands. I believe I really thrown him off when I told him, "You really hurt me and it's gonna take some time for me to get over that. First, I had to be for sure I could trust you because I knew it's a contract out for me." This crazy fool grabbed me talking about how sorry he was and how much he still loved me. I was saying to myself, "Tell me how much you love me after I turn your ass over to the organization!" I put a few false tears in with my act so it would seem a little more convincing. Then I pushed him away from me and started crying, "Take me home. This is too much for me now. I just want to go home." He had one of his buddies that went underground with him to take me home.

Yes, when I got home my two girls were awake waiting on me to return. So I spend the rest of the night with my girls watching TV. The next morning came I got up, cooked breakfast for my kids, and then sent them off to school. I did some cleaning around the house and start cooking my dinner for that night early. Once I sat down for a moment I called the godfather and told him of my plans. He agreed with it and told me be careful. Believe me I was going to be very careful because since this fool from another country still thought the contract was on me I felt like he might try to collect on it. I wasn't for sure if this fool from another country was going to try and see me again soon or what. Either way I will be ready. Well a few days went by before I got another phone call. This time it was this fool from another country himself. He told me that the reason he called was because he didn't trust his friend. We talked for a while but we didn't meet up that night.

It was until the following week we meet up. This time he asked if he could come over to my house. After that day this fool from another country and I had start seeing more of each other.I really had to play it off by asking my reddish hair male friend not to come around until I take care of this problem because I never knew when this fool from another country was going to try and seek over to my house unexpectedly. Well the plan was going along great. I felt I had all of his trust. It was about time because I was tired of looking at him and pretending like I was so in love with him. That night after this one fool from another country left I called the godfather and told him I was ready to bring him to them. The next night when this fool from another country came over to my house I asked him to take me to pick up my kids from a birthday party. Once we got there and got out of the car we went into the house; it looked like a party was going on. Only thing it wasn't the kind of party that he thought. This crazy fool from another country and I went into this one room and sat down. I remember this female came in and told me that my daughter wasn't feeling to well. I knew that was the key so I could leave the room.

The next thing I knew all I could hear was, "That bitch set me up." At first I didn't want to see what they were going to do to him; however, I went back into the room. I wanted to know if he was feeling as much pain as I was for those three months while I was on the run afraid for my kids and my life all because of his damn lie.

DIAMOND GLENN

After confessing the truth about the drugs and money this fool from another country was asked the question, "Do you want to live or die?" This fool beaten half to death, bloody all up chose to live which meant he was a servant, working for the rest of his life, free. I didn't care as long as my kids and I were ok and out of danger.

Chapter Eighteen
"Remorsing Reality Hurts: My Deep Will of Heart"

MAN WAS I ever so glad to get on with my life. I had so much to make up to my kids. After the huge scare I went through, my reddish hair male friend came back to Milwaukee to stay for a moment. Just when I think things is going to work out in my life something always happen. We were a happy family until one of my reddish head male friends got out of jail. Every time I turned around my reddish guy friend was at the door or on the phone. My reddish head male friend buddy didn't give us time to get out the bed before he was ringing the doorbell waking us up like an alarm clock. I would get so mad because my reddish head male friend would get up out the bed and go with his friend. I knew then that our relationship wasn't going to work out. I should have just left our whole relationship as an I'll see you when I see you kind of relationship. It's sad to say that every time I got really depress I got back more heavily on my drug habit.

I know it wasn't right but my drugs kept me in that I don't give a fuck what you do kind of attitude. I guess also because I went back bad on my drugs too. I also got back bad on my drugs to make my reddish head male friend mad because he was totally against me using them. I wanted him to fell how I be feeling when he do something that I didn't want him to do. Well, fat chance for me because all I did this time was made my reddish head male friend very mad only. Normally he will change his actions but not this time. After the kids all go to school I would put me on some clothes and leave. Hell, my reddish head male friend was gone so I felt I didn't have to stay at home all by my self? I would go to the tavern early, drink, get high, and then make it home before my kids got out of school.

I remember when he would come home and if I wasn't there my reddish head male friend would go in a rage and throw the bed covering off the bed. So now when I get home I have to hear his mouth, clean up my bedroom, and at the same time try to get dinner ready so the kids won't be so late eating once they come home from school.

I didn't care how he yelled because I would be so high till nothing he said bothered me. Just as long as he didn't put his hands on me he could say what the hell he wanted. So I'll keep on cleaning saying, "Yeah, whatever, now you know how I feel when you're gone all the time." I knew he was just going through a little phase because when the kids started coming in from school my reddish head male friend would turn that frown into a smile. I respected that in him because my reddish head male friend would never raise his voice when the kids were around.

As time went on I became back more so depending on my cocaine to get me through the day. I remember a few times when my reddish head male friend didn't go anywhere. I would try to find him somewhere to go so I could go down to the tavern. He would tell me, "Everywhere you go today I'm going with you, since you like getting drunk while the kids are gone to school." Now I knew I didn't want him to do that because his presence would interfered with my free high and plus I didn't want him to know my hangouts. So I stayed in the house all day but it didn't stop there. My reddish head friend use to tell me, "Lovely Faye, I think you're back on those damn drugs!" I would quickly say, "Look all I do is drink a fucken lot." I remember how upset my reddish head friend would get with just the thought of thinking I was back on drugs. I use to say to myself, "Damn, how am I going to keep him from finding out?" Plus I wasn't for sure how many days I could go without it before that monkey started riding my back. Well I found out soon. After about the third day of him being at home with me in the morning it happened, the monkey had started to jump on me. Every time I tried to go out the door my reddish head friend would block it. It was as if he knew what was going on with me. I remember how he uses to scream at me at the time and say, "What's wrong? Is it time yet?"

Man did I want to hit him in his mouth but I kept my cool. This one day he kept picking at me and teasing me. Talking about, "How long can you go? Does it hurt yet?" I knew then my reddish head friend knew all the time that I was back on those damn drugs. That monkey hit me real hard and I said, "If you don't get your ass out my way I'm going to hit you where it hurt at." My reddish head friend had made me so mad I exchanged some very hurting words with him. He then moved from in front of the door and said, "Go, go ahead, if you don't care about yourself why I should!" I left like a damn fool but only this time I didn't come home until late that night. Once I got home I felt like a big fool because this was the first time I wasn't home when my kids got there. I came in the house and quietly looked into my kids' room. They were sleeping so peacefully. Like they were the first time I came back home after being gone for those three months. Then I went into my bedroom.

When I looked in my bedroom my first thought was that I wasn't expecting my reddish head friend to be there. Then again I couldn't blame anyone but myself if he wasn't. So I turned on the light and found my bed empty. I sat on the end of my bed for a moment and cried because I knew I was wrong for saying all those bad things to him and running out the house like I did only because I had to get me some dope. Now feeling like a real ass hole and I didn't know where he was at or if my reddish head male friend was ever going to come back. I guess in a way I knew he was gone because the house was too dark when I first came home. So now I'm hurting, crying softly to myself and saying, "Why couldn't you be understanding in what I was going through?" I turned around and fell down on to the bed and cried into my pillows. I start screaming, "How could I be so stupid? Why couldn't I have been a little stronger and maybe I wouldn't have to be going through these pains?" Praying and wishing my reddish head male friend was still here so we could talk and hoping that he would be understanding enough to give me another chance to change my ugly ways!

Then I remember feeling the strong vibration in the pillows as I cried harder like a big baby and yelling, "I'm so sorry! Dammit, I didn't mean anything I said! Please just come back home!" Crying my heart out, screaming into my pillows, kicking, and beating the bed I was hurting for my lost love because I knew my whole world has came to an end. I felt no meaning or reasoning for life anymore. I knew life for me was going to be too hard for me to even try to accept without my reddish head male friend. Selfishly I only thought of myself. Tonight I lost everything I ever wanted and needed in a man to be happy when I walked out that door. Again I allowed my drug habit to mess up my life by giving me no for sure out look for my future. So I continued to cry like a big baby with my face buried in my pillows.

I jumped from the bed surprised and released the grip I had on the pillows when I heard his voice say, "How long? How long have you been back on that stuff?" All I could do was sit at the end of the bed and cry as I said, "I thought you left me." Knowing all the time it was the voice belonging to my reddish head male friend, he asked again, "How long?" I said, "A couple of months." Biting down on his teeth my reddish head male friend just stood there quietly watching me with that look that said, "I could kill you!" I sat there in this one stilled position sniffing because I was too afraid to say anything else or move. I remember how frightened I was when my reddish head male friend slowly walked to the bed and sat beside me. Till this day I never would had thought that these words of his would haunt me to be so true. My reddish head friend said, "Lovely Faye, I love you. The only way I'll ever leave you alone is when I die."

I gave my reddish head male friend a big hug and told him, "All I need is you not the drugs." From that night we started mending our messed up relationship. My reddish head male friend had promised to be there more for me and I promised him that I'll work on kicking my drug habit. I was so glad my reddish head male friend and I did try to work on our problems. My body went through a few changes while trying to get off those damn drugs but together we were able to stop my bad habit. Now I was clean from drugs and alcohol for about a few months. Well it's like me to get rid of one problem only to have another one walk into my life. Life seemed to be going along ok for my reddish head friend and I. We were getting along more like a real family. This one-day after the kids were gone to school I decided to go and do a little shopping before they came home. While I was walking around in the supermarket I kept feeling light headed and dizzy as if I was high on drugs. Sure right away I thought that my body was trying to test me to see if I would go and get some dope. I tried to rush through the store so I could hurry up and get back home. Only thing I believe I was rushing a little too fast because the next thing I remember was waking up in the hospital confused about why I was there but it wasn't long before I found out.

When I came through I knew where I was so I asked the nurse, "What am I doing here?" She told me I was brought here from the supermarket because I had passed out but I was going to be ok. The nurse then told me that the doctor wanted to know when I came through and then left out the room. At this point I'm even more confused. I didn't really care why I was at the hospital all I wanted to do was to get home before my kids got out of school. Then I thought about my reddish head male friend and what he might be thinking if he made it back to the house and I wasn't there. I didn't want him to think I was out screwing around again on drugs so I got up and started putting on my clothes. While I was getting dress someone knocked on the door, it was the doctor. I said, "Come in," and sat back on the edge of the bed, pulled, and held a sheet around my waist to cover the bottom half of my undressed body. Once the doctor came into my room he asked me what I remembered about today. I told him and then he asked me to lie back so he could examine me. I began telling the doctor I felt fine and I needed to get home because my kids will be getting out of school soon. I should have known something wasn't right when the damn doctor started asking questions about my kids and their ages. Then the doctor told me what was wrong with me and I said, "Is you sure?" The doctor said, "Yes, Lovely I'm very sure." I replied, "Well can I go home now." After the doctor said, "Yes, as soon as I made you a few appointments," I finished getting dress.

I didn't want to think about it now all I wanted to do was get home before my kids. While sitting on the bus ride home everything kind of begin to register. Then I thought to myself, "Oh my God, he going to kill me!" After the way my reddish head male friend carried on and left me the first time I got pregnant, I don't know how I am going to tell him I'm expecting again! Our son was twenty-nine months and I just found out I was four to six weeks pregnant. Then I said to myself, "Fuck it, I just have to deal with it because I'm keeping my baby!" When I got home he was there but just like a man in doubt my reddish head male friend didn't take the news to well. In a way I really didn't care about what he thought I knew for sure who baby I was carrying. As the days were coming and going my reddish head male friend started accepting my pregnancy. I remember how he would rub my stomach and say, "Lovely Faye, I hope you give me a little girl?" I would push his hand away from my stomach and sometimes say in a playful manner, "No, but you didn't want the baby at first, now you want you a little girl."

I don't know maybe it's just the vibes of a woman being pregnant that the daddy starts to get on your every nerve because it seemed that the bigger I got some of our little problems came back. I notice how my reddish head male friend had started staying out a lot lately but I wouldn't say anything to him. I mean I won't say anything to him at all. I was now giving my reddish head male friend the cold shoulder treatment. He had started hanging out with his no good friends again and I knew what that meant. Plus he would sometimes stay out all night and expect for me not to be mad at him. A lot of nerves I thought but my reddish head friend just didn't know, I was getting tired of our roller coaster riding ass relationship. One day I put down my laws and he felt that he shouldn't have to live under such strict pressure and went back home to his mama. Sure I was hurt at first but then I thought about it and said to my self, "I knew our peaches and cream relationship wasn't going to last long any was." The good and happy times never seems to last too long but I knew I had to go on with my life.

As the days went on depression started setting in on me. I felt that life for me could have been better if I wasn't pregnant again. Faced with no other choice but to make the best of my situation I knew now it was just me and my kids. Then the thought "if I wasn't pregnant I could fall back on my drugs for comfort and support," ran through my head but I knew it was only a thought. Well I tried doing the right thing I guess it wasn't meant to be. Anyway I knew I had to keep myself together for my kids sake. It was hard but there wasn't a day that went by I didn't miss and think about my reddish head male friend. In doing that only made me sadder. I would wish I never had put such hard demands on him but I was tired. Tried of the in and out of my life he was doing. True I loved him dearly but I couldn't stop the tears of pains from falling down my face. Unable to deal with the fact that my reddish head friend and I will never get back together caused stress and depression to become a major factor of my life. I would try to be normal around the kids but I knew deep inside even they suspected that something wasn't right.

As the days continued to come and go I worried myself half crazy and had a nerves break down. The doctors said I had a mild stroke. I lost temporary use of my left arm and I dragged my left leg as I walked with a limp. I remember how my mom uses to hit my hanging lifeless arm and say, "Baby you got to want to get better. You can't give up." I knew my mom was right but this aching empty space in my heart wouldn't let me accept or be part of the lovely life surrounding me. I really didn't care anymore if I lived or die! So now I'm going around as a half of a person, pregnant, and with the whole world weighted on my good shoulder. A few weeks had gone by. I remember my mom asking me have I been to the doctor. As I got up off the couch to go sit on the porch I sadly said, "No." I was so confused with life? I couldn't understand my purposes here on this earth? All I know was everything wrong kept happening to me. Plus I felt I wasn't a good enough mother no more for my kids. Even thou I loved my mother dearly it was more depressing and hard staying with her and my brother. Then again it was ok because the both of them helped really well with my other kids considering I couldn't even comb my girls' hair.

I guess you can say I was feeling totally sorry for myself. I remember how my mom uses to yell at me, "How do you think I feel seeing you giving up on your life! If you don't think about your self Lovely, think about the baby you're carrying?" Those words of hers did make me think a little more about my unborn baby life. For a moment I thought about how I really forgot I was pregnant and was focusing totally on the sorrow I was feeling for myself. Then I thought, "What or if any kind of damage did my stroke do to my baby I was carrying?" Now I started to really worry! I had a doctor appointment for the following week and this time I kept it. Well when I got to the doctor she said that everything seems to be coming along just fine and my baby appears to be growing fine. You see my doctor like my mother was more concern about my mental and emotional health. So now it was what am I going to do about it? The next few weeks I did a lot of thinking in regards to what am I going to do with my life? I even thought little of my reddish head male friend because now I too was worried about the damage my stroke caused upon my unborn child.

I begin to feel less sorry for myself and started working on getting back the use of my left half of my body. After the first couple of weeks I noticed a small change. Even thou I still walked with a limp I didn't drag my left leg as much but I knew I still had a long way to go. My mom had started rubbing down, bending, and exercising my left arm a lot for me. Now I wanted to get better so I watched my mom closely and would do the exercises myself. It wasn't that bad. It gave me something else to focus my mind on, which was getting better. I kept thinking while praying to myself, "Lord, all I want to do is get use of my arm again so I can get in my own house and have a healthy baby," even if it meant I will be alone. You know it's so funny because it seemed like every time you make up your mind to leave a nigga alone, he'll try to walk back into your life; every time. Yes, you guess right! My reddish head male friend came to Milwaukee to see me. I remember this one day when my kids and I had came from the store. I sat on the porch and watched them as they played in front of the house. It was nice. It felt good, like a real family in a long time only thing I was thinking was it would have been nicer if it was a father in the picture.

After about a few minutes I guess my mom realized we were back from the store because she came to the top porch and called down to me, "Faye is you ok? You don't need my help do you?" I answered, "I'm ok." I then heard the top porch screen-door closed. A few seconds later the sound of footsteps began coming down the stairs. As the footsteps got closer to the bottom of the stairs I said, "Mama, you didn't have to come down to check on me." I couldn't believe I was hearing his voice as the screen door to the bottom porch where I was sitting opened behind me. He softy said as if he was afraid and unsure of my reactions, "I'm not your mama." The first thought that came to my mind was, "Hell no!" Then super anger from the hurt of trying to get over him quickly jumped into my soul. In a blink of an eye it was as if the devil himself with total hate and punishing revenge had taken over my body. My heart started racing and beating really fast and hard.

As much as I still loved, missed, and was overly happy to see my reddish head male friend; the pain inside me which I was trying to bury wouldn't let me show my true affection that I so very much deeply wanted to express. Before I knew it I snapped and said, "What the fuck you come back for now!" Not like I didn't want him back but he just didn't understand and know the hell and pain his absence had put me through. Just seeing him reopened a lot of those aching feelings. Our break up, his absence was a major part of my stroke, and nerves break down. Look at me, I'm half handicap and carrying an unborn baby that I don't know is going to be healthy or not. He came out and sat on the stairs in front of me and said, "If you really want me to leave, I'll go?" As mad and hurt as I was I couldn't even tell my reddish head male friend to go. All I could say was "where you've been?" By this time my middle son was running from around the side of the house. When he stopped and looked from around the tree I could see my middle son eyes light up. I could hear the other kids coming and running to my middle son asking him, "what you looking at?" Once the kids had seen it was my youngest son daddy they all came running.

I had to stop my kids because they were asking too many questions to fast. I told them, "either you'al go and play or go upstairs!" The kids were mad now because I wouldn't let them greet my reddish head male friend and father of my youngest son to show how much they had missed him. I remember how my oldest daughter picked up my youngest son as he cried and said, "Come on you'al lets go up stairs." The kids stormed up the stairs while my reddish head male friend held the door open for them saying, "Lovely Faye, you know that ain't right!" I didn't care what he said. I just looked at him mad as hell and said, "Those are my damn kids. You're not going to keep running in and out of their fucken life!"

I even went as far as saying, "I'm the one who have to look at their sad faces when they want to know where you're at? Why you're not here?" Yes, my reddish head male friend trying to defend himself said, "Wait, it wasn't like that this time. Remember you were the one to give the strong rules I couldn't live by, but that's not what I came here about." That was when he reached into his pants pocket and pulled out some papers saying, "If you please just give me a few seconds I'll show you proof to where I've been." I really wanted to know so I gave my reddish head male friend his moment of proving to me. After hearing his story I found out that he had been in jail for a little over two mouths. Before I could ask the question of why you didn't write me, my reddish head male friend reached in his jacket pocket and pull out a small bundle of letters that had rubber bands around them. Then he said, "I wrote you several times but the letters kept coming back. I didn't know where you were." I just sat there silently holding my bad arm with my good hand, looking off into space, wondering how wrong I was about him.

When my red head friend grabbed me by my face and said, "Look at me. Did you think that I wouldn't come see about you?" At this time tears started forming in my eyes. I didn't know what to say. All the time I thought my reddish head male friend was with another woman and didn't really care about the kids or me anymore. I begin feeling even more sad and bad when my reddish head male friend said, "Once I got to mama house she gave me your mother's message. I went straight to see my probation officers and told her what had happened to you while I was locked up." I'm saying to myself I truly believe he is telling the truth because he showed me the paper but then again maybe him and my mom rehearsed this to give me more hope to get better? I was still some what confuse because in spite of everything we have been through I loved him deeply.

I wanted us to get back together so bad but I knew I wasn't ready for it, not now. Yet I'll never forget that sad serious look on my reddish head male friend's face and in his light brown crazy eyes when he told me how much he still loved me and nothing was going to stop him from coming to see about me. Well in a way I was glad my mom called his mom because my reddish head male friend and I would have been still feeling as if the other didn't want to see the other. This way we both found out the truth and decided to try and work out our difference. My reddish head male friend and I were talking again and he would come up three or four time out of the week to help me with the kids and look for an apartment. It wasn't easy but after about a month of looking I had my own house again.

Now I knew everything was going to be alright. My reddish head male friend, the kids and I were like a little family again. I made sure my kids understood that he was not going to be over our house all the time; only sometimes. This way I won't have to worry about the sad faces when he wasn't around. Our little agreement seemed to be working out just fine. I remember how my reddish head male friend was hoping so very much that I had a little girl. He would sometimes come back up to Milwaukee and stay for a few days or even two weeks and each time he came back he will talk about how he hoped

I have a girl. Anyway I enjoyed his company whenever he did come to see the kids and me. As I gotten closer to my due date my reddish head male friend and father of my kids was coming from Kenosha more regular. I remember he would tell me, "Lovely Faye you ain't ready to have that baby yet? You look like you are about to burst," and from then on he started calling me "Fats."

He just didn't know I wanted to bust him in the face with my fist when he called me fats. Instead I sometimes would tell him, "I'm gonna Fats you all right," and would try to beat him up knowing that I didn't have the breath too. He uses to run around the house until he made me out of breath and then he would tease me by saying, "Now you know that it's snow outside, if you keep this up I won't put your boots on for you." I would laugh at him and say, "Well then I won't cook you nothing to eat." I remember how he would have to put on my socks and shoes on for me because I was so big I couldn't bend. I couldn't even reach around my stomach to try and touch my knee; don't let me roll over on my back. God I was helpless. Sometimes he would reminded me of things I use to do to him and he would say that he'll get me back by teasing me so bad. He would playfully hit and poke me saying, "Remember when you did this to me," all I can do is tell him, "You know I'm going to get you back?" We had fun with each other all during my pregnancy whenever he was around.

I remember when he went to the doctor with me, I didn't know if I wanted to hit him in the mouth or roll under the table due to embarrassment. My baby's daddy was in the doctor's office saying, "Why wait, take her now. She's too fat," and then bump me with his shoulder and say, "Ain't that right Fats?" I wanted to right fist him in his mouth. My doctor just laughed and said, "She has a big New Year's Eve Party she was giving tonight and she could wait a few more days to have my baby." Even thou I wished I could have my baby today, I was kind of glad I didn't because I wanted to be with my kids for New Years and not stuck in the hospital.

I was now a few weeks past my due date and on January 3, 1985 I was suppose to be admitted so the doctor could induce my labor but the baby didn't want to wait those couple of days. My reddish head male friend and father of my kids had only been in Milwaukee for a few days before he left and went back to Kenosha. A few of his cousins came up to let him know about the big New Year's Eve Party in Kenosha. At first he didn't want to go because he knew I had to go into the hospital in a few days but then he asked me, "Can you wait till after New Year to have the baby?" I told him, "Yeah. Go ahead have fun and drink a few drinks for me. This baby hasn't come all this time we'll wait until you come back. Just make sure you're here by the third."

I was of course mad but it wasn't anything I could do to stop him because I knew he was going to go anyway. So he got his self together, rubbed my stomach and said, "Daddy see you next year." Then he gave me a kiss and said, "Happy New Year's Fats," and ran out the door so I couldn't catch him. Well now I was really feeling under the weather because everybody I talked to were going to a big New Year's Eve Party. Everybody I talked to also said, "To bad you're pregnant. Girl you're too big to be out on the streets anyways." As I laid in my bed feeling sorry for myself and said, "I hope every one of them get caught in the snow storm!" Later that night I had put my kids to bed and laid back in the recliner to watch TV. Well, the only thing about that is it didn't turn out that way. I laid back and went to sleep in the recliner since that was where I slept at when I was home alone with the kids. This way I could get up when I needed to and I really needed too! It must have been around ten thirty in the evening; I started feeling a few really bad cramps in my stomach. I thought and said to my unborn baby, "No you're not going to do this to me, not now?" So I got up out the recliner and started walking around hoping the cramps would stop but they didn't. Now I'm getting scared because everybody I knew had a party to attend so I didn't know who I could call on if I was really in labor.

Then I thought about my other kids that were in my bedroom sleeping. Oh my God, who gonna watch them if I had to go to the hospital? I didn't wait too much longer before I called an ambulance because I knew my baby didn't want to wait until the third; she was coming now. I called by my brothers' house who only stayed five blocks from me and told them, "I needed somebody to get over here with the kids because I was going to the hospital." One of my older brothers asked where my baby's daddy was at and I told him that he went to Kenosha. I remember my brother saying, "That little girl picked a fine time to come now. Somebody will be over there." The ambulance had come by the time I got off the phone talking to my brother. I walked down the stairs but my contraction had started coming so close and so strong that I couldn't make it back up the stairs. My oldest daughter woke up when she heard the paramedic in the hall with me. She came down to the bottom of the stairs where the paramedics had me laying and was crying as she screamed, "Mommy is you alright." I told her, "Don't worry mommy ok. I just need to go to the hospital to have your little sister," and she then sat down on the bottom stair next me.

The pains were still coming and one of the paramedic employees said, "Lovely we really need to get you to the hospital or otherwise you gonna have this baby in this hallway!" I told him I couldn't leave until someone comes here to be with my other kids. Then right away my oldest daughter said, "I'm a big girl now mama. I'll watch the kids and house till you come back." I was so proud of her because she was always trying to help out. Then one of the paramedic employees said and asked with concern, "Is some one coming to watch your other kids? How old is your daughter, maybe she can watch the house until someone get here?" I told him that someone was coming and they only stayed five blocks away. Then I told him how old my daughter was. After the one paramedic employees examined me again he said,

"Baby you're old enough to watch the house until your uncle come. We need to take your mama to the hospital now."

As the paramedic was taking me out the house I said to my daughter, "Don't open the door for nobody else," but by the time they got me completely out the door here come my younger brother out of breath. Once we made it to the hospital, they took me up to the labor and delivery area. I told them who my doctor was and the nurse said, "Let me page her because she just left!" My doctor came into my room taking off her coat, hat, and gloves. She said, "Well it looks like we might have us a baby after all? She couldn't wait a few more days and she beat the storm." After the doctor examined me she said, "Well Lovely, we gonna have us a baby. There goes my party." My doctor was fun, she always consider her patience as being very special and she always talked about her patience's unborn as if it was her baby. My doctor told the nurse, "Take her to the delivery area. I have to put on my scrubs. Looks like I might make my party after all." It was so funny because once I got in the delivery room it seems as if my contractions stopped. My baby acts as if she got lazy again. Now I was starting to wonder if she had put me through all these pains again and then I ended up going home like before.

My doctor was still in the delivery room making jokes saying, "Ok little girl, am I or am I not going to make it to the party before New Year's?" Then a few minutes later the contractions started back up again but this time they were very strong and hard. I remember hearing my doctor say, "Ok, we got us a big girl, at 11:31pm." My doctor examined me and she said everything was okay. She asked me, "Is it ok for me to go to my party now?" I said, "Sure." By the time I went home the streets were clear enough to travel on after the big snowstorm we got New Year's Eve Night. Everyone I talked to told me how they got stranded and had to leave their cars. I felt good because everyone was also saying I was in the best place because they wish they wouldn't have went out there in all that snow.

My baby's daddy did make it back on the third but of course I already had the baby. He asked me why I didn't call and tell him. I told him I didn't want to spoil his fun. He stayed about two weeks and went back to Kenosha. For the next few months my red head male friend and father of my kids was back and forwards from Kenosha to Milwaukee. As I started to get myself stronger I wanted out of the relationship but he told me I wasn't going anywhere with his kids. So one day while he was down in Kenosha I moved and told him nothing. Maybe if I wouldn't have moved just maybe what happened wouldn't have happened. I still kept in touch with my kid's daddy cousin, she promised not to let him know where I stayed. I would call my kid's daddy cousin off and on to check and see how he was doing. I remember telling me how mad he was because he didn't know where I was but deep inside I felt it was best for me.

What brought all this about was when I told him I was tired of this roller coaster relationship and I wanted out. He grabbed me around my neck and said, "Lovely Girl the only way I'm gonna let you be with another man is when I die!" For the first time in five years my red head male friend put fear in my heart. I knew then that I had to do what was best for my kids and me. It was hurting me not being able to see him but I knew time was going to heal all my old wounds. After about two weeks into my new house my phone was ringing late at night. I didn't answer it because my baby's daddy had gotten my number and been calling talking crazy. This one particular night I turned my answering machine on. Someone kept calling but I would only listen to them talk on the answering machine once it picked up. It was my kid's daddy cousins calling five or six times. Then another cousin called a few times.

I started feeling that maybe something was wrong but then again maybe it wasn't because my kids' daddy had them call me one night pretending like something was wrong so he could talk to me. The calls stopped but I still couldn't sleep so I decide to call down to Kenosha. Everybody's house I called I got no answer. So I started thinking that something must be wrong because I knew they had just called me and now I don't get no answer no where. I called information in Kenosha and asked for the number to the jail. My kid's daddy wasn't in there. Then something told me to call information again and ask for the number to the hospital and I found him. I got pissed off because I called the hospital in Kenosha a few times and they kept telling me, "Yes, he been through here and that's all they could tell me." So I kept trying to call his family to try and find out if he was ok but I was still unsuccessful. Then I decided to call back down to the hospital except this time I explained to the person that answered the phone who I was and where I was calling from. I further went into detail by saying how his family had called up to Milwaukee several times for me but when I called them back I got no answer. I told the other voice on the phone, "that I know he has been though the emergency. All I wanted to know is if he was alright?"

The voice said, "Could you please hold on for a minute, I'll get someone that could talk to you." For that moment of silence all I could do was pray that my kids' daddy was ok. The next time someone picked up the phone the voice on the other end stabbed me in my heart. The young lady that got on the phone identified herself as the nurse that had seen my kid's daddy when he was brought into the emergency department. After I explained to her my relationship with him, I'll never forget those words, "well it's gonna be public so I guess its ok for me to tell you." The way she said that statement I wasn't for sure if I wanted to hear what I was thinking but then she told me. The voice on the other phone told me, "Yes, my kid's daddy had been through the emergency." Right away I cut her off and said, "What you mean he been through the emergency? He just came in and out? What you mean through?" I guess what I was doing was trying not to accept the truth of what she mean by those words. Then she said, "Lovely, please listen and let me finish. I was trying to let you know in an easy way. Your kid's daddy was DOA." I dropped the phone and kept screaming, "No! No! He can't be! God no!" Unaware of how loud I was screaming and crying I heard little footsteps heading my way with these voices crying out, "Mama what's wrong?"

I didn't have the heart to tell them so I made up a lie and said, "You'al know how I'm always going around in this house hitting my toe? I kicked my foot this time a little too hard and it hurts like hell." My older kids always could find the words to make me get my act together real fast. My oldest daughter said, "Mama it hurt us to see you cry. When you hurt we hurt. Mama please don't cry?" Yeah, you're right I know you would have done the same thing. I stop crying. As I looked in those little faces their eyes were filled with tears all because I was crying in pain. I said to myself, "I had to stop crying for them because I couldn't stand to see my kids hurting like that." I gave each one of my kids a hug, a big thank you for caring kiss, and then sent them back to bed. I sat up most of the night crying silently to myself. I didn't want to talk to anyone but my mom. I knew she would have been sleep by now. I also didn't want to wake her up and having her worried about the kids and me. I lay down and held my baby girl who was turning three months the following morning.

I couldn't think straight the next morning because I was hoping all this was a nightmare. Here this reddish head man won my heart and love, plus made me very happy at once a pond a time. Then he stole my heart and caused me so much pain. Together we made warm madly passion love while enjoying each other's body. With the blessing of God, twice I gave birth to his two lovely children. In looking back, besides the good and bad memories, I'll forever have something very precious and dear to remember and treasure my reddish head male friend by. God it hurts! By the anger of a so call friend my reddish head male friend and father of my kids was killed.

My kids and my life, future, and heart was remolded, reshaped, and destroyed beyond destruction by evil rage! If it wasn't for my kids I don't know what I would have done. I was in the kitchen cooking my kid's breakfast and the phone rang; it was my dad. He asked me if the kids were awake and don't let them watch the TV. Not thinking I asked my dad why? Then my dad said, "Faye I'll be over there to talk to you." At the time I didn't want to talk to anyone but my doors were always opened for my dad.

By the time I hung the phone up my youngest son came into the kitchen where I was saying, "daddy," as he pointed. I wish I could tell him in a way so that he could understand that his daddy was dead. I looked at my youngest son and I wanted to cry. Instead I bend down to him and said, "Baby daddy is gone and he's not coming back, but my son kept saying, "daddy," and pointing. So this time I went to see what he was pointing at and I found my middle son sitting in front of the TV crying. When I came into the living room my middle son said, "Mama, he's dead! They said that he was dead!" I didn't know what to do or say that could dry up the tears on my middle son's face and take away his pain. I sat on the floor beside my middle son and said, "I didn't know how to tell you. Even thou he's dead we will always have him in our hearts and minds. Can't no body take away our memories." After I talked with my son to calm him down someone knocked at the door, it was my dad and my stepmother.

They had come over to see if I heard about my kids' daddy because it was on the news all morning. That was why my dad didn't want me to let the kids watch TV this morning. My dad said, "I know you want to go down there, that's why we're here. Faye I don't think you should take the kids down there, not now." So I called by my brother's house and explained to him what had happened to my kid's daddy. My brother told me he seen it on the news and was on his way to my house when I called. Sometimes I wonder if I was the younger sister and he was the older brother because I was always calling on my little brother for help and he would be there for me with no question asked. My dad took me down to Kenosha to face the horrible truth of what had happened to my kid's daddy. I was told how this guy came from behind my kid's daddy and grabbed him by the head and cut my kid's daddy throat. It was said that my kid's daddy then grabbed his neck and stumbled into the street where he got hit by a car. This mean and evil man armed with a knife cut my kid's daddy again after he fell off the car that hit him. My kid's daddy got up and made his way out of the street to be attacked again. A business owner came out firing gun shots in the air to make this armed person stop cutting at my kid's daddy. He was then put into a car and taken to the hospital where he was declared DOA. My kid's daddy and reddish high lighted male friend of mine were taken away from us for what reason we really didn't know. All I know is the guy that killed him was someone he knew very well.

If that's a so call friend then I'll rather be on this earth friendless. With a friend like that I hate to know what an enemy would have done. Now I had to get myself together to go to this funeral, I was hoping I would never have to do this. Once I got home I went to sleep only to be awakened by my mom. She told me she heard what had happened to my kid's daddy on the news in Chicago and took me in her arms as I cried like a big baby. When I really needed my mom the most she was always unexpectedly surprising me to be by my side. My mom then told me as she rubbed her fingers through my hair talking to me trying to calm me down. She said, "I knew you really needed me that's why instead of calling I felt I could help you better by coming up to be by your side." I remember my mom kept telling me, "Baby it's going to be ok, I'm here." I love my mom so much. I believe one phrase I got tired of hearing from everyone was, "you got to be strong for the kids." It seemed as if everyone was more concerned about the kids than me.

There were so many times I wanted to tell everybody, "Why

don't you all take the kids because I am hurting! I need to cry! You all don't know what the hell I'm going through!" Even thou I was trying to get away and over my kid's daddy, it wasn't no secret that I loved him very deeply. As the week seems to slowly come close to an end I knew I had to soon say my last good-bye to someone I loved so dearly. He have no more pain or suffering, no more worrying, or wondering about what's going on in my life. The only pain left is the emptiness in my heart that can never be filled the way he did. This was going to be one of the hardest things I ever had to do. To look at my kid's daddy, my friend, my lover, my strength all that I loved and forever will love, laying in a fancy decorated box, still, cold, and dead. Once this box is closed it would never open again and his face would never be seen again. It's hard! How can I take that last look?

If I could give him the kiss of life, he will breathe and be mine all over again. I wish I could just hold his hand to feel his pleasing squeeze just one more time. I wish I could alter the touch we shared that day he walked in my life to make sure I would feel his touch for life. I'll view life so much different if only God would let him breath again and give me back that man I fell in love with. If only I wouldn't had moved, how long would it have been before he came home for good, he kept telling me soon? All this week every time I started to cry I couldn't because I would see the innocent face of my child looking at me. He would tell me, "Mama please don't cry." Then I would dry up my tears as my heart silently cries with the worst meaningless empty painful ache of life. I know now that all I have in life to keep me going is my kids. I'm worry about how is my younger son going to hold up at his daddy's funeral. I'm hoping he won't take it too hard; after all he was only three and really didn't understand what was going on.

Even now he is missing his dad so much because he's always asking me about him. All I can say is, "Baby daddy had to go away for a long time." It's that time, as I slowly walked around getting my kids together for the funeral saying softly, "God why do I have to go? Why did this day come?" In my heart I really didn't want to see him laying up there dead but I knew I couldn't live with myself if I didn't go. When we first got to the church it was so many cars and people there. I remember my mom said, "Out of all my life I've never seen a funeral so big and for a young person." Yes, it was amazing to see how many people had come to pay their last respects to my reddish highlighted head friend and the father of my kids. He was deeply loved by many all over the United States. I went into the church and sat down in a seat where no one could block my view of him because I was to afraid to walk up there to see him. The way I was feeling at the time I knew I would have fallen flat on my face. So I sat there asking God to give me the strength to get through this funeral on my feet. I just stared at him as if I was in a trance, he looked as if he was laying in my bed sleep, and his whole facial expression was the same.

I remember my younger son said, "Mama, daddy sleep." I said to him in a soft like sad voice, "Yes baby, daddy is sleep and he will be sleeping for a long time," and then grabbed him around the shoulder pulling my son closer to me. I can remember while sitting at the funeral service for my kid's daddy I was getting upset holding on tightly to my baby daughter whom at that time was only three months. The pain, the suffering, the lost, the whole heart aching experience triggered a breathless cluster to form in my throat as tears rushed running down my face. To me I had seen no one but my reddish head male friend laying up there with a misty cloud surrounding him. I fadeless heard anything from people speaking while the service was going on. It was as if I was slowly leaving my body and going off into another world, except several times I kept hearing this soft distinctive voice saying, "Lovely, where are you? Come on think about the kids." It was as if this voice I was hearing was pulling against my spacey thoughts and desires of not wanting to live calming me down to face reality. I didn't care I didn't want to face the truth about life. All life surroundings looked so blurred. It was as if the whole church was empty and again all I can remember seeing was my kid's daddy as if he was lying in a mist of fog, a sleep, and I was trying to get to him.

In my heart I just wanted to be where he was even if that meant dying too. Regardless to what we had been going through I still loved him that much more than life. Aching with the worst pain of not being able to understand or knowing why this man had to kill my male friend and father of my kids? Why did he have to leave me so soon? Why? I didn't care anymore why; I just wanted to be with him where ever he was but this voice kept interfering with my decision. My deepest self-conscious was telling me, "Lovely, listen to the voice because it's telling you right." I remember feeling a warm touch as if it was rubbing through my clothes to the inner most part of my soul. It was as if this touch was fighting with another unknown part of me; pulling at me trying to help this voice redirect my thoughts. This warm relaxing touch continue rubbing me while in a far off distant I could still hear that unique voice saying, "Come on Lovely, where you're at? Come out of it?" It seemed like my kid's daddy was calling me to him and this voice was trying to stop me from going to him. For that moment I can remember it was as if a contest was being played with my mind, body, and soul to see which way I really wanted to go!

No matter how hard I tried to fight and struggle against temptation, something was still telling me, "No don't go, snap out of it." My heart was too heavy and filled with pain to listen. I just wanted to die. I wanted to crawl up there in that coffin with my kid's daddy and be buried with him. As I relived the moments of the funeral some of my emotions and feelings at that time is starting to come back to me. My body seems as if it is so weak. It was almost as if I was telling my breathing soul to leave me and I could slowly feel my body becoming lifeless. I know I was trying to run away from him but in reality I feel I don't have no life now that he's gone. I was forcing every ounce and strength of life that I had within my body to leave me. I was praying, begging God, to please let me die too because I didn't know how I was going to live without my kid's daddy. Yes, God answered my prayer and did what he felt was best for me in my situation. I started feeling as if I had total control of my soul and I tried to fight the battle of life and death within myself. I wanted to stop the hurt of these emptiness pains that were too unpleasant for me to deal with.

So I just sat there meditating myself into a deep comma while holding tightly to my three month old daughter and trying to make my body shut down on me. I was trying hard to closing everyone and everything out of my mind, heart, and sight. I just wanted to die but God said, no and sends an angel my way that knew how to win this quarrel that was being fought in my mind. The angel of my life which I loved so very much had this strong powerful magic voice talking to me and trying to control me; pulling me from this shell that only the angel knew I was slipping into. This wonderful magnificent, rare, irreplaceable, God giving, saving angel voice belonged to my mom. Again she was there to pick up my pieces and to put me back together again. I made it through that awful storm, even thou I was thinking negatively. I felt that everything for me had ended when I seen my kid's daddy laying up there dead and waiting to be put back into the ground.

A stronger will then mines reminded me that I still had six greater reasons to live than to die; my six kids. Once I got back to Milwaukee right away I started looking for me somewhere else to live. I didn't want to stay in my house anymore because of the hunting memories and the total emotional scared that my younger son was going through. I remember several times waking up either because my younger son was sitting or rocking at the end of the bed saying, "daddy, mama," or by rolling over onto a cold object. I would get up and grab my son and put him under the covers with me each time. I would hold him tightly while I rock him saying to him, "Daddy not here no more baby. He is sleeping somewhere else."

I thought for a minute that I was loosing my mind? I could never explain to myself how I was always waking up and finding knifes in the bed with me? I knew they weren't there when I first went to sleep? What was the meaning of this? Was I walking in my sleep doing things and not remembering? As the next few weeks went on by these occurrences with the knives in the bed started to be more frequently. I became even more confused one day when I got some explanation to most of my unanswered questions. I was cooking breakfast one morning and was looking for a knife. I asked the older kids have anyone seen my knives? Softly saying to myself as not for sure, "I know they were here because I put them back into the drawer this morning?" That was when my two older sons came into the kitchen where I was with my knives in their hands. I yelled, "Where did you get them from?" My middle son replied, "Alexis had them in his bed." Puzzled, shocked, and surprised I said, "What's Alexis doing with my knives?" I was even more shocked from the answer my two older sons had given me.

My boys told me Alexis had asked them to teach him how to use a knife. I was surprised because my youngest son hasn't said seven words since his dad funeral. At first I didn't understand why my youngest son wanted his older brothers to teach him how to use a knife; it just didn't register. Then my middle son said, "He said he was going to kill the man that killed his daddy." Now I knew I had another serious problem on my hands to deal with. I couldn't get my youngest son to talk about what my older sons had told me. It made me think back about comments that were being made while I was in Kenosha. People in Kenosha use to say how much my son looked like his daddy. I was also tired of hearing, "how my son was gonna be the one to avenge his father's death." I guess I never thought my youngest son was old enough to carry so much hatred in his heart and understand what was being said. I felt those who were talking should be the ones to go and kill, especially considering some of them were there when my son father was killed.

I looked at my youngest son and softly said, "Baby what am I going to do with you? How can I get through to you?" I didn't know where his little mind was. I knew he was hurting from the death of his father and I could see how badly he was. I know I'll never forget the sad and angry glowing look on his face when I woke up one night and he was sitting in my bed with a knife in his hand. Now you can image the scared, shock, surprised, and worried look on my face. His eyes were opened as if he was awake the whole time. What seemed even stranger was my youngest son was acting as if he was still asleep and unaware of what was going on. It was as if he was in a trance and I couldn't snap him out of it. I did get the knife away from him and then I put him under the covers next to me. He lay down with no fight or problems and went to sleep. Of course, after an experience like that I couldn't go back to sleep. So I stayed up most of the night thinking and trying to understand what was going on in my son's mind.

When morning came my youngest son was back to his same old self. He would sit or lay in the bed beside his little baby sister all day long as if he was her personal bodyguard. I could say when I wanted to do things around the house I didn't have to worry about the baby because she was well watched. If she moved or acted like she wanted to cry my youngest son put the bottle in her mouth. He was a good babysitter. I worried so much about my youngest son because I couldn't get him to talk. My youngest son was like a shell with no feelings, always just sitting, and shielding his life. It was as if he had closed himself off from the world outside of what was going on in his little mind and I couldn't help him.

Chapter Nineteen

"The Meeting of the Tall Dark Skin Lusty Build Brown Eyes Man"

MY COUSIN CALLED me and told me the apartment downstairs from her was for rent and if I wanted it she could talk to the landlord. I thanked her because later that evening she called me and said the landlord said I could have the apartment if I wanted it. Two and a half months after the funeral I moved into another house to try and start my life over alone. It was just my kids and I. It was hard but I knew I was a survivor and plus my kids needed me. By this time I had slowly started reintroducing my body back to my relaxing cocaine. I knew no other way of dealing with the death of my reddish head male friend and my shell shock son.

I called my son shell shock because I thought about how sometimes people act after being in the army and observing I really bad things happening around them during war. After my reddish head male friend died, my son had gone into his own little world. The reddish head male friend of mine was my son's dad. My son wouldn't talk to no one. He just sat in his bed as if he was frozen where he was sitting and he would watch over his infant baby sister.

He was unresponsive and I couldn't bring him out of it. I could tell him to lie down and he would sit for hours in a daze. I use to take my son and lay him down in bed as if he was a little baby. Most of the time, I felt as if I was the one that was loosing my mind. I even said a few times, "I wish I could do like my youngest son and close everything out? I wish my reddish head male friend was still alive!" I know whatever happened to have lead to my reddish head male friend's death could had been avoided if he could only see the mess his death has left behind. I was so burnable, sensitive, very unhappy, confused, and lost in life. Nothing seemed real to me anymore.

My cousin, bless her heart would come downstairs and check on me and the kids. I remembered how she would try to get me out the house. She used to say, "You should at least come out the house to just go for a walk!" I didn't, couldn't, and wasn't ready to deal with anything or anybody that was on the outside of my house door. I did allowed my kids to go out in the backyard to play but my youngest son always sat in the house watching over his baby sister. I just stayed in the house and only went out to buy food. I would wait until 2:00 or 3:00 a.m. in the morning to get up out of bed and go to the store. The food store I went to stayed open 24 hours. The store was usually very empty too. I could go through the store get what I wanted and be back home before the rest of the world decided they wanted to come to life. As far as paying my bills, what I couldn't mail I would give the money to my cousin to pay for me when she went to pay her bills. She'll give me the lecture about how I should go and pay my own bills every time.

I would sometimes say, "If you don't stop pressuring me, my door won't open for you." She would then fine something else to talk about. I remember this one very hot summer night the kids were all asleep and my cousin came downstairs to visit me. Since we were family I always left my back door unlocked but out of respect for me she still knocked before she came in. As I think about it, I did noticed something different regarding the way my cousin was calling my name as she walked through my house. I should have known she was up to no good and I fell in her trap. She came in talking about how hot it was upstairs and that she couldn't sleep. Then my cousin quickly changes the subject to ice cream. Talking about how bad she wanted some but was afraid to walk three and a half blocks to the restaurant alone. I just looked at her in silent because I knew what was coming next. It came out her mouth, "Come on Lovely walk with me!" I said, "No!" Then she said, "It's late. This time of night there's not many people out. Come on. Please! It'll do you good to get out for a few minutes." At first I wanted to take my cousin and kick her through my ceiling back into her apartment upstairs.

She knew how I felt on the topic of going outside but she continues to plead and beg. Then she said, "If at any time you feel too uncomfortable, want to turn back, and come home, we will. Even if I don't get my ice cream!" Still afraid of the outside world, I decided to take my cousin on her offer. I got up off my bed and started putting on some outside clothes. Then I said as if I had doubts, "I don't know why I let you talk me into this?" I could see this happy glow on my cousin's face once she seen I really was going out the house. She quickly said, "The air will do you good." When I first went outside I was very nervous. I believe I was more afraid of someone saying something to me. I didn't want no one to even say hi to me. That one word would be enough to put me on the edge of my nervousness, fear, and start crying. Well my cousin was right about one thing; there wasn't a handful of people on the street. After we got our ice cream and was walking back home, it was kind of a different story. People just started to come out of the air from all directions. My cousin had seen how nervous I had start getting and began to talk to me. She was trying to assure me that everything was going to be alright and I had nothing to worry about. I'm saying to myself, "Yeah that's what you think! You can't trust anybody. I don't care who or how good and nice they may look!"

I told her, "Every since I found out how my reddish head male friend got kill I really don't feel safe on the streets. People, even his relatives stood by and watched him die. No one did anything to try and help him!" Talking about the night of my reddish head male friend death upset me; it broke me down with emotions. So now I was walking up the street crying as my cousin put her arm around my shoulder trying to comfort me. She was telling me that God knew what was best. He left me here for a reason and that my reddish head male friend was gone for a reason." Then I remember her going on saying, "If he was here what would he want you to do?" I sadly said, "Take care of my kids." She did say a true and positive statement even thou I really didn't want to hear it. She told me, "You're now mama and daddy. Those kids need you now more than ever." I couldn't do nothing but agreed with my cousin, even thou I didn't tell her that. I know she was only trying to support me but what she didn't understand was the pain, the hurt, the emptiness, the lost, and the confusion with the kids. My life really had no meaning anymore except for my kids. They were all that I had and I couldn't wait to get back home where my kids were.

About one and a half block from the house my cousin decided that she wanted to stop in this one tavern to see if a friend of hers was in there. Wright away I said, "I thought he was upstairs?" Then she said, "This is my undercover lover." I told her, "I'll see you when you get home." Ok, remember I said I fell into her trap? My cousin said, "You can't go home without me because I will get in trouble!" When my cousin went into the tavern I sat down on some brick stairs to wait for her to come back out. After maybe about ten minutes my cousin came out and was trying to get me to go in the tavern with her. I told her I didn't mind waiting for her outside, besides it was rather quiet out here. A few times I got up and walked the little half of block to look down the street at my house. Just to make sure everything looked ok. Then I would walk back to the brick stairs to sit down, think some more, and softly cry. This time my cousin came out the tavern to check on me. After seeing how up set I was my cousin said, "I'm going to tell my friend I have to go. I'll be right out. I can't have you sitting out here like this for me." She when in and it wasn't even a good minute before she came right out.

I wouldn't have thought that, that moment would have been the start of my new life. As my cousin was standing by me and talking to me she was giving me time to kind of get myself together before we walked home. She was actually trying to give me hope that things are going to get better. It seems as if, at that very moment everybody and their mama wanted to walk by. I had no problem with them walking by seeing me with my head down crying. I wasn't ashamed. Whenever I felt like crying I cried. No matter where I was. After all they may never see me again in their life. Well, that statement didn't stand to be completely true. Out of all those people that looked and just walked pass me, one had to say something to me. I can't forget him. This one dark skin, slim, medium built male walked pass me and stopped. He stood over me and said, "Hold your head up. Life ain't that bad!" If I was in my right mind I would have told this dark skin, slim man a word or two. Believe me he wouldn't had liked those words neither. Being that I wasn't, the first thing I did was start crying even harder. I guess the way I started crying even more caused the dark skin, slim built man to say, "Damn baby it's not that bad!"

My cousin then grabs him by the arm and said, "Can I talk to you for a second?" They walked about ten or twenty feet from where I was sitting. My cousin and the man were so close that I couldn't clearly hear their conversation. I could barely hear their conversation; they kept fading in and out. My cousin had briefly explained to this tall, dark skin, slim built man my situation. He then came back over to me sadly and said, "I'm so sorry. If you ever need a friend to talk to, call me." I could see the figure of this tall, dark skin, skim built man, through my tear blinding, blurry eyes, hand my cousin something. As he started to walk away he said, "You take care of yourself. Everything will be alright." These words seem to be everybody's favorite words, "Everything will be alright!" They just didn't understand the emotional scare I was carrying. My cousin bends down to me and said, "Come on let's go home." She helped me up and kept her arm around me for moral support.

When we first made it to the house I went in side to see if my kids were still asleep. My cousin went upstairs to check on her household. A few minutes later she came back downstairs and said, "It's a nice night. You feel like sitting on the porch?" I softly said, "Yeah, I do. I think the air will do me some good." The next morning when I woke up I felt kind of different. I don't know if it was the walk, the time I had to cry out a lot of my locked up emotions, or the thought that there are some people who do care about other people. I thought about that figure of this tall dark skin slim man a lot that day. May be it was the way he presented his self as a gentleman. Plus I said, "he didn't know me from the man on the moon and offered me his ear."

Then I thought, "I wonder what he really looks like considering when I did peek out the corner of my eyes all I could see was a dark figure! I knew I wasn't ready for a relationship so that thought got flushed down the back of my brain real quick. Well, "maybe he could be a good friend considering that was what I needed right now?" Remember all those "maybes" were just thoughts; I went back to my normal routine. The next few days were pretty much the same for me. I cleaned, cooked, and took care of my kids. There were a couple of times I got teary eyed but I always felt it wasn't nothing that a little cocaine couldn't take care of. I had started depending on my drugs a little more than usual. While the older kids were gone to school I begin finding myself with too much quiet and sad time on my hands. Only now I had some thing else that I thought about. Or should I say some one else.

Being sad and depress, I knew wasn't good for me but I couldn't help it especially when loneliness set in on me. I really started missing my reddish head male friend. I start thinking about the things he and I would be doing if he was still alive. I know one day I'm going to find me another companion but right now a friend would just do me some good. I need someone to talk to. Someone with an open mind that I can boo-who on, share my pain, and emotions with. Someone that won't tell me, "Don't cry, you got to be strong." I need a real good friend right about now. My cousin is a good friend indeed but she has her own problems and family she has to deal with everyday. So I can't keep imposing on her.

Well as usual I found myself talking to myself, and believe me that was no solution to my problems. I remember this one night I was very sad and really needed someone to talk to. I got up out my bed and went upstairs to my cousin's apartment. The only thing is when I got up there the door was lock and I couldn't get in. I softly knocked on the door a few times and got no answer. It was kind of late and I knew my cousin's kids were sleeping so I started back down the stairs. Now I was really feeling bad because my cousin said, "Her door will always be open for me when I need her." Well, I really needed her tonight and her door was lock! I'm at the point where I didn't care if I live or die again. My heart is hurting so bad; I can't sleep. I didn't want to stay in the house because I was too depressed. Right about now I need some cocaine. I know it would help me relax.

The only problem is my cousin's boyfriend usually goes get it for me. This is one night I was so torn down I said, "fuck it!" I got myself together and went around the corner to get my own drugs. These people didn't know me from Adam and sold me some cocaine. I then went and sat on the swing in the playground directly across the street from my house and try to get high. This was one time it seemed like the more cocaine I put up my nose the more depress and sadder I got. My drugs couldn't comfort me anymore! I got off the swing, walked across the street and went into the house. I fell across my bed and cried myself to sleep.

When morning came it was business as usual. Only thing different was my cousin called to see what I wanted last night instead of coming downstairs and ask me. After she told me her situation, I kind of understood. I remember my moments of lovemaking too and how I didn't want to be disturbed by no one. Still in my mind I knew I couldn't continue to depend on my cousin to be there for me anymore. Then I asked her if she still had that phone number that guy gave her the other night! My cousin told me she had just looked at the number a few days ago. She also said she started to throw it away because she didn't think I was going to use it. She then said she'd get the number and bring it down to me. I was saying to myself, "She just doesn't know how glad I am she didn't throw it away!" I got off the phone and started my daily cleaning while my music was playing. You know the old say, "music soothing the vicious salvage beast?" I needed a whole lot of calming down.

A couple of hours went by and my cousin finally came downstairs. She had the number in her hand. First thing came out of her mouth was, "Call him. I got to see this!" I told her, "I will call him when I get good and ready. I just wanted to make sure you still had the number." Of course you know what the next question was and whom it came from? Me! I asked my cousin, "Girlfriend what do he look like?" She said, "Well he not that bad looking. I think he's kind of quiet and he might be too dark for you." I wanted to hit her in the head but in a way that was a true statement. You see I never went with a man that was darker than me. My preference was a light skin and slim but slightly strong built, long hair, good looking man. So I understood why she had made that to dark for me statement. Then I thought to myself, "He probably was ugly anyway?" As I think about our whole conversation more, my cousin never had a good-looking man in her life. She may think they were but every man she had was hurting when it came to look.

Now I'm thinking, "So much for that idea of even hoping maybe!" I threw the number on my dresser where it stayed until this one day I really was going to use it. I believe it was a week or so had gone by since I got the number from my cousin and never used it. This one night I was so unhappy and needed someone to talk to. I thought to myself, "I got to call him!" The only problem was I torn my room up looking for the number. Now don't ask what I did with it because I don't know! All I know was I wanted that number bad that night and couldn't find it. That reminded me of another old say, "Never put off until tomorrow what you can do today," because I should have used the number when my cousin was trying to get me to. Who knows, maybe he would had my number by now and would been calling me! It tears me up with anger and madness at myself for being so careless with this dark figure man's number. So I had no other choice but to fall heavy on my bottle and drugs to try to calm myself down and relax that night.

The drugs made me want to stay in the house. I believed once I started back on my daily alcohol drinking I began to get a little gustier. The drugs and drinking started to become a regular habit for me. I would leave the house late at night while my kids were sleeping. The night seemed so peaceful to me. Plus there were usually a handful of people on the streets, which didn't bother me. I was now going to get my own drugs when I ran out and sometimes I would walk by the tavern around the corner hoping maybe the dark figure man would see me and recognize me. This one night I got a little gutty and went into the tavern but I only stayed for a few seconds. I walked inside the door, went through the tavern and I went straight out the front door. A few guys were trying to holler at me but I kept going. You see what those few guys didn't know was they made their first major mistake by hollering at me!

I walked back to my house wondering if I would ever get the chance to meet the person who belongs to the dark slim figured body. I went into the house and checked on my kids. They were all still sleeping so peacefully. I poured me up a hard strong drink, got me a chair, and sat on the porch until I felt I could crawl in my bed and go to sleep. Well the drugs, alcohol, and the quiet night air did it for me. I went into the house and remember nothing until I woke up in the morning to get my kids off to school. I'm starting to feel a little more relax with myself but still so lonely. As long as my kids are home and woke I stay busy. Sometimes I wish they didn't have to go to school. Sometimes I wish they didn't have to go to sleep. During these moments is when all the hurts from hell invades my heart and life. I know deep inside one day everything is going to be all right. I only wish that day would hurry up and get here because life is really starting to deal me a loosing hand. I'm now becoming more than ever before totally depended on my drugs and alcohol to get me through both the nights and now the days too.

Yes, I am back. I am now the classiest, backslider, junkie, and alcoholic around. I wasn't trying to go back that route. It just happened. I needed a way to deal with life pains. My drugs and my alcohol together became the cure for whatever hurt me. Don't get me wrong, I still provided and took care of my kids but at night I was a totally different person. I would walk around the corner to the tavern only now I would stay and have me a few drinks. I would usually sit in the far corner of the bar. This way I wouldn't have to worry about too many people walking around or over me. I was really surprise once I gotten to know the tavern that there were a lot of nice looking men with gentlemen type of manners. Each man was different and unique in his own special way.

This one night I was sitting in my usual spot drinking and enjoying the music. Oh I forgot to tell you I meet one of my neighbors in the tavern. She recognized me but I didn't know her from Eve and the woman stayed directly across the street from me. Our front doors lined up with each other. Anyway she came into the tavern and started talking to me. I let the bar tender know that I'll be right back that way won't no one get my favorite seat. My neighbor and I made a quiet run to the drugstore and came back into the tavern. I was a little nervous at first but now I was feeling real good; enjoying myself. Drinking and not spending a penny. You know, I think I could really like this kind of life, I thought to myself! I'm just sitting in my usual seat talking with my neighbor that lives across the street from me. High as I wanted to be and getting very drunk thanks to this dark skinned, brown eyed man that was sitting at the other end of the bar.

It seem as if every time my glass got almost empty this dark skinned, brown eyed man will have it filled back up. For a moment there he was making me kind of nervous. I told my neighbor, "I hope he don't think he gonna get me drunk and take me off somewhere!" My neighbor said, "We going the same way and we are leaving here together." I said, "Cool. Now lets finish getting fucked up!" The miserable part about this dark skinned, brown eyed man was he did not once say anything to me. He kept buying me drinks and looking across the bar at me. Other females would come up to this dark skinned, brown eyed man to talk to them but he blew them off. He'll say a few words to them and then females would walk away. I couldn't figure out what he had in mind for me. After several more drinks his pretty brown eyes didn't temper with my fearful side anymore. Now I decided to play a game with him.

I told my neighbor to go over there to talk to this mystery dark skinned brown eyed man. I told her to make like she like him and ask him if he would like to dance. Well, she came back to her seat real quick. My neighbor told me, "Girl, he wants you! The man likes you!" I'm like, "Yeah right! He probably just wants some of what I got between my legs! Dunk and high as I am, I might just give him some?" My neighbor said, "Girl you crazy," and we laughed it off together. Strange but after our laugh I turned and looked in the direction where the dark skinned, brown eyed man was sitting and he was gone. At first I said to myself, "Damn I could have got his name!" Then a few seconds later I noticed him coming back to his seat. I'll never forget that night. I remember how he took a napkin folded it and placed it over the top of his glass. Now I'm wondering where is this dark skin, tall, lusty built, brown eyed man going. It wasn't long before I got an answer to my question. The music was playing and it sounded damn good. He walked over to where I was sitting and asked me, "May I have this dance?" I said to him, "Too late the song is going off."

Man was this dark skinned, tall lusty, built brown eyed man charming. He said, "I didn't want to dance with you on this song. I asked the DJ to play a special song for us." As the song started to play the DJ made a special announcement. He said, "This is a special dedication to Lovely." The dark skinned, lusty built, brown eyed man reached his hand out and said, "Lynn, may I have this dance?" I gave him my hand as he led me to the dance floor. The song was Two Occasion. It was the first time I ever heard it. While dancing I asked the dark skinned, lusty built, brown eyed man, "How did you know my name?" He said, "I ask the bar tender." While dancing I found out that this dark skinned, lusty built, brown eyed man had seen me in the tavern a few times before and has been watching me. He said, "I was a very respectful lady and he liked that most about me." He further told me about how mostly every guy in the tavern wanted me and he respected me because I stayed to myself and talked to no one. That let him know I wasn't one of those good looking females out here sleeping around.

When he told me, "that wasn't the kind of woman he was looking for," it made me feel special. This dark skinned, lusty built, brown eyed man said, "I want you to be my lady," I could have passed the fuck out. Right there on the dance floor in his arms. I don't know how serious he was but I really thought he was joking. I was saying to myself, "yeah you're good. Fill my head with all those good words. Spending your money on me like you're big timer. You're good but you're still ain't getting none." I just knew all he was doing was trying to lay those lines on me to get in to my pants. Little did he know I was strong as a bull! Even thou I wouldn't mind giving this dark skinned, lusty built, brown eyed man some; I had to stick to my guns. It goes to show you who got some kind of say so in the tavern. The song had stop playing then the DJ made the announcement, "we have an instance replay." Sure did. The song played again and I kept my high and drunken ass on the floor dancing in the rock hard arms of heaven. Enjoying every second of the dance it was as if my body began to get weak. I was now feeling like melting better in this dark skinned, lusty built, brown eyed man's embracement.

Tightly, squeezed, and secured but yet so gently held in his arms caused this warm feeling to flow over and through my body. After the song stopped I wanted to go directly back to my seat because now I really needed a drink to cool me off. I never felt like this before! Just by dancing with this tall, dark skinned, lusty built, brown eyed man, he made me very nervous, afraid of myself, and raised my body temperature to the max. If I would have stayed in that man's arm any longer I was afraid of what he might have talked me into doing! The rest of the night I was on the edge. I was so unsure of what had just happened to me on the dance floor. I do know this dark skinned, lusty built, brown eyed man had mixed up a recipe in my body that even I would eat. It was like every movement he made I was watching him. The way he walked, the way he stand, the way he sat, and the way he talked to others, I was watching him. I was focus but yet confused about this dark skinned, lusty built, brown eyed man! Could he be the one, I thought to myself. The tavern was about to close. As my neighbor from across the street and I started out the door this dark skinned, lusty built, brown eyed man stopped me. He asked if he and his friend could give us a ride home.

Of course the idea was running through my head, "I wouldn't mind letting you ride something alright!" I said, "No we only live a block up the street." Now tell me this dark skinned, lusty built, brown eyed man wasn't working overtime? He said, "Well can I walk you to your front door?" Ok now I'm thinking, "He thinks that once he gets to my door I'm going to ask him in? Wrong!" I said, "No that's ok. I wouldn't want you to leave your friend." Dude wasn't taking no for an answer. This dark skinned, lusty built, brown eyed man said; "I'll tell him to pick me up down the block. He wouldn't mind." At the same time I was thinking, you don't know which block I stayed down. He said, "If you feel uncomfortable with that then you don't have to tell me your address. I'll have him wait here until I come back." I then said, "No, that's ok. Just tell him to turn the corner and park at the end of the play ground." The dark skinned, lusty built, brown eyed man went over and talked to his friend for a few seconds. He then came back to where I was standing and said, "Ok, you're ready?" Was I impressed? Yes! My neighbor walked a little ahead of us. She said, "I'll walk ahead so you guys could have some privacy." The walk was nice. I really enjoyed his company and conversation. He seems to be a man with goals in his life and knows how to accomplish each of them.

When we made it to my house his friend haven't made it there yet. So I told the dark skinned, lusty built, brown eyed man that I'll be right back out. It was a nice and warm night, plus I wasn't sleepy. I went into the house to check on my kids. They were all still sleeping so peaceful. I put a speaker by the door and turned on some soft music. Afterwards I got him a chair and me a pillow to sit on. I then asked him if he would like something to drink. He said, "A cold beer would do just fine right about now." I went back into my house and got three cold beers out the refrigerator. One for me, one for the dark skinned, lusty built, brown eyed man, and one for my nosey neighbor who lived directly across the street. She decided to sit her nosey ass on her porch. I raised one of the two beers I had left in my hand as I started sitting down on my pillow. She knew what it meant and quickly said, "Yes." Before I could lower my hand with the beer in it, my neighbor was on her way across the street to get it.

She ran back across the street after I gave her the beer and sat her nosey ass on her porch. Doing what she do best, watching my house. I must say one good thing about that is whenever I went anywhere miss nosey could tell me who all came over and the time they came by. Burglary didn't have a chance as long as she lived on the block. Well, I sat out on the porch with this tall, dark skinned, lusty built, brown eyed man for a while. After a few beers I said, "Looks like your friend forgot about you?" He replied, "No he'll be here." I thought it was rather gentleman of him when he said, "I've kept you up long enough. Could I use your phone to call me a cab?" I went into the house and brought out my phone. The cab company must have him on hold for a while because he called a few other cab numbers before he finally said, "Give them your address." It was like radar timing. As the cab was pulling up in front of my house the tall, dark skinned, lusty built brown eyed man spotted his friend driving up the street. I thought it was really nice that even thou he didn't get in the cab he still gave the cab driver money for his troubles.

The tall, dark skinned, lusty built, brown eyed man gave me his phone number and asked me to call him sometime. He got into his friend's car and as they drove off I watched the car until it turned the corner. I started daydreaming about him being my prince charming. I took a big deep breath and my heart stated to flicker. I was telling myself, "I think I can really fall in love with that man. Of course, after he left my nosey neighbor came over to do what she does best, which was being nosey and trying to find out what she could. No matter what she asked me, I kept saying, "he's a real gentleman." I started walking my too happy, in love ass around deeply thinking about the tall, dark skinned, lusty built, brown eyed man. My neighbor helped me clear my porch. Afterwards I gave her another beer and send her nosey ass back across the street. For the first time in a long time I went to sleep with a smile on my face and in my heart. As I think about it, the thought of the fear that this man will hurt me didn't cross my mind. He was too nice. Also for the first time I went to sleep not silently crying about my reddish head male friend who had gotten kill.

This tall, dark skinned, lusty built, brown eyed man made me feel so good and comfortable that I didn't need my white friend (cocaine) to relax me. If nothing else comes out of this newly developed friendship with this tall, dark skinned, lusty built, brown eyed man he'll at least be a good friend to have. Of course, I only got maybe just three hours of sleep and it was time to get the kids up for school. This was one morning I felt good considering that I didn't get much sleep. The next few days my attitude was a little more on the cheerful side. Even thou many times I wanted to pick up the phone and call the tall, dark skinned, lusty built, brown eyed man but I didn't. I really didn't want him to think I was a pest. Also I didn't want him to feel he could use me either. Regardless of how nice he seemed I'm still going to keep my invisible wall up. I'm not trying to get hurt by him or no other man.

To get my mind off of this tall, dark skinned, lusty built, brown eyed man, I had to keep myself extra busy. It was hard because he put so much joy and happiness in my heart. I decided to change my bedroom around because I had a new attitude and a new view for living. I had my music playing in the background while I was changing my room around, dancing, and singing. At that moment I didn't have any man on my mind. You know how you move a piece of furnisher from its old spot you always fine something you've been looking for? I was surprised about what I found when I moved my dresser! I moved one dresser into a new spot and went back to the old spot where the dresser uses to be to clean up the mess that fell behind the dresser. I started picking through the things that fell behind the dresser. Who knows I might have some lost treasure or something within all that mess on the floor. Wishful thinking on my account. I picked up this piece of paper and begin to unfold it. When I opened it I smiled and softly said, "I don't need you now." This time I felt good throwing away a man's phone number. "Why?" I guess you maybe saying. Especially, since I was alone and needed the company of a good man from time to time! Well, remember that one number I had gotten from my cousin? That was the same number I lost and tore my room up looking for it. I found it in all that mess on my floor and I threw it away. Crazy you may say! It must not have been meant for me to use it because I would have never found out how much of a gentleman my new friend was. He cheers my heart up, puts a smile on my face, and he makes me feel good all over.

I was even happier to have found out that he was the same man that gave my cousin his number the night when she and I walked to get some ice cream. I guess faith said, "It wasn't meant for me to use his number!" How else could you or I explain it? It was a coincident, you could say! I've already memorized in my mind the same name and number on the piece of paper I found while cleaning my room. It was the same name and number as the one belonging to the tall, dark skinned, lusty built, brown eyed man I danced so warm and secure with. This man specifically dedicated the song "Two Occasion" to me, not once but twice. The mysterious number I thought I would never get the chance to meet the face it belonged to had reappeared last night. Well, I don't have to look no further or wonder anymore who this man was because I truly know now. That's why I said, "I don't need you now," because I had the information I was so frightfully wondering and looking for already. I would keep all that important information and more kept in a safe place where

I know I won't loose it again. Well my reader you probably put all the pieces together and came up with an answer about me and my friend. This tall, dark skinned, lusty built, brown eyed man and I became an idol. We became the idea looked good together couple.

He was so charming, good, and gentle. He very easily won the heart of my kids. As time went on I let the tall, dark skinned, lusty built, brown eyed man move in. Now we could spend a little more time with each other. Plus he didn't have to rush home early in the mornings to get his self together so he could make it to school on time. As far as my job, I did what I did best and that was being a mother and the lady around the house. Our relationship had become so nice and sweet. This tall, dark skinned, lusty built brown eyed man was a jewel to me; so precious and he treated me like a queen. What I really loved in the tall, dark skinned, lusty built, brown eyed man was his honesty about his past, present, and future planning. This led us into some very open communications and some very deep and serious talks.Sometimes these conversations got sensitive and emotional. Of course, it was I who would always be watery eyed. It was good to see he wasn't judgmental and had a very caring heart and open-mind. Me being who I was would try to be all hard and keep my true emotions from coming out. I remember how the tall, dark skinned, lusty built, brown eyed man would tell me, "Go ahead, and let it out. It'll do you good."

Surely but slowly my tears would start running down my face. He would grab me in his arms and hold me. Telling me, "Baby, that's what I'm here for." My face would be pressed snuggly up against his strong, soft, but rock hard muscled chest. It was like his heart was telling me, "every thing is going to be alright." Tightly secured in his arms I would begin to cry even harder. I felt so good in his arms because for the first time in years someone told me, "It was ok for me to cry." I thought I had died and went to heaven. As I cried with my face buried into the tall, dark skinned, lusty built, brown eyed man chest, it seemed so strange to me. I could feel years of releasing tension, anger, hurt, and sadness coming out of my deeply hidden inner soul and body. I though at that moment I felt as if I had just been reborn. Kind of like the release a woman gets from being in labor for many hours and then she gasp for that breath of air from pushing a big fifteen pound baby out of her. I could feel hurt being drugged out of me from when I was a child. I cried even harder when I thought about my deceased reddish head male friend. I thought about the pain, the suffering, the abuse, the want and the need for love I had needed, and so much missed. I even thought about the boy that killed my reddish head male friend. So many times I cried silently when I hurt and was in pain because life had made me that way. Now for once in my life I finally felt and believed that it was ok to cry.

This tall, dark skinned, lusty built, brown eyed man was good with whatever he did. He had a way of holding me that made me feel like I was floating on clouds. He would start squeezing and rubbing on me. I would for a moment forget why I was crying and drift off into this relaxing heaven he puts me in. One thing leading to another and oh, this tall, dark skinned, lusty built, brown eyed man would put my body in total exorcise. He kept me high on love. I didn't drink as much and I had cut back on my cocaine. He didn't like me doing the cocaine but I would tell him, "I need it to relax." What I say that for because this dark skinned, lusty built, brown eyed man told me, "Anytime you feel you need to put that shit in your body reach over and grab me. My high will last longer." A big smile came on my face and in my heart when I thought about the long time high he did give me. I mean I felt as if I'm in another world floating in clouds with him. Yeah, a girl like me can get addicted to the love drugs he has to offer. I started falling strongly in love with this tall, dark skinned, lusty built, brown eyed man so much. He was all I needed. He was all that I wanted or could have asked for. I felt God knew I needed someone to truly love.

An angel and he sent the tall dark skinned, lusty built, brown eyed man to me. Twice I let this angel get pass me but he came my way a third time. I said to myself, "I'll be a damn fool! I'm not gonna let you get away again!" Call it love, but I was now truly touched by a dark skinned, lusty built, brown eyed angel! Someone so kind, caring, sweet, understanding, giving, but most of all loving was sent to me. He had lots of very good qualities in a damn good man and I wanted him all for myself. Yes, my reader I felt that there was a God. I finally felt I was going to be happy for the rest of my life. I finally felt I had nothing to worry about again. All those bad hands that life was dealing me were over because with this tall, dark skinned, lusty built, brown eyed man I finally felt I can play the hands and win! Oh but reader remember this is my life! This is my story! What good last long in my life? Another horror story was being created.

Chapter Twenty

"I'm So Sorry: The Taking Back of Control"

THIS MADE IN heaven relationship I was now in turned out to be another one of those nightmares from hell. I guess the hell part about it was giving him my pussy and he still was kicking my ass. I couldn't understand it for the life of me, why he was doing this to me. This one night this tall, dark skin, lusty built brown eyed man had went out and didn't come home in time. It started getting late and I knew the taverns were closed. Sure, I was worried about if he was ok or not but then I started thinking he was maybe with another female. Of course, this was a thought my mind really couldn't deal with. So I walked around the corner and got a package of cocaine. Now I'm high, relax, don't really give a fuck but yet I'm still hurting. Feeding myself the thoughts, "I told you not to get involve with no one! I knew he was going to hurt me! Stupid! Stupid! Stupid!"

What could I do? I loved him too much to leave him, but it hurts too much to stay with him! God I don't know what to do? Maybe I'm just imaging everything? Image my ass! I'm not imaging these fucken feelings I'm going through and the cocaine didn't help! So I lay in the bed trying to go to sleep. I could sleep because I was constantly looking at the clock. Wondering where he could be?

Then, finally I heard him putting the key in the door. Oh but sister girl is too steamed and pissed in a way I wished he wouldn't had came home until I cooled off some! It was no hiding my attitude. I think it really only made matters worst when I did some cocaine in front of him. He yelled, "So this is what you do when I'm gone?" I told him, "Fuck you! I needed you! Where the hell was you at?" One thing lead to another! Back and forth the questions, which weren't getting answered, kept flying. Then before I knew it, POW!! I was hit. This tall, dark skin, lusty built, brown eyed man balled his fist up and hit me in my face!

That closed my mouth. I was more shocked and surprised then hurt. I was confused. Right away all kinds of thoughts started running through my head and they weren't anything nice. High and confused I sat back on the bed. I held my face as tears start running out my eyes and started crying saying, "Why?" Now all I wanted was to be left alone. The hurting part about the night was I couldn't believe that my prefect gentleman from heaven was really an angel from hell. I couldn't believe I was just hit, and he decided to sit his ass beside me on the bed. Then he tried to hold me while telling me that I'm sorry shit. I didn't want to hear it. I told him to get his shit and get the fuck out! My only problem was I didn't know this tall, dark skin, lusty built brown eyed man had an evil twin living inside of his body.

He told me, "I'm not going no where! You're not gonna make me fall in love with you, and then think you can kick me out!" Oh, but what a fool I was. He begin grabbing on my hand talking about, "Let me see!" I'm like, "For what? What am I going to tell my kids when they see my face looking like this?" Well, I did let him see and fell for his comforting me approach. By the morning the bottom of my eye had started swelling. I woke him up and said, "Look at my eye!" Oh yes, he was saying all that baby I'm sorry shit to me and all that other shit I didn't want to hear. Then all of a sudden his attitude changed. He said, "What you're going to tell the kids?" I said, "What you mean what am I going to tell the kids? You should be thinking what you gonna tell the kids for your reason why?" Then he started with this whole sad story about how he didn't want the kids to hate him. He didn't know how he'd be able to face them if they thought badly about him. Well, I only made things worst. The tall, dark skin, lusty built brown eyed man said, "Tell them it was an accident?" I looked at him and said, "What? I'm not telling my kids nothing you told me!" I went out the room to start breakfast.

It wasn't easy trying to cook and talk to my kids without looking at them but I did pull it off. Then the tall, dark skin, lusty built, brown eyed man came into the kitchen. "Hey baby," he said as he kissed me on the cheek. I said nothing and kept on cooking. I really wanted to hit him in his eye when he said, "I know my big baby ain't still made at me from last night?" Yes, all kinds of mutha fucks words started running through my head. I wanted to dash the whole pot of grits on his ass. Asking me that shit. He kept playing around and tried to kiss me. He started telling the kids to say things like, "Kids tell your mom I love her and don't be mad." Still playing around and trying to kiss me. I said in a low and soft voice to him, "You need to get the fuck away from me!" He still wouldn't stop. He kept on messing with me, trying to get me to talk to him. Then I thought I was going to say something to him until my son said, "Don't be mad at him mama." A bigger frown came on my face. I said to myself, "Boy if you only knew why I was mad at his ass, you'll turn the table on him too!" Oh, no it didn't stop there. The tall, dark skin, lusty built, brown eyed man said, "Baby, I'm not gonna stop until you tell me you accept my apology."

He had the kids all excited too. They too were now asking me to forgive him. My middle son said, "Mama why is you so man at him?" I told my middle son, "Ask him!" He asked him and I could have died when he gave my middle son an answer. He said, "You know how your mom always think she all hard and can whop the world?" Even I was waiting for him to hurry up and finish his little story. I was saying to myself, "You don't have the gouts to tell them the truth?" Remember I told you he was good in everything that he did! The tall, dark skin, lusty built brown eyed man had me believing his story and I knew the truth! He continues on by saying, "Well last night when I came home we got to playing a little too rough." Now I'm saying to myself, "And!" Then he said "And you all know how I be hollering and trying run to keep her from biting me? While I was falling out the bed I accidentally kicked your mom in the face." My eyes lit up with surprise and anger. I wanted to kick him in his mouth for that lie. The tall, dark skin, lusty built brown eyed man then start hugging on me trying to kiss me. Saying, "My Pooh not too happy because she woke up this morning with a little shiner and she's not speaking to me."

I don't know what the hell I was thinking about when I let him get away with that lie. I later found out that it was a big mistake on my behalf. Afterward he and I talked. He promised and assured me that he'll never hit me again. Things seemed to have gotten back to normal real quick. He would bring me little gifts and sometimes he did romantic things for and with me. Just for him being him I never could stay mad at him long. He'll always found some kind of way to win me over by making me happy regardless of what it took. As time when on it seems as if my relationship from heaven turned into a living nightmare from hell and it was no waking up! It became a pattern. I was constantly getting hit and beat on by this tall, dark skin, lusty built brown eyed man. I couldn't understand how I still loved this man when I feared for my life.

He had me so afraid of him till I wouldn't speak unless he told me to. When we would go somewhere don't let no one look or say hi to me because he would knock the dog shit out of me. I was now in a relationship I was too afraid to get out of. Plus this tall, dark skin, lusty built brown eyed man, as he said, "wasn't gonna let me out of the relationship." I was now a prisoner of love and it hurt! I became so badly strung out on drugs till I didn't care what happened to me anymore. I knew now that life was not ever meant for me to ever really be happy. Mind washed! Or was it sex washed? Either way I now knew and understood the old say, "A fool blinded by love." I done got my ass kick all the time! Sometimes I would sit and ask myself why I felt so guilty as if I deserved the beatings? He would talk that talk that made me feel so bad after he had done kick my ass. What really tripped me out was when he would point out specific things to blame on me for beating my ass. Like, "If you wouldn't have done this I would have not hit you." Or things like, "All you had to do was be quiet like I told you and maybe you wouldn't had got hit." I called myself stupid now but back then I was too afraid to even try to think or understand what the word meant.

With the beatings I was going through now in my life, made me think about my girl friend I went to school with. She uses to get beat on by her boyfriend all the time. Then I started thinking about another old say, "That once a man hit you, he will keep hitting on you!" I would sometimes say to myself, "You must like getting your ass kick?" I knew I was the only one to stop the beatings but I was too afraid of letting go of something I loved; he was causing me so much pain. Even my doctor was afraid for me. I remember how she would tell me, "Lovely, I'm just so afraid that one day this man is going to kill you." It hurts me even more when she things like, "I been your doctor since you were a young girl and delivered six of your kids." She told me, "Lovely, you got to do something because I'm getting tired of seeing you coming into the hospital beaten and broken up!" I can still hear the anger in my doctor's voice and see the sadness of concern and worry on her face. My doctor was right. To be honest I too was tired of the ass kicking. Deep inside I knew I was stronger than that. I had my mind made up and end up falling right back into that I love you shit of a spell he had on me.

Again I am treated like a queen until he decided he wanted to hit on me again! The ass kicking had started getting more serious. I can remember times when he would take care of the kids because he didn't want my kids to see how bad he had beaten me. I would lie to my kids numerous of times, while lying in the bed as if I was sick until my face heeled. When all the time I really wasn't sick but I was sick of the ass beating. I was sick of him hitting on me and it was time I did something about it. But what? I continue to do, provide, and take care of my kids. Only thing about the mother roles in my life, I wasn't truthful, or honest with, and to my kids. I knew it wasn't fair to the kids but I was more afraid of what he might do to them.

As long as I kept my kids out of my relationship I felt they were safe. Oh but it wasn't long before the butter start melting easier! I started noticing every time I got my ass kick by him I was high on that shit (the cocaine) and I was always talking big shit! I knew then I had to wake up and find myself before this man killed me. I started back focusing on my life and my kids. Plus they needed their mom and some cocaine addicted who always got her ass kick. I had to come up with a good plan and stick to it. Well, I kept trying to live my life as if I was happy. I felt my kids have been through enough bad times and hard suffering. The things I was going through in my life, I brought on myself. That's why I knew it's gonna have to be up to me to get myself and my kids out of this mess!

First thing I had to do was to build myself back up and build a higher positive self-esteem. The main thing I needed to do was to leave this damn cocaine alone. How I kept asking myself! How in the world am I supposed to break a bad habit that broke me down bad? I start think that the less money I had the less drugs I could buy. I knew then I had to keep all my extra money out my hands. The more extra money I had the more I spend on cocaine. The tall, dark skin, lusty built, brown eyed man and I had a very good conversation with no hollering or hitting. I explained to him how much I really do love him and how I really wanted this relationship to work. After talking to him I found out that he wanted the same thing. I explained to him how I really wanted to leave the drugs alone but I needed his help. That wasn't hard. He hurried up and said, "What do I got to do?"

I can say that as long as we have been together I never had to worry about him taking my money. I said, "If I give you my money would you not give it back to me especially when you know I want to buy drugs?" He looked at me and said, "You really are serious?" I replied sadly, "Yeah. I'm tried of us going through these changes. I really want this relationship to work." As time came and went by I started noticing a big difference in my relationship with him. I had seen the good gentleman coming back out of him. The only problem was I sometimes would let the ugly Lynn out of me. He was good to me but it was hard for me to shake that cocaine monkey that was riding my back. I would become so mean and evil at times to the point where he would leave me. I didn't mean it. It's just I needed some drugs bad in my body. What use to really piss me off was when he did leave he left me with my money. I would go through the house storming mad. Kicking and throwing things.

Then afterward I would cry like a big baby because I didn't get no drugs, done torn up my house up, and now I had to clean it up. It seemed as if he always knew when to come back. We would talk and everything would be ok again. I remember how the tall, dark skin, lusty built, brown eyed man would give me some marijuana to help me shake the monkey but it didn't work. I would start yelling and crying, while trying to fight the itch that my body was going through for the lack of cocaine. Oh but it got better. I started seeing what my withdraws were putting the tall, dark skin, lusty built, brown eyed man through. He would sometimes cry with me as he held me. Saying, "Damn, I wish I can do something to make this easier for you?" A bright light lit up in my head. I quickly said, "Baby you can. You can get me some dope." Right away he said, "No." Then I started begging; I was trying to make him feel guilty because he was the reason I was suffering. "Baby, I've been doing damn good because I love you more than the dope. Plus I want our relationship to work. All I need is just a little. Just enough to make this monkey ease off of me some. You see what it is doing to me. Baby please? It hurts. I promise I won't ask for no more."

Oh yes, I found his weakness and I played on it many of times. A matter of fact I ran over him. I now was getting this tall, dark skinned, lusty built, brown eyed man to buy me drugs when I wanted it. I knew it wasn't fair but I just wanted to get high. Well, that only lasted for so long until I really deep inside started feeling bad for my kids. Here my kids were saying how glad they were that I had stop getting high; when all the time I was really getting high more. I would lie to my kids and the tall, dark skinned, lusty built, brown eyed man about where my money goes. I would tell the kids I gave the tall, dark skinned, lusty built, brown eyed man all my money. I would tell the tall, dark skinned, lusty, built brown eyed man I bought the kids more clothes than what I really bought when I go shopping. So I was stashing extra money; stealing from myself just to get high. We agreed that he would monitor my cocaine use to wing me off it. This way I'll throw off doubts he may have about me getting high. By doing this I was able to play the monkey itch off with the tall, dark skinned, lusty built, brown eyed man.

If only he knew? I was now enjoying my high even more. I got high while no one was home but me and at night the tall, dark skinned, lusty built, brown eyed man would buy me more cocaine. Even that arrangement was working out just fine but something still wasn't right inside of me. I was getting unexplained pains; hurts of sadness, and bitterness was eating away at my heart. I couldn't stand to continue looking and remembering my kids' happy faces when they thought I wasn't doing drugs anymore. My kids were changing and growing up and I was staying too high to really enjoy those moments. Again I was telling myself I'm going to leave drugs along. This time I truly mean it. Each time I tried to leave drugs alone I will start back doing them more for all the wrong reasons. All this time I should have been doing drugs for myself; my entertainment. That's why I felt this time when I did the drugs it will be different but that didn't work either.

My mind was made up. I seriously meant it within my heart, "to shake the monkey and leave cocaine alone for good!" More determine to do it now for myself I had to come up with a sound proof plan to shake the monkey for good. I had to make sure when the monkey came riding my back, I didn't give him what he want but shake him. I knew the tall dark skin lusty built brown eyes man would give in to the monkey. I need somebody that was stronger than him and I. The biggest and best idea came into my head; my kids. I called the kids into the house and had one of those family talks. It wasn't as hard as I thought it would be. I told them the truth. I explained to my kids how I've been lying to them about my drug usage. I told them the reason I'm coming clean with them was because I now truly wanted to leave the drugs alone and I needed their help.

My middle son was always the joker of the family. He said, "You the mama and we the kids. We can't whop you if you don't do what we tell you?" I smiled and softly said, "Not really." I told my oldest daughter, "You are the oldest. I hate to put such a load on you but I need you to keep my money. No matter how crazy I get, no matter how much I beg you, you got to promise me you'll be strong and don't give me no money!" Then she said, "Why you not giving your money to your male friend?" I explained to her how I tried doing it but he would give into my cries. It made me very happy when my kids agreed to help me kick my cocaine habit. Now all I had to do now was just do it. The new plan was working out ok. I truly loved my oldest daughter so much for putting up with my mess. On days I knew I was going to get my check, I would keep her home from school. This way when I cashed my check she will be there with me. We will go pay bills, shop for the house, and buy the kids some clothes. My oldest daughter was good at keeping my money away from me. When we get home I'll give her all my extra money. She made sure I didn't get a dime of it.

She said, "Mama remember when we went into that store or this store," but she would say the store name. Then she would say, "You put the change in that pocket." I wanted to hit my daughter in the eye but I was glad she was watching me like a hawk. I would go through all of my pockets and even my bra to let her see I didn't have any money on me. She would then go into her room and close the door. I be trying to peek through the keyhole to see where she puts my money but she got hip to that and started covering it up. I believed I gave my money to the right person this time because she wouldn't give me nothing. Not one single penny! I would lie to her like I need to buy something for the house, she'll say, "No." I would talk crazy to her and even sometimes push her around but my daughter still held her ground lots of time with tears in her eyes and said, "I don't care what you do to me! I'm not giving you any money!" I would go into her bedroom sometimes and throw everything around looking for my money. My kids would stand there watching me crying, "Mama please stop!" There have been times when the younger kids would say, "Just give mama her money so she'll stop!"

My oldest daughter will still say, "I'm not giving her anything! It's for her own good!" Believe me the little girl was holding on to and for dear life and still told me "no." It was hard and I put my kids through straight hell but yet because I was their mother they put up with my shit and still loved me. I'll sit back and picture the fear I put into my kids while I was trying to kick my drug habit; I wasn't nothing nice. I really needed my ass kick! I remember the expression on their faces as tears ran out their eyes and poured down their little faces. I would sometimes think to myself, "How could I be so mean to my kids and say I loved them?" I knew it wasn't me; it was the monkey in me and on me that wanted the drugs. Those little faces, those watery eyes, and fearful wet faces were the strengths I needed to help me shake that monkey and kick my cocaine habit. I knew I couldn't continue hurting myself like I was doing but most of all I knew I had to stop hurting my kids like I was doing.

To my kids:

I love each one of you so dearly for hanging in there with me. Our closeness now allowed us to always find sometime in our lives to talk about our past, present, and future; the good and the bad. I'm glad I brought you up so each of you can talk to me about anything, no matter what. For that reason I knew I had to be honest about what was really going on in my life. By doing this I'm hoping none of you will make the same mistakes I have made in my life; or even if you should run into similar problems as mine own you will know how to deal with them better. I truthfully told you all of the good and bad things that could come with whatever lifestyle you choose to live. You all are including your seeds and your seeds' seeds will always be my life, my whole world, my family, my joy, my happiness, my reason for wanting to do right. You all are the only thing I have and I love you all so dear and deeply in my heart. I appreciate everything you all have done for me in my life. Most of all I treasure and cherish so preciously your love and the strength you all had in helping me through my fight with cocaine. Together we did it and 12 years later we still are doing it. Mama love's you all so much. Even for those of you that were trying to make your big sister give into me; I love you always and forever too. In your own way you were showing your love because you didn't want and couldn't stand to see me, your mama suffering and hurting.

After all the hell I put you, my kids through everything worked out fine. Those strongly spoken words of my oldest daughter rings in my ear even today, "it's for her own good." And my baby, you hit it; the bull's-eye, "it was for my own good." I love you so much. You know what? Your big sister was right. In fact she was very right about how she was handling my money. It was for my own good that I had to suffer some while going through my withdraws instead of feeding my aches and needs for the drug, cocaine. At that time I didn't want to hear the "NOs," but I knew it was only for my own good. When my daughter told me "NO," I knew what I could have done to my daughter and she did too. However, my oldest daughter still wasn't going to give me any money and I love her for all that and some. I love all my kids and their kids. <u>Again I thank you, my kids so very much for being there for me.</u> Without you all I couldn't have did it. A new life, a new start.

I was time to find a new house and leave all our bad past behind us. It didn't take me long before I found a new house for my kids and I to move in. My kids seemed so happy. They would go out and play with the good neighbor's kids. At first one or two of the kids uses to come into the house just to see what I was doing. I assured my kids that there would never be anymore drugs in our life and that was a promise I was going to keep; even, if it caused me my life. I believed my kids were coming into the house to see if I was doing drugs. After they seen I wasn't doing drugs they started playing more comfortable and enjoying themselves while outside. I would sometimes stand in the doorway just to watch my kids run up and down the street and playing with their little friends. The laughter in their voices while they were playing sounded like sweet music to me.

I remember how some stories of my life were so great to my kids that they would tell their little friends the stories too. Then that lead to, "mama tell my friend about the time you did this." I would sit down and tell the story to my kids and their friends. The surprising and amusing expressions on my kids' and their friends' faces each time I told the story warmed my heart. Sometimes my kids little friends would say, "Man your mama is famous." I'll smile as my kids will go back outside feeling all proud about their mama. What really uses to touch me was when sometimes the little kids would come by looking for my kids and they would bring a friend with them too. Nice and politely my kids' friends would say, "Could you please tell my friend about the time you did this," and I would tell the short story to the kids too. I told my kids these stories about my past so they would understand the outcome for making certain mistakes I did and reframe from doing them too.

I felt a lot better about myself because I was clean of drugs and my kids were smiling and happy. Plus I knew deep down in my heart and mind I would never use drugs again no matter what. My life seemed to be going along just fine. I was now enjoying every moment of watching my kids as they grew up. They were the stars that shinned in my eyes everyday and every night. My kids were so full of life now. It seemed as if they never got tired of running and playing outside. I really liked my life because it was telling me, "You are ok now," and I felt the difference. Oh, but remember, every time I try to change my ways for the better, something always throw a damn monkey in my life to cause me personal hell. Only this time it wasn't a white cocaine monkey that I was trying to shake and fight but a nigga monkey that was causing me bad vibes and heartaches. I got my kids out of one kind of abusive type of life only to summit them into another. Life was ok. My kids were happy, I was happy, and I thought the tall, dark skinned, lusty built, brown eyed man was happy with me now that I was off of drugs too.

Like I said I was damn proud of the turn around I had made in my life. I could now feel I was doing my best in whatever I did. I knew my kids were much happier with me, their drug free mom. The problem that started came from the tall, dark skinned, lusty built brown eyed man. I thought our relationship was going along just fine. I didn't go anywhere; all I did was stayed in the house. When I did go outside of the house it would be with the tall, dark skinned, lusty built, brown eyed man and or my kids. You see I also had gotten use to having someone with me when I did leave the house. Plus I didn't want to backslide on drugs. Lets just say I wasn't strong enough to take that chance either; therefore, I made sure somebody was with me when I left the house. I was only off drugs for a few months and I didn't really totally trust myself. Not yet at least. Even thou my mind and heart was made up, let's just say I haven't been put through the real test. I did get to the point where I was tired of staying in the house. I would become restless and needed something to do. My house stayed clean because every time you turn around I was acting like "Hazel;" cleaning even the cleanest part of the house. As the kids came in and out the door, I would go right behind them and clean up. I even cleaned my kids' rooms and folded all their clothes; plus I hung some of their clothes in their closet and ironed them too. All my kids had to do was be kids.

I really needed something to keep my mind occupy so I wouldn't fall back on drugs. To add to my problems the tall, dark skinned, lusty built, brown eyed man had started staying away from home daily until late hours at night. Sure I was wondering why and what he was doing but I would still give him the benefit of the doubt. This one particular night I wanted, no I needed a cold beer. The kids were all sleeping and I decided to walk around the corner to this one tavern; it was nice in the tavern. The people seemed to be enjoying themselves too. I decided to stay and throw some darts and have me a few drinks. I wasn't paying attention to the time and the hours had gone by so fast. I understand now what the old say meant, "time show pass when you're having fun." Once I realized what had happened I try to hurry up and get home. Now I was worried because I knew the tall, dark skinned, lusty built, brown eyed man would be at the house. As I turned the corner I could see him sitting on the porch. I'm saying to my self, "I know he's mad because I told him I wasn't going no where. I hope he'll be understanding!" I didn't do anything wrong; it wasn't like I was out doing drugs or with someone else! I just had a few beers and lost track of time. Well, I'll find out in a few seconds.

As I got closer to the porch I could see the angry expression on the tall, dark skinned, lusty built, brown eyed man face. I knew he was upset. When I got in front of the house I said, "Hey baby." The tall, dark skinned, lusty built, brown eyed man got up, said nothing, and went into the house. I asked him if he eaten yet and he told me not to say anything to him. The tone of his voice made me kind of nervous. That was all I needed to hear and I started taking my clothes off to get into bed. I was half asleep and the tall, dark skinned, lusty built, brown eyed man decided he wanted to talk and ask questions. Now I'm remembering what he said earlier about don't say anything to him. Of course I'm also remembering the past too; when I didn't give him the answer he was looking for, I got hit. All I wanted to do was to go to sleep. Then he said, "Don't you here me talking to you?" I said, "Would you make up your mind. Do you or don't you want me talking to you?" What I say that for because then it led to him saying, "Oh you're trying to get smart?" Back and forth words were being exchanged. Only I was scared to death that I might say the wrong thing even if it was the truth. We were now at each other throats.

Our loud mouths were ringing through the house and woke the kids up. They came into the room where the tall, dark skinned, lusty built, brown eyed man and I were. Yelling, "You better leave my mama alone!" I have seen the anger in my kids' eyes. If they had to my kids would really wanted to hurt the tall dark skin lusty built brown eyes man. I couldn't get my kids to go back to bed until I assured them that the tall, dark skinned, lusty built, brown eyed man and I wasn't going to be fighting. I came out the room to see my kids back to bed and then I went back to bed myself. Oh but that's just like a man wanting to have the last say so about anything. The tall, dark skinned, lusty built, brown eyed man started hyping the argument back up again. I kept asking him to leave me alone and just go to sleep. I promised the kids that we weren't going to fight. Leave it up to me to be the first to break the promise. I don't know what got into me that night but I guess I was having flash backs from the past.

Usually when I be trying to talk and defend myself, before I know it, POW. I would have got hit. This tall, dark skinned, lusty built, brown eyed man would always knock the dog shit out of me unexpectedly. I never would see his fist coming. My blood would run hot down my face. My nerves were shaken so bad until it felt like I had knots balling up in my stomach. I was so afraid that he was going to hit me even thou again I was telling the truth. Fear and reflexes reacted, two bad for that conversation. POW, POW! Before I knew it I had tightly balled my fist up, jumped up, and knocked the shit out of the tall, dark skinned, lusty built, brown eyed man. Then the fight was on. I for the first time wasn't taking an ass whipping from the tall, dark skinned, lusty built, brown eyed man. The fight was on and I mean it was on. Only this time I wasn't going to be the only one bleeding, black, blue, red, purple, and hurt. Then the kids came running back into the room trying to help me. They had brooms, bats, and anything else they could get their hands on screaming, "Leave my mama alone!" It was funny because the tall, dark skinned, lusty built, brown eyed man start screaming, "I ain't got your mama! Tell your mama to let me go!" From that night on I was the giver of the ass whipping and not the receiver. I thought to my self, "all this time I have been letting this nigga kick my ass. No more."

It's sad but I felt good to say that the fighting didn't end there. I submitted my kids to several beat downs and bloody fights that result in him or me going to the hospital. Sometimes it was me who had to go to the hospital but the majority of the time it was the tall, dark skinned, lusty built, brown eyed man that needed to go to the hospital. I had this attitude problem now. Anytime the tall, dark skinned, lusty built, brown eyed man came into the house saying anything to me I didn't like, I would knock the shit out of him and the fight would be on. This one time we were fighting and I mean I tore my house up with the tall, dark skinned, lusty built, brown eyed man. I was trying to kill him. I guess the neighbor thought it was the other way around and called the police. What they do that for? I almost went to jail. When the police came up on the porch they heard all the commotion that was going on inside the house. Talk about a brother was glad to see the police. The tall, dark skinned, lusty built, brown eyed man said, "Get her! I want to press charges against her!"

Those fools grabbed me and put me in handcuffs. I was mad and crying. Asking the police, "Why is you taking me to jail?" The one police officer said, "Somebody have to go to jail and from the look of him think it have to be you." I really started crying when my kids came into the front room crying, begging the police not to take me to jail. I asked them, "What is gonna happen to my kids?" The one officer said, "Either you can call somebody to get them or we can?" I wanted to hit him (the police officer) in the mouth for that smart-ass remark. I told my kids to call their granddaddy to come and get them. Then I asked the police, "What about him (referring to the tall, dark skinned, lusty built, brown eyed man)? What is you'al going to do with him?" The one officer said, "He'll go to the hospital and then he can go wherever he wants to go afterwards." I started crying, "That's not fair! You can't defend your self these days in your own house!" Then the one police officer that had me said, "What'd you say?" I told him what I had just said. The officer then asked, "Who name was on the lease?" I told him, "Mines. Mines and my kids." The police officer then took my handcuffs off. Man was I so happy I wasn't going to jail.

The officer took the handcuffs he took off of me and put them on the tall, dark skinned, lusty built, brown eyed man and said, "Ok buddy looks like we're gonna take you to the hospital and then you're going to jail." "Yes," I said. Once the police officer ran a check on the tall, dark skinned, lusty built, brown eyed man they found out that he had other warrants out for his arrest. You see each time in the past the tall, dark skinned, lusty built, brown eyed man had beaten me up I called the police. We would be right back together so they never could catch him because the police wasn't looking for him at my house. The tall, dark skinned, lusty built, brown eyed man would convince me in the past he wouldn't hit me again. What he didn't know was I had charges pending against him every time he hit me. I was just waiting till he really pissed me off and he would have been doing some time in jail. The only reason I never went through with the charges was because we got back together; this was a time I've been waiting for. Plus the police officer told me if I didn't go through with the charges this time the state would pick them up.

I loved when a good plan came together. The tall, dark skinned, lusty built, brown eyed man did about seven months in jail. Of course, I was going to see him. I was the tall, dark skinned, lusty built, brown eyed man faithful lady and did whatever I could for him while he was locked up. Once he did get out of jail we were back together again as man and woman. We still had minor disagreements but after the last battle or should I say fight we slowed down. Plus the tall, dark skinned, lusty built, brown eyed man would get the hell out my way real fast when he seen I was getting mad about something. The two of us decided to come to an agreement; therefore, when he seen I was mad he would leave me alone. Out of all the mess we've been through we still wanted to be with each other. Why you ask? Because deep in our heart we both truly loved each other very much.

Our relationship was now ruled as, "Don't ask me to do nothing that you won't do! Plus don't ask me any question if you don't want to answer any questions!" The tall, dark skinned, lusty built, brown eyed man and I got along damn good. The kids were happier again too. I was happy and I can say for sure the tall, dark skinned, lusty built, brown eyed man was very happy with me too. He had to be because he asked me to marry him. He asked me not just once but three times. Each time I said, "Yes." We had gone down to the courthouse twice and apply for our marriage licenses. By the time all the paper work came through and it was time to do it, I didn't because he made me mad. We still were together but living as common law husband and wife. I would tell him, "I don't have to marry you to get your name. By law I already have it. If you ever leave me and try to marry someone else, I'll have you lock up for bigamous. I am claiming my common law marriage." I loved this tall, dark skinned, lusty built, brown eyed man so much till I refused to give him up even if he wanted to go. I became a nightmare of his; he couldn't do anything without me checking him first. I would check to see if he was where he said he was. I remember how I use to tell him, "let me find out you're lying, I'm going to fuck you up!" Why was I so evil to him? Well let me tell you. Too many times I tried to get out this relationship and he wouldn't let me. The tall, dark skinned, lusty built, brown eyed man would tell me, "You had your chance to get out this relationship and lost it." I would sometimes say to myself, "I knew I shouldn't have taken him back." I don't know what it was but for some strange reason it seemed as if without this tall, dark skinned, lusty built, brown eyed man I was so sad, lonely, lost, and confused. I believe now he gave me true love, the true love I have been desiring so much for as a child but never gotten it.

Now since I found my security blanket I didn't want to let him go. So I asked the tall, dark skinned, lusty built, brown eyed man, "What you mean I had my chance and lost it? Hell you kept coming back to me!" He said, "That's it. I kept coming back. You should have gotten out before you made me fall in love with you. Now you can't go nowhere." I guess at first it was lusty, fantasy, desires, good company, mostly fear, and fulfillness the reasons why I wanted to be with the tall, dark skinned, lusty built, brown eyed man and because I only thought I loved him. Well now I feel different. I feel the same as he did. The tall, dark skinned, lusty built, brown eyed man had his chance to get out of this relationship. He should have let me left at least one of those times when I tried to but he wouldn't let me. Now I am so madly in love with him till it's sickening. I feel I'm not complete without him. He makes me very happy; regardless, of all the fighting and beating up on each other we did, we still were together and always crying behind it all saying, "I'm sorry and how much we loved each other."

Now I use to say to him, "If you wouldn't have done this or said that I wouldn't have acted the way I did." I guess now I was becoming a battering spouse. I would also always say, "I didn't want to but you made me do it!" I liked it because I would kick his ass and then he would kiss my ass to make up to me for kicking his ass. Strange! I don't know, call it crazy but I was determined to make this tall, dark skinned, lusty built, brown eyed man the best husband in the world. There were only a few catches to it. He's going to be my husband, my prefect man, my gentleman of all gentlemen, my king catering to his queen, which is me of course me. Wishful thinking, hey! Now I just got to put my plan to work and for it to work out the best for me. I sometimes still say to myself what did this tall, dark skinned, lusty built, brown eyed man do to me? How could I've been such a fool to fall for his gentleman charm? I was doing something right because whatever I wanted or needed the tall, dark skinned, lusty built, brown eyed man would go all out his way to get it for me. Who knows? Maybe this time it might work; the relationship of course!

Chapter Twenty-One
"What the Hell Happened"

WELL IT WAS a great life; a great plan. The kids were all growing up. My common law husband and I had become grandparents. We were really enjoying life; me and my family. I believe my common law husband enjoyed the grandkids more than I did. The grandkids did us good. Our favorite times were all of the time when we were with them. We did so many good things together and the family was still getting larger. If you ask any of our grandkids what you like to do most? I guarantee you they'll say fishing! They all love going fishing. Let me tell you about this because I feel it was so funny. One night my common law husband and our grandson dug up some night crawlers for bait for when we go fishing in the morning.

The next morning we had loaded all the fishing equipment in the car. My common law husband started asking about the bait that they had dug up last night. It was really strange that they just disappear out the refrigerator; they were no where around to be found. We gave up looking for the bait and decided that we were going to stop at a store to buy some bait. So he start gathering up our grandkids to take them fishing. When he found our grandson, my common law husband started yelling, "Baby come quickly!" I thought something had happened badly because the way he was yelling. So I ran in the direction I heard his voice. When I got there it was a sight to see.

Our grandson was sitting in the yard with the dog, a spoon, and a cool whip bowl. My common law husband had put the night crawlers in an empty cool whip bowl last night. Then he placed the night crawlers in the refrigerator. Cool whip was my grandson's favorite ice-cream topping. The boy would get him a spoon and eat cool whip out the bowl all day long. Let just say he felt cool whip tasted good on any and everything. The cool whip bowl with the night crawlers did not have any cool whip in it. Therefore, my grandson felt the bowl with the night crawlers did not have enough cool whip in it so he took it upon himself to open another bowl of cool whip. Then he took the cool whip and put it in the bowl with the night crawlers. By the time my common law husband had found our grandson, he had eaten mostly all the poor worms.

His little face had dirt and cool whip all over it. Now that was a pretty sight to see and it was funny because he helped himself to a spoon, cool whip, and a bowl. I asked my grandson did he know what he was eating. My grandson said, "At first it tasted kind of funny but after I put some cool whip on the worms they tasted good." That was my grandson's opinion but I'll never try it to see if it's good or not! Well, we did find the night crawlers, that is, what was left of them. We still had to buy bait on our way fishing. Even today we still laugh and talk about my grandson and his cool whip worm incident. Even after the slow start we still had a great time fishing. My grandson, now who is eight finds it so tickling and amusing to hear about his cool whip worm story.

We were like the almost prefect American family. We went to the zoo every summer, the festivals, all the parades, and any and everything that was kid related we went to. We made sure we never missed a parade down town. As a family we will pack a big picnic lunch for the long parade day stay and made sure we were early enough to get the front row. However, I believe some of the neighborhood kids liked our family outing just as much as we did. Mostly every time we went somewhere we took some of the neighbor's kids. All this enjoyment and love we for each other as a family was almost took away. My silent cries started all over again within my life.

How could the good times turn out to be something so badly! I had a car accident that left me off of work for a while. I'll never forget the sad times I lived through after my accident. Since I was unable to work I tried to get welfare and the system gave me such a hard time. I finally had a hearing about my case and the judgment was in support of me. Well, about a few weeks later I received back pay money that was owned to me according to the hearing courts. I cooked dinner and hurried the younger kids off to bed afterward. It was something about this night that was different. I couldn't really put my hands on it but I was feeling funny and was having lots of pains in my chest. You see I was on medication for my heart from a bad mickey slipped into my drink that left me sleeping for three days. Now back to that night. I was afraid. I didn't want the kids to see me if I was having a heart attack. I had medication but I didn't want to take it because it puts me in to a deep sleep for the first few hours. Since, I was the only adult home at the time I didn't want to sleep so sounded. Instead I took some of my other pain medication to ease the pains in my chest some. This way I could at lease relax slightly but yet still be alert until another adult came home.

Good thing I didn't take my medication. It wasn't a half an hour after I lay down before I was awakened by an explosion. Someone had thrown a gas cocktail bomb through my bedroom window and it was burning very fast. I woke completely up, grabbed the phone, and dialed 911 while I was violently ripping out of my burning dress. I started yelling at same time to get the attention of the kids that were sleeping upstairs. Once I got my dress off I begin hitting at the fire that was leading from my bed to my bedroom door hoping I could put the fire out some so I could get out. All within a few seconds I had seen that the fire wasn't calming down, I ran through the door of fire. By this time the whole house was full of smoke.

After I made it out of my bedroom I had seen that the whole house was filled with this thick black smoke. I couldn't see anything because the black smoke and the fire were spreading extremely fast throughout the house. I ran up the stairs in the darkness to wake the kids up and to get them out of the burning house. I was scared and praying silently to myself, "Lord please make sure that they are all alright." I went into each room and woke the kids up. I told all the kids to stay close by the wall as they went down the stairs. We used the wall as our guide to get down through the smoke filled burning house. I hurried all the kids to the back door because the entire front part of the house was in flames. I heard a big bang sound as if part of the house had fell down. I turned to look in the direction of the sound and it was my youngest son. He had kicked what was left of the front burning door and came in to help me. I opened the back door to make sure it was safe to go out. My youngest son and the dogs went out first and then the kids. As the neighbor was helping us get the kids away from the burning house, I noticed that one of the kids was missing. My youngest daughter had slept walked back into the house. I ran back into the house screaming and calling out my youngest daughter name but she didn't answer. The smoke was choking me. I was coughing a lot at this time. I felt as if I wasn't going to make it out of the burning house the second time but I wasn't gonna leave without my youngest daughter.

Each time I attempted to go up the stairs my feet went through them. I was now crying, screaming, coughing, and calling out my youngest daughter name hoping she'll wake up. Then it seems as if the fire had breath and became brighter. It was my middle son watered down coming through the fire to help me. He said, "Mama get out! I'll find her." I told him, "I'm not leaving until he gets her!" I told him the stairs would give away on him. So he walked the edge close to the wall. I later found out this was how they use to sneak out the house without me hearing them because the stairs squeaked. Back to the fire! My middle son yelled, "Mama, I got her get out of here!" I yelled, "You can't make it back down this way. Climb out the driveway window!" I ran out the burning house to the side of the house where the window to my youngest daughter bedroom was. My middle son broke the rest of window out. Then he put his youngest sister in the window. Only he wasn't handing her down to me. He started yelling, "Breathe," while doing CPR to his youngest sister. For that moment I stood there on top of my car as if my heart had fell in my stomach, frozen with my hands still up in the air as if I was waiting for him to hand my youngest daughter down to me.

He kept on saying over and over again, "Girl you better breathe!" She finally starts coughing and he handed her down to me. One of the neighbors got her from me. I yelled back up to my middle son, "Come on. I'll help you." As he started out the window it became filled with fire. My son was hollering as he fell back into the house away from the window. I couldn't see my son anymore. I yelled out his name asking him was he alright but he didn't answer me. Seconds later I heard a big crash! Then a big knot hit me in my stomach as I imagined what had just happen to my son. Now I was really going crazy because I knew I had just lost my son. I jumped down off the car and try to run back in to the house of fire. The neighbors grabbed me. I kept screaming, "My son is in there! I got to get him out! Please help, let me go." The neighbors finally got me clam down and told me that my son came out the house running so fast that one of the other neighbors jumped in his car to go catch him. If this one neighbor I trusted would not have told me this I wouldn't had believe it.

Her husband did come back with my son. He was ok. My family and I lost everything. The only clothes we had were what we had left on our backs. Except for me all I had was the under-slip that I was wearing. Even thou we had nothing, we still had each other.

Considering what could have happened, we were very blessed. The fire almost, could have but didn't take a life. This would have been something more disasters to my heart than the lost of all our materialistic things. I thank God, for this magnificence blessing. I believe God knew I was a strong woman and I will rebuild things back up for my family. The Red Cross people came and offer to put my family up in a hotel until we can find some place to stay. My two oldest daughters said, "No my mama is coming home with us." A few days after the fire, we went back to the house to meet the press. I knew everything was burned up and I didn't want to see the mess again. Even my fifty-six plants were gone; a few pieces of furnisher and some jewelry that belonged to my great great grandmother was gone, and never to be seen again.

As we started walking through the house my oldest son said, "Mama, here go some of your pages to your book. They were not burned." I told him, "For get it. It wasn't meant for me to write it no way." Then my kids started kicking through the burned trash and found more pages. One of my oldest daughter said, "Mama, you worked to hard on your book to just give it up." My kids seriously wanted me to finish my book. They kept on kicking and picking through the half frozen burned garbage left of what was once our home. I then start helping pick up and looking for the pages to my book. We got all the pages that we could find and put them in a plastic bag that we brought with us. We brought the plastic bags with the hope we could put some of our memories in them we found. Well, a few months after the fire I started putting the pages in order to see what pages were missing. It was so strange to me because they were all there. I still had every last page of the beginning of my book, the cover letter, the introductory, and each 190 pages afterward were all still there. Some pages were burned on the end and on other parts of the paper. Some of the pages had black footprints and smudge smoke from the fire on them. Just about every page had something wrong with it except for one thing; all the words were still readable. None of the words were damaged. Every letter was clearly readable for me to rewrite.

I said to myself, "Is God trying to tell me something? Maybe my book is supposed to be written? Maybe my story is supposed to be told?" Think about it my readers? You tell me what is the easiest thing to burn in a fire? I'll help answer it, "paper!" Paper flames up extremely quickly when fire hits it. For some strange unexplained reason the pages to my book was not burned nor wasn't any word unreadable to the eyes. Not one page had caught totally on fire to destruction. Help me out my readers if I'm wrong. The desk where I kept the pages to my book burned up. The same typewriter I used to type every page to my book, which sat at the desk burned up. Even the chair I sat in to type my book burned up. Again, help me my readers, if I'm wrong understand. Help me to understand why the paper that I had type part of my book on didn't burn up with everything else and paper is the easiest thing to catch on fire?

So I started doing some research. I retype the cover letter and introductory of my book and took the burned pages to a few people I felt would give me their honest opinion. I also explained to them how I felt that it is faith and it is meant for me to write my book. I told them about the fire and how everything my family and I owned burned up but the pages to my book didn't burn up. I left the pages with a few people and they said they would read the pages and get back with me. About a week later I received a phone call and was given information to get help so I could finish writing my book. I followed up on the information and took the steps I had to but in between then and the book getting where it is now so much had happened in my life. Many times I had to stop writing.

Over the few years I tried to put in time to faithfully write my book but life kept forcing me to stop. I was getting help from a young lady with some of the grammar and editing issues in my book but she moved out of town. So now again I was on my own. I also lost some very close relatives and friends whose deaths made it hard for me to get back on the right track with my own life. Two nephews, a niece, two grandmothers of my kids, three very close and dear friends, and an uncle who played a very important role in my life all died. Do you remember the uncle who house I would go over for summer breaks? Well, he had died. I'm going to miss him so much. He was like my second daddy. My middle son has been shot twice within a three year period. The second time the doctor didn't think he was going to make it but I knew he was a strong seed of mines. I prayed he would come back and fight of the thoughts of death. I prayed and asked God, "To please don't take him away from me? Not yet? Not now." By the will of God, my prayer was answered and my son pulled through.

I was in a car accident that messed my back up and torn my shoulder out of its socket. I was helpless for months. I couldn't even get out of the bed without the help of my kids. My two oldest daughters would cook food for me and bring it over on their way to work in the morning. Then late in the evening one of my oldest daughters will bring me over food to get me though the night. This way the younger kids that were at home didn't have to do too much for me when they got in from school. I was and still am blessed so much to have such caring and loving kids. How did I pay my bills? My four oldest kids even with houses and bills of their own made sure my bills were kept up and paid every month. Every time an invisible brick wall came up and knocked me down on my back, my kids and with the strength of God were there to help pick me up. Like I said before, "I am a strong lady. A fighter and I tried not to let nothing keep me down too long." After about a year and a half I was back on my feet and I was able to use my arm a little more. The doctor told me I'll never be 100% physically back to normal; I accepted his thoughts but I tried to be 100% of what I had to live and work with.

I knew I wasn't well enough to go back to work; therefore, I took some business and computer courses. My grades and skills got me a job right away after I graduated from school. While at work I'll use my break and lunch time to type on the computer so I could try and finish my book. Once I made it home sometime I would write and then go to work the next morning and put everything I wrote that night onto a disc. Everything so far seemed like it was moving along in the right direction. I loved when a good plan came together.

Oh and guess what? I forgot to tell you, I did marry the tall dark skin lusty built brown eyed man. He was the best husband to me. Of course I only had one husband in my life time and our love is now a true appreciated love. Not like that controlling love we once had and held against each other. Anyway the fighting stopped a long time ago and sometimes he use to make me sick but now I love him so much and now we can laugh, hug, kiss, and love each other instead of hitting. Until one day my husband allowed the same drugs that tried to destroy our lives at the beginning of our relationship, destroyed our happy marriage at the end. I offend wish I never knew what love felt like! I frequently regret that my heart knew how wonderful what true love felt like and was able to return a serious truthful happy love back. That tall, dark skinned, lusty built, brown eyed man who is now and still my husband put and left a bad deadly wound on and in my heart.

I found out falling in love is one of life's most powerful feeling there is in the world. When you fall in love everything around you seems brighter and more alive. Your heart beats faster and stronger. Every moment of your life with this person becomes a new experience that becomes more rewarding to your heart, soul, and mind. You feel like a child again with the joy of discovering new things for the first time. Or should I say, "You feel like a child with a very sweet tooth and just been let free in a candy store. Free to eat as much goodies as you choose." Yes, my readers, true love can be so beautiful as long as your partner truly loves you too. True love can bring you so much happiness and joy!!

I also learned how that same true love could easily turn to tarnish once your partner stops loving you the same! Sometimes I asked God, "Why did this tall, dark skin, lusty built brown eyed man have to be the one I feel deep in love with? Why did I have to fall so truly and deeply in love with this tall, dark skin, lusty built brown eyed man, who is still my husband?" I can go on and on and on with the why question but when all the time regardless of all the heartaches, pain, and suffering I went through with this man, I'm very glad to have gotten the chance to have known and be a special part in my husband's life.

I believe I liked myself better when I dogged men and didn't have any feelings for them; used them for what they were good for. I only thought of myself and my kids. The thought and knowing that my kids will always be there for me is all that matters to me now. Lets just pray that maybe this will bring me back some kind of peace of mind and happiness in my life, even if it's not the special love my heart wants for. I only wished when I was younger someone would had told me the horrible pains and sufferings of love because love hurts. I know it now; I feel it every day. I'm living proof of the pains and sufferings from love and the life that was dealt many loosing hands. Now the saddest part of my life is I love my husband so much and I know he is not right for me. This experience has caused me to close the doors to my heart forever and I promise I'll never allow my heart to open up again to such pains. I'll never love another again!!

I live a lonely but semi-happy life with my job, my kids, and my grandkids. I have great goals and intensions for me and my family life but I'm just too afraid of putting myself totally out in the world to accomplish them. I'm starting to feel if you go to fast, you might miss it, and if you go to slow it might pass you by. Me, I really don't know what pace I'm going to take in my life. Life is such a small word with enormous and unlimited responsibilities as a child growing up with no one and as a lonely adult. Sure I left out a whole lot of good, bad, hurting gossip, and talk about stuff that occurred in my life but some of those experiences are worst than some of the ones you have read about. I can write a library of books about the experiences I went through in my life. I just wanted my story to get out into the world to give those of you who are going through or experienced what I went through encouragement. Life may seem like hell when you are going through the drama but at the end as long as you continue to stand strong GOD will pull you through.

I hope I was able to say the right words that could reach out and touch someone who is going through life worst ends; I hope my life experiences could make a difference in someone else's life. Maybe my silent rides of life will give someone that little strength he or she needs to make a positive move in changing a confusing situation in their life. Just maybe someone who is reading my book can say, "Yes that's exactly what I'm going through! That's how I feel too!" Maybe I can get some troubled person or people thinking differently and understand that there is a better way. You can have peace of mind regardless of what you're going through. You can win with a loosing hand!

As I mentioned before, there's a lot of things I just didn't want to talk about or relive through this book. But regardless of what you are going through there is hope for a positive and stress free change. Who knows? Maybe it'll be a second book! It took strength that I didn't even know I had to go back into my past and relive some of those hurting moments. Some moments I had buried so deep in my mind that even I forgot about them on purpose. Once I started remembering, digging, and going back into the years of my life from a child all I could say was, "Oh how the past could catch up with you and eat you alive with hurt, sorrow, pain, guilty, and silent cries.

I realized through these experiences that the world was truly a mean place.

I was surprised in some of the many things I did remember from my past. I also was very deeply hurt and alarmed in the hands I had been dealt in life. Even now I know I wouldn't be able to rewrite this book because of the many tears I shed and pain I went through while writing it. I don't want to relive these broken memories again. Plus I don't think my tolerability is strong enough to deal with the pain I went through again while writing "The Silent Cry." Just reopening some of my life's darkest and deepest buried secrets and horrible moments, which I wanted to forever lock away, hurts. I want no one to go through what I have been though in my life and feel like you can't talk to somebody. No one deserves to be hurt by anyone intentionally. If people truly in their hearts lived by the "Golden Rule," none of these things would have happened to me and the world would be a better place for both young children and adults to live in. Just image living in a world without evil!

I've always remembered the "Golden Rule" as a child. I try my best to live by it so much till it's the rule I brought my kids up on and I explained the true meaning of the rule to my grandkids. Do until one as you want them to do unto you. "The Golden Rule," meaning treat people the way you want to be treated. I know easier said than done but it's the thought in and of the heart that really counts. This thought brings back to mind the promise I made years ago. Considering the things I have been through in my life I said, "Whenever I have any kids I'd watch them until they are old enough to watch themselves!" I didn't want anything to happen to my babies. Then when my kids started having kids my husband and I became the babysitters so the kids could go to work and go to school. A parent can't ever get enough of saying how proud they are of their kids and how much they love their children. I think and tell my kids everyday how much I love them and proud of their accomplishments.

Another reason I decided to finish writing my book is for my kids, my grandkids, and their seeds to come. I felt this book is a piece of my life tree to learn from and for them to always remember me by.

To my seven seeds and their seeds after:

Please stay together and be strong. For all you have is each other and I will always love you all even when I'm gone! I gave birth to seven bright, beautiful, caring, and loving kids, who are now strong young ladies and gentlemen. I am so proud of each one of you for whom you are. Remember, "Wisdom comes with age as it grows strong from its root in the heart and the mind." I loved and will always love you, my lucky seven.

I always shared with my kids the different stories about my life. They were the ones to inspire me to continue writing my book. Also, I wanted to express my feelings and emotions on how things can happen in our lives that can not only change our personality and attitude but also leaves and put fear in our heart. Confused and not knowing what to do are two deep emotions that can only hurt you more by keeping things all enclosed inside of you! Everybody needs somebody they can talk to. Everyone needs somebody who they can truly love and receive that same true love in return. No one deserves to be hit or abused by anyone, mentally, physically, and or emotionally. Life is a gift and God gave man a very special gift to love and treasure, "woman;" as a woman, all ladies deserve all the extravagance as a queen from the king, which is man, on earth. The female is a very important part of life and should be treated as so.

Like man the female has her most unique abilities, to carry, and birth life. After all the next female is always somebody's mother, sister, or daughter, who should be respected and treated as your own. God gave the greatest gifts of life to us; a father's love is to share, and a mother's love you can't compare. Again, it all comes back to us all being blessed with that unique woman.

I tried to share with you my reader signs and different things to watch for in your life and your love ones' life. Mood swings, loneness, unexplained out bruised of anger, and most of all the quietness. As you have read, I've been through it all. There is a reason for every mood a person is going through. To me the quietness is and was the most important and dangerous because it was my way of silently asking for help but I didn't really know how too. I was unknowingly silently killing myself inside as well as slowly and confusingly loosing my mind. So if you notice a change or something different about a child, a teenager, or even an adult take time out and try to talk to him or her. Who knows maybe they too could be "Silently Crying" out for help but don't know how to ask.

Life should be treasured and cherish like precious gold. Life should be appreciated and loved but not too tightly held. Life is a special gift that you only get once and only one good chance I was told. Make the best of your life by being the best in whatever it is that's your choice. I wish life would have been much better for me; not so many broken rules! Enjoy life, for which God has given you. Try to be positively successful with none or as less and fewer blues and mistakes possible. If mistakes have been made the best thing you could do for yourself is to learn from those mistakes. Remember what I've told you about my life and use my words as a learning tool. Please whatever you do, don't be cruel!

We all are going to be faced with some very easier said than done crossroads and decision in our lives. My personal advice to you my readers is when you do get to that intersection with many crossroads to it, please think deeply within your heart and make the right choice. Make sure you take the most acceptable direction that is pleasing to yourself. Although it may seem difficult at times to open yourself up and let yourself go, when you follow your heart, you will always be on the right path. Also remember, it is better to have experienced falling in love and losing it than to never have loved at all. If you are in doubt follow your gut instincts and do without. I know life isn't easy. It was and still is a struggle for me; from a child to an adult, to almost conquering life trials and tribulations, I climbed, ran through, crawled and a few times even try to take the pain and suffering out of my life by attempting suicide. With each attempt resulting in unvictorious, I only woke up day after day to add more problems and pains into my life.

I guess my life will never be complete no matter how happy or successful I become. I'll forever and always remember, wanting, and still looking for something that I lost, and can't ever get back; <u>my child hood.</u>

The anger of pain about the male species of evil taking advantage of a pure female species of good hardened my heart. The anger and pain that come from such a heartless, evil male species that robbed me of something I could never get back. Something that was so pure, clean, untouched, and good; <u>my virginity.</u> All my life has been filled with days of a lost childhood, memories, nightmares, anger, and pain that left me silently crying inside. I only wish that the world could have had a good, kind, and caring heart like mines.

I only wish that the world could have had a good, kind, and caring heart like mines. But in my life it didn't. So I'm left in a dark world where my anger and pain has left a mark on my heart from the evil male species I've encountered has left me silently crying inside.

If it's the Lord's will, then all my struggles, tears, pains, and battles of the unknown will, can, and could be a positive successful guide in someone else's life.

May God, bless you all…

www.ingramcontent.com/pod-product-compliance
Lightning Source LLC
Chambersburg PA
CBHW030359030726
47497CB00002B/407